LEGACY OF PROMETHEUS

LEGACY OF PROMETHEUS

ERIC KOTANI AND
JOHN MADDOX ROBERTS

A TOM DOHERTY ASSOCIATES BOOK
NEW YORK

LEGACY OF PROMETHEUS

Copyright © 2000 by Eric Kotani and John Maddox Roberts

This book is printed on acid-free paper.

A Forge Book
Published by Tom Doherty Associates, LLC
175 Fifth Avenue
New York, NY 10010

www.tor.com

Forge® is a registered trademark of Tom Doherty Associates, LLC.

Design by Lisa Pifher

ISBN 0-312-87298-4

First Edition: April 2000

Printed in the United States of America

0 9 8 7 6 5 4 3 2 1

LEGACY OF PROMETHEUS

THE JET WAS a corporate model, its color scheme red, white, and blue. These were not intended to represent the colors of the United States of America, but rather, those of the Republic of Texas. On its nose was blazoned a logo: a five-pointed white star trailing a stylized comet's tail. The logo was that of Lone Star Space Systems, and Lone Star was owned by Cash Carlson, a man with a reputation as colorful as his jet and a past full of dark rumors.

The woman who waited by the runway gate in the private aircraft terminal of the huge airport had heard all the rumors, and had discounted most of them: that he was an international outlaw tied in with the Mafia and Central American drug cartels; that he was a former secret agent, able to operate with immunity because he had found top-secret files that gave him the goods on everyone of importance in the American government, which he wielded for blackmail; that he was a mercenary whose private army had looted the vaults of several small nations. Those were only the ones repeated by the respectable press. The tabloids went into even more lurid flights of fancy, involving celebrities and visiting aliens.

The woman who waited by the gate was Asian, with the poise of a gymnast and the face of a fashion model. The bulky purse hanging from her shoulder looked like the sort that models carry to pack around the mass of cosmetics they need to get through a workday. But she was not a model. She was a journalist, and the purse contained the electronic paraphernalia of her profession: recorders, mikes, mini-laptop word processor and computer, portable fax, video camera for motion and still shots, and a portable phone that would put her in instant voice link with her European publishers. It even held a pad of paper and several pens.

She had scored a massive coup by getting an interview with Carlson, a man who thrived on speaking with crowds of reporters in public but was notoriously reluctant to grant private interviews. She had been amazed when her editor at *Paris Match* told her that Carlson's publicist had approved her request. She decided that it must have been the mass of background information about herself she had supplied Lone Star's PR people.

The jet drew to a halt and its hatch slid open, extruding a stair to the tarmac. First off was a burly, black-haired man in a long black overcoat despite the heat of the summer day. She recognized him as Jack Parker, an ex-U.S. Navy SEAL whose private security firm was rated one of the top ten in the world. For the last eight years, his firm had handled a single client: Lone Star. For half a minute, he stood at the foot of the stair. His head remained still, but she knew that his eyes were scanning behind the wraparound black sunglasses he wore. He made no signal, but another man came from the jet and walked easily down the steps.

Carlson, she thought, was even more impressive in person than in the pictures she had seen. Well over six feet tall, he had the spare but powerful build and hard-cut features always associated, rightly or wrongly, with American frontiersmen. His sandy, slightly graying hair was dense and close-cropped. It would have been curly, she decided, if he let it grow. Nearing fifty, the deep lines in his face were those of character and experience, not of age.

She left the gate and walked toward him, slowly, giving the bodyguard plenty of time to look her over. Carlson smiled and stuck out his hand when she was close. She took it, having to turn her face up sharply to look him in the eye. His eyes were deep blue.

"Miss Sasano? I'm very pleased to meet you. Isabelle at the *Match* tells me you're tops in your field." He spoke with only a trace of Texas drawl.

"She is too kind. And I feel very privileged to get an interview whereas all my colleagues have failed." His large hand engulfed hers and gripped it firmly, but he did not retain possession of it overlong, as so many men did.

"I have my reasons. Ah, here's our transportation."

A pair of white limousines cruised slowly across the tarmac toward them. Their blackened windshields gave them a sinister look despite the pearly paint jobs, and they rode low on what were plainly beefed-up springs. Armor plating, she guessed. The world was full of such cars these days. They bristled with exotic antennae.

The limos pulled up to them and Carlson opened a passenger door in the second car, gesturing for Sachi to precede him. She slid across the luxurious seat, which exuded an almost intoxicating scent of new leather. Carlson slid in after her, extending his long legs easily in the stretched vehicle.

"Morning, Toby," Carlson said to the driver.

"Mornin', Boss," the driver said. Parker got in next to him and turned his attention to the instruments on the dashboard, which looked, Sachi Sasano thought, like something that belonged on a high-tech fighter aircraft. The two limos pulled away from the plane in near-perfect silence, despite carrying enough weight to strain the limits of the internal combustion engine in each vehicle.

"Mr. Carlson . . ." she began.

"Call me Cash, please," he said. "People say 'Mr. Carlson,' I think they mean my father."

"Then you must call me Sachi, since we are to be informal. When may I start recording?"

"Anxious to get to work?" He grinned easily.

"Your publicist, Ms. Baird, promised access only between the airport and Carlson Tower."

"Relax," he advised. "It's never fast, driving between here and downtown Manhattan. You're lucky at that. I'd use a helicopter if the city authorities still allowed rooftop landings."

"Fast but inelegant," she said. "I much prefer automobiles."

"Good. May I offer you a drink?" He gestured toward a fold-down bar in front of them.

She shook her head. "Not while I'm working."

"Even better. Do you know why I picked you instead of all the others who want to interview me?"

"My qualifications?"

"Right. Oh, you aren't the first to express willingness and abilities beyond the norm. Some have offered to go to bed with me, both women and men. One lady from a Thai newspaper even proclaimed herself the oral sex champion of Southeast Asia, and willing to demonstrate."

Parker made a noise that might have been a derisive snort.

"But you're the first reporter to back up her credentials with a B.S. in bioengineering and grad work in closed ecosystems. It was a pleasure to find a reporter who actually knows something about science. A lot of them are enthusiastic about space work but they make embarrassing mistakes, which then get attributed to me."

"In Japan, it isn't unusual for reporters to have formal scientific training," she said. "It's less common in Europe, and even rarer here."

As soon as Carlson's party had disappeared into the limousine, a mechanic working on a Cesna at some distance pulled out a cellular phone surreptitiously, punched a number and spoke.

"They are on their way now."

The limos were making their way through the labyrinthian traffic tangle in and around John F. Kennedy International Airport. No wonder, Sachi thought, that Cash had reassured her they would have plenty of time to confer. In an age of supersonic passenger jets and bullet trains, wheeled traffic between major American cities and their airports was still in the nineteen-forties.

She felt that Carlson was studying her, weighing her. She was used to attention from men. They assessed her body, her face, her incredibly lustrous black hair. It could be a nuisance, but she was not above using her attractiveness to get men to open up to her, to say things they might not were they not distracted by her looks.

But somehow she knew this was different. Carlson's judgment would ride on the questions she asked and how she responded to his answers, not on her sex appeal. She took the mike from one of her recording units and clipped it to the lapel of her jacket. It was tiny and tastefully jeweled.

They pulled onto the Long Island Expressway, where the traffic, while dense, was at least moving steadily. Theirs were by no means the only specially modified limos on the road. Cars that would be stared at in small-town America didn't rate a second glance here, where persons of importance on all sides of the law and government required special protection, or at least the prestige that went with it.

The day was glorious, the sky a cloudless, pristine blue that set off the Manhattan skyline to perfection. An offshore breeze had been blowing all day, clearing the city of smog and haze, creating the sort of picture-postcard view that proclaimed New York to be exactly what its natives always claimed it was: a beautiful city. Beautiful from a distance, at any rate.

"You are in New York to address the U.N. concerning the upcoming vote on solar satellites, are you not?" she began.

"That's correct. Although the subject tends to put most people to sleep, I happen to feel that this could be one of the most momentous votes, for good or ill, ever to come before the U.N. If the vote goes the wrong way, the results could be catastrophic."

"You use strong language. Would you care to elucidate?"

"The era of superpower confrontation is over. For many decades, the peaceful uses of space were largely held hostage to the imperatives of U.S.-Soviet military rivalry. Now nothing stands in the way between the human race and the serious exploration of space, and the beneficial use of its infinite resources. Even so, a great deal of prejudice remains. Many people throughout the world remain almost reflexively hostile to space projects."

"Many of the opposition," she said, "will maintain that the terrible problems of hunger, poverty, and overpopulation here on Earth are far more important than space exploration."

"Those are indeed terrible problems, and they are exactly the ones I'll be addressing. See, it all comes down to energy. The universe consists of matter and energy. We have to have energy to alter matter into the forms that feed us, clothe and house us, and provide us with transportation. The energy resources of this planet are severely limited, and most of them are polluting to boot. There are no such limitations in space, and solar energy is clean."

He leaned toward her, growing animated even though he was delivering words he must have repeated a hundred times before. "I, and others like me, propose to go after abundant, cheap energy. This can only serve to help alleviate those problems you mentioned, because energy is absolutely crucial and as it gets scarcer, it won't get cheaper." He jabbed a finger skyward for emphasis.

"I plan to go out there and get that energy and sell it all over the world, dirt-cheap. And it's going to be a hell of an adventure doing it!" For a few seconds, something almost boyish showed through Carlson's craggy features.

"But there are other space—what is the word? Boosters?—who say your own project is impractical. I am thinking specifically of the Europeans and the Japanese, as well as the Americans."

"Of course," Carlson said. "And that's exactly how it should be. There's almost never a major problem with a single, simple solution.

The idea is to let the proponents of all the differing theories have their try at it. The ones that are truly impractical, or impracticable, will fall by the wayside. The promising ones will endure a winnowing-out process until one dominates the others."

"It sounds rather Darwinian."

"That's a reasonable analogy, but it's not all that ruthless. Because one comes to dominate, it doesn't mean that the others are exterminated. Space is unfathomably huge, and a great many niches exist out there. Look at the waters of this planet. You'll see up-to-date turbine vessels doing the biggest jobs and piston ships doing other work, and even a few paddle wheelers on the rivers. And everywhere, you see wind-powered boats and oar-powered craft used for work or recreation. I think my competitors are wrong, but that doesn't mean they're stupid. I expect to see them in business in the same environment for a long time to come."

In the seat before them, Parker touched a yellow symbol on one of the black screens in the dash.

"Query?" said a mechanical voice.

"Run a check on Connecticut license XBM two-five-one. Green late-model Chevy, mirrored glass."

Sachi looked back through the rear window and finally saw the car in question, eight or ten car lengths behind them. The heavily tinted, bulletproof glass made color difficult to judge. Carlson seemed to be paying no attention, so she went back to her interview.

"Mr. Carlson, your Lone Star Space Systems has been described by your competitor, Preston Reed, as a 'junkyard operation' in reference to your extensive use of surplus and abandoned materials: Proton and Energia rockets, jettisoned fuel tanks, et cetera. How do you respond to such aspersions?"

He smiled, but with a hard edge. "I prefer to think of it as recycling. Why waste perfectly good equipment, unless you suffer from misplaced vanity? Great fortunes were made in the years following World War Two by people buying up unneeded Liberty ships and transport aircraft to begin shipping lines and airlines. It seems to me the height of folly to go to all the expense of launching a fuel tank into orbit and then abandoning it just because its immediate purpose has been served. Not when it can be reused as a habitat or part of another vessel."

There was a beep from the dashboard console. "Queried vehicle reported stolen yesterday in Manchester County."

"Boss?" Parker said.

"No need to get excited just yet," Carlson said. "I doubt if more than two thirds of the cars on this highway would stand up to much scrutiny. Wait for a suspicious move."

"Right, Boss," Parker said phlegmatically.

"Is he always like this?" Sachi asked.

"It's what I pay him for. We're going to be exiting pretty soon. Last year in L.A. we got ambushed. I was giving a talk at JPL and they hit us at an off-ramp near Pasadena. Two of Parker's boys went to the hospital and the city managers were unhappy with all the bullet holes. They're a pretty stodgy bunch in Pasadena. Anyway, an ambush is no more likely here today than in any other time and place, but ever since Pasadena, the boys have been nervous about off-ramps."

They made it off the expressway without incident and soon were in a neighborhood undergoing gentrification; a former slum area being renovated block by block and ending up as elegant brownstones for the newly prosperous products of America's business schools. They stood four and five stories tall, most of them still uninhabited, window frames empty in their newly sand-blasted facades. Everywhere, manholes stood open, surrounded by curtained sawhorses and "Men at Work" signs in a half-dozen languages. Pedestrian traffic was thin, and even the wheeled variety was skimpy by New York standards.

"Looks like rain, Boss," Parker said.

Sachi looked up at the sky, framed between the high buildings. Not a cloud.

"Bodyguard talk," Carlson explained. "He means it's time to put on our raincoats. Yours is on the ledge behind you." He turned and took a bulky, folded object from the rear window ledge, handing it to her. Then he took his own and unfolded it. She did the same and discovered that it was a long coat, amazingly heavy. She had noticed the one Parker wore and guessed that it concealed weapons, but the weight tipped her off.

"Are these bulletproof?" she asked.

"Sort of," Parker said, still fiddling with his dashboard controls.

"How good is 'sort of'?"

"If we get bombed, it'll stop most shell frags. It'll keep out handgun bullets and shotgun pellets. High-powered rifle and machine-gun bullets will usually go right through, though it'll stop most ricochets."

With Carlson's help, she struggled into the coat and turned up its collar. It came to the tops of her ears. "What if you are hit in the head?"

Parker shrugged. "Nobody's come up with armor that'll make you immortal. You do what you can." She wondered how he saw through the black glasses, but then she noticed the thickness of the frames and the faint glow reflecting on the skin above his thick black brows. It was an electronic-imaging device. She had seen such instruments worn by soldiers, but none so compact or civilian-looking.

"Green Chevy still following," Parker said. "Rog, report."

"We got an armored truck a block ahead," said a voice over the car radio.

"Lose him," Parker ordered. Then, to Carlson: "We're taking evasive action, Boss."

"Paranoia," Carlson said to Sachi. "I hate it, but it's a part of modern life. New York City is one of the commercial centers of the world; it's full of armored trucks making pickups and deliveries. But we have a suspicious car behind us, so that makes an armored truck ahead of us a potential tank."

She could tell he was trying to put her at ease. "I've been in cities at war, Mr.—ah, Cash. Now, about the space station you have had in orbit the last two years: How large a crew can it accommodate?"

Carlson grinned. "You don't distract easily, do you?"

The car jerked into a tight, right turn and she leaned against the gee forces. "I would get no work done if I did."

"No more about the U.N. vote?" He sounded almost disappointed.

"Actually, it will be long over by the time my article appears. I just needed your statement for background. I am far more interested in your working projects. Your publicity department provides excellent materials, but the thoughts of the owner can be more enlightening."

"Well, we've had crews as large as twenty aboard so far, but when it's fully operational the station will house one hundred fifty—"

"Condition red," Parker said, his voice almost conversational.

No matter how expertly driven, an armored limo is not a fast vehicle, certainly no faster than an armored truck also driven by an expert. The vehicle in question had anticipated their evasion route and was stopped across an intersection ahead of the lead limo.

"What are we supposed to do?" Sachi asked.

"Just sit where we are and let the guys do their work," Carlson said. "It's what I pay them for. They're very temperamental and they get upset if we amateurs try to take a hand in things. Toby is our driver. That's his brother Thad driving the car up ahead. They raced on the stock-car circuit from their early teens. They were a top stunt-driving team for the movies and television when Parker hired them. Charlie, Rog, and Louis are with him, all top hands. We're—"

His calm monologue was interrupted by a squeal of tires, followed by a crash as the green Chevy hit their rear bumper. The massive limo rocked on its springs under the impact. Men piled out of the lead limo, weapons ready. Tubes poked from inside the armored truck and began to spit flame. The few pedestrians in the area, experienced New Yorkers all, hit the sidewalks and began low-crawling toward doorways, some of them dragging wounded limbs.

"Take out that armor," Parker said, his fingers dancing across his controls. Sachi heard a *whoosh* from behind them and turned in time to see a black cloud billow from the rear of the limo, enveloping the Chevy. "Impact didn't damage the paint spray," he reported. "They're blind back there now. Have to come out of that car pretty quick." He hit another control, and a hatch slid open in the limo's roof. He stood, lifting an angular, boxy weapon in both hands so that it cleared the roof before his head did.

The instant he was out, he fired a spray of bullets through the windshield of the Chevrolet. Sachi saw it dissolve into pebbles of safety glass as three men erupted from the interior. One of them went down instantly, his arms flying wide, sending a submachine gun pinwheeling through the air.

Parker's weapon made a muffled thump and something exploded inside the Chevrolet, spraying the area with more glass. One of the men from the green car fired at Parker with a heavy pistol, getting off two shots before being slammed down to the pavement. The third man was rocked by the explosion, but he recovered quickly and raised his submachine gun. He fired a short burst and bullets spanged off the roof of the limo simultaneously with Parker's return fire. The attacker was hammered to the pavement along with the others.

Parker turned to face forward as a man came from the far side of the armored truck, something long and rectangular balanced on his shoulder. Two of the guards were firing over the top of their limo. One of them was down on the street and another was trying to tug him to safety behind the car. Bullets spanged around them.

"Rocket launcher!" Parker said, raising his voice for the first time. "Get him!"

The man leveled the weapon straight at Carlson's limo, his hand tightening on the trigger. The front of the weapon had three gaping tubes. For an instant, it was rock-steady, then it shook as something struck the shooter. With a loud bang, an object shot toward the limo, skimming across its hood, impacting the facade of a building across the sidewalk. The security chief dropped back inside just as a tremendous blast sent glass and brick flying. A section of steel scaffolding attached to the facade gave way and crashed down onto the street.

One of the guards from the lead car dashed toward the rocket launcher, firing a continuous spray of bullets into the shooter. He dropped his submachine gun, snatched up the launcher and whirled to point it at the armored car. Bullets stitched his legs but he kept the weapon on-target as he depressed the trigger. There was a muffled *whump*, and fire burst from all the ports of the armored truck, followed by pillars of black smoke.

The silence was sudden and total. Then the sirens began. "Stay here!" Parker barked, jerking his door open and running toward the wrecked armored truck.

"Just sit tight," Carlson advised.

"I wasn't going to go anywhere," she assured him.

"At least you can't say I give a dull interview."

"No, but I still have a good many questions I intended to ask."

He laughed. "Single-minded, aren't you?"

Parker returned to the limo and opened Carlson's door. "You can get out now, Boss, but be ready to dive."

"Casualties?"

"Louis is hurt bad. He may not make it. Rog took a couple in the legs bagging the armor, but he doesn't look too bad." He glanced down at his own front and scraped the breast of his coat with his hand and came away with a number of dully glittering objects. He held them out for Sachi to see. They were flattened bullets.

"Ricochets off the roof. That's why we wear these things."

One of the guards came running from a building. "All secure," he reported. "I thought I saw some guy watching from an upper window, but he's gone now."

"Fine," Parker said in disgust. "And just what the hell were you trying to do, dragging in a wounded man in the middle of a firefight?"

"Louis was hit!" he protested indignantly. "Bleeding like a stuck pig! I couldn't just let him lay there!"

"Yes you could!" He poked the man in his armored chest with a big, blunt finger. "And next time, you will. You take care of the wounded after the shooting's over. I had four guns in the lead car. You going after Louis cut our forward firepower fifty percent. If Rog hadn't got the guy with the launcher, we'd all be dog food right now!" The guard stalked away, his face flaming.

"Charlie's a good man," Parker told Carlson. "Just a little sentimental, that's all."

"Civilians hurt?" Carlson asked.

"Looks like a few," Parker affirmed.

Carlson got into the front seat and called his New York headquarters and ordered his staff to make arrangements to handle the hospital care of innocents caught in the line of fire.

"Just watch," Parker told him when he emerged. "They'll all sue you. You'll be responsible for them for life."

Carlson shrugged. "I can't very well ignore them."

"Why didn't that man try to fire his rocket from inside the armored truck?" Sachi asked. "He exposed himself."

"You can't use a rocket launcher from inside a closed space," Parker told her. "The backblast would have fried everyone inside."

"Oh, I should have realized that." She seemed embarrassed to have overlooked the dynamics of rocket flight.

By this time, the police had arrived in full riot gear, their whirling lights lending an ominously festive air. The halted drivers gaped for a while and then, being true New Yorkers, began to honk their horns. The inevitable crowd gathered, drawn to the sound of gunfire like a herd of war correspondents. Connoisseurs offered analyses of bullet trajectories and blast effects to anyone who would listen.

A television news team arrived by helicopter and correspondents fanned out to take pictures and demand answers. Carlson was too busy answering police questions to field any from the media. A woman thrust a microphone at Sachi. "Were you in the car with Mr. Carlson when the shooting started?"

Sachi smiled dazzlingly. "So sorry, no speak English."

The woman turned away, not bothering to lower her voice as she sent her lead line to the station: "Who is the mysterious Asian beauty with Cash Carlson? Find out tonight on *News at Eleven!*"

Within an amazingly short time, the ambulances were gone, the greater part of the wreckage was cleared away, and they were back in the limo, which had sustained only cosmetic damage. The news teams left, disappointed. Carlson had promised a public statement later, Sachi had pretended ignorance to all who asked, and that left only the remaining guards. Theirs was an anonymous profession, and they preferred to keep it that way. Their wraparound shades re-donned, they grunted monosyllables or maintained silence when questioned.

"Any familiar faces?" Carlson asked Parker as they settled in.

"Two of the men in the Chevy were Paco Camarena and Michel Joffre. Both ex-Foreign Legion guns-for-hire with long records on numerous continents. Toby IDs the armored truck driver as an Austrian race-car competitor named Grundig. The Chevy driver and the rocketeer I don't know. There were three more in the armored truck but their mothers wouldn't know them at the moment. Forensics might turn up something."

"All freelancers?"

"That's how I read it. And none of 'em gonna do any talking now."

"What about the man Charlie saw?

"He says it was a squat, bushy-haired man, but he didn't have much attention to spare for him. Might've just been some wino sacking out in a vacant building and watching the excitement. Boss, I think there's a leak in your own organization and you're gonna have to let me go after it sooner or later."

Carlson shook his head vehemently. "It's been known for weeks that I was coming to address the U.N. If they were pros, they'd have no difficulty figuring out a good ambush site once they knew when I was coming in. There were only two or three exits we might've taken. The Chevy was spotting, directing the armored truck. If they missed cornering us today, they'd have hit us going to the U.N. or coming back or whatever. If they didn't get us here, they'd head on to Rio or wherever. These people know how to be patient, Jack."

Parker snorted. "Don't I know it. But you just don't want to think that any of your people would sell you out. You carry this loyalty stuff too far, Boss. Greed isn't the only motivation. Most people can be got to, one way or another."

Carlson sighed, but it came out as a cobra hiss. "Let it ride for now, Jack. I'd rather take the risk than encourage paranoia within my organization. First thing you know, they'll be spying on one another, personalities and old grudges will come into it, and a world-class operation will be in the toilet."

"Whatever you say, Boss." Parker was ready to let it rest, but only temporarily.

"Sachi, where are you staying?" Carlson inquired.

"Am I to take it that my interview is now terminated?" she asked.

"You left your recorder on, didn't you? You could sell it to any of the TV networks for a bundle. They'll run it as audio behind their evening report. Lots of gunfire and explosions."

"I am not a sensationalist television reporter, Mr. Carlson. I am a science writer for intelligent journals."

"We're back to 'Mr. Carlson,' huh? I'll tell you what. The evening before the big U.N. vote, I'm throwing a large bash for all the visiting dignitaries and the people I do business with. Would you like to attend?"

She smiled. "That's better. May I interview you there?"

He made a gesture of surrender. "I promise."

The limo pulled away from the curb. "Who were they?" she asked.

"That's something I intend to find out," Carlson said. "I've picked up a few enemies over the years. And kidnappers might think I'm worth holding for ransom."

"I know the difference between a kidnapping and an assassination," she said. "That rocket was intended to kill you. You said that your new project is all about energy. Was this all about energy too?"

His Western ease dropped for a moment and he regarded her with wary respect. "It might very well have been. When you talk energy, you're talking money. A lot of people stand to lose a bundle if cheap, abundant solar energy becomes available."

"Enough to kill you for?"

"People kill over nickels and dimes. We're talking billions here."

"This wasn't a nickel-and-dime attempt," she said. "But why you? Others are working in the same field."

He grinned. "I'm flattered. Maybe somebody thinks I'm the one most likely to make it possible. Or maybe the others are getting shot at too but it hasn't been as public. Or maybe one of them hired the hitters. Or maybe it's something else entirely."

"You live an uncertain life," she said as the limo pulled up in front of her hotel. The doorman rushed over to open her door.

"I find the uncertain life more exciting. Besides," he waved a hand, indicating the whole city around them, "people are being murdered right now, several dozen in the next twenty-four hours probably, without having nearly as much fun."

"I'll see you at your party, Cash," she said, extending her hand. He took it, and this time he held it a few heartbeats longer. Then she was out of the limo and walking through the glass doors of the hotel.

Carlson Tower, Lone Star's corporate headquarters in Manhattan, was a black-glass shaft overlooking Central Park, flanked by other office towers, some dating from the twenties, others even newer than it. At the entrance of the underground parking area, the building's security system checked the voiceprint of the lead limo's driver before opening the steel door. Seated in an armored booth, a security guard monitored a video screen, ready to halt the door, drop an inner barrier, or otherwise impede progress should he detect anything suspicious. As the cars passed the booth, their windshields and window glass flashed from opacity and became transparent, allowing the guard to make face ID.

"Lead car, you're two men short. Explain."

"In the hospital, Craig," Carlson said, bypassing the security net.

"I figured," the guard said. "Got word of a hit an hour ago. Don't hurt to make double sure."

The limos drew to a halt before a bank of elevators. Cash got out and walked past the express elevator that went directly to the top-floor penthouse. Instead, he went to another that took him to a hideaway apartment concealed on the executive floor. In accordance with established routine, one of the bodyguards took the penthouse elevator. He would turn on switches, open curtains, key a selection of music disks to play, and otherwise make it look as if Cash had moved in. At night, a sophisticated projector setup would cast moving shadows on the drawn drapes. To an observer in a nearby building, the penthouse would give every appearance of occupation.

The hideaway apartment was furnished to Carlson's taste, a combination of Scandinavian and modern-American styles. The exception was the room's centerpiece, a garish, overstuffed Victorian sofa-ottoman that looked like something out of a Storyville bordello. He tossed his jacket over a nearby chair, kicked off his shoes and sank into the sofa with a contented sigh, propping his feet on the ottoman.

"Rough ride in from the airport," he said, apparently to no one in particular.

A tall, chestnut-haired woman emerged from the tiny kitchen holding a tall, frosted glass, its contents transparent. "So I heard. Building security clued me and I caught the tail end of an on-site broadcast. Some network twit was making it sound like Beirut in the eighties. Was it that bad?"

"Bad enough for a couple of minutes. Louis may not make it, and Rog won't be dancing for a while."

"Was it a hit or a kidnap attempt? The TV report didn't say."

"A hit. They were going to take out my car with a rocket launcher. Jack says it's a Czech model, very successful against tanks in the Middle East. Someone wanted me dead."

Carlson knew that she would be tearing her hair out in great, bloody handfuls if it had happened on her watch. But Parker was in charge when Cash was on the move. She handed him the drink and he licked salt from the rim. It was tequila over crushed ice. Mixing drinks wasn't in her job description. She did it because she wanted to, and she did it, as she did most things, perfectly.

Cash's headhunters had found Pat Coogan in the Dallas police department, where she had done a stint as a decoy trolling for rapists. Apparently the work had suited her all too well. Bodies of known offenders began turning up all over the Dallas–Fort Worth area. Some in the department found this sort of individual initiative objectionable. She was headed for a catastrophic collision with an internal-affairs investigation and an ambitious district attorney when Cash snatched her away just before the grand jury was to convene. His political juice got the indictments quashed and he called in some old I.O.U.'s to mollify the D.A., giving him the goods on some high-profile offenders he could prosecute.

Cash had wanted her for his security force, but her organizational skills turned out to be even more valuable. She was now his personal secretary, doubling as bodyguard.

"Fix yourself one and join me," he suggested.

As always during working hours, she fixed something nonalcoholic. This time it was a concoction of fruit juices that looked like a milkshake, an old Brazilian recipe called a *"vitamina."* To Cash, it looked like a hell of a thing to be drinking at any time of day, but he rarely questioned other people's bad habits.

"So what's the score now, Pat? Have we got the votes?"

"The Russians are with us, of course, and the Chinese. In fact, all the space-faring nations. With those and a few more on our side, the others won't have the majority they need to pass their U.N. resolution."

"Shortsighted boobs," he said.

"We've been working on the others, wining and dining, flattering, offering, uh, financial inducements."

"What the hell, call them bribes. I can stand it."

"Right. Thibodeaux's been fixing some of them up with escort services. New York has some of the world's best."

"Amazing," he mused. "The world's oldest currency and it's still valid."

"Some things never change. Another margarita?"

He got up. "No, I'm going to hit the shower and rest for a while. Buzz me when the others get here."

"Right, Boss."

He undressed and stood under the needle spray, trying to force his body to relax. He was tired even though he felt he hadn't done anything all day. Maybe that was it, he thought. The flight, the forced inaction during the chaotic fight—not doing anything wore him out faster than anything else. He was a man used to unceasing activity. He thrived on it. A thorny engineering problem or dealing with some third-world nation's cutthroat internal politics left him refreshed and ready for more. But doing something as passive as sitting through an interview, with somebody else in control, was exhausting.

Thinking of the interview made him think of the woman. Sachi Sasano. An unusual name and an unusual woman. A knockout—in basic terms, almost too good to be true. Of course, that was the sort of thing that sent people like Jack Parker and Pat Coogan into frenzies of suspicion. To Carlson, it just made her more interesting.

Elsewhere in Manhattan, in a VIP suite of the Hyatt Regency Hotel, Jean-Claude du Mont, head of the European Space Enterprise, was seated on a sofa listening to a report from his deputy, Hans Krause, who had just arrived. Du Mont looked handsome and elegant in his designer smoking robe.

In fluent French with a hint of an Alsatian accent, Krause concluded: "So, whoever attempted to ambush Cash did not plan it well. They should have known Parker's reputation for preparedness in protecting his clients—he hasn't lost any as yet."

"Well, it would not have bothered me much if they had succeeded. I hear that a short while ago, there was a close call on his life in Pasadena. On the other hand, I would rather that he stay alive until after this meeting at the U.N. He can be of help to us in killing this idiotic motion by the third-world countries to control the solar-power satellite program."

He uttered the words "third world" with a combination of disdain and disgust.

"He is now safely ensconced in the penthouse in the Carlson Tower." Krause then added thoughtfully, "He would make an easy target there to a trained assassin with a rocket launcher on the rooftop of an adjacent building."

Du Mont smiled, looking smug and superior. "Well, Carlson isn't as smart as he thinks he is. I am not going to lose any sleep if he can't look after his own affairs."

Krause hesitated for a moment before yielding the last item of his report. "Ah, Mademoiselle Sasano was in the same limousine with Carlson when the attempt was made. She was interviewing him for *Paris Match,* I understand. He dropped her off at the U.N. Plaza Hotel."

A look of deep upset crossed du Mont's patrician countenance. It was unclear even to himself whether he was in shock to hear that she had been exposed to a great risk only a few hours ago or to learn that she had been in company with Cash Carlson, whose romantic escapades with women were not infrequent topics, even in the European society columns.

As soon as the Alsatian was gone, he was going to phone her at the hotel. Perhaps he would take her out to an expensive uptown French restaurant, squire her to a nightclub show, then bring her back to his suite to make passionate love. He ardently hoped that the novel environment would induce her to become romantic again. Why couldn't she be satisfied that she was Jean-Claude du Mont's sole mistress? Any civilized French woman would be, be she single or married. It never occurred to him that Sachi might have an entirely different perception of their relationship.

2

O Navigador, Brazil, and Earth Orbit, two years earlier

ON THE ATLANTIC coast of northern Brazil, a spaceship sat on its launchpad. As space facilities went, it was stripped to the basics, a far cry from Canaveral or the elaborate spaceports of Russia, Europe, and Japan. The coast had been all but deserted when Carlson had made it the launch site for Lone Star, and in the short time since, a boomtown had sprung up, enveloping it on the landward side. The town had been christened *Dom Enrique, O Navigador*, after the fifteenth-century Prince of Portugal who had founded the academy of navigation in Portugal that heralded the Age of the Great Voyages of Discovery by European adventurers.

Lone Star's site was located right on the equator, a few hundred miles to the north of the mouth of the Amazon River. Cash Carlson had cut a deal with the Brazilian government, offering a stake in his solar-power satellite program in exchange for a ninety-nine-year lease on the launch site, plus Brazilian contributions for the construction work at O Navigador.

It was a difficult place, remote and served by no roads capable of handling the necessary traffic. On top of that, Brazil was economically and politically unstable. It was just that the choice of ideal sites was not very large, and none of the nations with anything like an optimum location was in any better shape than Brazil was.

A solar-power satellite, in order to be geostationary, needs to attain an equatorial orbit at a geosynchronous orbital distance, which is some six times the radius of Earth. A geostationary orbit is always geosynchronous, but a geosynchronous orbit is not necessarily geostationary—for that, the orbit must be equatorial.

Despite the illusion created by televised launches in which rockets ascend vertically on their towers of flame and smoke, satellites do not go straight up into orbit. They must be launched in some direction, and the direction taken radically affects the orbit attained. A launch to eastward from an equatorial site can get a satellite into an equatorial orbit naturally. Launching in an eastward direction takes advantage of the rotation of Earth and adds an additional half-kilometer-per-second velocity to the rocket. Launching westward would subtract that velocity and be uneconomical. A launch from a higher latitude, say from Cape Canaveral, places the satellite in an orbit inclined to the equator at an angle.

In order to change an inclined orbit to an equatorial orbit, a considerable expenditure of additional fuel and reaction mass is called for. The larger the mass of the satellite, the greater the fuel requirements for the orbital modification. An industrial-capacity, solar-power satellite with a surface area of several square kilometers would be the most massive object ever to be placed in orbit. If the SPS were first placed in an inclined orbit, the cost for changing the orbit to an equatorial orbit would be stupendous.

Hence, O Navigador, Brazil. It had the equatorial location, it was possible to launch to the east, and that direction provided a fuel-saving over-the-water feature. Of the very limited number of nations affording such qualities, Brazil was the closest to Lone Star's headquarters. All other considerations were purely secondary.

By economizing to the max, cutting corners and with no one getting much sleep, Cash's team had managed to construct a bare-bones facility sufficient for launching a modified shuttle. Cash had made a special deal with NASA, which planned to discontinue the use of the shuttle shortly in favor of a coming SSTO (single stage to orbit), or RLV (reusable launch vehicle) fleet of space trucks. It was expected that the space trucks would eventually reduce the cost of taking a given mass into low Earth orbit (LEO) by a couple of orders of magnitude.

Carlson had lured several veteran astronauts from their NASA positions with promises of high adventure and frequent flights unencumbered by bureaucratic rules—in short, opportunities to play Buck Rogers. He paid them substantially higher salaries, but he understood that the best of them would not come and work for him just for the money.

He was also training his Lone Star men and women for launches and operations in space with reusable SSTO vehicles. These completely reflyable spaceships would make getting into LEO only a hundredth the cost of using throwaway rockets like Titans or the partially reflyable—but costly to service and operate—Space Shuttle. Cash was a major shareholder in an entrepreneurial firm that was developing SSTOs and expected to be shifting most of his space launches to the new vehicles as soon as they became available—possibly within a few years.

The O Navigador facility, as it stood, was not likely to draw tourists from far and wide. There was no luxury hotel, no museum, no theater, and no tour bus of any kind. Except for the gantries and the huge space-vehicle hangar, it looked like something thrown together on a Pacific island during World War Two as a way station for C-47s.

It would be a typical launch: routine and unspectacular, except in the purely visual sense. No matter what the mission, a space launch was still the most fabulous fireworks display in all of history.

"I wish I was going up with you," Carlson said to the assembled crew. They were in an air-conditioned prefab located as near as practicable to the gantry. It was one of the few air-conditioned structures in the area, necessitated by the heavy space suits the crew had to wear for launch.

"You always say that," Gudrun Dahlgren said. She was the lead engineer on this mission.

"Except when you're actually going along," James Esposito put in. He was the electronic engineer.

"I especially wish I was going along," Carlson continued, ignoring them, "because with this flight, not only will you be converting the first external fuel tank to a permanent orbiting habitat, but you'll be trying out the scooter. Since I did a big part of the designing on it, I should be the one to give it its first workout. But my schedule won't permit it, so you get to be the lucky ones."

"One hour to launch," boomed a voice over the intercom.

"Okay, I won't keep you here any longer," Carlson said. "I have to go butter up the press. Go on now and get the job done. And remember, I want some good footage of the scooter test. It's the sort of thing that'll really impress the TV audience, especially the younger viewers. You'll look like real spacemen instead of a bunch of overinflated Michelin Tire men."

The astronauts lurched to their feet as Carlson went out to the press briefing room. Media coverage of the O Navigador launches was minimal. As media assignments went, it didn't rate much better than a war zone in the third world. The only advantage to that, as far as Carlson was concerned, was that besides the dregs who couldn't draw better assignments, there were always a few hard-core space-shot junkies who were not only enthusiastic, but knowledgeable.

For Gudrun, Esposito, and the others, the only reality was the upcoming launch. They were veterans, with the nonchalant, almost catatonic attitude cultivated by astronauts since the beginning of manned space flight. The assumed casualness covered inevitable dread. Rewarding though it was, space travel was still an ordeal. Hardship lay ahead, most immediately during the launch-and-insertion phase. Besides the always present danger of catastrophic accident, there was the reaction to free fall. One never quite got used to it. No one looks forward to nausea.

Gudrun, like all space travelers, was grateful to the scientist who had come up with the first effective anti-nausea pill. Even so, it took time to work and it was more effective for some people than for others. There was always a certain degree of nausea upon leaving the gravity environment. Free fall, which looked so exhilarating on film, was a decidedly unpleasant sensation at first. It was much like the sensation felt when flying and one's aircraft hit an air pocket, the difference being that in free fall, the sensation never stopped. Earlier space travelers had had it worse. Some had stayed sick over the entirety of missions lasting for weeks, or even months.

As she finished her post-insertion checkouts and got unstrapped, Gudrun's stomach settled and she even began to feel a bit hungry. The faces of her companions were losing their pallor. It was time to start their mission.

"Okay, Jim, let's go," she said.

Gudrun led the way to where the new space suits were kept. The new suits fit both of them comfortably.

Normal air was used in the shuttle—in contrast to the Apollo spaceships in which a pure oxygen atmosphere was used. The oxygen pressure in the original shuttle space suit was significantly lower than the cabin pressure to avoid unwanted stiffening of the joints of the suit in vacuum. In consequence, several hours of pre-breathing of pure oxygen to purge nitrogen gases from the blood had been necessary in the shuttle whenever astronauts did extra-vehicular activities during the first two decades of their operations. It was done to prevent the crippling "bends" caused by nitrogen gas bubbles in the bloodstream, which would be induced by the lower gas pressure in the suit in vacuum. Women during their monthly periods and men with sickle-cell anemia in their genetic makeup were particularly vulnerable to this deadly affliction.

Earlier space suits requiring pre-breathing made it highly imprac-tical to perform macro-construction activities in space, such as the build-ing of space stations and the assembling of solar-power satellites. Now the air pressure within the new suit was the same as that in the shuttle. That meant no pre-breathing requirement for EVAs. The new space suit would not only make space more easily accessible, but also make it gen-uinely an equal-opportunity frontier to women and people of sub-Mediterranean ancestry.

Carlson had earlier invested in an entrepreneurial firm that had just become the first to perfect such an ideal space suit. Taking advantage of his position as a major stockholder, he took delivery of six new suits ahead of other customers such as NASA.

As lead engineer, Gudrun was the first to exit the spacecraft through the air lock into the cargo bay, where she was joined immediately by Esposito. The bay doors were already open, framing the sort of view that people on Earth could only dream about. The two gazed for a minute in awestruck wonder, dazzled as always by the sight that never palls.

The external tank had separated from the craft an hour earlier and floated a half-kilometer away. It was larger than their orbiter, about the size of a 747 jumbo jet. It hung there like a colossal torpedo against the background of half-lit Earth, whose bright blue hemisphere was rapidly gaining on the darker half as the orbiter traveled into the sunlit zone at a velocity of some eight kilometers per second.

The eastern extremity of the planet was a thin, dazzlingly bright crescent where the sun's rays reflected from the Pacific. The orbiter soared over equatorial Africa, with the Americas far beyond. Below them was the brown of the continent, with the Arabian Peninsula to the north, the view all but obscured by cloud. Over the Pacific to the east, they could see the swirling white of a big storm system. Against the jumbled, multicolored mosaic of Earth, the fuel tank stood out in surreal starkness. There are no soft edges in space, no fuzzy lighting. Nothing is out of focus. All is brilliant light or absolute shadow, with no filtering atmosphere.

"Enough gawking," Esposito said. "Let's get to work."

It was typical of Carlson, Gudrun thought, that he was more enthusiastic about trying out his scooter than he was about an historic first like establishing a permanent habitat in a fuel tank. It took the better part of an hour to get the little vehicle unloaded and checked out; then they climbed onto it and strapped in.

"*Vroom, vroom!*" Esposito said, pantomiming motorcycle handlebar controls.

"None of that," Gudrun said. "Nice and sedate, this trip." She sighted the skeletal craft's nose in the direction of the fuel tank and fired up. The scooter's low-yield booster kicked in smoothly and they accelerated to the maximum safe speed for the experimental run. It was not exactly at a heart-stopping velocity but more like the pace of an elderly accountant taking a leisurely stroll in the park. It would take several minutes to cross the half kilometer at such a speed, but this way, they would use a minimum of reaction gas jet to decelerate at their destination.

In the movies, spacemen zipped around in similar, albeit sleeker, scooters, accelerating, turning and decelerating just as if they were driving motorcycles, using a combination of friction, momentum, and gravity to maneuver with. In real space, only the momentum applied. If the braking deceleration were to fail, they would overshoot the target and keep right on going in an orbit around Earth. In that case, their only hope for rescue would be for another scooter, or the orbiter itself, to come for them.

Computing a precise orbit for the second scooter to play catch-up would be tricky, since simply going faster than the first scooter in the same direction would not get the job done: The two scooters would then be in different orbits. For the orbiter itself to come to the rescue would be an extravagant proposition in terms of fuel economy. All things considered, neither prospect was attractive. They had decided ahead of time that in case of deceleration failure, they would abandon ship. Even if they couldn't stop, they would pass close to the tank, and if they timed their jump perfectly, they might just stick to the metallic surface of the tank by the pull of the magnetized padding of their space suits. It was worth a gamble, anyway. And the best safety precaution was to fly very, very slowly. There was no big rush.

In the actual event, there was no problem. After a few small mid-course corrections, they came within a few meters of the tip of the tank. As Gudrun decelerated the scooter, Jim reached out to the hull and placed a magnetic anchor on its skin. By means of their magnetic boots and knee pads, they transferred themselves from scooter to tank without difficulty. It was neither graceful nor dashing, but it was safe and it worked.

Getting the tank open was a strenuous task. Its hatch was securely fastened by several latches, using the tried-and-true principle of backup safety systems. With tools from the saddlebag of the scooter, the two engineers pried the latches loose one by one. As always seems to be the case, several were more stubborn than others, and one was reluctant to come loose at all, but after a half hour of struggle, the last latch was free.

Gudrun contemplated the folding handle. "I wonder if this thing's gonna open."

"One way to find out," Jim said. "Turn the handle."

"Why didn't I think of that?" she muttered. No sense stalling. She tugged the handle into operating position, twisted it a half turn, braced her boots against the skin of the tank and pulled with her whole body. For a moment, her heart skipped a few beats as the door seemed to stick, then smoothly swung open on its single hinge.

"I'll be damned," she said. "It worked!" Then she flipped on her speaker and reported to the remaining orbiter crew, and to the world in general, in the clipped, test-pilot's voice made familiar by NASA cap-coms—capsule communicators—during the Apollo missions: "The hatch is open now. We are going in. I will radio you after reaching the Igloo."

The Igloo was the name given to the living quarters installed before launch in the intertank section between the forward compartment containing liquid oxygen and the larger aft compartment of liquid hydrogen. Quantities of both chemicals remained in the two compartments. Each would be put to good use by the crew.

As the lead engineer, it was Gudrun's privilege to be first "down" the hatch, despite the absence of any such direction in free fall. She crawled into a tunnel that ran through the length of the tank. It was roomy enough for her to move along on hands and knees without bumping her head on the "ceiling." She could even turn around, though with some difficulty.

Guided by the lamp in her helmet, she crawled about fifteen meters down the tunnel and found the hatch leading to the Igloo. There were no dogs holding this one shut. She turned its handle and pushed it open, then pulled herself in. She turned in a full circle, shining her helmet lamp over on all the interior surfaces. Everything looked intact on initial examination.

She was the first human being to enter what was to be Lone Star's space station in orbit, and she savored the sensation. "Come on in, Jim."

He pulled himself in and looked around. "I guess we've got a job to do now."

Indeed, the task ahead of them was formidable. First, they had to run a thorough check to make sure the Igloo had not suffered damage in the launch. Then they would prepare it for occupancy and stock it with the provisions they had brought up from Earth.

Second, they had to fit auxiliary boosters to the external tank so that its orbit could be adjusted as necessary. In time, more external tanks would be added to the first to form a working space station for the construction of Lone Star Enterprise's solar-power satellite. Some one hundred and fifty workers would eventually have to be housed in the orbiting environment.

Third, a module had to be attached so that orbiters launched from Earth could dock with the external tank on future flights.

Then they could prepare the inside of the external tank for the installation of various facilities. Carlson already had several contracts for the use of this space station; he badly needed the rent money to keep his solar-power program going.

That was in the immediate-to-distant future. For now, Gudrun had a message to deliver. She turned on her speaker.

"Orbiter, O Navigador and Houston: This is the Igloo. Looks like we got us a space station."

3

CARLSON'S INNER CIRCLE met in the plush executive conference room of Carlson Tower to map out its strategy for the following week. The problem was a move by an international group to establish a U.N. regulatory committee on power satellites. If established, the committee would have in effect a stranglehold not only on power satellites, but on virtually all future exploitation of space. It would establish a precedent granting the U.N. power over all space ventures, meaning, in essence, that nothing would ever get done.

Cash and his coalition of allies and odd bedfellows were determined to defeat the resolution. Backing it was an equally determined array of powers and individuals who were pushing for the socialization of space. Leading the movement were theorists who had seen their dreams of social engineering come crashing down in the ruins of the Soviet Empire, taking with it nearly all of the lesser nation-sized experiments. Having utterly lost the contest on Earth, they hoped to recoup their fortunes in space. Following them was a broad spectrum of enthusiasts whose motives ranged from idealism to simple greed.

When Cash came into the room, he found all the others seated at the conference table except for Parker, who stood at a window facing away from the others. Parker had been an early acquisition during the days when Carlson's work still involved more back alleys than boardrooms. The ex-SEAL had compiled a record for ruthless efficiency that was awesome even among that hard-bitten fraternity, and had carried the same reputation into his civilian security work.

Pat Coogan and Bob Thibodeaux sat in their usual chairs. Thibodeaux was Cash's New York hatchet man, in charge of enforcing policy and instilling motivation. He was small and sleek, with none of Parker's rough edges; he looked like one of those sharp-toothed animals capable of taking on other animals far larger than itself and sending them away bloody. He reminded people who met him of a wolverine. Even people who had never seen a wolverine thought he looked like one.

Across from them sat Alison Baird: plump, matronly, and a top-flight media expert. Next to her sat Adam Altieri, her personal secretary and right-hand man. He was poised with recorder and notepad. Alison had worked her way from weather girl at a local station to head of programming and vice president of one of the first international TV networks before being forced out by conventional network politics. Carlson had rescued her from the ignominy of teaching media communications at a university by making her his PR chief. Her job was to make him and his Lone Star Space Systems look good.

On her other side sat Auguste Chamoun, the money man. When his French–Lebanese banking family lost everything in the tragic devastations of Beirut, he had retained only his degree from Harvard and a devious head for figures. He had come to Carlson, promising to double, if not triple, every dime the Texan could raise. So far, he had been as good as his word.

Absent was the mystery man, the man none of them except Cash and Parker had ever seen. He was the secret weapon, essential to nearly every one of Carlson's enterprises. There were those who secretly thought that the man didn't exist, that Cash had made him up. But even these were forced to admit to themselves that the man, whom Carlson would refer to only as "Max," had to be real. It was hard to believe that anything human could accomplish what Max had done.

Carlson opened the proceedings. "Any new business?"

Parker spoke. "We got IDs on the other two stiffs: Boyd Flaherty, an IRA gunner with a flair for overseas work, and Basil Krylov, ex-KGB."

"It sounds like someone deliberately put together an international team, to spread the suspicion around," Thibodeaux opined.

"Not necessarily." Parker turned around and faced the table. "The mercenaries and international crooks have their ways of contacting one another. They hang out at the same bars and know the same people in common. They even have their own computer bulletin boards to keep current on who's got what projects going. If one had a plan to snatch the boss, it'd be pretty easy to put together a team like this. It's easier for them to get around if they never worked together. Six ex-SAVAK guys show up in New York all at once, even the New York cops will know something's going down."

"Then the question is: Were they freelancing their own operation or was someone else behind them?" Pat said.

"I've got my people working on it, but don't expect anything soon." Parker at last took his seat. "These guys don't go in for written contracts. Marseilles is still the major clearinghouse for mercenary operations, and I'm checking with my sources there to find out where these men last worked and if anyone was noising off about this operation."

"It's playing well in the news," Alison said. "Plenty of action, no innocent bystanders killed, the bad guys dead, and Cash survives another attempt on his life." She turned to him. "It adds luster to your flamboyant reputation."

"It's not the sort of reputation I need just now," Cash said.

"Flamboyance always goes down well with Americans, and there's no such thing as bad publicity," she told him.

"So how's my reputation as the space entrepreneur with the Midas touch?" Cash asked.

"Still the golden boy," she reported. "You know how Americans love swashbuckling men with murky pasts who come out of nowhere to attain riches and power."

"The down side of that being that they also love to see them toppled." Thibodeaux showed his feral smile.

"That goes without saying," Alison conceded. To her, reputation and publicity formed an ongoing process. Nothing was ever engraved in stone.

"Bob, how's our vote situation?" Cash asked.

"Looking good, but marshaling third-world votes is always touchy. Their U.N. people tend to be swayed by whoever greased their palms that particular morning. And there are so damn many countries now. The Euros are solidly with us. They dropped socialism so fast you'd never think they invented it in the first place. But it still has some cachet in parts of Asia, and in Africa and South America. The Middle East can sway either way. The real basket-case countries are going to be against us almost unanimously. The Balkans, led by Serbia, are going to give us trouble."

"If that's looking good, what looks bad?" Carlson asked.

"The numbers are still with us, Boss. I just want you to know that there can be some surprises yet in store."

"Good report. I've got my own strategy for dealing with them, and I've been talking it up with the Euros, the Russians, and the Japanese. They all think it's got promise and I'm sure of it."

"Max again?" Chamoun asked.

"No, no technological miracles this time, just old-fashioned politics."

"Enlighten us, Boss," Pat said.

Carlson leaned back in his chair and laced his fingers behind his head. "The world, as I'm sure you've all noticed, has changed enormously in the last decade or so. The last old-fashioned empire collapsed and divided into nations. Those nations, and others, subdivided into mini-nations, mostly along linguistic, or even tribal, lines. In all the reshuffling of borders, only Germany got significantly larger. The EEC formed the first modern-style confederacy, and others are shaping up in other parts of the world. So far, it seems to be a better system than the former coercive empires or stand-alone nations, but the reports aren't all in yet."

They endured the elementary social-studies lesson because they knew that he was about to get around to his point. For one thing, his Texas drawl, all but imperceptible in his ordinary speech, was growing pronounced. It was a sure sign that the message was on its way.

"Do you know what the new world is getting to look like?" Cash asked.

"Tell us, Boss," Parker said.

"It's beginning to look a little bit like the United States. What we have now is an agglomeration of states with representatives at the U.N., which now serves in the role of World Congress."

"The U.N. isn't a governing body," Alison pointed out.

"Lots of talk, not much action," Chamoun said. "That's pretty much like Congress."

"Exactly," Cash said. "Now, the men in my family served in the legislature of Texas from the days of the Republic. We had senators and representatives, both U.S. and Confederate, through the whole history of the state. Those men were experts at local, state, national, and international politics, and one of the great truths they learned and passed on is that at the representative level, all politics is local, every bit of it. And the U.N. is no different. Every member state is looking out for its own interest and will be swayed by appeals to that interest. The idea is to spread the interest out as far as possible.

"Let's look at the space programs of the past. Remember how the

Soviets did it? They had a centralized system headquartered at Moscow, and that government took no interest whatever in the welfare of the member states. The result was that even within the communist system, the local Parties became the enemies of the Moscow clique. When the clique settled on a space program, it decided where to locate it and put nearly everything in that spot: rocket-building factories, launching facilities, housing and training for the cosmonauts, everything. The people in the other republics got no immediate benefit from the project. It might as well have been happening in another country.

"Now, let's look at how it was done in the U.S. When the space program cranked into high gear under the impetus of the Soviet threat, the senators and representatives in Congress were all for it. Then they started carving it up. Pieces of spacecraft and their instrumentation were made in every state of the Union. Florida got the launch facilities, Texas got manned mission control, California got the bulk of the manufacturing, Alabama got one space center, Maryland got another. When the shuttle came along, it was launched from Florida but it landed in California at first, so that the whole contraption had to ride piggyback on an airplane, clear across the continent, before it could be launched again."

"Gross inefficiency," Chamoun snorted.

"But the U.S. was rich enough to do it that way and make it work," Cash pointed out. "There's no world empire, and the U.N. is no Moscow. What the new world does possess is a community of interest."

"You'd think they'd see that it's in the interest of the whole world to have abundant, cheap power," Pat said.

"Sure," Cash agreed. "But let's face it, most of the world has never had much of anything and they find it hard to believe that they ever will. Can you convince some guy in Bangladesh that a power satellite will make his water buffalo work better? Assuming he's the one in a hundred rich enough to have a water buffalo. What these people are going to want is immediate benefit, not literal pie in the sky."

"You've lost me," Thibodeaux said. "Are we back to just passing out bribes?"

"Uh-uh. I've talked it over with my principal allies and rivals and we've agreed to do this the good old-fashioned, deal-making, pork-barreling political way. We're going to get out there on the floor of the U.N. and promise everybody a piece of it."

"My god, Boss!" Thibodeaux said. "That's grotesque! Anything on that scale will be ruinously expensive and inefficient."

"It'll be big and audacious," Alison said. "It'll be new. It's just what people have come to expect from Cash Carlson." Headlines and sound bites danced in her eyes. She turned to the man seated beside her. "Adam, dear, take a note: 'Rumors fly that Cash Carlson will unveil a revolutionary proposal at the U.N.' See that it gets to the papers in time for the evening edition."

"How do we pull it off?" Pat asked.

"Since the earliest days of space flight, it's been acknowledged that equatorial countries are ideally sited for space-launch facilities. There're a dozen nations, most of them third-world, that have an immediate stake in our project. Everyone must have something to contribute, and we have to convince them of that."

Cash's Texas drawl gained speed along with his enthusiasm. "Does your nation have the sort of sand necessary for making the type of silicate we need for our orbiting power stations? Well, we'll just build our silicon-making plant right within your borders. And since it'll have to have power, you're going to get that hydroelectric dam you've been begging for all these years!" I want your teams working on this, people. I want you to find out what every little nation in the U.N. has to contribute to this undertaking so that we can let them know they stand to make a bundle out of it."

"We are talking here of money in almost mythical amounts," said Chamoun in his slow, all-but-inflectionless voice.

"The developed nations of the world," Cash said, "pour trillions into the undeveloped ones, and hardly anyone benefits from it. That's waste. This will not be waste. Besides, just think of what easy access to cheap energy can do to create economic opportunities for the developing world. We'll need extremely tight control to make sure that the loot is properly spent and doesn't get siphoned off into some generalissimo's brother-in-law's pockets. That's a nice plum for the U.N. itself. Did you ever see them turn down a chance at another bureau?"

"It could salve their sensibilities, wounded at losing their regulatory commission to strangle privatization of space," Thibodeaux conceded.

"I can see already that this is going to be a challenge," Chamoun said. "So many of those nations have nothing at all, not even location. And far too many of them are involved in wars."

"And for that very reason, foreign investors have been staying away in droves," Cash said. "Maybe this prospect will help them come to their senses and quit fighting. Put your minds to it. Hire specialists in the more remote parts of the globe. There may be possibilities out there we wouldn't dream of. If all they produce is people, we'll need contract laborers by the hundreds of thousands."

"And you got the others to agree with this?" Thibodeaux asked.

"Right. We each have different ideas about how we're going to get up there and grab the energy, but this is how we're going to pitch our projects to the U.N. The important thing right now is to assure that we can do anything at all. This planet needs that energy, that we all agree on."

"Which brings us to our next point," Thibodeaux said. "Right now, we space entrepreneurs are a band of allies with a common enemy. As soon as the enemy is eliminated, we become rivals again."

"That's the way it is with alliances," Cash agreed.

They spent the next few hours discussing the nuts and bolts of the upcoming operation. The conference room had its own computer terminals, with keyboards and folding monitors built into the table so that the participants could contact their nets and receive reports without having to leave. While Alison outlined a publicity campaign, Pat lined up a dozen high-powered think tanks and put them on retainer; Chamoun assessed the corporation's cash and credit reserves and set experts to work on an analysis of the developed nations' foreign-aid expenditures over the past decade.

While his aides conferred among themselves, Cash began to make telephone calls. Computers were fine for business purposes, but politics required personal contact and the human voice. In the space of two hours, he spoke with six senators, four key congressional committee chiefs, and eleven heads of state, including the President of the U.S. Last of all, he spoke with Helen Butterworth, incumbent secretary of energy and American delegate to the U.N. conference on energy satellites. For this call, he used the phone's TV screen. Helen liked to see who she was talking to.

"So, the prodigal returns," she said before he could say a word. "Where have you been the past week?" Helen Butterworth had an anchorwoman's looks and a diplomat's poise.

"Out working miracles, as usual, Helen. How're Mitch and the kids?"

She smiled. "They're fine, as if you cared. What are you after, Cash?"

"You wound me. Your family is as dear as my own. Actually, Helen, I need to know how you read the upcoming vote."

She sighed. "It's not like the old days, when nations A could be counted on to vote pro-U.S. and nations B would all vote pro-Soviet. They're like baseball players now: each a free agent who has to be courted. We'll give it our best pitch, but I can't be seen to favor Lone Star or any other American firm."

"That's understood, Helen." He glanced at Parker. The security chief was studying his own computer screen, this one loaded with the arcane graphics of his trade. He looked over at Cash and nodded.

"Line's secure at both ends and all points between, Boss."

"Is that your head thug I hear talking, Cash? Doesn't he trust my security precautions?"

"Jack's right hand doesn't trust his left, Helen. You know that."

"So what's the big secret? If I think you're about to lay me open to conspiracy charges, I'll blab it all over the media."

"Don't worry. The whole world will know all about it in a few days, but I wanted you to know about it going in." He gave her a brief run-down on the new game plan, and was delighted to see her jaw drop with dismay and her eyes fill with horror. It had been years since he'd seen Helen Butterworth's poise slip so thoroughly.

"You can't be serious! In an age of austerity, you're proposing a spending extravaganza such as the world has never seen! Nobody will go for it!"

"Don't be so sure. I'm proposing that the world start investing its wealth for a change, instead of throwing it away. This is an ambitious undertaking, I'll be the first to say so. But the initial investment won't be even a substantial fraction of the money the developed nations pour down the rat holes of the world without doing themselves or the rat holes any good. With my plan, everybody involved will profit. I'll be ponying up a big hunk of change myself, and the nations that'll be my biggest customers will put up the rest. The developed nations have the greatest need of energy, so it makes sense that they should be major investors."

"One little problem here, Cash. There are a dozen other contenders for the orbiting power-station business. Why should Lone Star get the entire world's business?"

"I've talked it over with most of them, and they agree that this is the best way to get the whole project funded. Whichever of us gets the nod will follow the plan."

"And how is the world going to decide which of you to hire?"

"We're going to do it the old-fashioned way, Helen: We're going to have a race."

4

THE U.N. LOOKED much as it always had: a white tombstone by a polluted river. Cars with diplomatic plates were happily double-parked for blocks around. Outside, as usual, demonstrators picketed. These days, most of the demonstrators were Americans of various ethnic groups protesting whatever was being done to their ancestral countries, either by foreign oppressors or by the current governments of those nations. Very few were demonstrating for or against the matter of the day's debate. It wasn't the sort of thing people got very excited about anymore.

Inside, much was changed. The number of nations had expanded enormously since the inception of the U.N., and more were created, it seemed, almost every day. This strained the space available, and the meeting rooms were growing ever more crowded. The Trustee Room had been chosen for the day's debate, since it was more spacious than most and there were hardly any territories left under U.N. trusteeship, anyway. Just at the moment, it was crowded with diplomats, industrialists, technical experts, and the press from dozens of nations, many of them vying for the few empty seats. A great many wore lightweight headsets attached to computerized translators. The proceedings would, as usual, be in English.

A murmur went through the room when Cash made an appearance. The other space entrepreneurs sent representatives to do the requisite arm-twisting, but Cash preferred the personal hands-on style. Pat accompanied him. Parker and his team stayed outside to monitor the situation. Security services tended to turn green when they saw Parker and his men coming. Armed men in street armor with grenades in their pockets gave the detection devices fits. Parker would spend the next few hours trading shoptalk with the other bodyguards while his team nailed down the approaches. It was standard drill to keep them all alert. Nobody had ever pulled a hit or terrorist action at the U.N., but there could always be a first time.

Cash saw a stylishly dressed European coming toward him with the obvious intention of speaking. He held out a hand and put on a grin of delighted recognition. "Who the hell is this?" he whispered to Pat.

"Hans Krause," she whispered back. "Rep and bagman for ESE. You met him in Zurich last year."

"Hans!" Cash said, gripping the fine-boned hand in his own more rough-hewn one. "Good to see you again! Are you all ready for the big debate?"

"We of European Space Enterprise have the highest confidence of success, Mr. Carlson." The accent was French, not German. Probably from Alsace-Lorraine, Cash decided. "However, we must expect trouble from the Balkans." His voice was tinged with the slightly exasperated contempt of the well-bred western European for his crass southeastern neighbors.

"I think we can deal with them," Cash assured him.

"It is to be hoped. People preoccupied with unresolved issues dating to the fourth century are unprepared to deal with the twenty-first. The Serb foreign minister is to be first to speak, I believe."

"I think I can guess what he'll say."

"Undoubtedly. Ah, Mr. Carlson, my chief was most impressed by your proposal. One expects audacity from the Americans, of course, but not such subtlety." It was one of those finely tuned statements that could be insulting or complimentary, or both.

"I think it's a very American sort of plan, Mr. Krause. I was just discussing it with my aides, and we all agreed that it's very American in concept."

"I must study the implications. In any case, my compliments on a most daring and original plan."

"And please convey my compliments to Monsieur du Mont." They shook hands again and the European wandered off to collar a few third-worlders.

"I don't like him," Pat said.

"He's nothing. It's his boss I don't like, and he really counts. Now, let's get to work. Got your list?"

"Right here. First target's sitting at a desk halfway up the slope, about six o'clock."

"Let's go get 'im."

Cash had Lesotho, Upper Volta, Chad, and Surinam in the bag before the Serb got up to speak. He was dickering with the Burmese—or was it still Myanmar?—representative when the meeting was called to order. The People's Republic still had strong socialist leanings, but it had the inevitable need for hard foreign currency, especially since the bottom had fallen out of the opium market with the development of cheap synthetics. Cash encouraged him to think of something truly beneficial that Burma really needed, and the man suddenly remembered that the long-moribund Irrawaddy dam project was just waiting to be reopened. Cash pointed out that with such a dam, Burma would be in a position to enter the labor-intensive ceramics industry, so essential to the energy satellites that he, Cash Carlson, planned to send into orbit in large numbers. The Burmese acknowledged that this bit of capitalist exploitation might indeed be the kick in the pants his nation needed to get it into competition with its high-tech Asian powerhouse neighbors. In exchange for a firm commitment, he might even consider reversing his government's stated policy concerning the U.N. regulatory committee.

"Damn!" Cash said as the two left the Burmese delegation amid smiles and handshakes. "Things are looking up. If we can get the Burmese, we can get anybody!"

"So far, so good," Pat agreed. "I think they're about to start." They were nearly two thirds of the way up the sloping, theaterlike floor. From this vantage point, they could survey the knots and huddles of deal-making in progress. To one side, Krause was chatting urbanely with some former colonial types. Smiling Japanese were glad-handing some South Americans, and a group of loud, laughing, backslapping Russians was overwhelming some frail-looking Malaysians.

"I have my doubts about those Russians," Cash said. "They're on the right side, but they come on like bulldozers."

"I'll talk with them," Pat said. "It's the country of Chekhov and Dostoevsky, so I guess they can be subtle and understated if they really try."

"No need to understate, but people from highly formalized cultures are insulted by that sort of boorishness."

Pat studied her boss from the corners of her eyes. As always, she was taken off guard when the education and culture showed through the surface of his frontier bonhomie. She thought she knew him as well as anyone did, but that wasn't saying much. On the surface, it seemed that there should be no mystery about him. As he said so often in his rambling briefings to his staff, he was from an old Texas family with branches in Karnes County in the south and Brewster County in the west. He had spent an apparently typical Texas boyhood doing whatever it was Texas boys did, going from high school to Texas A&M, where he took an undistinguished degree in engineering, followed by a stint in the Air Force as a lieutenant with an ROTC commission. Here he got into classified work and his record began to get murky. He left the Air Force and then simply dropped from view and from all records. Not so much as a single credit-card receipt gave evidence of the next five years of his life.

He resurfaced in Galveston, running a salvage operation. He claimed to have a map showing the location of a sunken Spanish galleon. The *Nuestra Señora de los Dolores* had gone down somewhere off Padre Island in 1615 with something like six tons of silver aboard, along with a half ton of gold in bullion form, plus the jewelry of the wealthy passengers and the treasure chests of the many merchants aboard, not listed in the royal accounts. The *Dolores* was the Lost Dutchman Mine of the galleon hunters, and everyone ridiculed the newcomer, assuming that he had been sold one of the hundreds of fake maps that were in circulation all over the world, especially on the Gulf Coast. Just another sucker, everyone thought. He wouldn't even show anyone his map.

From somewhere, Cash assembled a team of ex-Navy divers and off-shore engineers who had built and worked the oil platforms of the shallow waters. One morning they sailed from Galveston and stopped at an utterly undistinguished spot off the Texas coast where the water was no more than fifty feet deep. On the sandy bottom they marked out a precise rectangle and sank a cofferdam. Once the water was emptied from the cofferdam, they began pumping out the sand deposited by four centuries of gulf currents and hurricanes. Fifteen feet down, they found the *Dolores*, beautifully preserved.

The storm that had struck the vessel had arisen suddenly, so that the crew had not had time to throw things overboard and lighten the ship. She had heeled over in a phenomenally powerful wind, and a number of cannons had burst their breechings, punching holes through sides that were now under water. The sea had rushed in and the *Dolores* had sunk in minutes, taking with her five hundred crew, soldiers, and passengers.

The treasure of the *Dolores* had eventually realized nearly a half-billion dollars, and Cash was rumored to have a good part of the treasure hidden away in vaults somewhere. Of course, it had not all been simple. As soon as the *Dolores* was found, the State of Texas and the U.S. government had stepped in, impounding everything. At that time, Cash had displayed the political acumen for which he was later legendary. Origin in obscure, thinly populated rural counties did not mean political insignificance in Texas. Especially if your great-great-grandfather was with Sam Houston at San Jacinto. A few generous contributions to Texas institutes of higher learning, badly hurt by the various oil crises, had lined up the state on his side. Then Cash and the State of Texas had taken on the United States. After all, the Texas legislature reasoned, it wasn't as if some Yankee had come down to take the state's rightful treasure.

Cash had mollified the academic community immediately by erecting a museum in Galveston, where he transported the entire priceless Spanish galleon and all ancillary discoveries for display. To the Smithsonian he sent all the jewels and other artwork as a permanent display—though still available to Cash as security for loans. For conversion to currency, he used only the bulk bullion, which was of no archaeological interest save for a few dozen ingots, which he donated to various museums throughout the world. For the Catholic Church, he erected and endowed, in Galveston, the Church of Our Lady of Sorrows, for the repose of the souls of all the faithful who had died when the *Nuestra Señora de los Dolores* had sunk beneath the waves.

These masterstrokes of diplomacy had cleared his way, allowing him to use the treasure of the *Dolores* to found his commercial empire, rooted unexpectedly in the aerospace industry everyone had assumed was dead. Even then, there had been grumbles. That cofferdam bothered people. All the photos and diagrams showed the hull of the *Dolores* perfectly centered within the concrete rectangle. No map, people argued, could possibly be so precise. The treasure hunters who had spent their

lives searching for the wreck hundreds of miles away were especially bitter about it, but what could anyone argue? If Cash didn't have the map he claimed, the only other explanation was supernatural intervention. Several tabloids featured just that, along with the usual stories about how Cash was actually an alien from a UFO, possibly a reincarnation of Elvis.

In the years since, Carlson had built up a space service that had succeeded, against all expectation, without government money. He had taken absurd risks and had done things that seemed magical. And his risks always paid off. That was what rankled and puzzled people. Even his closest assistants wondered how anyone in his right mind could undertake the loony projects Cash regarded as everyday enterprises. He didn't hire yes men, and when they loudly demanded how the bloody hell he expected this particular piece of lunacy to pay off, he had a single answer: "Max says it'll work."

Max. Even now, Pat fumed when she thought of the name. Why wouldn't her boss tell her who Max was, maybe even introduce her to him? There were those who said that Max didn't exist, that it was Carlson's name for his own unique genius, but Pat didn't think so. Carlson was brilliant, but even he wasn't that brilliant. She was sure he had one of those idiots savants on tap, the sort who could do anything save live in the real world.

"They're starting," Pat said. The murmur settled down and people lucky enough to have seats took their places, adjusting the headsets of their translators. The young Dalai Lama intoned a secular blessing on the proceedings; then a Sri Lankan functionary announced the day's agenda, naming the lineup of speakers. The Secretary-General welcomed all participants and spoke of the grave importance of the matter under debate.

When the Secretary-General stepped down, the first speaker took his place. This was the foreign secretary of the Republic of Serbia, a squat, bullnecked man with a drooping mustache. He began by addressing a few general remarks, declaring the benevolence of the republic toward all the nations of the world. He further espoused the principles of universal progress through the equitable distribution of the world's wealth and resources—principles for which the republic firmly stood. Then he got down to business.

"Space," he declared grandly, "is the common heritage of all mankind. This is self-evident. If any country or private business establish-

ment wishes to exploit space by placing solar-power satellites in orbit, we the people of the world have the right to demand users' fees from them. I hereby make a motion for the establishment of a United Nations-based regulatory commission on solar-power satellites. The commission should be empowered to impose a U.N. value-added tax on the electricity from space power stations. I further propose that the money from the said tax be distributed among the developing or have-not nations for redress of wrongs done, and still being done, to them by the have nations."

A functionary stood up at a lower podium: "A motion has been made to establish a United Nations regulatory commission to oversee all orbiting power satellites, and endowed with the authority to impose a value-added tax upon the energy produced by said satellites, the proceeds for said tax to be distributed among the developing member nations. Is the motion seconded?"

By obvious prearrangement, the prime minister of Bangladesh stood and seconded the motion. The floor was thrown open to debate and the Bangladeshi was the first to speak, repeating the gist of what the Serbian had said and pointing out to the membership that Bangladesh was the have-not-nation standard by which all other have-nots were judged. He was warmly applauded, but the applause was entirely from the developing countries except for China and India. A slight frown betrayed his surprise at the indifferent reception of his proposal.

The next speaker was announced: American delegate Helen Butterworth, U.S. secretary of energy. The clicking and whirring of cameras greeted her. She was a favorite of photographers with her fashion-model looks and striking hair; she was a rare and genuine strawberry blonde. Interviewers often made the mistake of judging her by her appearance and expecting softball answers to their questions. It was a short-lived misapprehension. Unlike the others, she began without preamble.

"What the prime minister of Bangladesh and the foreign minister of Serbia propose is contrary to the accepted practice of the United Nations and contrary to the ideal of free enterprise. It is of course true that space is the common heritage of mankind; but it is there to be utilized by the human race freely. As long as nobody puts up solar-power satellites, the economic value to us of this common heritage is precisely zero.

"Entrepreneurs must risk their money to realize solar-power stations in geosynchronous orbit, and there should be a reward for it. As

long as there is plenty of free competition, the marketplace will make
sure that the inhabitants of this planet will get the best deal possible. Let
me point out that the United Nations has never considered a regulatory
commission on geosynchronous communications satellites. If we don't
need such a commission for ComSats, why do we need one for energy
satellites? The world is desperate for clean, cheap, abundant energy.
What possible excuse can there be for placing barriers in the way of
those who would go out and find that energy for us?"

"Hear, hear!" Cash said, applauding. A sizable rooting section stood
and applauded with him.

Butterworth went on for another fifteen minutes, embellishing her
original point with a salvo of impressive figures and quotes from acknowledged experts in the field. She stepped down, to be followed by a
Russian who presented his opposition to the proposed commission from
his nation's new capitalistic perspective.

So it went for the rest of the day. Politicians and statesmen, both
for and against the regulatory commission, urged their views. From the
first, the defining lines were clear. Practically all nations with space-
faring technology were against the commission. Those without such
technologies were split between those in alliance with space-age nations
and those without such alliances. The scheduled speakers read from
prepared texts, and it was clear from their stumbling delivery that some
of them were already getting conflicting signals from their governments.

Pat frowned when the delegate from the Dominican Republic spoke
up in favor of the commission. "I thought we had an agreement with
them!"

"We have," Cash assured her. "This is for the folks back home. They
don't get let in on all the fine print. They'll hear what their representative says and probably pay no attention to how he votes."

The day went on with speaker following speaker. The pressure
teams of the space-going nations worked the floor discreetly during the
speeches and energetically during the frequent breaks. Many years earlier, the U.N. had settled into a leisurely routine, broken only by international emergencies such as the invasion of one member nation by
another. Emergency measures were handled by the Security Council,
and this matter, momentous as it was, was no emergency. For this sort
of debate, the members preferred a slow pace, lots of talk, plenty of
backstairs politicking, rest breaks during which lines could be redrawn,
long lunches, and cocktail parties in the evenings. Most delegates were

on per diem, and the permanent staffs collected yearly salaries, so why rush things?

For two days, the politicians had their say; then the floor was opened to the expert witnesses. The world-renowned physicist from Princeton was the first to speak, as arranged by Carlson and his allies. His plea was impassioned: "Leave our last frontier open for exploitation by the free-spirited—our survival now depends on it. Even at the current rate of consumption, the world's petroleum reserve will not last more than five decades. A much-desired improvement in the standard of living in the developing world is increasing the energy-consumption rate exponentially. Billions of people living in the developing countries that cannot afford the oil are burning soft coals at an alarming rate, raising the specter of a massive ecological disaster. Safe, controlled nuclear-fusion power plants are not yet within our grasp—except the one in space, the sun. Let us reach out to the heavens with solar-power satellites and fulfill the legacy of Prometheus, who brought the fire from the sky for the human race."

He was followed by prominent scientists, scholars, and pundits from Ithaca (U.S.A.), Saint Petersburg (Russia), Tokyo, Utrecht, Montreal, Buenos Aires, and a number of other places, arguing for either side.

5

THE EVENING OF the second day, Carlson threw a massive reception for the delegates and the visitors in Carlson Tower. The hospitality rooms took up two entire floors, connected by broad stairways that were perfect for having one's picture taken by the press. Overhanging balconies allowed everyone to watch everyone else, and mirrored walls made it possible to see who was where and what was happening in all directions. Numerous convenient alcoves allowed small groups to break away from the main crowds for more-intimate communication.

"Not many of the scientists are here," Pat noted. She hovered at Cash's elbow, ready to prompt him with names, for which he had a terrible memory.

"Of course not. They want to feel that their participation is entirely disinterested. If they accepted my booze and buffet, people might think I was buying their support."

"Mallory is here." She nodded to where the boyishly handsome celebrity scientist was holding forth to an audience of adoring listeners.

"Mallory's different," Cash said. "He'd rather be here than at a scientific conference any day."

Quentin Mallory was one of Alison Baird's finds. During a visit to UCLA, she had heard about the young professor of astronomy whose classes were so popular that students had to take an extraordinary list of prerequisites before they could even apply for them. He was also the author of three best-selling books, only one of which was about astronomy. Of the other two, one was about evolution and the other about the nature of human consciousness. Intrigued, Alison had made inquiries. Mallory's colleagues sniffed that his professional work was shallow, that he spread himself too thin. She decided that they were jealous of his popularity and of the sales figures on his books.

"Boss, we've got to have him," she had told Cash. "The greatest scientists in the world put people to sleep when they talk and their writing reads like textbooks. This guy excites people. He talks and writes about science, and people get a sense of wonder and adventure from it. I talked to fifty kids on that campus who said that they'd decided to go into science after reading his books or attending his classes. Who cares if he's not the greatest astronomer in the world if he inspires a thousand kids a year to go into science as a career? If anybody can get what we're doing across to the public, he can."

On her advice, Cash had invited Mallory to his Texas space facility for a visit. He had already reviewed a number of Mallory's television programs and found him to be a gifted speaker with a hypnotic voice and an enthusiasm that was infectious. The man could make dusty fossils come alive without resorting to animation, and he explained the complexities of the solar system with a clarity that a ten-year-old could understand. He was without peer as a popularizer of science. In person, he proved to be affable, personable, and just as enthusiastic as he was when in front of the camera.

Before the day was out, Cash had agreed to bankroll Mallory's most ambitious work: a huge coffee-table book, lavishly illustrated, on the history of science. It had been an immense success both critically and financially. Brought out just before Christmas, it was in constant demand in bookshops all over America, and it sold well in foreign editions. An educational television series based upon it was in the works. His next book, scheduled to appear in time for the U.N. debate, was about orbiting energy satellites. It had come out two weeks previously and immediately shot to the top of the nonfiction best-seller lists.

Like many people whose greatest gifts are exercised before an audience, Mallory thrived on attention and adulation. Cash made sure to arrange for plenty of receptions and speaking engagements for the performer savant. He was to address the U.N. on the last day of the debate. By now, such was Mallory's popularity with the viewing and reading public that anyone who disputed him on scientific matters risked being perceived as an enemy of good sense.

Cash studied the crowd. To his relief, the high-fashion element was keeping its distance these days. That was because the austerities of the times made expensive fashion unfashionable, but he considered it an improvement. Many of the U.N. representatives had favored native costume in recent years, adding a splash of color.

A new arrival drew his attention. The newcomer was a man in his fifties, the stockiness of his body well disguised by a Saville Row suit of impeccable cut. His Italian shoes looked as if they had been carved from obsidian. Gold links winked from his cuffs. His graying hair was shaped to flatter the square, blunt-featured face. *He spends more on barbers than I spend on clothes,* Cash thought. He went to meet the man, hand outstretched.

"Preston, good to see you! You're a little late getting here, but the bar's still open."

Preston Reed took his hand. "I'm glad to see that you emerged from your recent escapade unscathed, Cash."

"Wasn't my escapade. Somebody else planned it."

"Still, no marks showing." Reed looked him over. "Cash, you really must let me recommend you a decent tailor."

"Doesn't suit my style, Pres. Pat had to browbeat me all evening to get me to put on a tie."

Preston Reed was the chairman of Space Technologies, Cash's principal American competitor. Behind him stood two young men who appeared to have been turned out by the same factory as some of Parker's team. They wore dark glasses indoors and seemed to look everywhere except at Reed. A pair of teenage waiters offered trays, and Reed took a cocktail and a canape.

"Old-fashioned, as always," Reed said when the waiters were gone. "Using real waiters, I mean. It's considered exploitative. Everyone uses those delightful robot servers from Hong Kong these days."

"I should do some college kid out of a job so that Leonard Fong can make a few more bucks? Hiring kids from CUNY helps them and the local economy both."

"At least the robots don't eavesdrop on sensitive conversations," Reed said.

"If you think that, you haven't checked out their circuitry," Cash informed him.

Reed looked at him sharply. "What do you mean?"

"Ask my man Parker. He can tell you."

Reed glanced at one of his security men, and the young man made a hasty exit. The CEO of S-T knew he had been maneuvered into an unwanted position of debt. His expression was sour as he bit into the canape, but his face smoothed instantly.

"Cash, your cook is a treasure. He or she must cost you a fortune."

"I pay him with what I save on tailors."

"Who's the lady in the green dress? She's stunning."

"That she is," retorted Carlson deviously, without hinting that he had already met her. Let the bastard salivate for a while, Cash mused to himself.

"Watch out, Cash," Reed said with an edge of malice. "She could be an industrial spy. There are schools and surgical clinics that do nothing but turn out undetectable technospooks. And you do have a reputation as a ladies' man."

"Why doesn't anyone just assume she's an idealistic young woman who believes in what we're doing and finds me outrageously attractive?"

Reed's expression was more eloquent than mere words. It said that years, perhaps decades, had passed since he had held such childish thoughts.

"How's the new project coming along?" Cash asked.

"Don't you wish you knew? Seriously, we're moving into the final testing phase. I'm afraid you've lost already." He seemed abstracted, unable to take his eyes off the woman in the green dress.

"People have said that before," Cash told him. "I've got the lightweight SP cells and before the year's out, I'll have the laser drive to boost them into orbit."

Reed favored him with a skeptically raised eyebrow. "Leave the disinformation to your propaganda staff, Cash. Laser propulsion is a good ten years off, and I'll have it before you do, anyway. Long before, since you'll be bankrupt by this time next year." He finished his cocktail. "Now, if you'll excuse me, I need to talk with Herr von Stoltz, whom I see over there by the fountain. I'll have some business to throw his way when you've gone under. That's going to leave him with a lot of surplus chemicals for which I'll offer him a favorable rate."

"I never stand in a man's way when he has business to transact," Cash said, gesturing graciously. "Enjoy the party." He grinned after Reed's back as the CEO made his way across the room, closely shadowed by the remaining bodyguard.

"I knew the two of you were rivals. I didn't know it was so public."

Cash turned to see Sachi in the green dress, standing by his elbow. She smiled hesitantly, as if she had been unsure of whether she might be butting into something personal.

"Preston and I understand one another. He's a sonofabitch, but he tells me to my face that he's going to drive me out of business. They're not all that honest."

"How interesting," the reporter from *Paris Match* smiled diplomatically.

"I'm just a Texas shit-kicker with wide-ranging interests, no need to be shy on my account." He caught her slight wince of distaste at his vulgarity. That was more like it.

"Is this the country-boy self-deprecation for which Southerners are famed? If so, I can't buy it. You have always impressed me as a visionary." Her eyes were refreshingly direct.

"Touché. You've found my secret weakness. I'm a closet intellectual with the soul of a poet."

"And do you never talk about yourself without irony?"

"I'd rather not talk about myself at all. I'd rather talk about you instead. You specialize in something space-oriented in France?"

"Only secondhand. I write science articles for a number of European journals. For the last two years, I've had a monthly column in *Paris Match*. I try to concentrate on space sciences, when I can get the editors interested enough. That takes some work. Usually they prefer nanotech or genetics or nearly anything that has medical applications."

"Medical, hmm?" Cash mused.

"Yes. They can't bring themselves to condemn anything that makes people live longer. They fear losing their humanitarian credentials."

"There should be a way to make use of that. Tell me, Miss Sasano, will you be on this side of the water a month from now?"

"With a good enough reason, I could arrange it."

"In one month, I'm going to throw a party at *Las Estrellas*. That's my ranch in Karnes County. It'll be an old-fashioned South Texas shindig to celebrate the SolarSat venture. I'll bet I can provide you with material for a few columns."

She smiled, showing perfect teeth. "I'd love to attend. Will you barbecue whole steers as they do in the movies?"

"Herds of them. Everybody of importance in Texas will be there, along with most of the American space industries people and some from overseas."

"How could I resist that? Of course I'll come."

"Just let me know where you'll be flying from and I'll send a plane to pick you up."

She smiled again and took his hand. "I've always heard that you do things in a big way. I'm glad to see that it's true. Europeans tend to be more stingy and calculating."

"So are Yankees. We know how to live better, between Brownsville and Baltimore."

"Until next month, then." She released his hand, but her eyes lingered for a moment before she was gone in the milling crowd.

As the evening wound down, Pat returned, holding a folded printout and wearing a faint smile.

"What did you get?" Cash asked.

"She's what she says she is. I'll have copies of all her articles for you by morning."

"Good. What are you smiling about?"

"She's more than just a freelance science writer, and she's a little closer to the European space effort than she admits."

"How's that?"

"She's almost certainly Jean-Claude du Mont's mistress." She expected an outburst, or at least surprise, but was disappointed when Cash just looked slightly bemused.

"Well," he said, smiling, "that makes her a lot more interesting, doesn't it?"

Sachi Sasano circulated among the guests with practiced ease, never lacking for attention. She was accustomed to the drill at this sort of function. You were sought out if you were powerful or beautiful, and in such gatherings, only world-class power and beauty counted. Even so, it had a flavor unlike the elegant soirees she had grown accustomed to in Paris. Seeking to find a word for it, she decided that it had an earthiness—no, a grittiness—to it that belied the swank ambience and efficient organization.

At the end of the evening, she found herself facing a pair of middle-aged aerospace contractors, each determined to see that she got back to her hotel without dying of loneliness en route. She tried to disengage without giving offense, but they were determined.

"Miss Sasano?" She glanced up to see a tall, youngish-looking man standing to her left. "We're all set up for that interview now. His Excellency is waiting upstairs." He didn't exactly wink, but he gave that impression.

"Oh, of course. I'm so glad he found a few minutes for us." She turned to her hapless pursuers. "You must excuse me. I am here on assignment, after all." She let the youngish man escort her to the lift.

"You looked in need of rescue. Never let it be said that Dieter Moyer passed up a chance to save a damsel in distress."

She made a quick assessment of the man, revising her first impression as she did so. She realized that he was not as young as she had thought. He had an unlined face and a full head of sandy-colored hair, but it was the sort of youthfulness that could be supplied by surgery. The rest was a boyish bearing and a brash demeanor, equally artificial. He reminded her a bit of the Kennedy clan—handsome men in their forties and fifties who somehow gave the impression of being just out of college. She classed him as Peter Pan. She had met many such men. They were especially common in America.

"How did you know my name?"

"I'm a writer, just like you. I was eavesdropping on you and Carlson talking." His grin was, of course, boyish.

"Well, thank you for rescuing me. Perhaps I'll be able to return the favor someday. And now I think it's time to return to my hotel. It has been good meeting you." She expected him to offer to escort her to her hotel, undoubtedly hoping to accompany her all the way into her bed. He surprised her.

"Glad to be of service. Good night." He turned and walked away as the lift arrived. She performed a mental shrug and dismissed him from her mind, the way she dismissed most unimportant men. When the lift doors opened, she was startled to see a neatly dressed young woman waiting for her. Something about the brunette's clothing and stance said "functionary."

"Miss Sasano? Mr. Carlson has placed his limousine at your disposal. Will you follow me, please?"

The white limousine waited at the curb. A burly, uniformed chauffeur stood by, holding the door open for her. He slid behind the wheel, agile despite his bulk. "Will it be the hotel, ma'am?" His manner said that he already knew which hotel it was.

"Yes, please." Was Carlson just being solicitous? Or was he letting her know that he had already had her investigated? Or was it Carlson's subordinates, letting her know what close watch they kept on anyone who got near their boss? That was likely. She knew how jealous the staff of a powerful man could be.

She was already feeling groggy when the limo pulled to a smooth stop before her hotel. The driver opened her door and waved off the over-solicitous bellhops. He walked her to the elevator, saw her inside, said, "Good night, Miss Sasano," and disappeared.

In her room, she peeled off her clothes and filled the tub with water a few degrees above body temperature. It was a cultural heritage, one of the few she had retained from her Japanese childhood and one she loved to indulge. Another was aikido. This characteristically Japanese martial art had lately become popular in Europe, particularly in France. There were a number of different ryu, or schools, of aikido. Sachi's dojo in Paris taught the Tomiki system, where students were trained in a program that included randori, or sparring. She put in three or four strenuous sessions every week, keeping her body finely tuned, taut but possessing a sculpted femininity.

In fact, she thought complacently, New York at this very minute was full of artists who would surrender their eyeteeth to paint her as she looked in the tub. She was dispassionately objective about her beauty. It was another resource, like her intelligence and ambition. She knew exactly how valuable it was to her, and how long it was likely to last.

She was luxuriating in the way the hot water leached the pain of fatigue from her body when the phone rang. The hotel had thoughtfully provided a phone she could reach without getting out of the tub, but she didn't feel like answering. The ring persisted and curiosity got the better of her. She picked up the handset.

"Hello. Sachi Sasano speaking."

"*Bon soir,* Sachi. I phoned a couple of times earlier but you weren't back in. I hope I didn't wake you."

"No, Jean-Claude, I am still barely awake. I was just about to get into bed. It's been a long day." She had arrived in the States only a few days before and she was not yet over her jet lag.

"Then I will make it brief. As you know, I came in on the Concorde a couple of days ago but have since been tied up meeting people on business. Let's have dinner at Sans Souci tomorrow evening. It's the restaurant on Fifty-fifth Street between Fifth and Sixth."

Jean-Claude invariably insisted on calling the Avenue of the Americas by its old name, Sixth Avenue. He said that was what it was called when he visited New York for the first time with his parents, many years ago. He saw no reason to change. Sans Souci. Why did that name always sound funny to her? Then she caught it and smiled at the multilingual pun. It was a French restaurant that proclaimed itself—in pidgin French-Japanese—to be "without sushi."

She felt a surge of irritation at du Mont's presumption. He took it for granted that she would drop everything to have dinner with him at his convenience. And yet it had been just this sort of arrogance that had attracted her to him in the first place. Maybe, she thought, she was just too tired.

"I must check my appointment calendar to see if I have any un-breakable engagements tomorrow evening. I can't do that just now. I'm soaking myself in a nice warm bathtub." She knew that would get to him, especially at this late hour at night. "I'll give you a call in the morning to let you know. *D'accord?*"

"*D'accord.* I will look forward to hearing from you tomorrow, then. Sweet dreams, Sachi."

She made a kissing sound and hung up.

It had been a mistake. The whole relationship with Jean-Claude had been a mistake from the first day. She knew that now.

It had begun two years ago, when she had been sent on her first big assignment: to interview the architect of the European space plan. He had dazzled her with his charm and a European sophistication that was just this side of decadence. His secretary had wedged an hour for the interview into his busy schedule, but when it proved too short, he had blithely canceled his business for the rest of the day, which had included meetings with some very important people. When even that had proved insufficient, he had invited her to accompany him to a din-ner engagement and in the course of the evening, she had found herself at a table that included the heads of three of the largest European aero-space industries.

Admit it, she said to herself, *you were flattered.* Studying her reflected perfection in the mirror over the tub, she could see clearly half the rea-son Jean-Claude had pursued her so avidly in the following weeks. First there had been little gifts: flowers, expensive chocolates that she had given to a hotel maid, but best of all, invitations to meet with the leaders of the European space effort.

She had thought that Jean-Claude had been attracted by her intelligence, education, and obvious enthusiasm for every aspect of the space program. It was amazing, she thought, how much worldliness a woman could acquire in a couple of years of such company. The fact was, Jean-Claude had his pick of beauties. He was bored by space enthusiasts. Thinking back, she realized that he had been intrigued above all by one thing about her: her refusal to be impressed by his repeated references to his aristocratic background. She now knew that he had had her investigated, and had learned why she was unimpressed. Sachi's was one of the oldest samurai families, descended from the twelfth-century general Shinra Saburo Yoshimitsu. Of course, peerage no longer existed in Japan, and she gave it little thought except when some upstart tried to emphasize his own breeding. She had a strong suspicion that had Jean-Claude learned instead that her grandparents had been fishermen from some little island, or factory workers from Yokohama, he would have lost interest in her quickly.

How could I have been so gullible? she thought. But she knew. She had been young, superbly educated, all too conscious of her own beauty—everything, in fact, except experienced. And she had been terribly vulnerable, just coming off the wreckage of a serious love affair in Japan. It had been her first, and painful as only the shattering of a first love can be.

Excuses, she thought in disgust. *There is nothing more futile than excuses. You made a stupid choice and the time has come to end it.* She had to face her own faults and do something about them. Despite her realization of his true nature, she was still attracted to Jean-Claude. She had always been attracted to powerful, dynamic men. But she could no longer be a mere moth circling such a flame. She wanted to be a part of what was happening ; better yet, she wanted to make things happen—the things that really mattered. People were stunned by her aura of glamour, but only the foolish and empty-headed could find glamour fulfilling in itself. The surface beauty of youth would fade soon enough, and she would not miss it. She intended to live for a great many years, and she wanted the coming decades to be filled with important work.

Jean-Claude du Mont, she now knew, would never want her to be anything more than his trophy.

THE PHONE WAS ringing again. Jean-Claude? Surely not. He was arrogant, but never obnoxiously overbearing. Her sleeping pattern was still upset. She had fallen into bed the night before dead tired, but she had not slept well, waking up once in the early morning hours and having trouble getting back to sleep.

"Good morning to you, whoever you are. This is Sachi Sasano's answering service." Her voice was still thick with sleep.

"Gee, I'm sorry if I woke you up, Miss Sasano. This is Dieter Moyer. I met you at Cash Carlson's party last night, remember?"

She frowned at the mouthpiece of the telephone. Did grown American men still say "gee"? It sounded like one of those horrid anachronisms from forties' movies, boyish nonwords like "golly," "gosh," and "swell."

"Wait a minute—I met so many people last night. I'll get it in a moment. You're the writer, aren't you? Peter Pan?"

There was a brief hesitation. "Peter Pan? Well, I've been called worse—oh, I get it. I rescued you from the bad guys, didn't I?"

"Exactly." If that was the way he wanted to interpret it, that was all right with her.

"Look, Miss Sasano, I had the impression that you wanted to know more about the inner workings of the U.S. National Space Council. A special meeting of the council is being held here in New York in connection with the U.N. debate on solar-power satellites. A good friend of mine will be hosting a dinner for some of them tonight. She told me I could bring a date. Would you be interested?"

She didn't hesitate for a moment. This was business and she never played coy when it was business. "I'd be delighted to join you for the dinner."

"Great! I'll meet you at your hotel lobby, say about seven?"

"That will be fine."

"Here's my phone number in case you need to reach me."

She wrote the number down as he rang off, wondering who his lady friend might be. So, she would have to tell Jean-Claude that she wouldn't be meeting him for dinner at Sans Souci after all. The U.S. National Space Council came first. She wondered if the American Vice President would be there. He was chairman, after all. Less than forty-eight hours in New York and things were getting more interesting. Then a thought struck her: How had Peter Pan known which hotel she was in?

Sachi stepped out of the elevator at seven o'clock precisely. Dieter was waiting for her. Instead of the hug-and-kiss she had come to expect as an escort tax from American men, he handed her an orchid corsage. She wondered whether he was supremely old-fashioned or if there was some sort of new civility in the air.

"How lovely," she said. "Just give me a moment to pin it on. This fabric is so delicate." The chiffon floated about her like a foamy black mist. Her long, tapering fingers worked the pin expertly as he looked on admiringly.

"I'd have needed five minutes to do that," he said, "and I'd have ruined your dress doing it. Which would've been a shame. It's a fabulous dress. Antonioni?"

"No, Loncour. It's from the new collection." So he knew Paris designers. And the slight rise of his eyebrows showed that he was impressed. He didn't need to be told that she was one of no more than five or six women in the world permitted to wear Loncour's new line even as it was being premiered at the Paris show. Few nations guarded their military secrets as the top couturiers guarded their new designs.

"Beauty and discretion both. That's a powerful combination." His own clothes were expensive without ostentation: a charcoal-gray sport coat, white-on-white shirt, black slacks, and casual Italian shoes. It was the sort of ensemble she expected from a man who could afford the best but wasn't really interested in his sartorial impression. At least he didn't affect duck-hunters' boots or plaid lumberjack shirts.

The car was equally unaffected: a white Mazda RX7. This sent her on another brief flight of fancy. Ahura Mazda, god of light, to carry Peter

Pan. Somehow, it seemed appropriate. She wondered how much he must have had to tip the doorman to let him leave it parked in front of the main entrance at seven in the evening. The man was certainly quick enough to open the door for her. Dieter comported himself with style, without making a show of it. Old-family money, she decided. A nouveau riche would have worn nothing but designer clothes, driven a Porsche, and let her see him passing a roll of bills to the doorman.

He drove west off First Avenue, then north up Park Avenue. At a stately building in a fashionable uptown district, he drove into the underground garage, passing the security guard with a nod. Sachi noticed that there was a nonuniformed man in the guard's booth as well, wearing wraparound dark glasses indoors after dark. There was a parking space miraculously available for the Mazda, right next to the elevator. Sachi said nothing, sure that all would be made clear eventually.

There was another man wearing shades standing next to the elevator. He paid them no attention as they went inside. Dieter punched a series of numbers into a computerized console. The doors closed and the elevator began to rise so smoothly that she barely felt the acceleration. There was no floor readout over the door. Silently, the door slid open onto a plush-carpeted foyer. They stepped out and Sachi noted a larger elevator to the right, presumably for guests coming from the ground-floor entrance. Dieter pressed the chime for the penthouse.

The door was opened by a uniformed butler. He gestured them inside and stood ready to take their nonexistent hats and coats. As soon as they were in the anteroom, Sachi saw a woman hurry across the larger drawing room to greet them. She was what Sachi classified as the fifty-but-almost-able-to-pass-for-thirty type, the inexorable advance of the years staved off with discreet surgery and untold pain inflicted by a personal trainer in a personal gym. The result was mature but sexy, and she was dressed to kill. Sachi wondered what prey she was stalking that evening. Or it might just be her personal style.

The woman gave Dieter an affectionate hug and kiss. It was, Sachi noted, a genuine kiss, not the sort where the participants smacked the air by each other's ears. It was also very slightly prolonged, causing Sachi to wonder about the implied relationship. Then the woman turned her attention to Sachi.

"Dieter, darling, I'm so glad you could make it. And this must be the lady you've been raving about since yesterday evening!"

"Surely not raving," Sachi protested.

The woman took her hands. "Yes, raving. That's the only word for it." She gave Sachi a once-over from toes to scalp, gauging everything from shoes to manicure to coiffure. A slight upward quirk at the corners of her mouth registered approval. She turned to Moyers. "For once, your taste equals your enthusiasm, dear."

"Sachi, this is my aunt, Gertrude Talbot. Try not to be too intimidated."

"I'm more than delighted," Sachi said. She recognized the name instantly. It was one prominent in the society pages, usually associated with good causes: endowing chairs and scholarships, medical-research drives, and so on. The source of Dieter's evident wealth began to emerge.

"Come along, you must meet the other guests. They're all supposed to be terribly important, but you're far more beautiful." She took Sachi by the hand.

"I take it the Veep's here?" Dieter said.

"Veep?" Sachi queried.

"The Vice President," Gertrude supplied. "Dieter thinks using vulgarisms like that gives him an air of casual sophistication."

"Aunt Gert, on the other hand, delights in puncturing pretensions."

"Lead on," Sachi said. This explained the mysterious security men: Secret Service. Not as flamboyant as Carlson's team but probably as good at their work. She felt a flush of excitement. This was an odd venue, and Dieter was hardly her idea of a dashing man of power, but he was getting her closer to the sources of power and action that intrigued her, faster than she could have imagined. To much of the world, the American vice presidency was a joke, an office without power or responsibilities, but the man was head of the National Space Council and as such, he had genuine clout.

By the time all the introductions had been made, the butler announced that dinner was served. Sachi found herself seated between Dieter and the Vice President. She assumed that Dieter had prevailed upon his aunt to grant her the privilege. The Vice President was refreshingly unpretentious, with a Southwestern informality that was not quite as earthy as Carlson's Texas manner. Even as she thought it, it occurred to her that she was judging most of the men she encountered against Carlson.

Mrs. Talbot artfully steered the dinner conversation, confining it to polite pleasantries. To Sachi's relief, the Secret Service men stayed away from the dining room. They were one aspect about life at the top that repelled her, not so much as a reminder of the ever-present danger of violence as the brutal assertion that the rich and powerful lost all right to privacy.

When the dinner dishes were cleared away, they were replaced with brandy snifters of Cardenal Mendoza, an exquisite Spanish product. With the brandy, the talk grew more interesting. The Vice President asked a DOE official about a report he would be sending the senate the next week on the fusion energy project. The VP was a youthful, handsome, dynamic man, in direct contrast to the elderly, affable but inspiring President.

"Good money after bad," the man said succinctly. He had been appointed to clear up the department's affairs, not to perpetuate them like the last several secretaries. "Every new discovery tells us that fusion energy is getting more remote, not closer. Even the most optimistic scientists are now saying it's a matter of decades, not years."

"I think Quentin Mallory's on the right track," said a scientist type whose name Sachi had forgotten. He was a professor of high-energy physics or something of the sort, and a member of the National Space Council. "There's a nuclear-fusion reactor that's been operating safely for around four and a half billion years, and we get most of our energy from it anyway, at one remove or other. The idea is to get out there and tap the photons more directly from the source. It can be done without hurting the environment, and the energy to be had is all but limitless."

"That's what the U.N. hearings have been about," the Vice President said. "So what's the problem?"

"Money, as usual," replied the professor. "Unless there's an assured market for the electricity from solar-power satellites, it will probably be a long time before private business will invest the necessarily huge sums of money—and we're talking about billions here—in such risky ventures."

"But I thought that was what all those arm-twisting business types were doing at the U.N.," Sachi said.

"What they were doing was arranging things so that the U.N. wouldn't try to stop them if they decide that their projects are feasible," said another council member who sat across from her. He was a Master of Business Administration, Wall Street type.

"But," the professor went on, "while you might have plenty of electricity to sell at competitive rates, the market could be effectively cordoned off by your rivals. Remember the problems the Iraqi revolutionaries had back in the fifties?" He looked around and got a tableful of blank stares. "They nationalized their oil fields and then tried to sell their oil. The big oil companies shut off the world oil market in retaliation and the revolutionary government went bankrupt and eventually collapsed."

Sachi suspected that the man was working up to a point, but she didn't want to appear ignorant by asking what it might be. He seemed to be saying in one breath that it was desirable for American business to get into the solar-power satellite race, and in another breath, to say that it wouldn't work.

"That being the case," said the Wall Street man, taking the bait, "why should the government be anxious to put up the money that American business is too timid to risk? The European Space Enterprise is already planning to put an industry-strength solar-power satellite in orbit in ten years. The Japanese consortium will soon be testing its early SPS, which I'm told has a ten-thousand-kilowatt capacity. Our California-based Space Technologies has its own plans, and its schedule is similar to that of the European program. What's the rush now? Why does the U.S. government have to get involved in such a costly venture? Right now, our national budget is so constrained that U.S. treasury bonds are selling at a record low."

"Haven't you noticed that our financial resources have been getting more and more limited in these last couple of decades?" the professor shot back. "It's no accident. Boys just out of business school make billions selling each other paper and getting out before the inevitable crash comes. Artificial booms on Wall Street, engineered by financial manipulators—corporate raiders, junk-bond salesmen and their ilk—who are only interested in paper profit and never in creating real value, they've deprived this country of the economic muscle it needs to compete in the real world."

The MBA type flushed slightly. "And your solution?"

The professor took a sip from his snifter. "We need to take decisive action now. We have to go on the attack instead of waiting to follow the lead taken by the Europeans or the Japanese. Some four decades ago, we sent twelve Americans to the moon and back and we left the rest of the world dazzled." He turned away from the MBA and faced the Vice President.

The point at last, Sachi thought.

"Mr. Vice President," he continued, "we ought to guarantee the first successful industry-scale supplier of electricity from space that there will be a substantial market for solar power. Let's say that the first company successfully providing at least half a gigawatt of electricity continuously will be guaranteed a market that can grow to fifty gigawatts in ten years."

Sachi made a mental note to find out how much a gigawatt was. She was not about to ask in this company. She knew the prefix "giga" meant a thousand million, but what that represented in terms of world energy consumption, she had no idea.

"That sounds good for the winner," said the Vice President, nodding, "but what about the losers? Is the chance of landing that contract tempting enough for them to take the plunge?"

"If it's taxpayers' money and not their own," said the Wall Street type.

The professor shot back with an answer. "It still should leave enough crumbs for the second- and third-place competitors to make it worth their while to have gotten in on the race, if we guarantee an open market. If we stiffen the antipollution laws, as we anticipate doing over the next decade, many of the existing coal-fired and even oil-fired power plants will be forced to close down sooner or later, leaving plenty of room for non-fossil-fuel-based electricity. And it's pretty evident that we won't have controlled-fusion power plants on this planet soon enough to fill the gap. Our economic competitors will surely see this and we'll set an example to them all."

"What about ground-based solar power?" Sachi asked. "Hasn't there been a great deal of experimentation in that area?"

"It would be fine for some limited objectives but would not be practicable for general purposes," the professor type said. "Solar energy as it reaches Earth is diffuse, and the atmospheric absorption takes its toll. It requires enormous acreage to obtain even a minimum of power, and much of the world doesn't have the acreage to spare. It's heavily dependent upon the seasons, and it's unfeasible in a cloudy climate, so that lets out Japan and most of Europe. There is also the all-important diurnal cycle to consider for supplying power on an around-the-clock basis. And ground-based solar power might have to be transmitted from places like Arabia and Saharan Africa, and nobody wants to be dependent on those nations for their energy. No, though it might be expensive in the short run, in the long run, power from solar satellites is the best plan."

"Actually," the Vice President said, "the President and I have already discussed this at some length. He is quite favorably inclined toward a major federal initiative on the solar-power satellite concept."

"And he thinks he can sell this to Congress?" asked the Wall Street type, eyebrows raised. "As a member of this council, I know that the word 'space' has been poison on Capitol Hill—in some quarters at least—for years."

"When he talks to Congress, he won't be talking space," said the Vice President. "He'll be talking energy and environment. These are getting to be very powerful words indeed. Cash Carlson has shown what private business can do in space—"

"There are those who think Mr. Carlson is a better poker player than businessman," interrupted the MBA. "And he didn't build his famous private space station from scratch. He used jettisoned external fuel tanks from space shuttles. When the Russians were desperate, he bought their Energia and Proton heavy lifters for launch capability. That's not building, that's scavenging."

"And what of that?" asked the professor. "They were paid for with that taxpayers' money everybody is so concerned about, and they were being used once and thrown away! Buying up government surplus and reusing it has a long and honorable history. The Greek shipping magnates, Niarchos and Onassis, got their start after World War Two by buying up serviceable but unneeded old Liberty ships and employing them as commercial freighters. Does anyone accuse those two of being poor businessmen? All over South America and Africa and Asia, airlines were founded by people who couldn't hope to buy new aircraft from the manufacturers. Instead, they bought up C-47s and other cargo craft turned out by the thousands for the Allied forces and no longer needed after the war."

"Beautifully made planes, too, by the way," said the Vice President. "On my visit to Africa last year, I saw several of them still in use after more than half a century."

"Exactly," said the professor. "If Carlson has found a way to make use of these supremely expensive artifacts, I say more power to him!"

Sachi was beginning to wonder whether the professor had been coached by Carlson himself. So far, everything he had said was in agreement with what she had come to think of as "the Carlson line." But it just might be that a number of people simply thought along the same lines. She found a place to interject herself into the discussion without seeming too ignorant.

"I must confess that I've never been lucky enough to attend a shuttle launch," she said. Instantly, all attention was on her. It was something she was used to. Truly beautiful women got attention for even their most inane statements. "I have no idea of exactly how large those fuel tanks are. The films give no sense of scale."

"I've seen a number of launches," the Vice President said, "and even that doesn't give you much of an idea. It came as a surprise to me to learn that those tanks are the size of Boeing 747s with all the seats removed."

"Incredible!" she said. "I had no idea they were so huge. Just a few of them would make a very sizable space station."

"I've heard that Carlson's already making money selling free-fall laboratory facilities in vacuum," said the Vice President. "He's even leasing space in his space station back to NASA for use on our moon ferry project!"

"That seems a backward sort of way of doing business," said Mrs. Talbert.

"It wouldn't have been necessary if NASA had ever had the authority to build a midway station in space for journeys to everywhere else in the solar system," said the professor. "Carlson had the vision to do it in the first place, and the business savvy to do it cheap. He stole a march on everyone, but that was because he believes in the future of manned space operations."

The Vice President looked around the table and saw approval from everyone except the MBA, who obviously wanted to see black ink on the bottom line of a properly prepared balance sheet before he was going to approve anything. "In three months, I'll be attending the next environmental summit at Iguazu Falls right after the next Rio Conference," the Vice President went on. "I plan to use the occasion to float a trial balloon on this."

All around the table, political antennae stood up and quivered. Why was he announcing this at a private dinner party instead of earlier in the day, when the National Space Council was in session? *Three months, hell,* she thought. *He's floating his balloon right now.* It occurred to her that this might be aimed at her. He could well know of her writing for European journals, her connection to Jean-Claude du Mont, maybe even her recent encounter with Carlson. It was all but impossible to keep secrets these days, especially from people with access to first-class intelligence organizations. Not that she was trying to keep anything particularly secret.

"I think I see where you're leading," she said. "The solar-satellite idea will be repugnant to those who are reflexively hostile to anything involving manned space programs. So you are going to pitch energy to the U.S. Congress, and environmentalism to the environmentalists."

"Exactly," he confirmed. "Even the hard-core environmentalists will be hard put to find objections to something that reduces dependence on fossil fuels. Most of them don't like hydroelectric power either, with reason. It really isn't very good for river systems. Objections to nuclear fission power have been getting even stronger because of its perceived risks. There's even a growing objection to hydrothermal projects. This bypasses all of that. Whatever else they may be, solar satellites are nonpolluting, they don't interfere with any sort of ecosystem, and they sure as hell aren't going to be sited on anyone's sacred burial grounds."

A few minutes later, the Vice President took his leave, pleading a heavy schedule the next day. The others left in what seemed to Sachi a well-understood order, impenetrable to non-insiders, leaving only herself, Dieter, and Aunt Gertrude. It occurred to her that having set all this up, Dieter had said almost nothing during the evening. It certainly wasn't because he was intimidated. He seemed perfectly at ease even in this exalted company.

She wondered if he simply didn't consider himself an authority and didn't care to venture an opinion among acknowledged experts. She had no idea of what his educational background might be, but she was beginning to think that he was a dilettante, fascinated by the idea of space exploration, unprepared by his education to take an active part in it, but allowed by family money, connections, and influence to engage himself peripherally and help it along in his own way. She guessed that it gave him great pleasure to bring her and the Vice President and these other influential people together.

It was almost second nature to her to classify men by their place in power structures. A few were leaders wielding power, most were followers. She had always been drawn to the leaders. Dieter was not so easy to classify. He was more like something out of an old English novel. At least he seemed comfortable with what he was. She certainly couldn't fault his manners. His behavior toward her was positively Edwardian, although it was plain to her that his interest in her was romantic. At another time, another stage in her life, she might have felt inclined to reciprocate.

But now? She was no longer content to be an observer. She was ready to take an active role in events. On the other hand, this evening might not have been just a public-spirited event on the part of Dieter and his wealthy aunt. They might have been discreetly exploring opportunities to invest their multibillion-dollar fortunes in the future of the world. There was perhaps considerably more than met the eye.

And she was more interested than ever in attending that Texas barbecue.

7

FROM THE HOUSTON airport, Cash's helicopter took him to the Lone Star Space Systems' control facility in the city. The main technical operation was to the south of Houston, in Ford Bend County. Control was a squarish building of gleaming, mirrored glass set in the middle of a landscaped park. Employees called it the "Glass Box," or simply the "Box." It was like a thousand other office buildings in the booming city except for its purpose, and its unique full-time inhabitant.

The chopper landed on the pad in front of the main entrance while Parker hovered overhead in his own bird. Cash exited the chopper and ducked beneath the rotors as he made his way to the front door. When he was inside, Parker flew on to Cash's Houston residence, where Pat was making arrangements for his stay.

The change from the muggy exterior heat to the air-conditioned interior was a jolt, but a welcome one. Cash greeted the employees, all of whom seemed to be busy. He knew it wasn't the fake activity that took over in most organizations when the boss showed up. With the new project, everyone would be putting in overtime for months to come.

Cash's office suite took up most of the fifth floor. Like the office in New York, the suite in the Box included living quarters, small but comfortable. It also contained an elevator to which only Cash had access. After tossing off his jacket, fixing himself a drink, and with glass in hand, he crossed to the elevator and pressed his thumb against its ID plate. It was time to visit Max.

The plate read his thumbprint and the door silently slid open. Cash stepped inside and the door silently closed again. The elevator began to drop. There was no floor reading, nor did the lift pass any landings before it halted in the deep subbasement. The supersecret elevator had only two accesses: Cash's lofty suite and Max's subterranean lair. The elevator halted and the door opened onto a dim, cavernous room, its principal illumination provided by a number of computer screens. Some showed arcane symbols, others were set up for sophisticated computer games.

Max sat in the center of the largest console. He didn't turn around when the elevator opened. His fingers danced over his keyboard, and Cash could see nothing of him but the back of his pear-shaped body and a head of unkempt, frizzy red hair.

"C'mere and look at this, Cash." As always, Max spoke as if Cash had stepped out five minutes before.

"And a gracious good afternoon to you, Win." Max's real name was Winston Crumly. He was Cash's secret weapon and the real reason for Cash's meteoric streak to the heights of space tycoonship. Cash figured he would have made it anyway, but he wasn't fooling himself. He knew he sure as hell couldn't have made it as fast as he had without Crumly.

Cash went to the chair next to Crumly's and dumped a load of Chinese restaurant takeout cartons onto the floor. As always, the place was a pigsty. Pizza boxes, taco wrappers, fried-chicken tubs full of well-gnawed bones, plastic forks, and throwaway chopsticks were strewn everywhere.

"How can you live like this?" Cash asked for the thousandth time. "If this building wasn't sterile, the mice and roaches would walk away with you. Let me send someone down to clean up."

Crumly shook his head solemnly, not taking his eyes off the screen. "Uh-uh. Can't do that. They'd bring in germs. Get me one of those Hong Kong robot maids."

"Fong loads those things with spy circuitry." What a world. Parker worried about spies and assassins, Pat worried about strange women, Crumly worried about germs.

"I'll fix it."

"I guess you can, at that. What've you got?"

"I've been running Brazil through my set." This, in Crumly-speak, meant that he had fed every conceivable fact about the nation of Brazil through his computers in search of correspondences and trends. He had sources of information most governments could not tap. More correctly, it was information collected by governments that they did not share with one another.

"And the results?" Cash intended to expand his small Brazilian launch facility greatly for the SolarSat project. He was highly interested in anything having to do with Brazil.

"Look at the figures on these fifteen states." The screen in front of Crumly lit up with incomprehensible gibberish. "I've got here agricultural and industrial figures from the end of the Brazilian Empire in eighteen eighty-nine to the present. Now, look at this." The screen split and more nonsense appeared, figures and symbols that meant nothing to Cash. "Military and political operations in the same states over the same time period." He split the screen two more ways and added revolutionary and Catholic Church activities, along with the dispossession and removal of various Indian groups, and native, non-Catholic religious movements, Marxist incursions, and the movements of neighboring nations along Brazil's borders. He moved the multiple segments around on the screen to show where various symbols seemed to click together.

"Win," Cash said patiently, "just tell me what I'm looking at. Keep it simple."

"What you're looking at is revolution in eight to ten years unless the economy gets a really big kick in the butt."

"Local uprising?" Cash asked hopefully.

"Revolution. Big, bloody, and years long. Look how it's gonna progress." His fingers did their ballet on the keys and the figures changed. "Bloody fighting in Minas Gerais leads to famine, which spreads to Goias, Para, and probably all the rest. The catastrophe gets so big it's right off my screen. It's a big country, about as big as the U.S. Some parts will break off and form independent states, others will be grabbed by Uruguay, Paraguay, Peru and Colombia, maybe by Bolivia, too. Complete banana republicism."

"My God, Win! Are you sure?" Crumly just looked at him. The question was meaningless to him. Finally, he realized that some sort of elucidation was in order.

"It's been happening everywhere, Cash. The really big countries are having the same problems as the empires. They can hold together only as long as they're prosperous, strong, or both. Take one of those factors away and they fly apart by cultural centrifugal effect." He took a doughnut from a box and bit into it, showering the front of his shirt with powdered sugar.

Cash didn't doubt that Crumly's assessment of the situation was accurate. He had never known him to be wrong where his computers were concerned.

"So what do we do about this?"

Crumly just shrugged. His field was spotting trends. Solutions he left up to Cash. Sometimes Cash wanted to strangle him, but he couldn't afford that any more than he could afford revolution in Brazil.

Winston Crumly had come into Cash's life when Cash was trying to put together a deal to buy discarded space-shuttle fuel tanks to build his own space station. He'd had patchy success with launching other people's satellites but it was a shoestring operation, and his ambition required major capital backing. Cash was a talker and a wheeler-dealer in the old Texas tradition. He knew he could raise the money. What he would lose in the process was total control of his operation. That he was not willing to do. This had to be a Cash Carlson operation or nothing.

He had been dealing on a computer net shared by like-minded businessmen, trying to locate some cheap, secondhand government equipment, when an anonymous query had appeared on his screen: *"Mr. Carlson, how would you like to make a billion dollars quick?"* The symbol at the top of the screen indicated that the interloper had accessed him by way of a secure code number Cash shared with only a half-dozen close cronies. Some teenage hacker, he decided. But Cash had a weakness for audacious entrepreneurs, so he decided to give him or her a chance.

He keyed: *"Make your pitch and keep it short."*

"I know where you can put your hands on a minimum ¾ billion in unclaimed gold."

"Why should I believe you?"

"Two years ago, you were team leader on the Ramirez hit in Yucatan."

Cash had felt sweat spring out on his scalp. The Ramirez job was why he'd left military intelligence. Ramirez had headed a separatist movement that would have plunged Mexico into a catastrophic civil war, and eliminating him had caused Cash no qualms. But the operation had been wildly unlawful and was headed by a born-again fanatic in covert operations. Cash had sworn off all such government lunacy and had thought, until now, that all records of the operation were destroyed.

"Okay, you have your sources. Let's meet."

"No. We can do this over the screens."

"Face-to-face or no deal."

He had waited a long time, then: *"All right."* An address in southern Florida had appeared on the screen along with a time on the following afternoon. Cash arranged for an airline ticket and packed a toothbrush and a gun. The gun was undetectable by airport security, a souvenir from his government-spook days. He fully intended to shoot the interpoler, lacking any fully satisfactory explanations.

The house was a shabby, wooden affair in a nondescript neighbor-hood. At his knock, a voice had called, "Come in."

He walked in. "Close the door," the voice said, oddly uninflected. "I can't stand bright light."

He could just make out a blobby figure hunched before a bank of glowing screens. The place smelled of mildew and decay. "Okay, I'm here. What's the pitch?"

"You don't have anything I could catch, do you?"

This was getting unreal. "Since you know so much about me, you ought to know that."

"You never can tell about germs. Come over here and I'll show you how to get the gold."

The screens showed the type of satellite photos familiar from weather broadcasts, but some were infrared or broken down into sym-bols requiring special skills to interpret.

"Your name is Winston Crumly," Cash said as he studied the screens. "You're twenty-eight years old, you graduated from the local high school, and you lived here with your mother until she died two years ago, which I presume is why this place hasn't been cleaned since. I have my sources, too."

Crumly ignored him. "This is a sequence of images of a stretch of the Texas coast over the last twenty years. Lots of storms, and the sands shift all the time, the water changes depth. See this?" His cursor indi-cated an oddly symmetrical bump in the offshore sand. "Look what hap-pens when I run these overlays." The images flashed by, each dated. The bump faded, sometimes disappeared, but always reappeared as the water depth increased, indicating that a thinner layer of sand lay over whatever it was. The thing was elongated—almost, Cash thought, like a ship.

"You're talking about sunken treasure?" he asked, incredulous.

"Uh-huh." Then Crumly told him about the *Nuestra Señora de los Dolores*. Cash wasn't sure whether he should laugh or just put the mad-man out of his misery, but something about the sheer nuttiness of the situation had tickled his fancy. This was just the sort of wild gamble that appealed to him. Then he recognized a few security symbols at the top of some of the screens and his scalp started to sweat.

"My God, Crumly! These are some of our top-security satellites!"

"Uh-huh. Lot of the satellites are sort of old. They don't get the clarity of image I want. These're designed to look for submarines and they're real up to date."

"If they look for submarines, why are they looking at sandbars on the Texas coast?"

"I had to sort of reprogram them."

Cash was aghast. "Crumly, they'll put you in prison for a thousand years for this. They'll put me in with you just for knowing about it!"

Crumly shrugged. It was a gesture Cash was to learn well. It stood for all the ordinary, everyday matters that Crumly found uninteresting. "Uh-huh. It's sort of illegal. That was why I contacted you. You don't seem to worry a lot about illegal stuff. I mean, you don't need to worry. They'll never know that I'm using their hardware. They don't even understand how to use it themselves."

"If you only knew how that comforts me," Cash said. Then his gaze went back to the bump in the sand.

It had been the start, as the movie had it, of a beautiful friendship. Except that Cash wasn't entirely sure that Crumly was capable of friendship, or even of truly rational thought or behavior. For one thing, the computer genius seemed to possess every phobia known to science. Germs were the least of it. Agoraphobia and the fear of crowds kept him at home. Strong light upset him. When Cash had built the Box, Crumly had designed his subterranean lair, and then had been terrified to travel to it. He was afraid to drive or fly, and he even feared elevators and escalators. Parker had waited until he was asleep and then had sedated him and carried him to his new home unconscious.

Now they had to worry about revolution in Brazil. Cash kicked a pizza box in irritation. Crumly, who was terrified of germs, feared nothing he could eat, however dubious its origin. He ordered anything he wanted and it was delivered by dumbwaiter. Rumors were rife in the kitchen as to who was ordering all the junk food, but it was thought to be at least three terribly unhealthy people.

"Will the expanded launch facility help out the economy enough to stave off disaster?" Cash asked.

Crumly fiddled with his computer. "No. It'll help."

"They'll need a lot more manufacturing," Cash mused. "What else would help?"

"A rise in demand for beef," Crumly said. "Maybe a plague."

"Plague?"

"If there were less people, there'd be more to go around."

"Oh. Well, we don't want that." He ran his fingers through his hair. "Why this? All I want to do is build the first working solar-power satellite and now I have to figure out a way to stop a civil war."

"Life is never simple," said Crumly, who coped with life by avoiding it.

"I'll put my people to work on it. I'll have Chamoun access your figures and put together a think tank. There has to be a way out of this."

"Why?"

"Why what?"

"Why does there have to be a way out?"

"There always is," Cash assured him. "It's an old Texas saying."

Cash's Houston home was a large suburban house of no special pretension. Peripatetic and unmarried, he saw no point in maintaining a princely establishment where he slept no more than a week out of each month. As a result, the place always had the look of a house that was for sale, kept and cared for by conscientious realtors. He met with Parker and Pat in the master dining room, a spacious salon with picture windows looking out over an impeccably tended garden. At Parker's insistence, the windows were opaque from the outside. The Mexican housekeeper laid out coffee and iced tea and withdrew. Briefly, Cash outlined the new problem. Parker was unimpressed. Immediate danger was his line; dangers eight to ten years in the future might as well not exist.

"Are you serious?" Pat demanded. "This Max may be able to see through water and mud, but do you really believe he has a crystal ball?"

"He hasn't steered me wrong yet. Five years from now, the bulk of the Lone Star will be invested in our Brazilian launch facility. I doubt it would survive the Balkanization of Brazil."

"There are alternatives," Pat pointed out. "The Kenyans practically promised to give you Mount Kenya if you'd locate there."

"None of the equatorial countries are any more stable than Brazil—most of them are probably a good deal less so. And none of the others have Brazil's infrastructure and abundance of nearby resources."

For insurmountable reasons of physics, equatorial sites were indispensable for launching geosynchronous power satellites, taking advantage of the earth's rotation to help the massive loads along into the most advantageous orbits. This gave the equatorial nations real leverage, since there were so few of them. The vast majority of Earth's equator lies on the oceans. Of those nations on the equator, the most desirable—until SSTOs became fully operational—were those with water splashdown sites to the east, further narrowing the choice of sites. Cash had made the Brazilian site one of his first priorities upon going into the space-launch business.

"With most of the world bawling for U.N. aid, it's going to be difficult to drum up relief for a nation as relatively rich as Brazil. And you'd better not even be seen trying it, since you've already gone way out on a limb with your everybody-gets-a-piece space policy."

"I imagine you're right about that," Cash conceded. "But something has to be done, and I'm not talking about handouts. Get Chamoun on it. I want him to put together a think tank, and what we're looking for is real investment that will create real jobs and real prosperity, not just some sort of temporary buyoff. We all know how that turns out. Tell him that when he has some prospects lined up, I'll get right to work doing some arm-twisting. There's no excuse for a nation as rich in re-sources as Brazil to be in such a bind."

"Right away, Boss," Pat said.

"Not my line, Boss," Parker commented, "but I've worked in a lot of countries and when they're screwed up, often as not, it's government inefficiency and corruption that's at fault."

"You think I don't know that? That part of it I'll look into personally. I don't flatter myself that I can reform a bad government, but maybe I can convince enough people that there are better things than winning second place in a revolution and getting shot by a firing squad."

8

LAS ESTRELLAS WAS a sprawl of rolling grassland in Karnes County, south of the San Antonio River. The land had once been a dusty waste of caliche pits and prickly pear. For a while, flax had been raised, but the rainfall in South Texas was always too chancy for crop raising. Cash's land was now plowed and sown with drought-resistant grass. The transformation had been radical. He sort of missed the prickly pear, though. It had been atmospheric, if nothing else.

He clumped out onto the veranda wearing the high-heeled boots he never wore except for affairs like this. Texas garb was de rigueur at a traditional barbecue. Besides the boots, he wore jeans and a gambler-striped shirt with a string tie. He drew the line at a Stetson. Cash had never liked to wear hats of any kind.

The party was just getting cranked up, with guests still arriving hourly. They arrived by plane, by helicopter, by motorcade, and by less pompous means. Some came by humble personal automobile, a few by motorcycle, and some even walked. Cash had invited his neighbors as well as the business, scientific, and political notables.

At various spots on the property, no fewer than three bands provided mariachi music, square-dance tunes, and music of no particular provenance. In a corral, local vaqueros gave riding and roping demonstrations for guests from benighted lands that lacked a cattle culture. Over long fire pits, as promised, steer and sheep and hog carcasses turned on spits. For those with less heroic appetites, chickens, ribs, and hamburgers grilled over the mesquite coals. Cooks used brooms to baste everything with red barbecue sauce from galvanized washtubs. Cash didn't believe in sending guests away hungry.

He stepped off the porch to greet the latest arrivals. Everyone was checked out by Parker's team, as surreptitiously as possible. In the middle of his own briarpatch, Cash didn't feel threatened by anything far short of a ballistic missile. The security was mostly concentrated on the periphery of the ranch. Parker strolled around wearing his grandfather's Colt Peacemaker in a low-slung holster.

"Chopper coming in, Boss," Parker reported. "It's your Tokyo-by-way-of-Paris lady friend."

"Then let's go meet her."

To keep the dust down, Cash had designated a landing spot a half mile downwind of the party site. He and Parker climbed into Cash's favorite ranch vehicle—a WWII-era Jeep, complete with a big white star on the hood. In a mount next to the driver's seat was a Thompson submachine gun of the same period. Like Parker's six-shooter, it was mainly for atmosphere, but it worked.

By the time they were halfway to the pad, they could hear the helicopter's engines over the throaty growl of the Jeep. A silvery flash appeared in the northwest, coming in from San Antonio. The Jeep and the helicopter arrived simultaneously, forcing Cash to squint against the flying dust and debris. Parker, behind his wraparound dark glasses, was undisturbed.

The engines shut down and the whirling rotors slowed to a lazy rotation, their tips drooping. Cash climbed out of the Jeep and went to the passenger side of the craft, stooping low. The Plexiglas door opened and Sachi appeared. Cash took her hand and helped her out. She was wearing Levis and a cotton shirt, and her eyes were hidden behind a pair of expensive European sunglasses, a concession to the fierce South Texas sunlight.

"Welcome to *Las Estrellas*, Miss Sasano."

"I'm so delighted!" Her wide smile seemed genuine. "The Wild West at last!"

"It's not as wild as it used to be, but we do our best."

Parker loaded her luggage into the rear of the Jeep.

"What a . . . a quaint vehicle." She raised her sunglasses and eyed it skeptically. "Is it a Jeep?"

"Built in nineteen forty-four. Back when Detroit still made a decent product. Have you ever ridden in one?"

"I'm afraid I've never had the privilege."

"Then hop in. I'll drive and Jack can get in back and watch for enemy aircraft." Parker perched on the luggage and Cash punched the ignition button. The Jeep made its inimitable noise and he revved the engine impressively. Then they were off in a cloud of dust.

"Air-conditioned, too," Sachi said as the wind whipped her long black hair behind her like a banner.

"It has all the options," Cash agreed.

It took less than a minute to drive from the pad to the huge, circus-sized tent cover that shaded the buffet and socializing area. An Hispanic employee came from the main house to take Sachi's luggage.

"Those transatlantic flights can be hell," Cash noted. "Manuel will show you your room. If you'd like to un-jet-lag for a while, I won't be offended. We'll be carrying on far into the night."

"That's very thoughtful," she smiled, "but I've been in Miami for the last week, and I took a morning flight to San Antonio. A real Texas barbecue is just what I came here for. Give me five minutes to adjust my makeup and I'll be right with you."

As Cash expected, the five minutes turned out to be half an hour, but he was still impressed with her ability to keep her appearance despite the ordeals of travel.

"Ready for the tour?" he asked.

"Lead on." She had exchanged the cotton blouse for scarlet silk, and her Levis had been tailored to fit like paint.

"I've got to play host for a while. It's a good chance for you to meet some of the VIPs." Within a half hour, she was introduced to the governor of Texas, the senators and representatives of that state, and the High Sheriff of Karnes County. The presidents of Mexico and Brazil were in attendance, and the President of the U.S. was expected to make an appearance sometime during the weekend.

"This is a high-powered group," Sachi said as they strolled toward the barbecue pits.

"Don't let all the Washington and foreign brass dazzle you," Cash cautioned. "The High Sheriff's the real power in these parts."

An errant breeze blew smoke over them.

"I didn't know how famished I was," she said. They came to a booth where, incongruously, Polish sausages were heaped beside trays of sauerbraten and kraut. "You feature an eclectic menu."

"No, it's all local. Within a few miles of here there are towns named Cestohowa and Kosciusko, settled by Poles. A ways north of them is New Braunfels, a German settlement. They weren't all Anglo and Mexican in the old days. Did wonders for the local cuisine, anyway. Back during the First World War, my grandfather had the task of making sure that nobody spoke German in public."

"You're joking!"

"Not a bit. There was a lot of that sort of hysteria when we first got into the war. The high school cut pictures of the Kaiser out of the history books, that sort of nonsense. Anyway, Grandpa thought he heard someone speaking German over in Karnes City and busted up a conversation between a couple of patriotic Poles. He was so embarrassed that it was the first and last time he exercised his authority as enforcer of language purity."

"It looks wonderful, but I'm in the mood for something more Southwestern." They went to the pits and heaped plates with barbecued beef and pork ribs. The servers added baked beans and potato salad without being asked. "I might as well banish cholesterol from my mind for the duration," she said.

"You'd be well advised to. Nouvelle cuisine never caught on in these parts, a true blessing. This is the apotheosis of plebeian food, intended to be a pleasure rather than a torment."

"That's a refreshing change." As they ate, they wandered over to the corral, where a determined young man was demonstrating the fine art of bulldogging—diving from the back of a running horse onto the horns of a running steer, grasping said horns and twisting the animal's head until it was forced to fall.

"Isn't it dangerous?" Sachi asked, fascinated.

"There are safer ways to get a cow to fall over," Cash admitted. "I never saw much point to it, but it's a skill highly thought of in some parts."

"Do you own a lot of cattle?"

"A few. Would you like to see my herd?"

"Of course."

"Then toss the plate and let's get in the Jeep." She threw the paper plate, which now bore only clean bones, into a trash can and wiped her hands on the seat of her Levis. They climbed into the Jeep. Parker tried to accompany them, but Cash waved him off.

"Sometimes I like to think I can take care of myself," he grumbled. He started the Jeep and shifted into gear. The little vehicle sped along a dirt road, raising a plume of dust in their wake. Within a few minutes, they were on a stretch of rolling ground where the grass was long. Cash turned onto a side road that led through a barbed-wire fence. There was no gate, but where the road passed through the fence, there was a cattle guard of parallel pipes that clattered when the Jeep rolled over them.

He turned off the road and drove across the tough grass to a low rise, beyond which was an open meadow where several hundred crude-looking animals grazed placidly. Sachi had been expecting massive, prize beef cattle, but these were rangy, almost scrawny beasts, with piebald hides and tremendous horns.

Cash shut off the engine. "I never liked cattle. Dumbest animals in the world, next to sheep and horses. Most of my family chased these stupid beasts all over Texas and up to the railheads in Kansas and points north. Mainly what they got out of it was a lot of heartbreak. The animals that survived the blizzards and the droughts mostly got run off by rustlers or Indians or Mexican raiders, if hoof-and-mouth disease didn't kill them first. I think half the men in my family ended up trampled or shot or drowned in rivers because of cattle. These are longhorns. They're a museum breed, useless for beef or dairy or much of anything else."

"If you dislike them so much, why do you raise them?" she asked.

He grinned at her. "Nostalgia for the good old days."

She smiled back at him. "I think they're very picturesque."

"They are that," he agreed. "Come on, let's get back to the party. This is all yesterday out here. I'm not interested in yesterday. Tomorrow is what concerns me."

As they drove back, a huge helicopter passed overhead. Its silver sides bore a scarlet logo: a stylized sun and stars. "I see the Japanese contingent's arriving," Cash commented. He turned onto a road leading to the helipad and got there in time to greet the dozen businessmen who emerged from the craft. Minibuses were on their way from the main house to pick up the new arrivals. Cash got out of the Jeep and walked up to a man about his own age, to whom the others deferred. The Japanese smiled and bowed slightly as he shook hands. A puzzled look crossed his face as Sachi approached.

"Sachi, this is Kazuo Yoshino, head of—"

"We know each other," she said, extending her hand. "I interviewed Mr. Yoshino two years ago for *Paris-Match*."

Yoshino smiled and took her hand. "And I knew your father, too."

"*Mata dozo yoroshiku,*" Sachi said with a slight bow.

"*Kochira koso dozo yoroshiku,*" Yoshino replied, returning the bow.

Cash studied the helicopter. "It's a beauty, Kazuo. Did you bring it here just to show off?"

"Our newest and fastest. We like to travel in style. Besides, there may be some people here interested in ordering a few."

"I don't doubt it. I'm one of them."

"I thought you might be. I will put you in touch with the manufacturer while I am here. The range of options they offer is dazzling. I am sure you will find something to suit all your needs."

Yoshino declined an offer to ride in the Jeep, not wanting to get his expensive suit dusty. The Japanese contingent boarded the minibuses and Cash drove the Jeep back to the ranch house.

"Yoshino thinks it's a wasted trip if he can't sell someone Japanese aerospace products," Cash observed.

"That's probably why he's where he is today," she said.

While the new guests were freshening up in their quarters, Sachi sounded out Cash on his relationship with the Japanese. "I take it you and Yoshino are not quite as hostile as you and Preston Reed are?"

"Our relationship is cordial and businesslike. On the SolarSat project, we're rivals, but it's a may-the-best-man-win sort of rivalry, to use an archaic and sexist phrase."

"But he heads a major consortium of Japanese businesses. If you or one of the others win the SolarSat contract, he and his colleagues won't be put out of business. Lone Star is a one-man operation and you're betting everything on it. If he wins, you lose everything."

"That's by my choice. He and his friends like a safe game. That's not my style. If I bet the ranch on one turn of the cards, it's because that's how I like to play."

"Is that the Texas style?"

"That's it." He grinned again. "Besides, I can always find me another sunken galleon."

Her well-schooled face showed the faintest flicker of eagerness. "That's something I'd like to get the real story on."

"I was in a dockside bar and met an old guy with a lot of tattoos, a fascinating yarn, and a map to sell."

"I don't believe that and neither does anyone else. There was something unprecedentedly high-tech involved. What was it?"

This was getting better. Was she a spy? Not necessarily. A columnist looking for a scoop would ask the same thing.

"If I had some secret technology at work, why would I tell anyone?"

She smiled as if she knew more than she should. "I know a man . . ." She let it dangle off meaningfully.

"I'll bet you know a good many."

"A man in Europe. He thinks you have good reason to hide the truth behind a preposterous story."

"Why does he think that?"

"He thinks that somehow you used spy satellites, that there's some sort of collusion between you and American military intelligence."

This was getting too close. It was du Mont. Had to be.

"Then he greatly overestimates the esteem in which I'm held by my government."

"You have a history of intelligence work, some of it in covert operations. You could still have friends in that line."

Cash had made a point of studying how the best interviewers tricked interviewees into unintentionally revealing statements. He remembered how Orianna Falacci got Henry Kissinger to admit to his "lone marshal" fantasy.

"No go, Miss Sasano. I bought a map. Ah, here are our guests."

Yoshino and his party had emerged from the house, having resisted any temptation to change into more casual clothes.

"Well, Kazuo, who won the great Pacific sweepstakes?" A crowd of small nations lay on or near the equator between Australia and the Asian mainland, all of them vying to provide the location for the Japanese launch facility.

"We will launch from Borneo, near Balikpapan, but we will have other support facilities in the nearby nations."

"Good policy. Is the political situation there stable?"

"Not ideal, but very few states are perfectly stable these days, especially those along the equator."

Cash saw that Parker had his head tilted to one side, an attitude that meant he was receiving a message. "The Prez can't make it," he reported, "but the Veep's coming in this evening."

"You'd better make arrangements for his security," Cash said.

Parker grimaced. "Okay, but I hate dealing with amateurs." As far as Parker was concerned, the Secret Service people were government flunkies who couldn't cut it in the private sector.

"You can live with it, Jack," Cash said. "Get to work."

Parker grabbed a handful of his own hair and drew a forefinger along his hairline in a scalping gesture. This accomplished, he turned and stalked off.

"What was that all about?" Sachi asked.

"Jack claims to be a descendant of Quanah Parker. He was the last of the big Comanche war chiefs. Jack says Quanah scalped my great-grandpa, and when he's pissed off at me, he lets me know he'd like to do the same to me."

"You have an . . . eccentric staff, Cash," Yoshino observed.

"You aren't the first to notice."

The gathering continued well into the night, with a respectful pause in the proceedings for the arrival of the Vice President. By the time the moon was directly overhead, the bulk of the guests began to drift off toward the nearest suitable accommodations. Cash had thoughtfully reserved blocks of rooms in all the local hotels and motels, but many opted to drive or fly to San Antonio, a town with first-class hostelries. The festivities would recommence early the next morning.

A few privileged guests were put up at the ranch. Among these was Sachi, and she wondered why she had been thus favored when so many important people had to seek a roof elsewhere. She suspected she would learn soon enough. She stood on the veranda enjoying the cool night-time breeze, listening to the shrill singing of the crickets that infested South Texas, when she heard the distinctive sound of the Jeep returning from the landing strip. Cash had gone to see off the last of the departing guests and now the little vehicle pulled up before her. Cash climbed out the doorless passenger side.

"Park it and go get some sleep," he instructed Parker. The Comanche just grunted and drove off.

"He won't sleep until the Vice President and all the rest of them are gone," Sachi told Cash as he mounted the porch steps. "He's a pro."

"He's a damned prima donna, is what he is," Cash said. "At last I've got time to relax and talk. Will you join me in the living room for a drink?"

"I'd be delighted." She had noted with approval that Cash had only sipped at an occasional beer all day. She liked to see self-control in a man of responsibility.

The living room was a vast, flagstoned expanse with a wood-beamed roof high overhead. In its center was a sunken area surrounding a circular hearth in which a mesquite fire crackled invitingly. The fireplace lacked the chalet-type cowling she was familiar with, but the room was not smoky. She decided that there was a hidden ventilation system somewhere, sucking up the smoke. She took a seat on one of the couches facing the fire and Cash brought her a goblet of white wine. He sat down with a contented sigh.

"A day like this is worse than five days on an offshore oil rig," he said.

"I noticed that you were fretting. It isn't your sort of work, is it?"

"No, but it's necessary and there's nobody else to do it. If I had my way, I'd do all my work in my offices and plants and launch facilities. I could get away with that when I was starting out with a shoestring operation and a small group of employees. We all knew each other and we knew what we were doing, and why. But this is a huge, multinational operation. When you think about it, it concerns the whole world. That means diplomatic and media involvement."

"And your personal style demands that you take care of all of it," she pointed out.

"Exactly," he said ruefully. "I got myself into this. And that's just what I wanted to talk to you about."

"It is?" So it was not to be merely a simple seduction.

"Yes." He leaned back and steepled his fingers. "Back at my reception in New York during the U.N. hearings, you said something that started me to thinking."

"I suspect that you are thinking a mile a minute all the time, but I'm flattered that something I said started you thinking in a different direction."

"You mentioned that the European media have a weak spot for advances in medicine, that they just can't bring themselves to criticize a project that contributes to longer life or better health."

"Yes, that's true," she said, wondering what this was building up to.

"How would you like to work for me? I need a PR specialist and press liaison for Lone Star's medical-experiments section. The job's yours if you want it."

She blinked, taken aback at the suddenness of it. "I don't quite understand. I had no idea that Lone Star even had a medical-experiments section."

"It does now. It's something I'd been planning for a long time. Just about all of the developers plan the same thing. These are big orbiting stations we'll be building, with lots of space for things besides solar power generation. Companies, universities, and foundations having free-fall projects in the works are already bidding for space."

"I'm flattered, but I'm not sure that my European publishers would treat my work as legitimate journalism if I was merely one of your employees. I don't write advertising."

"Nobody's asking you to lie. And you wouldn't just be putting out press releases. You'd have a voice on the planning board and would attend all the top-level planning sessions with the rest of my staff. And I need the media exposure. You've taken a special interest in space exploitation for years, and you didn't know that medical research was involved. Imagine how ignorant the general public must be."

The hook was irresistible. Not merely to be reporting on new developments in space, but to be involved in the planning. To be at the very center of things!

"I accept," she said, smiling. Then she felt the elation drain. She knew that Jean-Claude would expect her to spy for him. She pushed the thought from her mind. She could handle two men, even two men like Jean-Claude du Mont and Cash Carlson.

"Good," he said. "As a matter of fact, you might be qualified to take an even more active role. I'd been meaning to ask: Since you studied journalism, how did you come by your interest in science?"

"It's my deepest, darkest secret," she said conspiratorially.

"Shameful as all that?"

"Worse. But since you're taking me into your inner circle, I fear I must come clean. I'm not just a journalist, Mr. Carlson. I have a Bachelor of Science Degree in bioengineering from the Tokyo Institute of Technology."

"TIT, eh? Better not use the abbreviation in your resume."

"And I did graduate studies in closed ecosystems. That was in Europe and here in the States. I'd have gone for my Ph.D., but I found I just wasn't interested in an academic career. In Japan, it's not at all unusual for a science reporter to have a formal education in science from a reputable university, although it's rare in Europe, and even rarer here in the States. By reporting, I could keep up with the things that interested me without becoming an academic drudge."

"An excellent decision. But why be so secretive?"

"Because I learned very early that men are highly intimidated by women with brains, especially if those women are trained in hard science. That's when men can become hard to interview."

"Closed ecosystems, you say?" Cash pondered the possibilities for a while. "Sachi, in a few weeks, I need to make a trip to my orbiting facility. I can't take any deadweight, but I can sure wedge in a closed-systems specialist." He gave her one of his infectious smiles. "Want to come along?"

9

JEAN-CLAUDE DU MONT looked like the man for whom the word "distinguished" had been coined. He was tall and almost spectrally thin, with an aristocratic face graced with a salt-and-pepper mustache, and graceful wings of graying hair above his ears. The polished tropical hardwood of his desk reflected his handsome countenance faithfully, unobscured as the surface was by so much as a single sheet of paper.

Nothing about the office hinted that he was the head of the European Space Enterprise. It looked like the office of a nineteenth-century minister of state. The fact was that du Mont despised the twentieth century, which he associated with the decline of Europe and the rise of upstart nations such as America and Japan. He was determined that the twenty-first should see the reascendancy of Europe, especially that of France.

It was his considered opinion that at least fifty years had been wasted worrying about the boorish Russians and the remote Chinese, to the neglect of important matters, years during which the intelligentsia of Europe had slavishly given themselves to an alien political-economic philosophy, while the youth had surrendered to the equally pernicious American popular culture.

It had been a deplorable setback for Europe, much akin to the invasions of Huns, Magyars, Moors, and Norsemen, but du Mont was determined that the effects should not be irreversible. Already, Europe, despite some fragmentation by ethnic and linguistic splinter groups clamoring for independent states, was pulling itself together.

The only fly in his ointment was the fact that the dominant economic power was Germany. At least the Germans were Europeans, and better them than the English!

There came a discreet knock at his door. He did not like intercoms and buzzers. "Come in."

The newcomer was Hans Krause. The Alsatian bowed slightly and took a seat facing his chief.

"Carlson claims to have the lightweight solar-power cells and says he will have the laser drive to get them into orbit by the end of the year."

"Your source for this information?" du Mont asked.

"Preston Reed. I met with his administrative assistant in Aspen yesterday and he passed this on to me."

"And does Reed believe this to be true?"

"Apparently so."

Du Mont sat back and pretended to be considering the information. Actually, he was trying to decide who was lying. Sachi had told him of the claim days before, but she had said that Reed was highly skeptical. So why was the man passing it on as if he believed it? Was he making use of a rival's disinformation for his own ends? If so, it would not be the first time. Du Mont had made use of the tactic from time to time himself.

"If true, he has a decided advantage from the start."

Krause nodded gravely. "That is so. But how could he develop these things in advance of everyone else?"

Du Mont snorted. "It is simple. He met a tattooed old engineer in a JPL bar who had blueprints to sell."

Krause laughed sycophantically at his chief's witticism. "It is no less likely than his other claims."

"Cash Carlson!" du Mont said with a curling lip. "What sort of name is that? A cowboy name, something out of a bad Western film! He probably sees himself as John Wayne defending the ranch from marauding redskins. They all think that way, as if their pioneer ancestors emerged victorious through superior valor and the favor of Providence. It would never occur to a cowboy fantasist like Carlson that his precious Texas was won by virtue of disease and the New England factories of Colt and Winchester."

"Just so, Chief," Krause said. He knew that Carlson was nothing of the sort. Furthermore, he knew that du Mont knew it as well, but he had learned not to interrupt or dispute these diatribes. The advantages of working this close to the centers of power made putting up with the man's tiresome and rather crackbrained Eurocentrism a small matter. In most other respects, du Mont was the soul of clear-sighted pragmatism. That was just as well, because the next item on the agenda was rather delicate.

"Mademoiselle Sasano—"

"What about her?" du Mont asked icily.

"It seems that she keeps . . . perhaps too much company with Carlson."

"What of that? She still works for me."

"Ah, I see. Well, if that is the case, then all is well."

"Perfectly. Is there anything else?"

"The, ah . . . gentleman from the former Soviet Union has arrived. Do you wish to see him?" Krause's distaste was palpable.

Du Mont gave a Gallic sigh. "I suppose I must. There is some work one cannot entrust to a civilized person. Send him up."

Krause left and du Mont brooded about Sachi Sasano. Was she truly getting too close to Carlson? He could scarcely believe that someone of Sachi's refinement could be attracted by a man as crude as Carlson, but one never knew about women's taste. There had been a time when the most popular actor in France had been Charles Bronson. He shuddered at the thought.

But Sachi? She had been little more than a schoolgirl when he had found her—a starry-eyed graduate student who had a passion for science and, he reflected complacently, good taste in older men. He had taken her in as his protégée, training her in the higher social arts, providing her with the contacts she would need for a career in journalism, should she choose to continue on that course.

Naturally enough, she had become his mistress. That was only to be expected in such a relationship, and it was a privilege to which du Mont believed himself perfectly entitled. He had a wife of suitable breeding whom he saw several times each year, usually at functions involving their two grown sons and daughter. It was a cordial and convenient relationship. He pursued his own interests as she did hers, each maintaining an acceptable level of discretion. She had for many years been exceedingly close to a prominent Italian statesman, a man married to an equally famous Italian film star. It was a civilized arrangement, du Mont thought; a very satisfyingly European arrangement.

He dragged his attention back to the task at hand. The Russian. The continent was full of such men these days: thugs of the old regime and its satellites who needed markets for their arcane skills. They hired out as "security specialists" and "intelligence analysts," and even as "interrogation engineers," to whatever government or firm would have them. The more primitive—and less hypocritical—governments of the third world simply hired them as assassins, torturers, and spies. Those of the more developed world had to be more circumspect. One thing was for certain, du Mont noted: The deplorable swine never seemed to lack for employment.

The one he was meeting with was named Sergei Kuprin. At least that was the name he was using this year, in France. Like so many of them, he had a Macedonian passport. The little Balkan republic had become to passports what Panama and Liberia were to ships' registrations. Anyone lacking a passport but possessing a certain reasonable sum of money could purchase one quite legally. It was understood that no one who was not of Macedonian ancestry need expect any help from Macedonian consuls or foreign-department officials should the passport holder encounter trouble during his perigrinations.

It was not that du Mont approved of such people, or advocated employing them on any regular basis. It was just that certain distasteful matters had to be accomplished from time to time, and there were some things one did not ask a civilized person to perform.

The knock at the door was loud and peremptory. "Come in," du Mont said.

The Russian was a stocky man whose dark, coarse hair stood out from his scalp like a wire brush. He swaggered to a chair and sat down without being asked.

"Good day," the Russian said. "What sort of work do you have for me?" His French, unlike his manners, was excellent.

Losing their empire has cost them none of their arrogance, du Mont thought. *But then, perhaps arrogance is all they have left.*

"Let us not be so hasty," du Mont said. "I must know a few things first."

"Why? It was your man who contacted me, not the other way around. You knew about me from someone, so presumably I come highly recommended."

Du Mont let none of his anger or impatience show. This was like dealing with a trained dog—it could accomplish certain limited tasks, but only in its own way. He would have to do things the Russian's way, at least for now.

"So you do. However, the matters upon which my colleagues have employed your expertise were somewhat different from the task I have in mind."

"Go on."

"First of all, have you had any experience at all in aerospace operations?"

The bushy eyebrows went up. "Aerospace? Not at the operational end. But in intelligence matters, yes. From the very first, it was recognized that space operations were of primary concern to state security. Protecting our own secrets and learning about those of the enemy were routine."

"How did you spy on the American space program?"

"They published an amazing amount about it. For the rest—" He shrugged. "Paid informants were by far the best and the most cost-effective method, and the safest. There are always people willing to sell out for money."

"You didn't have many committed ideological allies on the inside?"

"You mean the way we infiltrated British intelligence in the thirties and forties? No, that was a fluke; a little clique of upper-class homosexual Cambridge students who passionately needed to destroy the system that gave them such privilege. In America, the sort that gravitated toward the Party were not the type to take a serious interest in engineering and the hard sciences. But you can always count on greed and desperation."

Kuprin, not bothering to ask permission, took out a crumpled pack of cigarettes and stuck one in his mouth. He lit it with a match and looked around for an ashtray. Not finding one, he dropped the match on the floor. "This is ancient history. What do you want me for?"

Du Mont wrinkled his nose at the foul-smelling smoke. Was the man truly this crude, or was he just testing a prospective employer?

"What do you know about Cash Carlson?"

"The cowboy rocket man? Only that he's one of those colorful capitalists one always reads about in the popular press."

"Do you think you could infiltrate his operation? There are several matters of great interest to me for which I am willing to pay generously."

"This is something a little unusual, but I can do a preliminary assessment in the next few days. The only difficulty may be the locale. Houston is not exactly a great international metropolis."

"Carlson is moving most of his operations to Brazil for the solar-satellite project."

The Russian grinned. "Much better! If I can't plant agents among the South Americans, I should be in another line of work. What is true of the Yankees is doubly true of their southern neighbors."

"Carlson himself has a background in covert operations," du Mont pointed out.

"But he left military intelligence to go into private business, so something about the occupation must have disagreed with him."

"His chief of security is a man named Parker."

Kuprin made a rude noise with his lips. "I've seen his dossier. A red Indian with a reputation as a wild man. Security is not the same thing as intelligence. The man is just a glorified bodyguard. Never fear, if the information you need is to be found in Brazil, I'll get it for you. Now, what is it I am supposed to be looking for?"

Du Mont told him about the lightweight solar-power cells and the laser drive. "But more important than these is the way Carlson found that treasure galleon. I think that there was collusion between him and American military intelligence. That means corruption on a massive scale and if I can prove it, I can get the U.N. to bar him from the solar-power satellite competition."

"With him out of the competition, you are sure to win?"

"With the others, it is more a matter of organization and expertise. None of them has a decided technological edge. I do not wish to compete against some shadowy alliance of business and the American military."

"Then if we can agree on my fee, I can find what you need," the Russian said confidently.

"You seem very sure of yourself."

"Of course I am." Kuprin smiled and spoke as if imparting an elementary lesson to someone very naive. "There are certain things one can always count on. One of them is corruption. It is always there, one must merely find it."

"Then find it for me. Bring me the proof."

"This Yankee is a fish bone in your throat, eh?"

"That is of no concern to you," du Mont said icily. "I wish to hire your services as a spy, not as an analyst."

When the Russian was gone, du Mont sat and fumed for a while. The presumption of the man! As if Jean-Claude du Mont needed to be lectured upon the nature and prevalence of corruption! Well, if one had to ascend a Himalayan peak, one hired a Sherpa guide and did not bother oneself about his primeval level of culture. It was always thus.

But could so blunt an instrument accomplish a delicate and subtle task of infiltration and espionage? He could only hope that the man was capable of assuming a façade of civilization for the duration of the operation. Resigned, he turned to the next duty of his long, busy day.

As he left du Mont's office, the man who this year called himself Sergei Kuprin was engaged in an analysis of his own. Unlike du Mont, this sort of character reading was his profession, and was correspondingly more insightful. His real name was not Kuprin, and he was not Russian. He had been born in what was now the Georgian Republic, a place where he was no longer welcome. His birthplace was within twenty kilometers of Stalin's, and while he had no memory of the Stalin years, he had absorbed the man's lesson well: Nothing was desirable save power, and power meant the Party.

Young Ilia Choloquashvili had joined all the Party youth organizations and had done well in school, despite his distaste for most academic subjects. He had concentrated on the truly important things, such as learning to speak Russian like a Muscovite. After a compulsory stint in the army, he had won appointment to the KGB, where his natural talents and inclinations raised him quickly through the ranks. He had headed an interrogation team in Afghanistan and had displayed suitable brutality, although he preferred the subtler arts of espionage and the running of agents in foreign countries.

The collapse of the Soviet Empire had not caught him completely off guard. With a number of colleagues, he had made arrangements to ensure his survival and future livelihood. He knew that the end of the corrupt, inefficient old empire would not greatly change international rivalries. There would always be a demand for his skills and for the worldwide web of contacts he had built up during his career.

From du Mont's Paris office, Kuprin caught the Metro and fifteen minutes later was on a bullet train for Marseilles. The ancient port city was to questionable international freelancers what Paris was to couturiers. There was a shift toward the Balkans, where toleration of one's activities outside the area was broad, but Marseilles had tradition, a fine central location, and far better restaurants.

His new employer was a man of a type with which he had become all too familiar: aristocratic Europeans, forever resentful of the loss of past glories, convinced that their culture was the highest achievement of human history. For many years, they had been peripheral to European affairs, but with the resurgence of the continent, coupled with the disgrace of the left, they were reasserting themselves. It was as if they expected to resume their nineteenth-century prominence, this time somehow without the benefit of colonialism.

Kuprin had no particular objection to working for such people—they were no worse than the Party apparatchiks he had served for much of his life. They certainly had better taste and manners. What rankled was the way they despised those whose services kept them in place. This du Mont, for instance, obviously felt that he was not sullied by his own dirty work so long as he farmed it out to others.

Well, Kuprin reflected philosophically, it was not as if he usually expected to like the people he worked for. He had gotten over the expectation of bonhomie somewhere during his first year in the Young Pioneers. He was a professional, and he would do the job for which he was hired.

Near the waterfront of Marseilles was a bar called "Camerone," owned by an ex-Legionnaire named Guenter Schwartz. Its clientele consisted mainly of mercenaries and espionage freelancers like Kuprin. It was known to the French police as "Alexander's Headquarters," because a raid on the place would yield a huge number of Macedonian passports. Schwartz assured the loyalty of his customers by conducting daily sweeps for bugs. A sterile meeting place was an invaluable resource for these people.

It was midafternoon when Kuprin arrived, a quiet hour when most of the customers were in their homes or other quarters sleeping off lunch, too early for serious drinking. He found Schwartz behind the bar, discussing something with a pair of hard-faced bartenders. Schwartz poured him a vodka without being asked.

"*Bon jour*, Andrei."

"It's Sergei now. Sergei Kuprin." He knocked back the shot and held out the empty glass for a refill.

"Sergei, then. How goes it?"

"Business is good. It's why I've been away since last year. I have a local client now." This had an elastic meaning in Kuprin's world. Usually it meant French, or at least Western European.

"Good. Then we'll be seeing more of you." Schwartz knew better than to ask for specifics.

"Maybe. It may keep me traveling, in which case I'll be needing a mail drop and a secure telephone line. The usual terms?"

"Done. I'll have the numbers for you by evening."

"Excellent. Do you know anything about the abortive hit a few months ago on the Yankee rocket independent, Carlson? It involves my new job."

Schwartz frowned, turning his blocky Prussian face into a mass of deep lines. "A disgrace. Joffre and Camarena were good men once, old comrades from the Legion. These last few years, they would work for anybody. Did you know Krylov?"

"Only by reputation, which wasn't great. A drunk and a thug, good for little but strong-arm work."

Schwartz nodded. "That was my impression. The IRA gunman was never in my place and I never heard of the driver. But Joffre and Camarena met in one of the back rooms with a purported businessman from Bolivia about three weeks prior to the attempt. I never saw the Bolivian before, or since."

"Most likely a professional go-between," Kuprin said, wondering if du Mont had had anything to do with it.

"If so, he picked the wrong men. Parker and his team have a limited sort of practice, but they are very good at it."

"Personally, I think Parker is overrated, like most of the American operatives. They are as much a product of their own films as of training and experience. But then, one must admit that he and his boss are still alive, which is more than can be said for a number of men who have graced your establishment."

"Too true. And you aren't the first to ask. Two days after the shoot-out, men arrived, making discreet inquiries."

"I suppose Parker had to try. Did they learn anything?"

"Not from me. As for my customers, they talk or keep quiet as they see their own interest." He refilled Kuprin's glass.

"Are any of the South American operators around?"

"Are you looking for the Bolivian?"

Kuprin shook his head. "No, this is something else. Much of my new job will involve Brazil."

"Then you won't want to talk with the Argentines or the Chileans?"

"No, but contacts in Venezuela, or in Suriname or the Guianas, could be useful. Possibly even in Colombia and Ecuador as well."

"All equatorial countries," Schwartz noted without inflection. Kuprin said nothing. "Vargas is in most evenings. So is Santos. They've both done a great deal of work in that part of the world."

"When do they usually arrive?"

Schwartz glanced at the clock above the bar mirror. "About two hours."

"Good. That leaves me time for something to eat. I've had nothing since breakfast in Paris." Even at the thought, his stomach rumbled. "If they arrive before I return, tell them I want to confer with them."

Schwartz nodded curtly. "In the block behind this one there's a little restaurant called 'Chez Maurice.' It looks like a dump but they make bouillabaisse the way God intended it to be made."

Kuprin went there and tried the bouillabaisse, which was, as Schwartz had indicated, superlative. For Kuprin, one of the charms of foreign service with the KGB, always excepting Afghanistan, was that one got to eat decently for a change. Well, barring an utterly unlikely communist counterrevolution, he need never concern himself about a Russian diet again. Now that he thought of it, even reestablishment of the old KGB would not make him welcome at home, as his activities since the collapse had hardly been conducive to the resurgence of Marxism. He had worked for pay and nothing else. The collapse of the Soviet Empire meant that the world's few remaining Marxist regimes and revolutionary movements were unable to afford his services.

After dinner, he took a stroll, making frequent, random changes of direction, reversing himself often. When he was satisfied that no one was following, he headed back toward Camerone. He knew it was unlikely that he was being tailed, but a man of his profession neglected the habits of a lifetime at his mortal peril.

When he entered, Schwartz nodded toward a round table set in a tiny alcove off the main room. Two men sat at the table. Each appeared to be in his mid-thirties. One was plump and clerkish, his eyes wide behind round-rimmed glasses. The other affected the style of an international drug mercenary, with a suit of armor fabric and a belt full of high-tech communication equipment. Kuprin knew that the clerkish one was Vargas. He had had some minor dealings with the man before. So the other had to be Santos.

"May I join you?" Kuprin took a chair without waiting for a reply.

"Schwartz vouches for you," Santos said, shrugging.

"It has been a while since you have been active in our part of the globe," said Vargas.

"My new client has interests there. It involves the new space-launch facility." With these men, he had no need to talk in circumlocutions. "Are you acquainted with it?"

"Of course," Santos said. "I expect it to be an even greater resource than the French facility in French Guiana."

"How is that?" Kuprin asked, fairly sure that he already knew.

Santos leaned forward, elbows on the table, fingers laced. "Much of my work involves facilitating movement of merchandise from Colombia and northern Peru to the United States and Europe. A space facility means great air traffic, many aircraft that arrive loaded and leave empty. They are given amazingly little customs attention."

"A splendid resource, as you say," Kuprin commented. "And you, my friend Vargas? As I recall, you are the fixer, the greaser of palms, in that part of the world. Has this new launch facility come within your purview?"

"Everything that involves jobs, or money, or government action in Brazil may call for my professional services. This project, you understand, will be most desirable for a great many people. It may well involve the largest number of government contracts in the history of Brazil: construction, catering, services of all sorts, utilities, land purchase and lease, the list goes on. The influx of workers, both native and foreign, will be great. There will be much foreign money flying around. Needless to say, the opportunities for graft will be unprecedented."

"Here is what I need," Kuprin said, getting right down to business. "I have been hired to set up an intelligence operation within the Lone Star operation. I wish to be on the spot myself, as controller. I must have people who are trustworthy and skilled."

"Do you wish to recruit here?" Vargas asked.

"I may pick up one assistant here. Except for that one, I would rather work with locals."

"How many?" Vargas asked.

"I will require an overview of the whole operation. Say a minimum of five people, at least one of whom must be a computer expert and employed in Carlson's computer center."

"On the launch pads?" Vargas queried.

Kuprin shook his head. "All that will be quite public. I can watch it on television. No, the nerve centers are far more important: the computers, the financial department, anything to do with planning. Make up a list of likely personnel. I will take rooms in Rio and begin interviewing."

He leaned back and knocked back a vodka. "I will wish to plant my own bugs, and the best way to do that is during construction. I'll need access to all blueprints, especially those of the administration building and the on-site quarters of the top people, especially those of Carlson and his staff."

Vargas steepled his fingers and thought for a moment. "You will need to have a cover that will give you continuous access to all the sensitive spots. Would a supervisory position in the engineering-and-maintenance section be acceptable? In such a job, you would have ample excuses to go nearly anywhere at any time. You can arrange for small accidents, breakdowns, and minor crises to allow for your presence wherever necessary."

"Would Carlson's people not become suspicious of so many emergencies?" Kuprin asked.

Vargas shrugged. "Not as long as you don't overdo it. After all, we are dealing here with Latin America, where incompetence is a way of life."

"Then make it so."

"One more thing," Vargas said. "Will your activities involve sabotage or acts of violence? If so, I must know in order to arrange for suitably skilled personnel."

"Not at the moment," Kuprin said. "So far, I am employed for intelligence work only and I'd rather not use people who might have compiled intelligence or police dossiers for such activities. In the future, I may well be doing such work. I suspect that my employer will not be satisfied with just knowing what is going on, but will want to take steps to assure himself of an edge. If so, I will want to put together a separate team for any such operations. Have a list of suitable personnel for me to contact at need."

"Done," said Vargas.

Kuprin turned to Santos. "Your operations seem to involve cargo space predominantly. Do you move people as well?"

The man nodded. "Yes, both as crew and as passengers. A valuable shipment must have an escort. Sometimes it is a crew member, even the pilot."

"Passengers, you say?" Kuprin asked.

"People will pay handsomely to emigrate to America. With properly recompensed officials at both ends of the flight, this is a very safe way to facilitate their travel."

"I believe I will find your services very valuable. I may require cargo to be shipped out of the country without having to trouble the authorities, and I wish to have a quick means of escape should something go wrong."

Santos nodded. "I can arrange that. Would a specific destination be of primary importance?"

"For the cargo, France most likely. For me—" he performed a Slavic shrug, "—there may not be leisure to select a destination. Anyplace safe will do for a start. Some amenable nation in Central or South America would be suitable."

Santos favored him with a white-toothed grin. "In that part of the world, my friend, they are all amenable."

Kuprin turned and called over his shoulder for another round. When their glasses were refilled, he raised his in salute. "My friends, I think we shall all do very well out of this business. Here is to the future of man in space!"

Laughing, they raised their glasses and clinked them together.

10

WINSTON CRUMLY SAT in blissful communion with his beloved screens, munching on pizza. Most people would have been baffled by his multiple screens and keyboards, but Winston's thought processes were not those of an ordinary human being. Linear reasoning, proceeding in an orderly fashion from point A to point B, had little if any role in the way his brain worked. He was one of those people who had been designed to function in symbiosis with the computer. Had he been born at any earlier period, he would have been insane, a hopeless drunk, or an early suicide. The effect would have been as if half his personality was absent.

As it was, here in his den, he could function with incredible efficiency and do things probably no other human being could do. Not that many of his fellow humans would have considered him either sane or socially acceptable. Their brains just did not function along the same lines as his. That was their loss as far as he was concerned, when he bothered to think about his fellow humans at all. He liked Cash Carlson because Cash appreciated the things he could do with his computers and didn't give a damn what he ate, how he dressed, or whether he bathed frequently.

Crumly took a big bite of pizza and studied the screen in front of him. It was his favorite: onion and Italian sausage with plenty of extra garlic. Crumly knew that garlic protected him from all sorts of germs. He knew that the AMA was keeping that a secret so they could go on raking in the bucks selling medicine and performing unnecessary surgery. He intended to break into their computer banks someday and expose them. He reached for his keys but paused when the flasher over the elevator lit up.

"Who is it?" he asked the empty air.

"Parker," said a voice.

Crumly didn't like Parker. Parker scared him. Parker was one mean dude. But Parker was loyal to Carlson and he had access to Crumly during any reasonable hours. The elevator door slid open and Parker came in. He was dressed in slacks, boots, and sport coat, casual but a little heavy for Houston. He needed the extra fabric to cover his hardware.

"Hello, Winston."

Crumly didn't say anything. He went back to watching his screen. Parker pulled up a chair next to him and Crumly edged away. No telling what sort of germs the man might have brought in.

"What are you doing now, Winston?"

"Checking out the European launch facility. Their road net, mostly." He had an overview of perhaps four square kilometers, the picture looking almost like a map on his screen. He isolated a thousand-meter square and blew it up to screen size.

"You're not using the spy satellites again are you, Winston? You know the boss says you're not supposed to do that."

Actually, he was, but he knew that Parker wasn't familiar with the government's code symbols. Even Parker couldn't be an expert on everything. He turned to face his visitor for the first time.

"What do you want, Parker?" He noted with satisfaction that the bodyguard recoiled slightly from the garlic. Maybe Parker was really a vampire. Vampires hated garlic.

"Winston, I think the boss may have problems he's unwilling to deal with, and that's a mistake."

"He makes mistakes?"

Parker nodded solemnly. "Yeah, even the boss makes mistakes. It's always a mistake to present your back to an enemy, especially one in your own organization."

"Enemy?" Crumly felt his scalp prickle. This could be worse than germs, worse than flying in an airplane. If Carlson had internal enemies in his own company, then Crumly was vulnerable, too. His safe little den might not be so safe.

"Exactly. Whoever it is, he's good. I haven't caught 'im yet, so he's gotta be good."

"It's a he?"

Parker shrugged. "He, she, maybe even they, but I doubt that. What he's doing doesn't take a team, and more than one would just increase the danger of exposure."

"What is it he's doing?" Nervously, Crumly picked up a doughnut and nibbled on it.

"Not a whole lot. He's cagey, he doesn't act often, and he's subtle."

"What's he done so far?" Crumly blinked owlishly behind his round rimmed glasses.

"He's been tipping assassins and snatch teams about the boss's travel schedules and routes. We've been getting hit too many times, by people who know exactly where we're going and when we're gonna be there."

Crumly's stomach lurched with dread and it took another doughnut to calm it down. Killers and kidnappers. This was definitely worse than germs.

"I want you to help me find him, Winston," Parker said patiently, used to Crumly's multitude of eccentricities.

"I dunno. I'm not very good at working with people. Especially bad people."

Parker leaned forward, his face hardening. "Uh-uh, Winston. This guy's not bad, just greedy. I'm bad. Remember that, Winston." His look softened a little. "No, you don't need to mix with people, or even talk to them. I want you to work with your computers."

"Oh," Crumly said, relieved. "That's different. I like computers."

"I know you do," Parker said soothingly. "And nobody in the world can use them like you do. Can you monitor the computer traffic in this building?"

"This building?" Crumly said contemptuously. "I can monitor all the computer traffic in any Lone Star facility anywhere in the world."

Parker grinned. "That's the kind of talk I like to hear. I want you to go over all that stuff, look for anything suspicious—unauthorized access, that sort of thing."

"That's an awful lot of traffic," Crumly said doubtfully.

"I trust you, Winston, I know you can do it." He patted Crumly on the shoulder and the eccentric flinched away from the hand. "And don't trouble the boss about this. It's for his own good."

Parker got up and walked to the elevator. Before he went in, he turned around. "And, Winston—I better not find out it was you." He stepped into the elevator and the doors closed.

Crumly got out of his chair and tore off his shirt; jamming it into the disposal slot in the wall. With a suck of air, it was whisked toward the incinerator Crumly had insisted on. The man had touched him, contaminated his shirt with germs! He yanked off the rest of his clothes and jumped under the shower. With the water running as hot as he could stand it, he scrubbed down with carbolic soap.

The shower calmed him and he began to think as his panic subsided. A spy in the organization? Somebody threatening Carlson? Well, he'd just see about that. It was an intriguing problem, trying to find a single, cagey enemy agent in the huge babble of computer traffic of Lone Star. And the guy could be using other facilities—his home phone, for instance. Well, no problem there, either. As he warmed to the puzzle, he smiled and began to hum. One thing was for certain: He could sure make this bozo sorry he'd ever fallen afoul of Winston Crumly.

Parker was well satisfied as he stepped from the elevator onto the main floor of the Houston facility. He hadn't been serious about his little threat. Crumly could start a world war with his computers, but he was pretty harmless otherwise. And nothing could ever persuade him to betray Carlson, who had saved him from the real world. No, that was just to light a little fire under Crumly, who tended to lose touch with reality unless it was brought forcefully home to him.

Half-consciously, he checked the time readout in his electronic shades. That was a design feature he'd insisted on when he ordered the shades for his team. Parker had once known an assassin whose technique was incredibly simple and effective: He'd walk up to the mark and ask for the time. When the mark looked down at his wrist, the hitter would waste him. It was time to meet with Pat.

She was waiting for him in the secure conference room. As far as Parker was concerned, the rest of the building, apart from Crumly's crypt, was a security disaster area. Carlson's refusal to cultivate paranoia meant that he did without most security guards, ID checks, scanners, and so forth. He said he didn't want his employees to feel they were working in a fort and being watched all the time. Parker told him he was being hopelessly naive, but Carlson was the boss. This one room was as tight as the security chief could make it.

He drew a cup of coffee, strong and black. Some of his old Navy habits stayed with him. Pat sat at the conference table with a cup of herbal tea in front of her, along with an opened portfolio. She glanced up at him coolly, which was okay with Parker. He didn't demand warmth from colleagues, only competence and professionalism. Pat had plenty of both. Plus, she wasn't shy about getting her hands bloody if that was what it took.

"Here's the schedule," she said, passing him the papers for the environmental summit. Parker thought the whole thing was a waste of time, but the boss insisted that they would have to sell the SolarSat idea to the environmentalists, and the meeting was going to be in Rio anyway, and Carlson was determined to be a big figure in Brazilian events from now on.

Toward the end of the stack of papers, Parker frowned. "He's going to this Iguazu Falls thing?"

"He says it's important."

"Ever been there?"

"Uh-uh. It's some sort of resort. Lots of conferences are held there, scientific gatherings, that sort of thing."

"Crap! I hate resorts. Big spaces, limited pathways, great fields of fire. I thought I'd have a heart attack when he went to tour all those game parks in Kenya."

"The Veep's going to be there. The whole place'll be crawling with Secret Service."

Parker snorted. "Them! I wouldn't trust the Secret Service with my grandpa's old hound, and I hate my grandpa's old hound. I'll have to go down there myself ahead of time, scope the place out, put my own people in the important spots."

"You'll manage," she said, used to his griping. If it was up to Parker, she thought, the boss would spend his life in a maximum-security prison where the Comanche madman could keep an eye on him all the time. She closed the portfolio. "I think we've got other problems."

"I know we have. What's yours?"

"That Japanese woman." She glowered while Parker grinned. "It's not funny. She shows up at a party and the boss turns into a teenager. He invites her to the ranch, he offers her a job at the top level of company work—he's even planning to take her up to the Igloo! He's gone nuts."

"He can be impulsive."

"It's more than that. First off, it's bad business relations to jump some stranger over the heads of people who've worked for him for years."

"I wouldn't presume to advise him on that. Security is my field."

"Then doesn't it bother you that she's Jean-Claude du Mont's mistress?"

He shrugged. "Her morals aren't my concern. I've checked her out from every direction and it doesn't look like she ever did any dirty work for du Mont. Maybe she's just some bimbo with a taste for rich, powerful men."

"That doesn't sound like you, Parker," she said. "When did you ever exempt anyone from suspicion just because they looked innocent?"

Parker peeled off his shades. For a moment, the interior display winked colorfully, then darkened as the batteries shut down. To save power, they worked only when worn.

"Look, Pat. One thing me and the boss both know: The safest place to have a spy is right next to you. You don't keep them right there, who knows what they might be up to?"

She wavered, not sure if he was leveling with her. "You really think that's what he's doing?"

"Could be. He doesn't tell me everything." Actually, Parker didn't worry much about Sachi—he knew Pat would be watching the woman like a hawk. He sort of liked the woman's style. "Sure you're not just jealous?"

She glared at him icily. There were some things about which she had no sense of humor.

"Okay, sorry I said that. Now, about my problem: I'm going after that mole, no matter what the boss says. Sasano hasn't been around long enough to fit the bill." Pat shared his suspicions. They had discussed this before.

"I'll back you. I think he needs to be caught, too. The boss is dead wrong this time."

"Thanks. You got any candidates?"

"About fifty. No motives, just opportunity. If the motive is greed, that's all that's necessary. Too many people have access to our movement plans. Have you eliminated Max as a suspect?" It still bothered her that Parker had access to Max and she didn't.

"Believe me, I'd suspect you before I'd suspect him."

"I'm not sure how to take that."

"Let's just say that he has more to lose than anyone else if the boss gets it or Lone Star fails."

"I'll buy it." She laced her fingers on the table in front of her. "Now, let's get to basics. What do we have? We have a traitor in the organization, with access to certain sensitive information. This person has a desire to sell this information and has been doing so to person or persons unknown." Her eyebrows went up. "It is still unknown, isn't it?"

He nodded. "We've hit a dead end in tracing who organized or hired the teams."

"So, is seller contacting buyer or vice versa?"

"I'd say the former. It's fairly easy to get services like that out into the market these days. But if there was a recruiter working Lone Star, trolling for sellouts, he would've been reported by now."

"How does our man let it be known he has something to sell?"

Parker sat back, smiling approvingly at her excellent cop technique. "Freelance espionage work used to be the field of a tight little clique of international operators. They knew each other and traded information among themselves. They had their regular drops and meeting places. Even during the height of the Cold War, the big national spy agencies depended heavily on the independents. The CIA and KGB and MI-Five and the Sûreté got all the publicity, but half the time, they were all buying from the same little bunch of pros."

"I see. But this is all changed?"

"It's changing. What did it is the computer. It's the world info net. People all over the world can contact each other through bulletin boards. They learn the latest access codes and they can find out anything they need, or put out any information they want to, including things they have for sale. It's unregulated and unregulatable, too big to monitor. It allows people to operate in a state of total anarchy."

"Sounds scary," she said.

"It is. You want to know what's scariest about it?" he asked, grinning.

"What?"

"Most of the people doing it are lots smarter than anyone trying to police them."

"So you think our man could just be making himself available through a computer bulletin board and contacting his customers that way? No meetings on park benches or in smoky, dim-lit bars?"

"Could be. He could conduct his whole operation in a few minutes out of the week, never even leave his console. And when we catch him, we may not even know his buyer."

"What?"

"No need to. He delivers the goods over the net and they deposit his pay in his bank account the same way. No personal contact, no dealing with the end user. Far as he knows, the buyer might be du Mont, or Reed, or the government of Tibet, or the Martians."

"My God, Parker! How are we going to catch this bastard?"

"It won't be easy. But if he's greedy, he'll trip up. You can always count on greed."

"Greed isn't the only possible motivation," she pointed out. "There's always revenge."

"Maybe. But I'm putting my money on greed." He didn't mention the job he'd given Crumly. Between a greedy blunder and the loon's computer savvy, he thought, I'm gonna nail this bastard.

Auguste Chamoun ran a hand over the top of his shiny, bald scalp. He was as close to utter imperturbability as it was possible for a human being to be, but this one trivial gesture was a sign of distress. Few people knew that, but the man who sat across from him did. Bob Thibodeaux had a negotiator's skill at reading body language. He knew all the attitudes and gestures of his employer's close associates, and he knew that Chamoun's palm across the scalp meant bad news.

The two sat in Chamoun's office high up in Carlson Tower. It was a spacious chamber, one side of which was an immense, bowed, floor-to-ceiling window with a stunning, panoramic view of Manhattan and the New York harbor. It was, arguably, the most spectacular office in New York. Chamoun had insisted upon quarters even more impressive than Carlson's own. This was not from personal vanity. "When you want people to give you money," he had explained, "you don't go hat in hand like a beggar. You get them to come to you and you overwhelm them with your substance and dependability. You make them *want* to give you money, so that they can share in your glory."

Now his confidence had been shaken, and Thibodeaux wanted to know why. "Let's have it."

"We seem to be under attack."

"Attack? Well, there has been a good deal of shooting lately, but that's not your field."

"Worse. It's easy to shoot back at gunmen. This time, somebody is trying to subvert our financing. In the last six days, three major investors have backed out of the project, even at the risk of legal action being taken against them. Thank goodness, at least some old-money people, like Talbot and Moyer, are still sticking with us."

Thibodeaux leaned forward. "How big?" Chamoun pushed a stack of readouts toward him and he looked at the figures on the bottom lines. His eyebrows went up. "This is substantial, but not catastrophic. People often get cold feet going into a high-risk project. The boss's pep talk wears off and they start thinking about all the money they have riding on a dream. This may be nothing."

Chamoun shook his head. "Bob, you are a political specialist, not a financial specialist. Mr. Carlson is a dreamer and a man of action." Of Carlson's top aides, only Chamoun insisted upon referring to him formally. "Neither of you understand this sort of thing. This is not the end of it. Three well-established firms of venture capitalists—one Spanish, one Saudi, one Greek, each with about the same amount invested— backed out within a few days. Someone is approaching them with . . . who knows? Threats maybe, or temptations of higher profit if they will abandon this venture. I am telling you there will be others. This is a coordinated effort by someone who knows what he is doing. Not all terrorists use guns and bombs."

"What steps are you taking?" Thibodeaux asked.

"I have our representatives in those three countries investigating, trying to find who is behind this. I have others alerted to move as soon as the next one backs out."

"You're telling me this for a reason."

"Exactly. I've sent a memo to Mr. Carlson. As usual, he ignored it. He thinks I am being an alarmist. He has no patience with people who panic too easily. I think he is leaving himself open to enemy action."

"So do I," Thibodeaux affirmed.

"My contacts are among bankers and financiers. But the enemy here may not be a business rival. This could be political action."

"And that's why you're conferring with me." Thibodeaux showed his wolverine teeth in a smile that utterly lacked humor.

"It is your field. You must make inquiries at once. We have to find the source of the threat and put an end to it."

Still smiling, Thibodeaux said, "It'll be a pleasure."

*   *   *

In her own office in the same building, Alison Baird was conferring with her staff. She was a bit annoyed because her personal secretary had called in sick for the third time that month. She knew she would have to do something about Adam very soon. She shook off the annoyance. She was at the center of her little domain and doing the sort of work she liked best. Her conference room featured huge television screens where the latest Lone Star ads could be viewed. Her suite, which took up most of two floors, also featured facilities for film and video editing, a small television studio, a number of artists' studios, and extensive research and recording facilities.

Blissfully unaware of any threats to Lone Star, Alison and her crew were brainstorming. She sat back in her thronelike chair at the head of the table, twirling a pencil in the long, nervous fingers of both hands, looking up at the ceiling as if for inspiration. They had just viewed the latest promotional videos for the Lone Star SolarSat project and she was not satisfied.

"They lack something," she said. "The camera work is wonderful, the editing is world-class, the narration likewise. But something is still missing. Think about it, people. What do we need here?"

There was silence for a few seconds, then a young man spoke up from the far end of the table, where the most junior team members sat.

"We need music," he said.

Alison looked at him. "They were fully scored. They had music."

"No, I meant we need music!"

Alison tried to remember the boy's name, then it came to her: Peter Narvik. A recent graduate of the USC film school and, for a blessed change, not interested in making big-budget movies with lots of special effects. His student project had been a short short about a heart transplant and it had garnered an Oscar nomination, thus gaining her attention.

"Elucidate," she ordered.

"It's something everybody's lacked," he said, showing some excitement. "Even as a kid, I always thought NASA needed theme music."

"Theme music?" she echoed.

"Yes. Everybody in the world knows the Olympic march, don't they? Why shouldn't the space program have one? We need rousing rah-rah music, so distinctive that anyone will recognize it within the first three or four notes. That's so we can preface even the shortest bulletins with a few bars. For longer programs, we can have a five- or six-minute version to play over the titles and closing credits, and a full symphony-length version to use as background music for feature-length productions. It's important that every theme be memorable and melodic, each one evoking a specific emotion."

There was silence for a full minute. All attention was on Alison, who sat with a faraway expression. Her fingers had stopped twiddling with the pencil. Finally, she spoke.

"I like it. More than that, it's brilliant! Who shall we get to compose it?"

"John Williams does that kind of work better than anybody else," said the woman who sat to Alison's left.

"Jerry Goldsmith," said another.

"We could have a contest!" said a rather geekish-looking young man from the video editing section. "Like when there's going to be a monument or a civic center or a museum project."

Alison considered it for a minute. "No, I'm afraid not. Contests are wonderful for building excitement, but for this, we want one of the top musical pros, and they don't enter contests like artists and architects do." She turned to her secretary. "Send out feelers. Find out who their agents are. Let them know it will be the most important commission of their lives."

"Whoever it is, he'll charge a bundle," Alison's accountant warned.

"So what? We're Lone Star, we do things in a big way."

The accountant winced.

"Besides," said the film-school boy, "we'll recoup it all if the publicity's handled right. We'll put out a CD of the music, sell models of the spacecraft and the satellites, run a line of Lone Star action figures—"

"And we'll sell commercial time on our major television projects," Alison said, catching the enthusiasm.

"Sell advertising on our advertising?" asked someone.

"We'd better if we're going to run hour-long, prime-time programs," she answered.

"That's where we'll premiere the music!" said the pride of USC. "For months ahead of time, we'll leak it that it'll be the biggest musical event since *Rite of Spring* opened in Paris in nineteen thirteen."

"Let's do it!" Alison said. Peter Narvik. She decided she liked this boy. She'd have to find him a chair farther up the table. She glanced at the one next to her, Adam's chair. That one might do very well.

11

THE CITY OF *Dom Henrique, O Navigador* had no true harbor, only jetties
for glorified barges that transshipped big cargoes from Belém, the port
city at the mouth of the Amazon River, which had a harbor deep enough
for oceangoing freighters. Transporting high-tech space hardware by
barge might sound a bit primitive, but NASA's gigantic Skylab, about
the same size as a Saturn V rocket, had been shipped to Johnson Space
Center on a barge.

The most conspicuous structure on the sandy beach was the mon-
strous launch tower for Energia. Energia was the Russian answer to
America's Saturn V, although even the brutish Energia could not quite
match the big American rocket for lift capacity. With Energia rockets
came Russian engineers and technicians to the tropical beach of O Navigador.

Russian and Portuguese were only two among the many languages
to be heard in the ever-expanding streets of O Navigador. Adding to the
gold-rush atmosphere was the colorful, polyglot population characteristic of boomtowns the world over. Almost as good as a sudden oil or
mineral strike was a new technology, building a community from the
ground up. A small community in which a sizable proportion of the
population held exceedingly high-paying jobs drew hustlers like sharks
to a bucket of blood emptied into warm waters. Beside the more or less
legitimate hotel keepers, restaurateurs, and retailers of all sorts, there
came the saloon keepers, gamblers, con men, whores and their pimps,
and labor strong-arm specialists. After these came the plain thieves, drug
dealers, and cutthroats.

O Navigador, and practically everything in it, was the brainchild of
Cash Carlson. He had talked the Brazilian government into contributing
land and other locally procurable capital goods, as well as a part of the
manpower for the construction of the O Navigador space facilities, in

exchange for a substantial share in his solar-power satellite enterprise. Carlson's corporation had an ambitious charter to cover further exploration of the solar system. He knew that the Brazilians were getting tired of being known as "the people of the next century." He persuaded *o Presidente dos Estados Unidos do Brasil* that this was going to be "the Brazilian Century."

Carlson had paid hard cash for Russian Energia and Proton rockets at a bargain-basement price, when the Russians were desperate for hard currency. He pointed out to the Russians a simple truth—that once the new, extremely economical SSTO fleets of reusable launch vehicles got into operation in a few years, the financial value of their throwaway rockets like Energia and Proton would depreciate dramatically overnight. They would be better off—in fact, much better off—selling them to Cash at discount prices before that happened.

To minimize his cash outlay, he also offered the Russians a share in his SolarSat project. In addition to these monetary temptations, Carlson laid out a few hard facts: Even Americans, who had all but lost interest in space exploration after the spectacular accomplishments of the mid-twentieth century, were getting back into it in a big way. Both the Japanese and the Europeans were gearing up for a massive space effort. Reasonably enough, the Japanese looked at things from an Asian viewpoint, while the Europeans, rallying around Germany's powerhouse economy, thought in terms of western and central Europe, still regarding everything east of the Urals as alien territory. Everyone was developing lifters equal to or exceeding Energia in capability.

Cash had pointed out further that Russia's best bet to get in on the ground floor and not be left behind was to team up with the American wildcatter, getting some use out of their remaining Energias and Protons while new lifters were under devclopment. It would also keep their unemployed scientists and technicians together, working on the Lone Star project rather than scattering to work on the projects of any nation that offered them pay.

At the end of the negotiations, after the handshakes, signatures on contracts, and endless Russian toasts in high-proof vodka, Cash had turned to his team members and said: "I wonder what my father would think, seeing his boy Cash sitting down at a table with Russians and literally offering them the moon." He had shaken his head in wonder at the way the world had changed.

*   *   *

The corporate jet landed gently on the newly finished landing strip of Bartolomeu Dias airport. The buildings were still little more than white-washed sheds and semicylindrical huts of corrugated galvanized steel, their plating still new enough to flash in the sunlight. The jet halted before the terminal, the roar of the engines dropped to a whisper, then to silence, and the stair lowered to the tarmac with a hiss of hydraulics.

Cash was first to descend the steps, followed by Sachi. He was dressed in a business suit, since there was always a danger that Brazilian officials might ambush him and carry him off to a meeting or a business lunch. Latin American custom did not tolerate informality in a man of business or official importance. The sight of a doctor or an architect changing his own flat tire could scandalize a town for weeks.

Sachi had taken a more practical attitude and dressed in a safari outfit of cotton khaki, topped with a broad hat to protect her delicate complexion. Like everything else she wore, it looked like an outfit from a Paris couturier's salon. In this case, the effect was bestowed by the wearer. She had picked it up at a Banana Republic store in a Houston mall.

Cash gestured broadly. "It may not look like much now, but just wait! In ten years, this place will make Cape Kennedy and the French Guinean launch site look like poor cousins. O Navigador will be the number-one spaceport in the world!"

Sachi looked around and tried to stretch her imagination. What the place looked like at the moment was a dump. Building refuse lay every-where, and much of the landscape consisted of mud. Work gangs were all around, but they seemed to consist of men in some sort of charge who harangued and shouted at an approximately equal number of other men, who stood about with expressions of confusion, boredom, or sullen indifference.

"Well," Cash admitted, "it's getting done in a third-world sort of way, but it is getting done."

She smiled. It was almost impossible to resist Cash's enthusiasm. "It's certainly colorful." She felt the way she had upon first seeing his Jeep. It might be rough, but Cash was in his element.

Parker came from the terminal building. He and his team had flown ahead to clear the way.

"Well, Boss, nobody's trying to kill you today, but they just might do it by accident. There's been six shootings in the barrio since sundown last night."

"Barrio?" Cash said. "We've got a barrio already?"

"Several," Parker affirmed. "All of the rougher part of town, which is most of it, is now called the barrio. It's actually *bairro* in Portuguese, but we call it barrio here. It was the Mexican workers started that. And there are several sub-barrios, consisting of the little enclaves of the various Central and South American groups. They like to live together in their own neighborhoods. That's not even getting into the Chinese, Vietnamese, Korean, and Russian communities, all of which are pretty quiet and safe."

"It sounds like the Wild West," Sachi said.

Cash shrugged. "It's the frontier, for sure. Until things settle down here and the workmen bring in their families and law enforcement takes hold, it's going to be pretty unruly. That's old history to us, but Brazil has had lawless gold and emerald camps for the last century or more."

A massive van rolled up then and they got in. "Let's take the long way to the hotel," Cash ordered. "I want to see how this town's developing."

"Boss—" Parker began.

"Let's see the town, Jack. You said yourself nobody's trying to kill me here."

Parker sighed. Another headache.

Carlson looked out over the sprawl of shanties that reached almost up to the spaceport gate. "Last time I was here, there was a half mile of open land between the port and the town. Where did all these people come from?"

"They are squatters, Mr. Carlson," the driver said. "All the good land has been bought up by developers and is too expensive to live on, so they stay out here and pay nothing."

"Who owns this stretch of land?" Carlson asked.

"You do," the driver answered.

"Oh, hell," Carlson grumbled. "I remember now. I didn't want anything built this close to the port, so I optioned this land. Now if I run these people off, I'll look like a *Norteamericano* capitalist ogre."

"Life's tough," Parker commented.

Most of the shanties seemed to be made out of cast-off building materials from the port site: scrap lumber, corrugated iron, plywood, plastic sheeting and so forth, anything to keep the tropic rains out. The people were obviously poor, but none of them seemed to be hungry or raggedly dressed. Most of them likely had work at the space facility or in the town. Carlson made a mental note to look into the land-speculation situation. These people probably squatted here simply because rapacious speculators had driven land values sky high for the sake of a quick profit. A little arm-twisting in the right quarters should produce some cheap land and low-cost housing.

Sachi was grateful for the air-conditioning in the van. Cash was used to the climate of Houston, called "Calcutta West" by the locals with a self-flagellating sense of humor. She preferred more temperate climes. She observed the shantytown with detachment. It did not shock her. She had traveled extensively in India and Africa, and she knew what real poverty looked like.

The town of O Navigador itself was far more interesting. The streets had been laid out as broad, straight thoroughfares, but that did not prevent them from being jammed with traffic. Trucks, vans, cars, motorcycles, motor scooters, bicycles, even riders on horseback, crowded the pavement, sometimes venturing onto the sidewalks. Horns hooted and squawked, people shouted and gesticulated. Traffic lights hung at all the intersections but they had not yet been turned on, and Sachi doubted that anyone would have paid attention to them anyway.

The first district they entered was Mexican, and they could hear loud brass-band music coming through the open doors of the numerous cantinas. Off-duty workmen wandered the streets with the hectic, holiday air of men with money in their pockets and no wives to tell them how to spend it.

The Chilean, Ecuadorean, and Colombian districts were similar, with slight alterations of dress and music. The Chinese district was more sedate and the cooking smells were different. The area catering to the American technicians and contractors looked more expensive and made great use of neon, although it appeared rather raw and drab in the daytime.

"It's coming along," Carlson commended. "A little rough around the edges at the moment, but before long, it'll be a resort town. Orlando South. Let's approach the Disney people. We'll pitch it as the latest Disneyland site. They haven't had a go at South America yet. After all, a space launch is the biggest fireworks display in history. They can build a whole theme park around the spectacle. We'll be running a regular schedule, none of that NASA stuff, calling off a launch because somebody in Bangkok sneezed."

Sachi enjoyed it when he was like this, spinning off ideas, even some fairly silly ones, as his mind and his enthusiasm fed off each other. And he always meant what he said and was an incredibly persuasive salesman. She was willing to bet that construction would begin on a new Disney park within a year or two.

"Where are we staying?" she asked.

"The Hotel Carioca," Cash told her. "It's the closest thing to a modern hotel the town has at the moment. There's a Hilton and an Oberoi under construction, but they won't be open for months. At least the Carioca's air-conditioned. The older places you ventilate by opening the windows and turning on the ceiling fan."

"Local color has its attractions," she said, "but in this climate, I'll opt for the modern amenities." She knew the tropics. The novelty of watching lizards chase bugs across the window screens had palled long ago. The prospect of dysentery had no appeal, nor did cold showers, or toilet facilities down the hall on the floor below, if not in the backyard. All in all, she thought, there was much to be said for the twenty-first century.

The hotel proved to be adequate, its VIP suites about equivalent to the rooms of an average American hotel. Carlson had reserved the top floor, with himself and Sachi in adjoining suites and Parker's team sited strategically here and there. She surveyed the spartan bedroom and reflected that she was not here for a luxury vacation. She was here to take a trip into space.

The thought filled her with excitement mixed with dread, and she sat down on the bed to think things over. Since girlhood, she had dreamed of going into space, but she had never seriously believed that she would ever have the chance. Now it was here and she was wondering if she had been too quick to accept the offer. It was one thing to fantasize about hurtling into space on a rocket. Actually sitting on top of a gigantic bomb waiting to be hurled into a hostile void was another.

The Energia booster was an immense, looming presence. It was hard to believe that anything so large could move at all, much less fly. Yet there it was, wreathed in down-curling clouds of liquid nitrogen. The searchlights trained on the booster somehow made it seem even more imposing, bulking against the outer blackness.

The Lone Star launch facility was built near the beach, so that during quiet periods, it was possible to hear the surf breaking on the sand. To those with long memories, it resembled the early days at Cape Canaveral—basic, but functional. At this stage, Carlson could not afford frills.

"You know," he said, looking up at the booster, "I never had much regard for Russian bureaucrats, but sometimes they showed a lot more brains than ours did."

"How is that?" Sachi asked. They had driven out to the launch site after dinner at the hotel. They had only two days in which to prepare for the launch, and he wanted a look at the facility as soon as possible.

"They didn't throw away their most expensive space assets. Those fools in Washington axed the Apollo program while we still had three fully functional Saturn-Five launch vehicles. They were the greatest rockets—and the most expensive—ever built by human beings. You can still see them, taken apart, at the Kennedy Space Flight Center, and the Johnson Space Center, and the Marshall Space Flight Center. They're just museum displays now. I've seen tough old astronauts with tears in their eyes, looking at those exhibits. Utter waste."

"No need to preach to the converted, Mr. Carlson," she said.

He grinned ruefully. "Sorry. It's about the only subject that still gets me indignant. Come on, let's go get measured for our suits."

"It all seems so unreal," she said as they drove to the hangarlike building where the suits and much other gear were kept. "I'm not an astronaut. I'm just a journalist."

"That sort of attitude is one thing we have to get rid of," Cash told her. "All that stuff about astronauts having to be supermen is nonsense. It was okay in the early test-pilot days, 'the right stuff' and all that. But we're pushing space as an ordinary working environment. Any healthy person ought to be able to travel in space with no more than a routine medical checkup. Ah, here we are."

They got out of the van and went into the building, which turned out to be the one tolerably complete structure at the launch site. A technician guided them to a room where space suits stood in ranks like a miniature army of aliens, held up by armatures. These suits, Sachi was informed, were "industry rated," meaning that like the facility itself, they were both inexpensive and highly functional. They came in basic sizes and did not need to be custom tailored for individual astronauts.

It was not as if anyone was going to be carrying out complicated scientific experiments on the moon, after all.

"Don't you have a special suit of your own?" Sachi asked Carlson.

"I'm an engineer, not a scientist or a pilot. I just get one off the rack like everyone else."

She looked around the room while technicians went over her with a tape measure. "Where is Mr. Parker's suit? I thought surely he would have one, armored and covered with missiles and ray guns."

"Don't give him ideas," Carlson said, laughing. "He'd like exactly that. He's pouting right now because he's not going along on this trip. I guess he thinks I need protecting from Martians or something. I've promised him that he can go up and establish a security system as soon as our facilities and personnel are large enough to require it."

"And you said you couldn't take deadweight up there? Why would a space station need security?"

"Eventually," Cash said, "we'll have a large number of stations, with hundreds, maybe thousands, of people working on them. There'll be traffic back and forth from one facility to another, not just from the ground. Jack thinks the situation will be ripe for espionage, sabotage, and terrorism. He may well be right. He usually is about his business. Remember, we're going to be dealing with a very precious commodity—energy. There's certainly plenty of dirty dealing in the oil trade, so we can expect the same in solar energy, once there's enough money in it."

"Strange," she said as she tried on several pairs of gloves. "When I was a child, I always saw space exploration as adventurous, but straightforward. I thought that the astronauts would be a brotherly band of scientists, facing dangers that came with an unknown and hostile environment. I didn't think that it would turn into an extension of Earthly problems."

"It goes with the species," Cash said. "We may be flying around in space these days, but we're still territorial apes competing for limited resources. I used to be pretty idealistic myself, but I've come to doubt that we'll ever be free of our essential nature. If I were of a puritanical frame of mind, I'd say that we're cursed with Original Sin, but I think we've just been doing it for so long that it's imprinted in our genes."

"Hindus would say it's our bad karma coming back to haunt us," she noted. She was having trouble with the gloves and decided she had better shorten her nails before the final fitting. "I had a little Shinto upbringing as a child, but a little upbringing is all you are likely to get in Shinto. It is an uncomplicated religion as religions go—'Keep your soul and body clean' just about covers it all. And, of course, 'Revere nature and live in harmony with it.' Shintoism doesn't go in much for sinfulness or inherited guilt."

"Whatever the reason," Cash said, "we're stuck with ourselves for the foreseeable future."

Carlson's measurements were on file, so he didn't have to undergo any measuring once the technicians were satisfied that his weight was the same as the last time he had gone up.

"We'd better head back to the hotel and get some sleep," he said when Sachi was fitted. "We start orientation early tomorrow. The day after, up we go."

Again her heart lurched at the thought. This couldn't be real!

But it was.

By mid-morning, the press and other media people were swarming all over the launch site. As Cash, Sachi, and an engineer who was making the flight with them came out of the suiting facility, the reporters descended like locusts. The pilot and a second engineer who served as emergency pilot had been aboard for hours, going through endless systems checks. Cash was the main target of the paparazzi, and he played them like an expert.

Sachi was a journalist, but she was accustomed to one-on-one interviews, not this sort of pandemonium. She noticed that the cameramen seemed to prefer her as a subject, no matter what the ones with microphones might be doing. For once, she wasn't sure why. The industry-rated space suit had proven to be the one garment she could not glamorize. It fit like a potato sack and would have looked no different on a teenaged boy. Her hair was confined beneath a cap that tied under her chin like an old-fashioned bathing cap, and she had forgone any cosmetics. Even so, the cameras stayed on her. From hairline to chin, she was the most beautiful human being ever to venture into space.

"Mr. Carlson, will you be carrying out any important experiments on this voyage?" asked a breathless young woman.

"No, this'll be just a routine inspection trip," he answered, exaggerating his Texas drawl. "I'm a hands-on engineer, I like to see close up how things are going. But mainly I'll be keeping out of the way. We all know how specialists hate it when the boss shows up at the job site, don't we?"

"You make it sound like it's just a job!" said another.

"That's all it is. Space is a working environment now, like the land or the sea. Pretty soon we'll be hiring lots of skilled people to work up there. They'll have to be willing to put up with some hardships or inconveniences, but it'll be a lot more agreeable than working in Antarctica."

"But what about the danger?" asked a man from one of the all-news networks.

"Hell, space isn't dangerous," Cash said. "New York is dangerous. The Los Angeles freeway system is real dangerous. In space, you just have to be careful and not too inclined to claustrophobia. Once we've got our really big facilities operational, even that won't be a problem. Look, over the last eighty-ninety years, probably a hundred thousand people've served in submarines, from the little tin fish they had in World War One to the huge nuclear boats they have now. Does anyone consider that very remarkable anymore? I can guarantee that pretty soon working in space will be a lot more pleasant than living on a sub."

By this time, they had reached the bus that would carry them to the pad. Before she could board, a reporter who appeared to be barely out of his teens jumped in front of her.

"Miss Sakamoto—"

"Sasano," she corrected.

"Miss Sasano, as a Japanese, does working in an American space project cause you to feel any sense of conflict?"

She was taken aback by the question, which seemed not merely rude, but irrelevant. "Why do you consider me Japanese? I was born in Japan, but I've spent most of my life in Europe or America."

Carlson stepped in smoothly. "People, we're not engaged here in an American project. Lone Star is primarily American, but I have investors in Japan, Russia, Europe, the Arab nations, and of course, Brazil. Getting working solar-power satellites into orbit is a worldwide project, and the whole world will benefit from it. All of us in the race feel that an open competition is the best way to accomplish this, but it has nothing to do with competition between nations. And now, if you'll excuse us, we have a rocket to catch." Smiling broadly, he mounted the bus with the others.

"Thank you," she said as she sank into one of the bus seats. They were oversized to accommodate the extra gear some of the astronauts had to carry. "I can see that in this business, you have to cultivate patience with the press."

"It can be difficult sometimes," Cash told her. "Alison's spent years drilling me in how to behave with them. Remember, they're not always ignorant. They're just addressing an audience they assume to be ignorant. Often with a good deal of justification, I might add."

"To tell you the truth, it's good to have something petty to occupy my mind. I'm terrified."

"If you were terrified, you wouldn't have come out of the hotel this morning. You just have butterflies in the stomach."

She laughed. "Butterflies in the stomach! What an apt phrase. Is that an American colloquialism?"

"I guess it must be."

"Actually, it feels more like circling vultures."

"You'll get over it," he promised.

She wondered if she would ever master his composure at the prospect of a launch. The engineer, an obvious veteran, actually looked bored. He was thumbing through a stack of papers and sipping at a plastic cup of coffee. Probably needs it to stay awake, she thought enviously.

The bus halted at the base of the launch platform and from that moment, they were in the capable hands of technicians who did everything but hold them upright. With one at each elbow, Sachi was guided to the tower, warned every time there was a turn or a step to negotiate, provided with every assistance possible. She half expected to see a busy little man with a broom sweeping the path in front of her. She understood that this was primarily to allay the last-minute jitters most travelers experienced, and for once, she was grateful for excessive solicitude.

Almost before she knew it, she was reclining on a couch, strapped in like a mummy. Cash was next to her, and the two engineers were nearly supine in couches that, at the moment, were above them. The pilot reclined in lonely splendor at the apex of the roughly conical compartment. To her surprise, Cash began to speak to the empty air in front of him. Then she realized that the tiny television camera mounted on the rear of the couch in front of him was broadcasting outside. He was talking to the reporters again.

"The SolarSat project is still in its infancy," he said to the unseen audience, "and Lone Star is running an even tighter operation than the others. No frills permitted at this stage. As a matter of fact, the passengers are strictly secondary on this flight. What this rocket carries is primarily cargo. We're ferrying construction materials for building our first SolarSat in low Earth orbit. We're also taking supplies and equipment for the crew already living up there." He stopped speaking, and Sachi could tell that he was listening to a voice coming through the minute speaker clipped to his ear.

"Yes," Cash went on. "The first operational space station, the flagship of our fleet if you want to call it that, will be Lone Star. At the moment, it's a single space-shuttle external fuel tank with a habitat rigged up inside. The living quarters have been named the Igloo, a fairly apt bit of terminology. One of our technicians suggested it, as describing a spare and basic habitat in a hostile environment. They've been working hard up there, making the place habitable and operational." He was silent again, listening.

"No, there's a lot going on besides getting the solar-power operation on line. To tell you the truth, at this stage, I can't afford it. While we're waiting to have our shuttle tanks fully pressurized, there are plenty of lab projects and experiments that specifically need an airless, sterile, gravity-free environment, which is exactly what we have outside the Igloo. We've sublet lab space to several pharmaceutical and chemical and bioengineering firms. We have negotiations proceeding with NASA to rent space in Lone Star as a staging area for the NASA orbital operations." He listened again.

"Thank you, thank you very much. I'm afraid I have to sign off now, I just got the signal that the countdown's starting."

Countdown! The word carried the sound of utter finality, although on a conscious level Sachi knew that it meant nothing of the sort. Everything had been proceeding "nominally"—NASA jargon for "perfectly." They could stop almost any time up to the instant of main ignition. Still, it seemed that an irrevocable step had been taken.

". . . five, four, three, two, one—ignition!"

She felt the rumbling vibration, but there was no motion. She was sure something had gone wrong. Then she remembered that the initial acceleration is low for a massive rocket such as Energia. Then the huge thing began to lift, at first with the gentle acceleration of an elevator. It was an oddly familiar sensation, but instead of stopping after a few seconds, the pressure continued. She felt as if a heavy weight had been pressing against her. It would have been difficult to breathe, had she been breathing at all. For a moment, things got very bright, then very dark.

"Held your breath, didn't you?"

She looked over at Carlson and realized that the pressure was gone and there was no sensation of weight at all. Then she understood that she had fainted. She was embarrassed and felt that she had missed the best part of the launch. At least all her trepidation was gone.

"How long was I unconscious?"

"Just a few seconds. You didn't actually pass out from acceleration. You held your breath at the end of the countdown and then didn't breathe again until you fainted. Just about everybody does that on their first launch."

But by now, she was looking out the small window next to her couch. The sky had a blackness she had never known before in her life, the stars making solid, intense points of brilliance, utterly undiffused by atmosphere. At the rear corner of the window she could just make out a blue fragment of the planet below. She was in space!

"Can I loosen these straps? I can't really feel the effects of zero-gee. I've been waiting for this all my life!"

"Not just yet," Cash said. "We've got to go through all kinds of systems checks before anyone can loosen up. There's not much room for floating around in here anyway. There'll be lots more when we get to the Igloo."

"Then it seems I must be patient." She turned and looked out the window again.

As THEY APPROACHED and matched orbit with Lone Star, Sachi was impressed by its size. It looked huge, much larger than the 747 to which it had been likened. A few hundred meters away drifted several more shuttle tanks, awaiting their turn to be assembled into the growing space station.

Inside, the residential quarters were disappointingly spartan and cramped. She could see that it would be some time before the accommodations in Lone Star approached those of the palatial starships named *Enterprise*. But then, those ships, unburdened by the scientific rigor of the present world, possessed mysterious internal gravity fields and were unaffected by inconvenient things like the stresses of acceleration and deceleration, not to mention the speed of light.

Once inside, with the lock shut behind them, they climbed out of their space suits. The first thing Sachi noticed upon twisting off her helmet was an intense mixture of chemical and organic odors, a sort of refinery-cum-locker-room smell. This was something her lifelong reading about living in space had failed to mention.

"You get used to it," said a technician, noticing her wrinkled nose. The speaker was a young woman of chunky build with short, curly, blond hair. "I'm Marian Harlowe, biotechnician. I've been assigned to help get you oriented."

"Sachi Sasano. I hope I won't be too much trouble."

"Are you kidding? Do you know what it's like living in a tin can for months at a time, seeing the same old faces? I'm dying to talk to someone new." She seemed friendly and good-humored, although with that underlying core of dead seriousness that always seemed characteristic of astronauts, especially when working.

And, like soldiers on duty, these people were always on work status. Leisure time was scarce, and even when sleeping, they were at all times ready for immediate action. Sachi had read that nervous stress was an abiding problem among astronauts. It was due to the ever-present knowledge of the fragility of their habitat and the unrelenting hostility of their environment.

"I leave you in Marian's capable hands," Carlson said. "She'll give you the basic drill. I'm going to see what's been done to my space station since the last time I was up here." He went off with a small group of technicians into the depths of the Igloo.

Marian helped Sachi out of her space suit and showed her how to stow it in one of the racks. "They're stowed by size and gender," the woman explained. "In an emergency, you don't want to have to fumble around finding your own suit. Just grab one your size and get into it, quick."

Then Marian led her to a partitioned area lined with bunks. "Pull yourself along with your arms at first," she warned. "Until you're used to zero-gee, you'll tend to push off too powerfully, using your legs. Then you bash your head against something and maybe damage delicate instruments. In fact, you should always move slow. You get things done faster by moving slow, out here. Move fast and you waste time overcoming your momentum."

"There is so much to learn!"

Marian shrugged, an odd gesture since from Sachi's viewpoint, she was upside down. "There's not much technique to be taught. It's mostly a matter of feel." She looked Sachi over. "You've had dance training?"

"Yes, and gymnastics and martial arts."

"Good. The more movement training you've had, the quicker you'll adapt out here. People who've never had to train their bodies to do difficult things can have a hard time of it. I was a distance swimmer and scuba diver back home, so I took to zero-gee with no problems. You shouldn't have any."

Sachi eyed the racked bunks. They looked more suited to cargo storage than to sleeping. "Do you ever get used to the nausea?" In the excitement, she had almost forgotten about it, but now she was getting decidedly uncomfortable.

"Did you take your pills before launch?"

"Yes."

"Then your stomach should settle down before long. You'll be okay for the duration, but don't forget to take your pills on schedule."

"Is it possible to sleep on these things?" Sachi asked, running a hand over the unyielding surface of a bunk.

"You don't so much sleep on them as lash yourself to them. They're mainly to keep you from floating around and to give you instant orientation. When you wake up, you know exactly where you are. That can be important in an emergency."

It seemed ominous to Sachi that these people gave so much thought to emergencies. But then, it might be far worse if they didn't. The compartment they were in was roughly cubical, about four meters on a side, with bunks for six people. A folding partition separated it from other, similar compartments.

"This is the women's quarters," Marian told her. "There are others. We change them around as personnel density and makeup shift. We can put aside quarters for married couples, too. Right now, we don't have any of those."

"And couples who aren't married?"

"Whatever suits them. Privacy is to be found even here. But take it from me, most of the time, you're just too tired to be interested. I mean, most people want to, you know . . . experiment. It's kind of intriguing, don't you think? What it's like in zero-gee?"

"And what is it like?" Sachi asked.

"You get over the novelty real quick. And this isn't a really romantic environment, as you've probably gathered by now. You probably won't even be tempted on your first stint up here. You never feel quite well even after your stomach's settled; just wait till you try tackling the zero-gee toilet."

The glamour was already wearing off Sachi's dreams of space exploration. It was, as Cash had said, just another working environment, and a very tough one at that.

The Igloo, it turned out, was a walled-off section of a space-shuttle external fuel tank, uncolorfully named "Tank One." The remainder of the tank was now fully pressurized and several areas had been set up as labs for various projects, some of them actually in progress.

As a closed-systems specialist, Sachi's first job was to go over Igloo's life-support system. The external tank was a long way from having a closed ecological system capable of supporting life for extended periods with a minimal replenishment of essentials. She had to make sure that Igloo's system, at least, was operating at maximum efficiency.

After that, she had to go over the entire external tank and its sub-structures to see if the closed ecosystems designed by Max and a team of Carlson's bioengineers would actually work. If it turned out that modifications would be necessary, she wanted to figure out at the very least the basic changes to the design while she was still in Lone Star.

Then she would have to help begin construction of the free-fall biological laboratory that Cash wanted to lease out. Finally, and not least of all, she would have to keep track of everything so that she would be able to write exciting articles about Lone Star when she returned to Earth.

She found that Marian's predictions were accurate: Her stomach quieted down, but she never felt quite well. She suffered chronic headaches, sore eyes, and an unending stuffiness of the sinuses, as if she'd been perpetually about to come down with a bad cold. These were standard zero-gee symptoms and she was assured that they would fade in time. The only problem was, she wasn't going to be in orbit long enough for that.

Despite these annoyances, she enjoyed the work. She was too busy to brood over her aches and pains.

Meantime, Carlson was at work on his own projects. Despite his coy protestations to the media, this was far from being a routine inspection trip. He intended to try out the ion drive about which he had been hinting so mysteriously. He didn't like the idea of announcing technical experiments in advance. Something could always go wrong, especially in the early testing stages, and that could mean unwarranted adverse publicity.

It was an electric-impulse rocket, but Cash preferred "ion drive" because it sounded more glamorous. It would—if it worked—move the satellites from low Earth orbit, where they were assembled, to the far higher geostationary orbits. Compared to the conventional fire-belching, chemical-burning rockets, the ion engines were very slow, requiring days or weeks to cross distances the old-style rockets could cover in hours, but they were far more economical. Chemical burners ejected a large quantity of reaction mass at relatively low velocity, whereas the ion-drive engines would expel ions—actually, atomic nuclei—at extremely high velocity. They were ideal for moving an immense structure like a solar-power satellite through space. For this purpose, a slow, smooth, gentle means of transportation was perfect.

Cash's personal version of "Waste not, want not" was "Risk is better than waste." In practice, this meant that he disliked expensive experiments that yielded only confirmation that a process would work. In this case, he planned to test his ion drive by using it to propel three communications satellites from a low Earth orbit to a geostationary one. They were to be placed in orbit 120 degrees apart from one another—with respect to Earth—so as to provide a continuous communications network for Cash's space station and orbiting satellites. These three satellites would link them all to his Houston headquarters. It would also enable the coordination of Lone Star's worldwide empire without depending on someone else's communications satellites.

Maximum self-sufficiency was always one of Cash's primary goals. He would achieve a good-sized chunk of it with this experiment—providing that it worked, of course. It was risky, but that was okay with him. He liked risk.

As with most of his projects, he planned for it to pay for itself far beyond his own uses for it. With his electrical-impulse engines, Cash planned to launch a number of inexpensively produced communications satellites from the cheaply achieved LEO to the far more complex and costly geostationary orbit at a fraction of the old cost. He would then publicize his ComSat program aggressively, relying on Sachi and Alison for a big media boost. He knew that there had to be a huge market for his low-cost, no-frills communications satellites, especially among third-world countries that hadn't a prayer of affording one at the moment, but that desperately needed modern communications links with the rest of the world.

The three satellites, each equipped with its ion drive, had been towed to a distance of about ten kilometers from the Lone Star Space Station. The boosting of a solar-power satellite from a LEO would always take place at a safe distance from the command center in Lone Star, and this ComSat launch was to be a dress rehearsal for the big event. It would also minimize any launch hazards to the rather fragile external-tank space stations, as he would have ample time to take corrective measures with the slowly accelerating satellites in case of an ion-drive misfire.

A young engineer—but then, they were all young—studied the panel of colored lights in front of him. "Why don't we just go now? Start the countdown from T minus four? Everything checked out perfectly before we towed the sats out to the launch sites."

"Uh-uh," Cash grunted, studying the board. "We keep to schedule. For one thing, orbital elements have been precalculated. Start countdown now at T minus two hours." There was no rush, and he recognized the difference between acceptable risk and stupid corner-cutting. Right now, time was their cheapest commodity and he saw nothing to gain by speeding things up.

For an hour and fifty-six minutes, they went through routine systems checks, the tension building by the second. Then, at T minus four minutes, the countdown was halted.

"Oh, crap!" said the engineer who had wanted to start early.

"Checked everything, did you?" said Cash, looking at a warning light that told him a computer chip controlling one of the ion drives might be faulty.

"Double-checked!" the engineer insisted. "Everything was working perfectly before we carted them off. It's probably just a glitch in the telemetry. It's happened before."

Sachi had abandoned her own work for a few minutes to be present for the big moment. "What now?" she asked, disappointed.

"Somebody's got to go make a house call," said the engineer. "Chuck, you want to suit up and go with me?"

"Who's gonna watch the Christmas tree?" Chuck asked, waving at the control panel. The term had been borrowed from the old submarines, which had had a panel with red and green lights. When all the lights were green, the sub could dive. If any showed red, something was open and could let the sea in. The panel aboard Lone Star was a great deal more complicated, but the multitude of colored lights made the old name apt.

"Just stay where you are, Kim," Carlson said, it seemed to Sachi a little too hastily. "I'll suit up and go with Chuck."

"You're the boss," Kim said.

Although he would never admit it, Carlson was happy with the glitch because it gave him an excuse to use the space scooter. He had been itching to try it out for a simple reason: It looked like something Buck Rogers would use. Like most adventurers, Cash had never truly grown up. His one regret was that according to a rule he had written himself, a scooter had to be operated by two riders at all times, in case of an accident.

"Shouldn't one of the engineers—" Sachi began.

"I'm an engineer," he snapped. Then, to Chuck, "Let's go suit up."

"Forget it, Sachi," Marian told her when the two were gone.

"There's something about EVA that makes them revert to about ten years old. You might as well try to take away his favorite toy. Believe me, I raised five brothers."

The space scooter was essentially a crude spaceship with no provision for remote control. It had to be piloted by a live human being in full possession of his faculties. Like most space-oriented hardware, it lacked the sleekness that the illustrators of old had given their vehicles. Vacuum made streamlining irrelevant. It was a collection of struts, engines, and nozzles, with provision for the attachment of cargo pods. There were seats for two riders, but these were more to provide orientation than out of any real need for seating.

Still, Cash thought as he strapped himself to the contraption, it was a Buck Rogers gadget and he'd overseen its design and development. While he would have preferred to pilot it himself, Chuck was the senior astronaut and Cash had never been checked out on the scooter. His previous visits to Lone Star had been too crammed with work to allow for what, for him, would have been mere self-indulgence. Sometimes, he thought as he finished strapping in, being the boss had serious disadvantages.

As Chuck cautiously took the scooter away from the space station, Cash savored the sensation of traveling independently in space. It made him realize that this was what he was doing it all for. All of his scrambling and fast-talking, all of the arm-twisting and wheeler-dealing was for a single purpose—so that he could get out into space and have fun. It was customary for tycoons to protest that the money and power were really nothing, but in Cash's case, it was true. In practice, he was broke most of the time. When he got his hands on money, it was to invest it in his space projects. Now that he was out here, it just beat the hell out of trailing cows and drilling oil.

The problem was, the boss was sort of redundant on this type of operation. The astronauts probably considered him deadweight, and the investors would have a collective heart attack if they knew he was risking his precious money-generating hide on an EVA best left to the pros.

Hell with 'em, he thought.

The trip out to the satellite was routine. The scooter gave little sense of speed beyond a gentle sensation of acceleration. From time to time, Cash turned to see Lone Star dwindling in the distance. Other than that, it was almost like not moving at all. The satellite showed up as a brilliant dot that swiftly grew into a spiky, semicylindrical object hanging above the blue arc of Earth's horizon.

Chuck fired the braking rockets expertly and they came smoothly to a halt within arm's reach of the ailing device. The computer-control device was in an easily accessible unit and Chuck removed the insertable section containing the malfunctioning chip and replaced it with one clipped to his belt.

"Check?" Chuck asked over the suit-to-ship intercom.

"All green," Kim reported.

It was so easy it was almost disappointing. They restrapped themselves to the scooter and Chuck got it turned around with deft touches to the attitude rocket controls. Then they set off for the space station. They had gone no more than a half-kilometer when Chuck jerked violently.

"What's wrong?" Cash cried.

"I've been shot!" Chuck's gloved right hand gripped his left biceps.

"For Chrissake, Chuck! Nobody gets shot in space!" Cash insisted.

"Yeah? Look at this!" Chuck twisted around and opened his hand. Sure enough, there were two tears in the arm of his space suit, just as if a bullet had entered and exited. Thick fluid seeped and bubbled from the rents. Cash didn't think it was blood. It was probably the self-sealing goo that was sandwiched between the two surface layers of the suit. No way to tell how much damage had been done inside until they got back and took the suit off.

It was orbiting debris: a piece of rock, a pellet of metal from a spacecraft, it didn't matter what. The quiet and vast distances of orbital space gave a deceptive sense of tranquillity. In reality, everything out here was hurtling along at tens of thousands of miles per hour, relative velocity. At those speeds, even a paint chip was a deadly missile.

Their space suits were designed for such emergencies. The sealing agent was one such safety feature. It would rush into any vacuum created by a break and coagulate there, effectively sealing the suit for an hour or so. Assuming, of course, that the hole wasn't too big. If the hole was too large to be sealed, the suit's controls would sense the pressure drop and cause the helmet's lining to contract around the astronaut's face, adhering tightly to the skin and allowing him to breathe, at least. Simultaneously, throughout the space suit, similar devices would be activated, compartmentalizing the suit so as to minimize the exposure of the body to vacuum. Any such prolonged exposure could cause irreversible damage, but this precaution gave the astronaut a chance.

This didn't look all that bad, but for all Cash knew, Chuck could be bleeding heavily inside the suit. They had to get back to Lone Star, fast.

"Uh, Cash, can you take over the controls? I'm getting a little lightheaded." Coming from the imperturbable astronaut, that sounded ominous.

"Sure. Can you hang on for a few more minutes?"

"Guess I'll have to."

Cash had spoken with more confidence than he felt. *Well, what the hell*, he thought. *How hard can it be?*

The major problem to be overcome was first the dislocation caused by the slight momentum transfer from the space debris striking Chuck, and second, his spasmodic reaction to it. They had caused the attitude of the scooter to shift slightly. Even a very minor change several kilometers from the station could make a significant difference at the end of the journey and cause them to miss the docking bay. Steering a tiny spaceship wasn't like parking a car.

"What the hell's going on out there?" asked someone at the station.

"I'm a-bringin' in the stagecoach," Cash reported, "but the driver's been shot." This was greeted by a deafening silence.

"Chuck," said the voice, "check the boss's breathing mixture. He's babbling."

Cash knew better than to try to correct the attitude error all at once and risk making things worse. He made adjustments incrementally as they traveled. Chuck was no help, drifting in and out of consciousness, and disoriented when he could speak at all.

Cash was congratulating himself as he herded the scooter into the docking bay and its deceleration net. Striving for a featherlight "landing" in the net, he overcompensated for his forward movement and started drifting backward at the last moment. A delicate touch on the accelerator reversed the motion in time. With a slight jar, the scooter landed in the net.

Cash unstrapped himself, then Chuck, and maneuvered his companion into the air lock. As it pressurized, he told the others to stand by. There were long-practiced procedures for dealing with such an emergency, although this one was a first, to the best of his knowledge.

The instant the lock opened, Dr. Parsemian took charge. It was Lone

Star policy to have an M.D. on-station at all times, plus a minimum of three other personnel with extensive paramedic training. The doctor and the designated three efficiently stripped Chuck's space suit off. As his left shoulder and arm came free, big globs of blood drifted up from the sleeve. One of the paramedics sucked it out of the air with a vacuum device, quickly filling an attached plastic bag.

"He's lost at least a liter," the medic reported. "Must've nicked an artery."

Chuck was pale but conscious. "Do I get a Purple Heart?"

"You're out of luck," Cash said. "This is peacetime." Then, to Parsemian, "Shall I send him down in one of the emergency lifeboats?"

At this stage of the construction of his space station, Cash had two lifeboats—a modern version of reentry vehicles that could accommodate six passengers each—on hand and ready to go in case of emergencies. If the capacity of the lifeboats should turn out to be insufficient, all the aerospace firms and agencies had a cooperative rescue agreement, although calling on them would cost him a bundle.

Parsemian probed the wound. "It went clean through, so I won't have to cut it out. Doesn't look like it left any debris behind. It may take a little debriding, not much. The arterial nick's not too bad, nothing's been severed. No chance of infection—space debris is sterile almost by definition. I can purify that blood and pump it right back into him. How about it, Chuck? Want to stay up here with a few stitches in your arm?" Parsemian obviously had an ulterior motive: If Chuck stayed, the healing process of a unique laceration under zero-gee conditions could be charted.

"Long as I don't have to do any heavy lifting," Chuck said.

Sachi, drifting well out of the way near a wall of the chamber, looked puzzled.

"Astronaut humor," Cash explained.

They went to the dining area for some coffee while the medics did their work. Sachi wanted to hear all about the brief but harrowing adventure, recording Cash's words for her next article. One thing about his explanation puzzled her.

"Who is Buck Rogers?"

"A space adventurer from the old comic strips and Saturday matinee serials of the thirties and forties. Never as famous as Flash Gordon, but I always liked him. People used to disparage anything having to do with space as 'Buck Rogers stuff,' but I thought that was a compliment."

"I see. Of course I know about Flash Gordon. Alex Raymond is a highly regarded artist in both Japan and France."

"Really?" Cash said.

"Oh, yes. And the artist who used to draw the Tarzan strip just before the war."

Cash frowned, trying to remember. "Burne Hogarth?"

"Yes, that's the one. There have been several Tarzan retrospectives in Paris galleries. The French regard American popular culture more seriously than the Americans do."

"The French never cease to amaze me," Cash admitted.

With Chuck strapped reluctantly into a bunk for doctor-ordered rest, the satellite launch proceeded. Everything went off like a charm. The ion engines worked flawlessly, and the sats would achieve their geostationary orbits exactly on schedule. Not so satisfactory was the report on the malfunctioning chip.

"Mr. Carlson," Kim called, "would you come here, please?"

Cash went to the nest of computer consoles Kim called home. "What's up?"

"That chip you and Chuck brought back wasn't defective."

Something made Cash's scalp prickle. "So what was it?"

"It had been infected with a virus. I don't have the lab equipment here to tell more than that, but this much is certain." He tossed the chip to Cash, who snatched it from the air.

"I don't suppose it was some teenage kid pulling a prank?"

"Not with something this sophisticated. Whoever did it knows his stuff."

"I've got some people who know their stuff, too. I'm going to trace this chip back to the place where its silicon was mined."

Just as Cash and Sachi were getting ready to return to Earth, he told her about the virus.

"Well, we knew you had enemies," she said.

"And me with such a sweet disposition. I guess when billions of dollars are at stake, the rivalry gets a little stiff."

"Another job for Max?"

"He'll love it."

A burst of excited chatter reached them from somewhere within the cavernous interior of the station.

"Sounds like teenagers playing a video game," Carlson said, mystified.

Marion's head appeared in the doorway, upside down from Sachi's perspective, but Sachi no longer noticed such things. "Mr. Carlson! Come quick!"

"Oh, Christ! Not another emergency. Do we need to suit up?"

"No! No! C'mere, you gotta see this!" If there had been any gravity, she would have been hopping up and down with excitement.

"Teenagers, hell. She's reverted to a twelve-year-old," Cash muttered.

They followed Marian as she pulled her way through the station with her arms, agile as a fish. Carlson kept up, but Sachi had to make her way more sedately. They came into the communications center, where half the crew was trying to shoulder its way closer to a screen, gabbling excitedly in what sounded like an exotic language, but which Sachi recognized as the specialized jargon of astronomy and higher mathematics.

"You remember *Heisenberg*, the X-ray satellite?" Marion asked. "It's the one you launched a few months ago, gratis, for the MIT–Max Planck–ISAS [Institute of Space and Aeronautical Science] team."

"Of course I remember. What's happened?" Periodically, Carlson donated Lone Star's asset to support astrophysical research from space. It sometimes took the form of offering free launch services. In return, the experimenters kept him apprised of their major findings. He endured many lectures from Chamoun on the folly of this costly practice, but there was no gainsaying Carlson where his scientific manias were concerned.

"Latest news from the ground, Boss," said someone at the screen. "*Heisenberg* has detected strange, modulated signals from the direction of *eta Cassiopeiae A.*"

Sachi closed her eyes. "Let me think. *Eta Cassiopeiae:* a binary system, right? Two stars, A and B, widely separated. A is a sun type."

"Bingo," affirmed the mission astronomer. "They orbit one another every four hundred and eighty years."

"The hell with that," Carlson said. "What do these 'strange, modulated signals' mean?" He pushed his way to the screen, shoving everyone else aside.

Marion answered, "Professor Mallory thinks the signals could quite possibly be artificial."

Sachi saw Carlson's face flush with excitement, something he never showed even during a space launch. "Does that mean what it sounds like?" she asked. "Communication from an extraterrestrial civilization?"

"Could be, could be," Cash said. "But why the hell are they transmitting in X ray? The SETI people have been scanning for ET communications in radio wavelengths. This is odd." He said nothing for a while, and the rest chattered in lowered voices. Then he said, "If this pans out, boys and girls, it's going to be a whole new ball game out here."

13

ONE OF THE world's great natural marvels lies on the border of Brazil, Paraguay, and Argentina. Rio Iguazu flows westward through the vast Brazilian plains toward its confluence with the Paraná River. In the triangle formed by the two rivers, Brazil, Paraguay, and Argentina come together, for reasons best known to sixteenth-century diplomats and prelates.

The triple border could not have had a more spectacular and dramatic setting, for just before the Iguazu joins the Paraná, its waters tumble off the Brazilian plateau in a series of cataracts unmatched anywhere in the world. Just before the precipice, the Iguazu flows into a vast swamp, so that instead of reaching the cliffs in a single stream, it topples over in a horde of falls interspersed with small islands. On the Brazilian side, the falls are known as *Foz do Iguaçu*. On the Argentinian shore, it is called *Catarata del Iguazu*. The name comes from a Guarani word meaning "Great Water."

The name, Sachi thought, was certainly apt. It had been too late to see the falls when they arrived the night before, but Cash had made sure that she got a room facing the cataracts, rather than the jungle on the other side. She had left the balcony door open all night to hear the rumble of thousands of tons of water pouring over the lip of the precipice every second.

Now, in the light of morning, the sight of the falls was stunning even at a distance. When she heard the knock at the door, she left the balcony reluctantly. She expected someone from room service to clear away the breakfast dishes, but she was wrong.

"Good morning, Sachi." It was Parker

"Good morning, Jack. Please come in." She walked back toward the balcony. "There's half a pot of coffee on the table. It should still be warm." Parker was beginning to thaw a little toward her. She could not say positively that he liked her, but he seemed to be no more suspicious of her than he was of most people.

"Thanks," he said, pouring a cup. He came out to join her. "You want to be careful when you go out to see the falls."

"Oh? Are they as dangerous as everything else?"

"You never know. I was talking to the hotel manager last night. Earlier this year, a couple of newlyweds came up from Buenos Aires. The honeymoon lasted only a few days. They went out to see the *Garganta del Diablo* and the bride sort of fell over the cliff while her husband was looking the other way. Her body washed up downstream the next day. She was a socialite, and he inherited a substantial fortune. Nobody could prove anything, though."

"Hotel people usually don't like to spread stories like that," she said.

"They were staying at a rival hotel. He was happy to tell me all about it. They lose a few just about every year. Bozo tourists climb over the railing to get a better photo, dumb students show off for their girlfriends by doing handstands on the rail, that sort of thing."

"I promise to be careful."

Uncharacteristically, Parker fidgeted. "Yeah, well, the boss said—"

"Tell Cash," she said patiently, "that I will be perfectly safe for a few days. This place is crawling with security, and I took care of myself for a good many years before joining Lone Star."

"I agree you can handle yourself," Parker said. "And you know I think the boss is entirely too lax when it comes to security. But after what happened up in the space station, he's getting downright paranoid."

"It's frightening," she admitted, "but I think the last thing we need to worry about is an attack on me. I don't count for anything."

"Look, I'm leaving a couple of guys to—"

"Assign them to guard Cash," she insisted. "If he is in more danger than usual right now, he needs all your personnel."

"Okay, if you insist. Just watch yourself."

She smiled. "I always do."

The night before, they had just settled in and Cash was about to join her for a late supper, when an emergency call came in from O Navigador. There had been a launchpad fire, possibly sabotage, and it might be serious. Cash and Parker were leaving and might not be back for three or four days.

After Parker left, Sachi savored the sensation of having a whole day to herself with nothing to do. It seemed like months since she had enjoyed such a luxury. It had been months. She checked the hotel directory and called for a morning appointment at the hairdresser's. Confining her hair under a cap had done it no good and she hadn't had an opportunity to rectify the situation. The endlessly recycled air of the space station had proven hard on her skin as well. She would have herself redone to her toenails.

Seconds after she set the phone in its cradle, it rang again. "Hello?" She expected to hear Cash calling from the telephone in his airplane.

"Sachi? How good to hear your voice!" It was not Cash.

"Oh . . . hello, Jean-Claude. I wasn't expecting to hear from you. How did you find me?"

"I knew the Lone Star party was proceeding to Iguazu Falls, and there are only three or four hotels there that Carlson would use. I found you on the first try. How did your venture in space go?"

She described the launch and her work in space, but when she came to the emergency, something caused her to gloss over it. It was not that she was suspicious of Jean-Claude, but she had absorbed some of Parker's reluctance to give out unfavorable information.

"How exciting it must have been for you," du Mont said. "And all went routinely?"

"Like clockwork. It was almost dull after the first two or three days."

"And what are your plans now?"

"To relax, take a couple of days to repair my appearance and learn to live like an Earthbound human being again. This afternoon I plan to go see the falls close up."

"Excellent. I have never been there, but I hear they are a marvelous sight. Will you be visiting France anytime soon?"

This was delicate, and she had been wondering how she would handle it. She decided she would have to be direct.

"No . . . in fact, I plan to make my permanent residence in the U.S. I will be visiting Europe often, of course. But now I work for Lone Star and I can't do that and be a resident of France, can I? The tax situation alone would be too complicated."

There was a pause. "I see. Our Mister Carlson must be a very persuasive man."

She knew she should have expected it. "He is. He has given me important work, close to the center of the solar satellite race. He's given me the chance to go into space myself!"

"Sachi," he said with exaggerated patience, "space is the venue for the cowboys and adventurers of this age. It is becoming merely another sweaty workplace. You are meant for better things than that. Come back to Paris."

"And do what? What 'better things' am I meant for? To be an ornamental addition to the Paris social scene? How much longer can I be ornamental, Jean-Claude? Five years? Perhaps ten, with the best surgery? Besides, being a social butterfly is not my idea of a life worth living. This is a career doing something important, not attending parties and writing fluff pieces for journals." Until she said it, she had not realized how important Lone Star had become to her.

"Very well. It is your life. I simply think you are making a mistake."

"Perhaps I am. But as you say, it is my life, and mistakes are mine to make, Jean-Claude . . ."

After a long moment of pause, she heard him say, "Au revoir, Sachi." There was a click and a dial tone.

She replaced the phone in its cradle. She knew that she had taken an irrevocable step, cutting ties that had held her for the past two years. She felt sad and free at the same time. She felt that she had grasped the reins of her life. But was she escaping the control of one man only to surrender herself to the control of another? Somehow, she thought not. Whatever Cash's peculiarities might be, however overbearing his enthusiasms, he showed no inclination to control anyone. Even his closest aides were simply given their tasks and told to accomplish them the best way they could. He picked capable people rather than obedient drudges, and he assumed that getting the job done was more important than doing it his way.

She was not so naive as to think that her looks and charm had had nothing to do with her getting so far so fast in Lone Star, but she was sure that Cash would never have taken her on if he had thought that she was not fit for the tasks she had been assigned. And he had kept her busier than she had ever been in her life. Not once had she been expected to stand around looking beautiful, to greet people, or to hang on Cash's arm as his escort.

In fact, now that she thought of it, had it been any man other than Cash Carlson, she would have considered it odd behavior. He had no jealous wife watching him like a hawk. She was accustomed to men making passes at her on first meeting. Granted, men of wealth and power had good reason to be suspicious of women anxious to parlay beauty and charm into a share of the bounty. But surely by now, she had demonstrated that she was nothing of the sort. Gentlemanly restraint was admirable, but there was a limit!

She brooded on the question as the hairdresser fussed with her dense black hair. Was there someone else in his life? Possibly some might have suspected that Carlson was a secret homosexual, but Sachi's antennae were too fine-tuned for that. Had that been the case, she would have known that first evening, before she was halfway across the room.

Pat Coogan? She was with Cash a great deal. She clearly was jealous of Sachi's sudden intimacy with her boss and suspected her of being a gold digger. Sachi idly wondered whether that expression was still current; she had heard it used in old movies. She made a mental note to find out what the current expression might be.

She decided it wasn't Pat. If the woman was Cash's mistress, she would be more secure than she seemed.

Then she thought about Max. Nobody ever saw Max except Cash and Parker. Everyone assumed that Max was a man, but there was no evidence for that. Suppose Max was Maxine? The more she thought about it, the more sense it made. Cash was based in Houston, and that was where Max was. In Houston, he was always either conferring with Max or away on unexplained absences. And Lone Star had always been something of a partnership, with Cash as its very public head and the mysterious Max responsible for most of its coups and breakthroughs, the function of an equal partner, not of a mere employee.

"Maxine!" she hissed.

"I beg your pardon?" asked the woman who was buffing Sachi's nails. From her client's tone, she wondered whether she should be sharpening them instead.

"Nothing," Sachi mumbled.

Coiffed, buffed, and feeling like a new woman, Sachi stepped through the entrance of the hotel. There was enough left of the day to see at least the most famous of the falls. *Garganta del Diablo,* the Devil's Throat. The doorman, anxious to practice his French, told her that there was a local bus stop a short walk from the hotel. She could call a cab from the nearby township, he said, but the wait could be a long one and it would cost more, so why bother?

Impressed by the doorman's persuasive logic, she walked to the bus stop. Even this mild exercise felt good. What she really needed, she thought, was a hard workout at a real dojo, though she doubted that this area provided any such resource. She would have to find other ways to stay in shape.

As she made her way to the bus stop, exotic birds with huge beaks were flocking to the nearby treetops. These, she decided, must be the famous toucans. They were colorful, with the raucous voices that seemed to be standard for tropical birds.

She managed to jump onto a bus just as it was about to leave, and found a seat. The ride took her along a dirt road next to what appeared to be a swamp. She knew from a guidebook she had read that morning that it was actually the Rio Iguazu, spread out and shallow, flowing sedately toward the cliffs.

It seemed almost contradictory to her. Standing out on the hotel balcony, seeing and hearing all those unthinkable tons of water surging over the cliffs and pounding on the rocks below, she had expected to see the waters of the river running rapidly toward their sudden tumble. Well, she thought, perhaps the water flow would pick up its momentum as it got closer to the cataracts.

After a ride of just a few miles, the bus let her off at the approach to a jetty. The low walkway was built out over the swamp and extended for what seemed to Sachi to be at least a mile. The sun was getting low, but there were still some people strolling about. She passed a boat tied up to the jetty. Two men lounged in it, apparently more concerned with the bottled beer in their cooler than in the fishing poles leaning against the craft's gunwales. As she walked, the roar of the water grew in volume, but the water below her still moved at its snail's pace.

She passed by ruined jetties near the one she was on. Apparently a recent flood had destroyed the older structures. The scenery was calm, almost placid. Except for the noise, it was hard to believe that she was near something called the Devil's Throat. She could see that the jetty ended at a platform, and beyond the platform rose a white mist. Relieved that the walk was at an end, she crossed the platform and leaned over the rail. Only then did she experience the full impact of the *Garganta del Diablo*.

An immense tonnage of water poured from several directions over a horseshoe-shaped cliff. The toppling waters were mesmerizing and for a while, Sachi was oblivious to all else. To her amazement, birds swooped through the mist, diving through falling water to their nests on the cliff behind the wet curtains. At least, she thought, their eggs were well protected from predators.

When she could tear her gaze away from the falls, she looked beyond the cataract to the quiet water beyond. The swamplike river flowed
lazily to within a few meters of the precipice, so placid that a careless
boatman could be sucked over the falls before he even knew they were
close. There would be no warning except for the noise. She wondered
if a few Spanish explorers had discovered this peril the hard way.

The spectacle was so hypnotic that she took little notice of her surroundings. When she arrived at the platform, she had noticed two
groups of tourists wandering around, gawking and taking videos. While
she watched the water, one group, sated with the view and the omni-
present roar, wandered back down the jetty. A lone tourist passed them,
coming toward the platform. A camera hung from his neck, sporting a
telephoto lens the size of a man's forearm. A straw fedora shaded his
vaguely Indian features. Even as he arrived, the second group decided
they had had enough and began to make their way back to the "mainland."

It was beginning to get dark. Sachi wondered where the day had
gone. It seemed like only an hour or two since she had stood on the
balcony of her hotel room, listening to Parker lecture her on the dangers
of exploring the falls alone. The memory made her look around just in
time to see something moving toward her much too quickly. It was a
fleeting impression, glimpsed from the corner of her eye, but it sent an
instant adrenaline rush into her system. From that instant, reflex took
over.

She bent her knees to lower her center of gravity and moved to the
right, her mind flashing a warning that it was a man rushing toward her
with his arms outstretched, hands poised as if to push her over the
guardrail. He was tall, undoubtedly strong. Even as her brain registered
the fact, she continued her rightward movement, pivoting as his right
hand went past her, getting behind him enough to push at the lower
center of his back with both hands, her hips low in a powerful aikido
posture, boosting his momentum. Caught by surprise, his forward rush
unchecked, he hit the guardrail.

Had he been a little shorter, or had his rush been less impetuous—
most of all, had he not had Sachi's added vigorous push to increase his
forward speed—the guardrail might have caught him. He bent double
at the waist, his hands grasping at the top rail, but he was unable to get
a firm grip and his body continued its outward course over the rail.

With his right hand, the man got just enough of a grip to twist his body around so that he hit the slight rock protrusion beyond the rail facedown. Then the rail jerked from his grasp and he scrabbled frantically at the wet face of the rock. He hung there for a few agonizing seconds as Sachi watched, unable to move, instinctively wanting to save his life but too shocked to do anything but stare with horrified fascination as he slid off the slippery rock and fell into the mist, to be swallowed up by the *Garganta del Diablo*. If he screamed, she could not hear it over the roaring of the waterfall.

She stood there for two or three minutes, her knees trembling with reaction, holding herself up with a white-knuckled grip on the upper rail, the rail that had done the would-be assassin no good. It seemed unbelievable. The scene was exactly the one she had been admiring. The birds still swooped through the falling water to their nests, the white mists still rose, and the tumbling waters still roared.

When her breathing was almost normal again, she straightened and turned around. The last group of tourists was still in sight, about halfway shoreward on the jetty. It seemed impossible that they had noticed nothing. But the action had lasted for no more than a few seconds, and the noise of the falls numbed the brain to anything else. It was as if nothing at all had transpired.

Then she saw that not everything was the same. Someone had left a camera on the platform. It looked like a professional model, the type with a tremendous telephoto lens. She was more accustomed to the cameras used by fashion photographers, but she knew enough about cameras to realize that such a lens alone could cost hundreds, even thousands, of dollars. It was not the sort of thing a careless tourist would leave behind. The man must have been carrying it and set it down to be out of the way while he carried out his work.

She was about to leave it lying there when the thought struck her that this might be important. For once, she wished Parker or Pat Coogan were around. This was something that called for police instincts. As she left the platform, she bent and slung the camera over her shoulder.

Walking along the jetty, she thought about what had just happened. She even allowed a note of complacency to enter her thoughts: For someone feeling sluggish and somewhat out of shape, she had reacted swiftly and dealt successfully with a killer much larger and stronger than herself. Standing at the guardrail had something to do with it, she decided. It was like standing on a subway platform, always alert, even unconsciously, for a push from behind that might topple her into the path of an oncoming train. And she had been thinking about Parker's warning.

One thing was certain: This time, she had been the sole target. Cash and the rest weren't even in the same country.

She quickened her pace, nervous that another assassin might show up. Then she told herself that had there been another, he would have accompanied the first in order to ensure a thorough job. But the man might have a driver waiting for him at the end of the jetty. If so, what would the driver think, seeing the victim turn up alive and his confederate nowhere in sight? She suppressed her growing anxiety. What must Parker's life be like, thinking this way all the time?

She got to the end of the jetty just as the tourists were boarding a bus. To her relief, there were no cars in sight. The assassin must have taken a bus or been dropped off by a cab. Then she remembered the boat with the two beer-drinking "fishermen." Had it been there when she walked back? She had been too shocked to notice. She climbed aboard the bus and sat with the camera in her lap, trying not to tremble and attract attention. For the duration of the ride she stared out the window, seeing nothing, lost in thought.

Back at the hotel, she found the manager and showed him the camera. "I found this on the bus. Did any of the tourists here lose it?"

The manager glowed with delight. "Thank heavens! One of the reporters here covering the American Vice President's visit reported it stolen this afternoon. It is quite valuable and he wanted to hold the hotel responsible. Absurd, of course. We are responsible only for items locked in our safe. Still, it was embarrassing. On the bus, you say?"

"Yes. Left on a seat."

"How strange. I suppose it must have been taken by a boy from the town. He probably never took anything so valuable, realized he had no way of getting rid of it without getting caught, and abandoned it."

"That makes sense," she said.

"Anyway, thank you very much, Miss Sasano. The owner will be very relieved to get it back."

Later, in her room, she sipped at a martini and tried to analyze the sequence of events. Had the man followed her? He hadn't been on the bus she had ridden out to the jetty. Of course it was possible he had been dropped off by a driver. The boat was still a possibility. If she had not been followed, how had he known where to find her? To whom had she spoken of her intention to visit the falls? She thought hard.

Parker, of course. She was willing to believe that such a man could be suborned, but he knew so many ways to kill people that he would consider this clumsy attempt insulting. Had she said anything to the hairdresser or the manicurist? She thought not. The doorman! He had been so helpful, so thoughtful to see to it that she took the bus, not a cab. A taxi driver might have waited for her, noticing who went out on the jetty and who came back. This made sense.

Then the glass paused as she was about to take another sip of her martini. She had told Jean-Claude.

Surely not him. But the air of constant suspicion that hung around big-business operations had infected her. No one was above suspicion. Certainly he was too civilized to go into a homicidal rage over losing her to Cash. But there were many factors at work here. She knew it was a mistake to assume that she herself was at the center of this—not when matters of power and money and international prestige were at stake. These were things that people routinely killed other people over. She could not imagine how she fit into the picture, but someone else might see things differently.

She opened her suitcase and took out the secure phone she had been given. It was linked to a communications satellite and equipped with a scrambler-descrambler device. She punched the combination she had been given, hoping its range extended to O Navigador.

"Parker here."

"Sachi here. Jack, we need to talk."

14

WHEN I LIVED in Dallas," Pat was saying, "I always envied the jet-set life. I used to wonder what it would be like to just casually get on a plane at a moment's notice, jet off to someplace thousands of miles away, stay an hour or a couple of days, then fly off somewhere else you hadn't even been thinking about the day before." She looked out through the limo's window at the rainy, neon-filled Tokyo night. "I didn't think it would make me this tired." She gave a jaw-cracking yawn, not bothering to cover her mouth. "Do you ever get used to it?"

"No," Sachi said, smiling. "The human body evolved in a slower-paced world. It was never meant to compress time zones. I think part of being a jet-setter is in making it look easy."

"I'm glad it's not just me." The attempt on Sachi's life had inspired Cash to pack her off to Japan, amid a lot of I-told-you-sos from Parker. He had assigned Pat as assistant and bodyguard, much to her resentment. The ostensible reason was to make arrangements for an upcoming conference Cash had scheduled with Yoshino and some other Japanese businessmen, but the real reason was to get Sachi somewhere safe. He thought that Japan would be much safer than the wide-open environments of the Americas.

"Don't worry," Sachi told her. "Whatever else it might be, this evening won't be strenuous. Otherwise, I'd have tried to beg off. Besides, this sort of informal socializing is very important in Japan. Think of it as our version of Mr. Carlson's Texas barbecue."

"Do you think Yoshino will talk about anything important?"

"I think it likely that he will float something our way, as a preamble to the serious talks between his organization and Lone Star."

"Is this that subtle Asian indirection I've always heard about?"

Sachi laughed. "Something like that. But it won't involve how somebody holds his fan, or the color of plum blossoms floating down-stream."

"I didn't mean—"

"I know what you meant. Yes, people here usually prefer something more leisurely than the direct, cards-on-the-table deal-making that prevails in the West, especially in America."

"I've met Yoshino," Pat said. "I'm not sure who these others are. Do they represent . . . what's the word? *Zaibatsu?*"

"The *zaibatsu* were prewar organizations, very tightly organized and controlled, virtual monopolies. What we have now are *keiretsu*. *Keiretsu* are much more loosely organized. They aren't all that exclusionary, but they are very large and powerful anyway. They have great influence on the Japanese business world. Mitsubishi is a *keiretsu*. So are the Mitsui, Sumitomo, and Fuso groups. There are one or two others. I believe Fuso was formed to give groups outside the big three a cooperative venue."

"It doesn't sound like the American way of doing business," Pat said uncomfortably.

"It isn't, but it suits the Japanese. Each *keiretsu* has at least one world-class bank and a worldwide trading firm. But the trading firms aren't exclusive. They can sell merchandise not produced by members of their group."

"Sounds complicated," Pat commented.

"Business usually is. I'm afraid that's about as much as I know about it." Sachi was glad she wasn't alone. Like Parker, Pat had thawed a bit toward her, especially when she was told about the incident at *Garganta del Diablo*. She had made it her business to comfort Sachi, who was suffering from delayed reaction and remorse. Pat had assured her that she had no cause to regret "wasting a sleazeball," as the ex-cop so quaintly put it.

"Believe me," Pat had said, "if you have to deal with one, go ahead and kill him. If they live, they sue. Well, maybe not in Brazil, but in the States."

The black limo had picked them up at their hotel. The drive was not a long one. "What part of Tokyo is this?" Pat asked.

"The Akasaka district. Here we are." The limo pulled up before an undistinguished-looking entrance surmounted by a modest sign. The driver got out and opened the door for them.

"Not very fancy looking," Pat noted.

"That doesn't mean much," Sachi said. "Some of the best New York and Paris restaurants look like dives from the outside."

"That's a kind of reverse snob appeal. Is it the same here?"

"More like tradition."

A kimono-clad woman bowed them inside. The entrance hall was as understated as the exterior, making it difficult to tell how large or lavish the place was. They left their shoes in the hall and stepped up to a highly polished wooden floor where two pairs of slippers had been laid out for them, pointed in the proper direction. After making several turns along a meandering hallway, also floored with impeccably polished wood, they were shown to a small, detached house that was connected to the main building by a roofed corridor.

The room inside was covered with immaculate tatami. Its design was traditional, but the furnishings were subtly altered to accommodate Westerners as well as Japanese. Beneath the low table was a sizable pit so that those who preferred to could sit as on a chair, instead of on their legs in the Japanese fashion. The cushions were furnished with small backrests for the further comfort of those accustomed to non-Japanese seating.

Yoshino and two colleagues, men in their fifties, sat at the main table. In a small alcove near them, another, younger man sat at a smaller table. As the two women entered, Yoshino and his companions drew their legs from beneath the table and sat in traditional Japanese fashion. Sachi lowered herself to sit on the tatami floor with the elegance of an accomplished Japanese tea master. Pat followed suit, not quite as smoothly but with the ease of a trained athlete. The Japanese seemed impressed.

They bowed formally, then Yoshino introduced his companions. The one with brush-cut white hair was Mr. Ishida. The other, a burly man with a salt-and-pepper military mustache, was Mr. Yamabe.

"Miss Coogan, I fear that we must speak Japanese this evening. My colleagues at this table speak little English. On the other hand, Sugiyama, my special assistant," he gestured at the young man seated at the smaller table, "speaks a little English. He lived in the U.S. for a few years. If it would not offend you, he would be most happy to be your companion for the evening. Of course, the shoji partition will remain open. We certainly do not wish to exclude you." The young man smiled and bowed.

Pat didn't like the idea at all, but she realized this was not the time for a show of temperament. She knew she wasn't being shunted aside because she was a woman, since they were going to discuss matters with Sachi. Pat still didn't fully trust her, but she saw little likelihood of double-dealing here. The boss had frequently expressed his confidence in Yoshino, which he never did about Preston Reed or Jean-Claude du Mont. Besides, she had a small recorder in her purse, equipped with a directional mike. She had Japanese-speaking subordinates who could assure her whether Sachi faithfully reported the matters discussed.

Pat smiled. "Not at all. I wouldn't want to sit here like a stump while everybody else was talking. I'll be more than happy to join Mr. Sugiyama." She rose in a single smooth motion, grateful that her daily workouts kept her knees from popping.

The dinner began ritually, with heated sake and dishes of delicacies of numerous sorts. The better part of the meal was taken up with the leisurely process of getting acquainted. Pat learned that her companion for the evening spoke nearly accentless English, had spent time in Dallas and was a Dallas Cowboys fan, and liked bluegrass music.

Sachi learned, somewhat more significantly, that Mr. Ishida and Mr. Yamabe were chief executive officers of the lead or primary corporations in the two most powerful *keiretsu*. Among them, the three represented an awesome industrial capacity and financial muscle.

Then Yoshino shifted the direction of conversation. He was red-faced and appeared slightly inebriated, but Sachi knew that was how a Japanese sometimes wanted to appear when broaching a delicate or an important subject, one that he had to discuss with candor.

"I knew your father well, Miss Sasano," he began indirectly. "I grieved over his untimely passing." Sachi's father had died in an airline crash when she was in her teens. "If you will pardon my putting it this way, I have come to regard you as a favorite niece."

This seemed overdone, but it hinted that he was leading up to something important.

"I will be as frank with you as I would be with him. May we rely on you to keep this conversation in strictest confidence?" Before Sachi had a chance to say anything, he went on rapidly, raising a hand as if to forestall anything she had to say. "No, no, I am not asking you to keep anything from Mr. Cassius Carlson. In fact, we would very much like for you to tell Mr. Carlson all that we are about to say to you tonight."

It struck her that this was the first time she had heard anyone use his real name. She knew what Yoshino was getting at. He wanted assurance that she represented Carlson and nobody else. Especially not Jean-Claude du Mont.

"Certainly, Mr. Yoshino. No one but Mr. Carlson will be privy to this conversation."

Apparently, the waitresses had been instructed beforehand. No one entered the *hanare*, the detached room, from that point on. Sugiyama kept the heated sake flowing at the main table by means of a porcelain bottle placed in a kettle over charcoal in an elegantly shaped ceramic hibachi. This, he explained to Pat, who was trying to eavesdrop on the conversation at the main table, was the true hibachi. The crude little charcoal cooker known by that name in the U.S. was called in Japan a *shichirin*.

Yoshino began his proposal. Within five minutes, Sachi understood that there were a number of men in the world—du Mont among them—who would gladly kill for the information she was receiving.

"Miss Sasano, here in Japan we are ready to commence production of our own solar-power satellites. Mr. Carlson knows this. However, the nation finds itself in a difficult position internationally. Our very competitive success has made us a lone wolf among nations. It is imperative that we show the world Japan can be part of an important team effort that will be of great benefit to all." He paused for a sip of sake.

"It hardly needs to be said that we cannot do this by taking a combat role in even the best-intentioned peacekeeping military mission on behalf of the United Nations. Our constitution forbids it, and our people, for good reason, have a fervent aversion to war. After long debate and discussion among both political and industrial leaders, it has been decided that the peaceful exploration of space forms an ideal arena for such a cooperative venture, and the solar-power satellite program is an excellent venue.

"Worldwide cooperation in the venture under the auspices of the United Nations is of course a wonderful ideal, but it is quite unrealistic in the current competitive climate. It could never work, not with the notorious bickering and the infamous bureaucracy of the U.N. alone. To involve the ponderous government bureaucracies of dozens of member states would make the whole enterprise excessively cumbersome. Financially, it could become too costly to make it a practical alternative to conventional sources of energy.

"So we have considered three major candidates for an international collaboration on a private, or at least a semiprivate, level. These are du

Mont's European Space Enterprise, Preston Reed's Space Technologies, and Cassius Carlson's Lone Star Space Systems."

Sachi listened attentively, quietly, her face revealing nothing.

"The first two we rejected after brief consideration. They are truly not interested in a team operation, certainly not on any sort of equal basis. Besides, both are already so large and ponderous that they amount to government bureaucracies themselves. We know that in this sort of quickly evolving, high-tech field, any organization in order to not go under has to be ready to move with great alacrity and to adopt the latest and hottest technology.

"Besides, and perhaps most important, we were not sure we wished to entrust our future to men like Jean-Claude du Mont or Preston Reed. They are ruthless men, not only ambitious, but unscrupulous. Former superiors, subordinates, and business associates agree that both men are quite capable of treachery and double-dealing. They have left behind numerous ruined careers in climbing the ladder of power and success.

"We investigated Cassius Carlson most carefully. He, too, is a battler, and he has a mysterious past. But he has never betrayed a business partner or an associate. He deals fairly with his employees. I take it that this has been your own impression of Mr. Carlson, Miss Sasano?"

"Yes, it has been. Mr. Carlson is highly unorthodox, both personally and in a business sense, but he is a meticulously ethical man."

"Excellent. "Unorthodox" is hardly the word for him. Some of the things he does, such as finding that treasure galleon, look like magic. But it is exactly that sort of magician-entrepreneur that the times call for. The strong points of Lone Star and our own Uchu Kaihatsu complement each other nicely. For instance, over the last few years, we have developed amorphous silicon technology for manufacturing solar cells economically. Since an immense acreage of solar cells will be needed, this alone will drive down substantially the final cost of the electricity produced from the solar-power satellites."

He left unspoken the fact that Carlson's recent loss of his own silicon plant had left him desperately in need of their product.

"Originally," Yoshino went on, "we had intended to use our beamed energy thruster to move our power satellites from low Earth orbit, where they are less costly to assemble, to their geostationary orbits. However, we have encountered a technical problem that may require a few years to solve before these thrusters are available to us."

Surely, she thought, this admission was setting her up for something.

"It is our understanding," said Mr. Ishida, speaking for the first time, "that Mr. Carlson has tested the ion drive he has been hinting about for years, and that it works as expected. Is this true?"

Sachi felt her heart lurch to a stop. They had admitted that their SolarSat effort was almost at a standstill. In return, they wanted assurance that Carlson's ion drive was operational. Could this whole scene be a charade to trick such highly confidential information out of her? Her next words could doom Lone Star. On the other hand, Carlson had told her that he needed people who could think on their feet. It came down to instinct, and she trusted Yoshino. No hint of inner conflict showed on her face.

"It is true. Just a few days ago, I was present aboard the Lone Star Space Station when the drive was tested. Three ComSats were boosted from LEO to geostationary orbit. The engines performed flawlessly." No need to mention the sabotaged chip.

The three at the table with her seemed to exhale as one. There were smiles and relaxation all around.

"This is wonderful news," said Mr. Yamabe.

"Yes," Yoshino agreed. "Please tell Mr. Carlson that we think it would be in the interests of both our organizations to, shall we say, merge our hardware. We wish to participate as full partners. Of course that means that we will put up all funds necessary to make the Uchu Kaihatsu–Lone Star SolarSat the first operational solar-power satellite in history!" They all raised their sake cups.

The denouement of the dinner passed by Sachi in a haze. After effusively polite good-byes, she got into the waiting limo with Pat.

"Well, what happened?" the other woman asked impatiently. "All I could make out was somebody using the boss's real name. He hates to be called Cassius."

Sachi shook her head slightly and inclined it toward the driver. Pat understood and they switched to small talk. When the driver saw them inside their hotel, they waited until he drove away.

"Now let's take a walk," Sachi said, going back out through the hotel's main entrance. Again, Pat didn't need to ask why; their room might be bugged. A gentle rain was falling. Between the rain and the traffic noise, even a directional mike would do eavesdroppers no good.

"Let's have it," Pat urged. Sachi gave her a brief but complete report on what Yoshino and the others had said. To her amazement, the taller woman stopped in her tracks.

"My God!" Pat said. "We're saved!"

"What?" Sachi had no idea of what she was talking about.

"Okay. You've been straight with me, so I'll repay the compliment." She told Sachi about the raid on Lone Star's financing and the precipice of catastrophe it left them on.

"I had no idea!" Sachi admitted.

"That's because you're always with the boss," Pat said, resuming their walk, her high heels clicking loudly on the pavement. "You never get together with Chamoun and Thibodeaux. They've been in a frenzy for weeks. Auguste's sources have dried up and Bob's standing there with his knife sharpened and nobody to stab. If this Japanese deal goes through, we'll be financially untouchable."

Sachi went down a short flight of steps and into a small, smoky bar. They took a table and ordered drinks from a kimono-clad waitress. The predominantly male clientele stared but nobody had the nerve to approach two such formidable-looking women.

"Mr. Carlson never hinted that we were in such financial trouble," Sachi said.

"It isn't that he doesn't trust you," Pat told her. "It's just that he doesn't care."

"What?" Sachi said, incredulous.

"It's true," Pat admitted, sipping a Kirin beer. She would drink nothing stronger while on duty. "He's a Texas horse trader when it comes to raising money, but once he's got it, he takes no further interest. He drives Chamoun crazy. He just doesn't care about money. He only wants to get into space and play with his toys."

Sachi smiled over the rim of her glass. "I found that out when we went up to the space station. Buck Rogers."

"Exactly." Pat pondered for a few minutes, then: "Sachi, there's something else you should know." She told her about Parker's mole hunt. "Keep it quiet, unless you think the boss's in immediate danger. You know how he is about fostering paranoia inside his organization. We think he's wrong."

"I appreciate your confidence. Does this mean I am now a full member of the team?"

"I guess it does. The boss has considered you so from the start, but I think you know by now that we don't always trust his judgment."

"I seem to be learning a lot of valuable things," Sachi said. The two women clinked their glasses together.

JEAN-CLAUDE DU MONT sat grimly behind his desk. Like the other furniture in his office, the desk dated from the reign of Napoleon III, the Belle Epoque that saw French civilization at its height of influence and prestige, before the disasters and humiliations of the twentieth century. The other furnishings of the office were from the same period, as was the demitasse of coffee on the desk before him. He had not touched it since the Russian ape had entered two minutes before. Somehow, it seemed a desecration to use so elegant an artifact in the presence of this uncultured oaf, to whom it could mean no more than a soldier's tin cup.

In fact, Kuprin knew exactly what the cup meant. He knew that it was part of a china set that du Mont had coveted for years and had finally managed to acquire at an auction held by Hotel Drouot six days previously. He knew that the set had once belonged to Madame de Stael, who had given it as a gift to Talleyrand, a man in whom du Mont detected many similarities to himself.

Kuprin knew a great deal about du Mont. With his usual care for self-preservation, the Georgian had done some research on his employer. He knew that du Mont was from Autun, like Talleyrand, but tried to give the impression of being a native Parisian. He knew that the man had graduated from the Sorbonne and had held a number of positions in the French aeronautics industry. With ten years of administrative and sales experience behind him, he had left to found his own company, selling French aircraft, military and civilian, on the brutally competitive international market.

By dint of energy, cunning, and the extravagant use of bribery and blackmail, he had made French sales soar far beyond those of Great Britain and the United States. He was frequently accused of treaty violations—selling military craft to outlaw nations and aggressors worldwide—but his extensive web of political contacts protected him from any meaningful censure.

When the European aerospace consortium was formed, Jean-Claude du Mont was the natural choice to head it. He had taken to the post with the zeal of a crusader. If exploitation of space was to be the destiny of mankind, then he would see to it that that destiny was dominated by Europe. He had not gone into business simply to make money, after all. It was to restore France to her ancient glory, a task for which he felt eminently suited. And Europe's right to dominate the world had been manifest since the Dark Ages. The new Europe, risen from the ashes of World War Two, purged of its ancient divisions, would dominate the second millennium.

Of course, the new Europe was in turn dominated by Germany, but du Mont was certain that couldn't last.

Kuprin knew all of this and a great deal more, while du Mont knew almost nothing about him. That was the way Kuprin liked to keep things. Just now, the Frenchman seemed a little too agitated. Kuprin thought he knew why.

"The Yankee's silicon-production plant is a heap of junk now," Kuprin reported. "According to the post-fire analysis, it will be at least a year before he can gear up for full production again. That ought to set back his schedule for solar-power cells."

"What about the launch facilities at O Navigador?"

"So far, security there remains tight. My cover job gives me access to the place, but that is all. The security team watches everyone like hungry vultures. I have spotted Parker's people among the ground crews in every department."

"So he is not proving to be the pushover you anticipated?" Du Mont's tone was not quite as acerbic as usual. He seemed preoccupied. "And is it not true that some of your people have been apprehended by Parker's security?"

So, du Mont had his own sources inside. Well, it was to be expected. "That is so." He hid his irritation. "But they are expendable."

"Come now, Kuprin, you don't even know if they are alive. Parker could have them under interrogation at this very moment. He is not known for his humanitarian leanings."

Kuprin flicked ashes on the floor and was rewarded with an aristocratic wince. "Monsieur du Mont, this is my realm of expertise. Credit me with knowing what I am doing. I have many people planted in Carl-son's organization. No single one of them is crucial. Parker is not tough enough or ruthless enough to use really effective interrogation proce-dures. And, most important, none of those people know that I am their controller. The agent who hired them is no longer in Brazil, and as soon as any of them become compromised, I change reporting procedures and personnel. Even if they talk, they can only lead Parker to a dead end. Nothing can lead back to me, much less to you."

"All right, you are a master of your trade," du Mont admitted. "But what about Sachi Sasano? Her byline appeared this morning in *Paris Match*. Surely she isn't filing from your hideout in the Mato Grosso?"

So that was it. In the middle of operations of great delicacy and world importance, the man was half out of his mind with jealousy over a woman less than half his age! *Sometimes,* Kuprin thought, *I just don't understand people.* That did not mean he could not use their weaknesses to his own advantage.

"I sent in a professional kidnapper to get her at Iguazu Falls. The location was excellent, Parker was elsewhere, but the man failed to make the snatch. Security there during the summit was like the Kremlin before Gorbachev."

He reported in a bland, bored tone, as if this were no more than an ordinary glitch. Inwardly, he seethed with anger and mortification. There was no way he was going to tell du Mont how the job had been bungled. Carlos and José had moored their boat to the long jetty. They were supposed to wait until Sachi returned from the falls, then hustle her into the boat. Carlos was supposed to be expert at his work. Should there be any other tourists around, it was to look as if they were meeting her for a boating trip somewhere. The roar of the falls would drown out any cries she might make, and an ether-soaked rag, deftly applied, would quiet her.

But Carlos, it seemed, was no longer the steel-nerved kidnapper he had once been. He had grown too fond of the famous product of his native land, Colombia. From the time they got in the boat, José had reported, Carlos had been sniffing from an inhaler, growing more glassy-eyed by the minute. He had seen their quarry at the hotel and kept babbling about what a beauty she was. Carlos, a noted womanizer, was looking forward to a long and intimate acquaintance in the Mato Grosso hideout.

As the tourists trickled back from the overlook, Carlos had grown impatient, taken a last, heroic snort and announced that he was going to go get Sachi. He paid no attention to his partner's protests. Taking up the hat and camera he had stolen for protective coloration, he had climbed from the boat to the jetty and disappeared toward the falls. A few minutes later, José had seen Sachi return, a stunned look on her face. She never even glanced at him, and he was too astonished to attempt the snatch on his own.

Three days later, Carlos's bloated, fish-nibbled body had washed up several kilometers downstream from the falls. Kuprin would have believed that the worthless fool, in his drug-induced haze, had simply fallen from the jetty and been swept over the falls, except for the woman's clear state of shock as related by José. Could she have actually overpowered the burly Colombian? In his condition, maybe he wasn't all that difficult to handle, capable only of making trouble and embarrassment for his employer, Sergei Kuprin.

"I suppose it is hard to get good help these days," du Mont said, his poker face back in place. "I expect to hear better news from you soon, Kuprin." He picked up some papers and pretended to study them, the interview obviously at an end.

Kuprin rose, dropped his cigarette to the expensive carpet and ground it out with his shoe. "If you could find a better man for this job, you would be talking to him now, not to me. I'll be in touch."

As the Georgian left, du Mont fumed for a moment, then sighed resignedly. Even Louis XIV, he thought, had had to rely on brutes for some tasks.

16

CRUMLY'S SUMMONS CAME while Parker was supervising the monthly sweep of the Lone Star Houston headquarters. The sweep was thorough, turning up six new bugs, about average. They weren't very sophisticated, just the small but crude sort easily planted by someone making a delivery. A genuine mole would have been able to plant something far better. But whoever it was, he was being very cagey, avoiding anything as clumsy and easily detectable as mechanical listening-and-recording devices.

As Parker was listening to his team's wrap-up, a message blinked on the heads-up display inside his shades: *"See me: Max."* The corners of his mouth quirked up into a near smile. *The crazy little bastard's telling me he has access to everything, even to my security hardware.*

"Wait here," he told his team. "I'll be back in a few minutes."

He took the special elevator down to Crumly's lair. This time, the troll was prepared. A path had been cleared to the computer terminal, the junk-food wrappers swept aside, and a plastic mat laid down. A chair was covered with a drop cloth and reeked of disinfectant. Crumly sat in the chair beside it, wearing a surgical scrub suit and mask.

Parker sighed and sat down in the covered chair. "Glad to see somebody around here takes serious security measures."

Crumly didn't even look at him. "I found him."

"So I figured. Who is it?"

"Let me show you how I found him."

Parker knew he'd have to be patient. The nutcase wanted to show off. It was understandable. He damn sure got little enough pleasure out of life. "Okay, show me."

"Look at this." Crumly grew animated. In fact, Parker was wrong. Crumly, operating his computers, was in a state of ecstasy an ardent drug addict would envy. The screens lit up with bank statements, telephone bills, and spreadsheets. The images froze. "Adam Altieri."

Even as Crumly pronounced the name, Parker was running it through his mental filing system and came up with a face: bland, youthful, cheeks lightly dusted with freckles beneath wire-framed glasses. "PR, right? One of Alison's people?"

"That's right," Crumly affirmed. "One of her closest aides. More important, he's in charge of setting up interviews, photo ops, things like that. He has near-complete access to Mr. Carlson's traveling schedule."

"Show me more."

"Here's where he withdrew twenty-seven thousand from his bank account. Over here's his phone bill. See that number that he calls almost every day?"

"It's local," Parker noted.

"Uh-huh. It's listed to a dry-cleaning establishment belonging to a Mr. Rudolph Valentino Washington."

"Let me guess. He doesn't really have a thing about his laundry, does he?"

"Uh-uh. Here's the New York police file on Washington. He's been indicted repeatedly for bookmaking. No convictions." Above the rap sheet was a picture of a man in a black suit with a tight white collar and narrow black tie. He looked like a stereotyped preacher from an African-American-oriented sitcom.

Parker leaned back against the drop cloth, his fingers steepling. "So our man Altieri has a weakness for the ponies?"

"Not just that. Look at this phone-call density." The largest screen lit up with a breakdown of Altieri's calls to Washington's number over a yearlong period. The calls were color-coordinated by month, day, and hour. On some days, there were multiple calls. Crumly touched a key and several of the numbers turned white. "These are the races. Look at the corresponding withdrawals on the other screen. You can see the season on all the major tracks. Plus, he bets big on the Triple Crown races. He dropped a bundle on the Belmont and Preakness. Actually won big on the Kentucky Derby, though. Big deposit the next day."

"Even a bozo gets lucky once in a while," Parker noted.

"But get this. Those red fall numbers? Notice the weekend concentration?"

"Football," Parker said. "And the green winter numbers are basketball, and in summer, there's baseball. What's that yellow figure?"

"Indy Five Hundred."

Parker chuckled humorlessly. "It seems that Adam is a degenerate gambler. When did this start?"

"In a small way, looks like eight or nine years. But suddenly the numbers get big in June three years ago."

Another fact clicked into place. "Pasadena."

"Uh-huh. That was the first big correspondence that got my attention. It led me to all the rest. But I don't know why he started just then."

"That's because it has nothing to do with computers or numbers, Win. It's psychology. What we have here is a classic junkie, and gambling is his fix. He goes along for years thinking he's got it under control, keeps his losses tolerable, probably not even his friends know he's hooked. Then one day he loses it and plunges in deep, makes crazy bets, always loses and has to bet more in hopes of covering his losses. He married?"

Court records came up on the big screen. "His wife divorced him for nonsupport last year."

"Figures. And Mr. Washington is a bookie with real juice. That many arrests with no convictions means he has serious mob backing. You think to check hospital admissions?"

Crumly looked surprised. "Yeah, I found his emergency-room bill but I didn't connect it with this." He tapped the keys, and a hospital admission form appeared. Altieri had shown up with multiple contusions, three broken fingers, and some loosened teeth. A hospital photo showed a face swollen beyond recognition. Crumly had appended the police report. Altieri claimed he was attacked by muggers on a street near his Manhattan apartment and severely beaten. He could not identify his attackers.

"That was the first warning," Parker said. "The media call them, 'legbreakers,' but they don't usually do serious damage until the second warning. They don't want to harm the earning power of a valued customer."

Crumly looked astonished. "You mean he'd go back and bet with them after they've done that to him?"

"He's a junkie," Parker said. "He'll cross a minefield on his knees over broken glass to get his fix. But he knows he doesn't dare welsh. So he has to cover his bets, and it no longer matters much to him how he does it."

"Well, he solved his problem," Crumly said. "Look at these airplane tickets. More than twenty weekend flights to Las Vegas in the last two years."

Parker noted that Altieri had paid cash for the tickets. No checks, no credit cards, and Crumly had found them anyway. He shook his head. If the man wasn't as crazy as a bedbug, what an asset he'd be to the security staff. He noticed something out of place.

"Those flights," Parker mused. "Six last year, five in the first half of this year, then all the rest in the last four months."

"He's found some new information to sell?" Crumly hazarded.

"Maybe. Or maybe somebody has him on retainer now. A nice fat wad of bills every month and he can almost normalize his addiction, at least until it takes another leap and he has to start betting the whole wad on the first high-school football game that comes along after he picks up his drop. See there? The calls to Washington have slacked off since he started making the regular Vegas trips."

"Yeah, I noticed that. I just figured he found a new way to have fun."

Parker got up. For the first time, he truly smiled. "I'm going to show him what fun's all about. Win, I want you to keep a close eye on all his records from here on in."

"You mean you're not going to get him now?"

"Oh, I'll pay him a visit, point out the error of his ways, maybe. But a guy who's got himself into this kind of position can be more valuable where he is than at the bottom of the bay. If somebody's keeping him on a retainer big enough to bankroll these Vegas trips, that's the guy I really want to learn about, maybe feed some false information." He almost clapped Crumly on the shoulder, then thought better of it when the nerd winced away from him.

"You missed your calling, Win. You should've been a detective."

"You really think so?" Crumly said, blinking.

"You need to work on your social graces; you're no Sam Spade with the dames. Other than that, you're a natural."

Parker left the lair and rejoined his team, bringing the sweep to a hasty close. Within a half hour, they were in a company jet on their way to New York. The others wondered about the sudden change in schedule, but they said nothing. Their chief, even more reticent than usual, spent the trip deep in thought. Carlson would be in Japan for a few more days. The island nation was just about the safest place on

Earth, so Parker had requested the time to see to the company's far-flung security net.

He was pondering the implications of Altieri's behavior pattern. The early, random betrayals made plenty of sense. The degeneration of this sort of gambling junkie was a well-known phenomenon, taught in every criminology course. It usually led to embezzlement, but in this case, the perp had valuable inside information to sell. He'd undoubtedly put his goods up for bids on one of the underground info nets, probably one of those used by international hustlers and mercenaries. It all jibed, in the earlier years.

The abrupt change of lifestyle looked more ominous. It seemed as if Altieri had been put on retainer by someone with real money, and it had begun at the same time as the devastating attacks on Lone Star's SolarSat program. He'd known for a long time that the attacks were coordinated, but the sabotage operation had been set up by a pro, somebody who hired his flunkies through intermediaries. Every time Parker's team had caught a spy or a saboteur at work, they had run into a dead end because the hiring or controlling agents were too deeply concealed.

The cell structure made Parker suspect a mastermind from the old Eastern bloc. But he couldn't be certain, because terrorist organizations worldwide used similar systems. This was too methodical and cautious for ordinary terrorists, though. Whoever was running this operation, he was no fanatic, nor was he ego-driven like so many of the terrorist masterminds. This had to be a mercenary, probably freelance, working for one of Carlson's numerous enemies. He would be the hardest sort of foe to catch.

Now, just maybe, Parker had a line to the bastard. He smiled at the thought. It wasn't a pleasant smile.

Alison Baird smiled when Parker came in, but she was a little puzzled. He had phoned from the airplane as he neared New York and she had said sure, she'd hang around an extra hour or two if it was important. Parker was someone she almost never saw except with Carlson. Security and Public Relations were two branches of Lone Star that rarely intersected. But friendliness and sparkle were parts of her job and her smile was bright.

"Good evening, Jack. We don't see one another often enough. To what do I owe the honor?"

"I won't keep you long, Alison, but this is important."

"So you said. How can I help you?"

"I'm investigating one of your people, Alison. Adam Altieri."

She pushed away a little from her desk, leaning back in her chair. The smile was gone. "Adam. I see. Is he in trouble?"

"He could be. How's his work been?"

"Uneven. He was wonderful when I first took him on—hardworking, imaginative. He was my right hand for a long time."

"And then?"

"And then he grew erratic—missing work, turning in sloppy work, borrowing against his next paycheck. At first I suspected drugs. I've seen them get like that when they move into cocaine and other drugs. Three or four times I've decided to fire him, but he always gets a grip on himself and straightens out. I don't expect it to last. Lately I've had my eye on a new boy, first-rate material. I've been planning to ease him into Adam's job, as soon as I have an opportunity to send Adam packing."

She leaned forward. "But that's my department, nothing to concern security. What's this all about?"

Parker gave her a brief rundown on what he had learned about Altieri, leaving out Max's participation and leaving unspoken the implication that he himself was acting on Carlson's direct orders. As he spoke, her expression grew more alarmed and she raised a hand dramatically to her forehead. From long professional experience, she had a broad range of gestures designed for the camera.

"My God!" she said when he was finished. "I should have seen it coming. That beating, the way his wife left him. But you know the boss's orders about not concerning ourselves with the employees' personal lives."

"I've warned him about it enough times," Parker said, shrugging.

"But I never dreamed it meant espionage and sabotage, maybe even murder! Has anyone been killed?"

"Not on our side," Parker said, remembering the man Sachi had sent into the *Garganta del Diablo*. "But we might easily have lost a lot of people. It was pure luck that nobody died at the silicate plant. We found explosives at one of the O Navigador fuel-storage facilities. Somebody lost his nerve before he could plant and arm them. If they'd gone off close enough to those tanks, we might've lost a hundred workers, probably some firefighters, too."

Alison was quick to pounce on an inconsistency. "But that has nothing to do with the boss's schedule. I can see the kidnap attempts, but—"

"It's all tied together," Parker told her. "Somebody's running Altieri here in New York and a whole bunch of people in Brazil. It's time he and I had a little talk."

"He's not here," Alison said. "He's probably at home."

"I'll just pay him a little call."

"Jack, you're not going to do anything awful, are you? I mean, you'll turn him over to the police, won't you?" She looked a little green.

"Police?" he said, grinning. "You mean arrests and trials and all that? That wouldn't be very good publicity, would it, Alison?"

She turned greener. "No, it wouldn't."

"Well, don't worry. I'm going to keep this quiet, and I won't do anything really messy to him just yet."

She still looked green as he closed the door behind him. Then she began to run damage-control scenarios, just in case something went wrong. She began to sub-categorize the scenarios: sabotage, international terrorism, industrial espionage. Then she gave them a favorable spin by stressing the heroic efforts to thwart the nefarious plots.

Short of utter catastrophe, she knew she could make Cash Carlson come out of this looking good.

Parker punched the combination for Altieri's apartment.

"Who is it?" queried the voice through the tiny grill.

"I got some materials from Alison Baird's office. She says you gotta take care of this stuff right away." There was a buzz and a loud click, and Parker opened the door and entered the building.

Altieri's apartment was situated in a six-story brick apartment block in Washington Heights. Everything about the place was typical New York. Even though the location was much better than average, the elevator Parker rode to the fifth floor had a small, parabolic mirror in an upper corner. That way, before a prospective rider committed himself to getting in, he could check the mirror through the tiny window in the door to see if anyone was lurking in the blind corner.

The hallway was clean and well-lit. Without thinking about it, Parker checked out the possible ambush sites and escape routes. He'd already checked the apartment from outside: There was a small balcony with a fire escape. He didn't know if there might be access to adjacent apartments, but that would be most unusual in New York. Knowing the terrain was habit with Parker. He didn't expect to need it this time—Altieri wasn't the sort of crook likely to turn pugnacious.

Parker knocked and put on his meanest face: eyes slitted, mouth almost lipless. There was a sound of locks being turned and bolts being drawn, quite a few of them. Also typical New York. The door began to open.

"Why didn't Alison—" The visible eye widened at the sight of Parker and the door began to shut. Parker pushed it open easily. He walked inside and shut the door behind him.

"Mr. Parker!" Altieri seemed torn between terror and relief. "You scared the hell out of me! I mean, I was expecting a delivery boy, and you . . ." The confusion dissipated and dread took over. "What's this all about?"

"You've been a bad boy, Adam. We need to talk about it."

"I . . . I don't know what you're talking about! You'd better get out of here or I'll call the police" The attempt at sternness fell flat, tapering off into hesitant bluster.

"Sure, call the police, Adam. They'll want to hear my story. I have evidence tying you to attempted murder, attempted kidnapping—hell, I can probably nail you for insider trading. And that's just what I've found out about you since this morning." He stalked toward Altieri, who backed away until a chair stopped him. Parker put his fingertips against Altieri's chest and gave him a little shove. He sat abruptly.

"That's it, Adam, sit down. This isn't going to be pleasant. For you, that is. I'm going to enjoy it a lot." He reached into a side pocket of his long overcoat and came out with a stack of printouts, which he dropped in Altieri's lap.

"It's hard to hide your little peccadilloes these days, Adam. Everything's on computer, even when you pay cash. You've been selling your information to some very nasty people, Adam."

Desperate to avoid Parker's eyes, Altieri flipped through the sheets. As he did, he got a grip on himself and his voice firmed.

"You've got nothing here, just circumstantial evidence."

Parker grabbed him by the front of his shirt and lifted him from the chair. "What do you think I am, Adam, a court of law? I don't give a damn about circumstantial. This is proof." He let go and Altieri collapsed bonelessly into the chair. "Besides, I don't need to do a thing to you. I just stop your paycheck. And I have a friend who can make your bank account disappear. Then what'll you say next time Mr. Washington's boys come by to collect?"

Altieri turned pale. When he spoke, it was almost in a whisper. "I've heard about you, Parker. They say you can just make people disappear if you want to."

Parker hauled up a chair and sat almost knee-to-knee with Altieri. His bulletproof coat gaped open to show the massive machine pistol beneath his arm. "They say right, Adam."

Altieri raised his head and met Parker's gaze steadily, his fear under control. "You're not doing that. What do you want from me?"

Parker favored him with a bleak smile. "Good boy, Adam. You're smarter than I thought. If you cooperate and don't try to screw around with me, I not only won't make you disappear, I may even let you keep your job. As much of it as Alison's willing to let you have, anyway."

"What do you want me to do?" He sat a little straighter, thinking he might get out of this alive somehow.

"First we need to talk about your little problem with the ponies and the dice and so forth."

"It's not like I'm nuts or anything," Altieri said defensively. "It's just for fun, a little relaxation. Everybody in this town gambles a little. Nothing illegal about it. It's just that once I bet a little too much and I had to cover it. All I ever needed was one big win and I could have cleared everything, gone back to betting only on weekends . . ."

Parker leaned forward and slapped him, hard. "No-no, Adam, none of that. Every junkie and drunk and degenerate gambler has an excuse, I know that. But you don't have any excuse. You won big more than once. It never made any difference, though. You always had to bet it and lose it."

Tears came into Altieri's eyes. "It's not my fault! I can't control myself. I'm sick and I need help."

Parker sighed in disgust and slapped him again. "Nobody gives a damn about your mental problems, Adam. You're going to need help breathing if you don't come clean with me."

Altieri held his hands out, palms forward. "All right, all right! What do you want?"

"Up until recently, you jerked around like any other damn-fool adrenaline junkie. You'd get in the hole and sell your information over the info nets for whatever you could get. Then about four months ago, your trips to Vegas got more regular and a lot more numerous. Must be nice, with a gambling jones, having a nice, regular income over your regular paycheck. Who's got you in his pocket, Adam?"

"I never see him," Altieri said hastily. "I never see any of them, or even know who they are. They make deposits in my account by computer, same as I send out the information."

Parker reached into a pocket again. This time, he came out with a pair of fingerless black-leather gloves. They were reinforced over the knuckles with leather-covered pyramidal plates. "Now you're going to make me get rough with you, Adam. I mean, give me credit for a little brains. Your bank records are sitting right there in your lap. The other payoffs were made by computer, but somebody's been giving you cash lately."

Altieri held out his hands again. "No! Wait! Yeah, I've been getting cash, but it comes in an envelope, he doesn't deliver it by hand. It gets delivered to my mailbox at the Tower on the first of each month."

Parker grabbed him by the front of the shirt, yanked him forward and punched him lightly on the nose. The result was a smacking sound and a severe nosebleed. While Altieri sat groaning and watching in horror as the stain spread across the front of his white shirt, Parker went into the kitchen and wrapped some crushed ice in a dish towel. He returned to the living room and handed Altieri the ice pack.

"Hold this against your nose. The bleeding'll stop in a couple of minutes. Sure hope you're not a hemophiliac."

"Jesus Christ, Parker," Altieri groaned. "You didn't have to do that."

"Yes I did. Because you're still trying to diddle me around. Sure you get a regular envelope of cash now, but you're being run by a pro. I know all the signs. He'll have wanted to confront you personally when he hired you, or maybe sent a trusted emissary to make the buy. He was paying big money for important information, so he'd want to know what kind of weasel he was buying. Tell me about it, Adam."

"I . . . I can't."

Parker felt a tingling sense that he was getting close. It almost had to be his adversary.

"You can't tell me because he scared you?" Altieri didn't say anything. "Adam, I can't have this. I need a line on that man. I need to know all you know about him."

"He's a scary guy," Altieri whined.

"I know. The top operators usually are. He's like me. The difference is, I'm in your living room and he isn't. Tell me, Adam, or you're going to get real uncomfortable."

All the stuffing seemed to go out of Altieri. When he spoke, it was without feeling or inflection. "He approached me when I walked out of the Tower one evening. Said he was buying information and had plenty of money to pay for it. I tried to brush him off. Thought he was maybe one of your people. But he took my arm and steered me into a bar. It was like he had me on a leash. We had a few drinks and he laid out his proposal. He'd pay me cash on a monthly basis and I'd be his exclusive source. Never said how he'd found me."

"You've left an electronic trail like a buffalo through a lawn party. Describe him."

"Big, but with a squat build so he looks short unless you're standing close to him. Square face, kind of pushed in like a bulldog's. Slavic-looking, I'd say. Piggy little brown eyes and bushy black hair. Smiles a lot, but you can tell he doesn't mean it."

"Voice? Accent?"

"Deep voice. His English is fluent but with a heavy accent. Eastern European, I'd guess. He talks the way Russians talk, with a lot of mouth and lip action. I noticed some silver-looking teeth in the back of his mouth."

"Stainless steel. That's Eastern Europe, all right. You're doing good now, Adam. Keep going." At last he was building up a picture of the man he was facing.

"He was smooth, in spite of all the rough edges. Acted very businesslike, like this was an ordinary transaction, something he does every day. Maybe he does. He told me what information he wants and how to send it to him."

"How's that?"

"He told me not to use a company computer or my own PC or modem. Instead, I encode the information and send it over a commercial fax machine."

"I want the code and the fax number," Parker said.

"The code's a simple one, but the fax number changes every month. The month's new number is on a slip included with the cash."

"You're doing good so far, Adam. Keep it up and you may get out of this alive yet."

"Sure," Altieri said, dejected. "Big choice. You're gonna kill me or he will."

"You got to learn to look on the good side. This guy and I may kill each other, and the boss is too tenderhearted to waste you. After all, you're a gambler, so you've got to be an optimist. Now, here's what you're going to do to earn my goodwill and keep breathing a little longer: You're going to keep on sending out the information, but it's going to be what I give you to send."

"He told me what can happen if I don't play straight with him," Altieri said. "He went into detail. This guy knows all about torturing people."

"What do you think I am, Adam, Amnesty International? I don't care if this guy majored in torture with a minor in genocide. He's been using sabotage and terrorism against Lone Star and you've been helping him and I'm pissed off at both of you. Just because I'm being nice to you now, don't think I'm your buddy. I'm still waiting for that fax number."

When he had the number, he rose. "Now, Adam, don't you even think about skipping town. I'll find you. You've seen how I got all these records, even when you thought you were being smart, using cash instead of checks or your credit cards. I want you to show up for work every day as usual. Put in your hours, collect your money. You can even go on placing bets with Washington if you feel like it. Your new employer's watching you, too, and he'll notice if your habits change radically. We don't want that, do we?"

Altieri shook his head.

"I'll give you the info to send, and you turn over the new fax numbers to me as you get them, along with any instructions that are passed along to you. Have you ever seen who puts your cash envelope in your box?"

"No. It hasn't been there when I've worked late at night, but it's there early in the morning, before the regular mail delivery."

"So whoever's doing that may be keeping an eye on you, too. Walk lightly, Adam."

"God, how can I live like this?" Altieri agonized.

"Maybe it'll all do you some good. Learn from it. The worst that can

happen is you'll get killed, and you were heading that way anyhow."
He turned and let himself out. "Sweet dreams, Adam," he said before
he closed the door. Behind him, Altieri buried his face in his palms and
sobbed.

17

JEAN-CLAUDE DU MONT did not like this boardroom. The long table was made of highly polished wood, but it was of the modern type, with computer terminals under folding covers. The whole room was ultramodern, which was why he disliked it.

Nor did du Mont like the building that held the room. The headquarters of the European Space Enterprise resembled, to his fiercely prejudiced eye, a lunatic's vision of an alien spacecraft: all struts and cantilevered ledges and blue mirror glass. It was, he decided, just what one must expect when choosing a design by holding a vulgar contest, judged by a panel of art critics, of all things, and then, inevitably, awarding the contract to a twenty-year-old Italian student who had never built so much as a doghouse and who believed that he received instructions from a fifty-thousand-year-old being from Atlantis, an alien astronaut who hailed from Proxima Centauri.

Du Mont had protested the whole thing vehemently. The backers of the Enterprise had said that the public would not stand for yet another neoclassical marble confection or an austere, Bauhaus-style box of glass and concrete. For something as cutting edge as a space program, they would want something more modern than the day after tomorrow. Du Mont had pointed out, reasonably, that nothing ages as quickly as the latest fashion. Within ten years, the building would look hideously outdated. He wanted something of a more permanent, dignified nature. Something, for instance, more like Versailles. What he got was the Italian juvenile delinquent's undoubtedly drug-induced hallucination.

He was drawn from his architectural musings by the secretary's announcement that the meeting was called to order. Seventeen men and women drawn from various nations made up the board of directors of the European Space Enterprise. The general atmosphere was somber.

First to speak was Jan Ten Boom, a rotund man who was oversensitive to the smallest setbacks.

"Is it true, Monsieur du Mont, that we are nearly one year behind Lone Star Space Systems in our solar-power satellite program?"

Du Mont replied equably. "Surely you understand that phase one of our program is precisely on schedule. We carry out our procedures with utmost attention and care, methodically. Inevitably, this takes time. Monsieur Carlson of Lone Star, on the contrary, does not follow established procedures. He cuts corners. He may appear to be ahead now, but he is certain to encounter debacles down the road. In fact, he is experiencing them already. His whole operation, especially the Brazilian phase, has been plagued with accidents. That is the weakness of a headlong, one-man operation, in contrast to an experienced team such as ours." Dutchmen, he thought, should stick to what they know: selling diamonds and raising tulips.

"There are rumors of sabotage," said a woman from Poland, a nation du Mont considered to be artificial: a plaything for diplomats and a convenient place to conquer when one was in an aggressive mood.

"An obvious excuse," he said, shrugging. "Bunglers always shout 'Sabotage!' when their own stupidity is manifest. When the Challenger blew up, there were people hoping for evidence of sabotage, or of a missile launched from Cuba, so that NASA's ineptitude would not be exposed."

"Speaking of rumors," said a russet-haired Swede, "there is one going about that Carlson has struck an alliance with the Japanese space consortium. Would the Japanese tolerate the shoddy workmanship that you imply?"

Du Mont maintained his patrician poker face. "Surely this is but an idle rumor. We know the Japanese are not fools, and only fools would even consider teaming up with Carlson's harebrained operation. No, I assure you that our only real American competition is the California-based Space Technologies. Preston Reed is both an engineer and a man of sound business sense. We, however, have a slight edge over his operation. Space Technologies is entirely dependent on the new single-stage space truck, provided by NASA. According to our latest reports, the funding cuts of two years ago are hurting the schedule for completion of the space-truck fleet."

"True to the traditions of NASA," said the Swede, raising a polite laugh from the group.

"Now, I will be first to admit that we have had our funding problems," du Mont said expansively, "but these are nothing to compare with the roller-coaster funding that characterizes America. It seems to please the Americans, but they are an incomprehensible people. Discipline and attention to long-range projects do not, it appears, suit the frontier mentality."

"They suit the Japanese mentality," said the representative from Great Britain, Lady Elspeth Hughes. "Rather notoriously so, in fact."

Du Mont smiled at her benignly. *English aristocracy,* he thought. *An appalling people: tweedy, horse-toothed rustics with squawking voices and no taste in clothes. What other people could have invented a middle-class royal family?*

"The Japanese virtues are those of an ant heap," he said. "They have a rigidly hierarchical, near-military management structure, supported by an army of faceless drones. Their excellent aesthetics fail to make up for a personal style utterly lacking in elan. A strong color sense is no substitute for an adventurous spirit." That he had completely contradicted himself in denigrating America and Japan did not bother du Mont in the least. The point was not, however, lost upon his listeners.

Their deliberations were interrupted by the arrival of servants pushing refreshment carts. The guests were offered a choice of coffee or tea, served in demitasses of eggshell-thin porcelain. On matching plates were slices of exquisite French cake. The silverware was Rosenthal. Du Mont took deep satisfaction in observing such civilized amenities. He could not picture an American or a Japanese or British board of directors ceasing work for beautifully prepared refreshments. *Just the coffee break,* he thought—*instant coffee from a machine, or tea in bags. Disgusting.* When the plates were cleared away and the servants gone, he resumed.

"Even in the unlikely event that Lone Star gets its large-scale power satellite working first, it is virtually certain that it will not have the capital to take advantage of the immense market open to it. It is very doubtful, in fact, that Carlson would even be able to serve half the market that would be guaranteed by the U.S. government."

Du Mont was not at all confident of his predictions, but he spoke with unshakable authority. He did not, of course, tell them that he had no intention of leaving his victory to the uncertainties of ordinary industrial and technological competition. In the non-ideological, Darwinian modern world, the future belonged to the most ruthless. It was time to take off the gloves and acknowledge that this was war. He was prepared to give Kuprin orders for far more drastic action than the sort of petty harassment the man had indulged in until now.

He was forced to admit to himself that he had underestimated Carlson. He had thought that with a bit of trouble here and there, the American could be toppled. He had thought that Carlson had reached his eminence through a combination of blind luck and the collusion of the American intelligence community. He had been wrong. The man had unsuspected resources. Still, these were not without limit, and he would soon break. No mere destruction of a silicon plant would do now.

More than his career and the honor of Europe were at stake. When Sachi left him, she left a void in his life impossible to fill. He had thought her no more than one of a long succession of mistresses, but now he knew that was not so. He must have her back. It seemed that she had the unerring female instinct to attach herself to the most powerful, virile male. What was the term the zoologists used? The alpha male, that was it. Jean-Claude du Mont would destroy Carlson's financial empire and leave him with nothing but debts. Then Sachi would come back. There could be only one alpha male in the space community, and that would be Jean-Claude du Mont. His expression betrayed none of these musings.

"I assure you, my friends," he said, smiling, "that our solar-satellite program is proceeding as scheduled and is all but defect-free."

Karl Ehlers, chief engineer for the space ferry at the French Guinean launch site, felt like tearing out his hair in great handfuls. He said so, loudly.

"What's the matter this time, Chief?" his assistant asked.

"The software that just arrived for the data-display system is useless! Those turkeys have no concept of quality control!"

"Who was it this time?" the assistant asked. "The Portuguese?"

"The Danes. You'd think that Danes at least could come up with reliable software. It was probably Hans Christian Andersen's birthday or something and they took half the day off and were drunk for the rest of it."

He knew he should not be surprised. The space ferry was a European Space Agency program. In practice, that meant that all participating countries demanded a conspicuous role in some aspect of the effort.

Theoretically, all European countries were equal. In reality, some were a good deal more equal than others, especially when it came to technology. Since the major components, such as rocket engines and attitude-control systems, had to be ordered from Europe's leading aerospace companies, the relatively minor items were supplied by the lesser firms.

They might be relatively minor in the mind of a bureaucrat, Karl thought, but there was no such thing as a noncritical component in a spaceship, as the Challenger booster rocket's infamous O-rings had so tragically demonstrated. If only, he thought, everything could be manufactured by experienced outfits like Phillips, Siemens, or Fokker.

"Sometimes I envy the Japanese," he mused, sipping at the day's twentieth cup of coffee. "Imagine, having no country but your own to contend with. It sounds like paradise to me."

"Since we aren't Japanese," his assistant said, "what do we do next?"

Ehlers punched a button on his console. "Guido!" he barked. "Get in touch with Paris. Tell them the software for the DDS is full of bugs and incompatible with the hardware, to boot. We can't possibly keep to the schedule for the first test-launch of the space ferry unless we get new software, viable software, within two weeks."

There was something about country clubs, Preston Reed thought, that brought out the best in American business. His favorite was the Royal Palms in Palm Springs, and he was enjoying its amenities even as the thought ran through his mind. He was seated on its broad, flagstoned patio, enjoying a magnificent sunset, a chilled Coors in one hand.

"Mind if I join you, Preston?" He looked up to see Armand Chilson, CEO of one of California's largest aerospace manufacturers and an important subcontractor in Reed's SolarSat project.

"Delighted to see you, Armand. Pull up a chair." Of course there was no need for Chilson to touch a chair. One was swiftly tucked beneath him by an Hispanic club attendant. There followed a polite exchange of amenities, then the inevitable business talk. In keeping with country-club etiquette, it was not of the deliberate, boardroom variety. Rather, it was of the indirect, offhand sort that was more in keeping with the surroundings. An amazing amount of American business got transacted in this manner, Reed reflected. Industry gossip that would be out of place in the boardroom was easily circulated in the more relaxed venue of the golf course, patio, dining room, and club bar.

"I hear Carlson's caught his tail in a crack," Chilson commented. "Nothing confirmed, of course, but people are getting very concerned about the soundness of his financing."

"So the golden boy is losing a little of his shine, eh? It's to be expected. The contenders that come out of nowhere and rise to the top without paying their dues usually drop just as fast. All style, no substance—you can't last in the business world that way. You need staying power."

Reed knew Chilson was probing at him, trying to learn if he was behind the poisoning of Carlson's money well. In fact, he was. He had precipitated the raid on Carlson's investors and had circulated rumors, through third parties, of his rival's shaky underpinnings. Perhaps not the most ethical undertaking of his career, but nothing illegal, of course.

"I'm sorry to see it, in a way," Chilson admitted. "I'm like everyone else, I have a soft spot for flashy hustlers like Cash."

"Yes, men like Carlson make all our lives a little brighter. But sometimes it takes a catastrophe to improve things. Look at that sunset." He gestured toward the western horizon with his beer. "Beautiful, isn't it?"

"Sure is. I don't know when I saw so many colors." Chilson wondered what his colleague was getting at.

"It comes to us courtesy of three big volcanic eruptions last year: one in Hawaii, one in Alaska, and one in the Philippines. Entire cubic miles of dust blown into the upper atmosphere, and it results in these beautiful sunsets."

"Rough on the people near the volcanoes, though," Chilson said.

"True. But then, that's the way the world works. One man's catastrophe is another man's blessing. That's the way it's going to be when Lone Star crashes. One overmatched contender will be off the scene and the field will be roomier for the rest of us. We can pay more serious attention to our work without distractions like Cash Carlson's magic stunts. It gives people the wrong idea, you know—all this dashing space-cadet stuff, as if colorful adventurers really mattered."

"Can't help it," Chilson said. "Always had a weakness for cowboys. By the way, how's the microwave-receiving station coming along?"

"Right on the money so far, and I don't anticipate any trouble. I'm thinking of going over there tomorrow or the day after for a look-see.

The heat's godawful this time of year, though." Reed's station was located in the Mojave Desert, not far from Palm Springs by helicopter, but it might as well have been on another planet as far as terrain and climate went.

He knew he was a little behind Carlson in spite of all the Texan's problems, but a corporate juggernaut like Reed's took a while to get rolling and build up momentum. Its virtue was that once rolling, it crushed everything in its path.

A few minutes after Chilson went into the clubhouse, Reed's personal aide approached, carrying a portable telephone. He looked just the slightest bit tense. Reed found beepers both annoying and vaguely degrading, as if he were at someone else's beck and call. In consequence, an aide always dogged his steps, even on the golf course. The aide had the duty of answering a beeper.

"I told you I wasn't to be bothered this afternoon short of an emergency," Reed said, annoyed.

"I'm afraid this is an emergency," the aide affirmed.

Reed took the receiver. "Preston Reed here. This better be important."

It was his executive vice president on the other end. "There's been a slipup in the delivery of the microwave transmission system for the power satellite."

"Are you serious? I thought the delivery date was firm."

"So did I. They did everything but swear on the Bible they'd be on time. And that's not the worst of it."

"Oh, hell. What is it?"

"Congress voted on NASA's budget this morning. There's been a big cut in funding. That means another delay in the first space-truck flight."

Reed sighed. "How long?"

"They're saying several months, but time is pretty elastic when it's NASA talking."

"Don't I know it. Listen, Henry, this is an unsecured line, so let's not discuss this further right now. I'm going to scrap the visit to the Mojave site. I'll get back to L.A. as quickly as I can. Can you meet me in my office?"

"I'm at headquarters right now. I've already dispatched a helicopter to Palm Springs to pick you up. It'll deliver you straight to the roof."

"Thanks, Henry. Let's not get all excited about this."

"Right, Preston." There was a click and Reed handed the receiver back to his aide. He sighed. Why couldn't the government ever perform as smoothly and efficiently as his own organization did?

He had leisure to think about it as the helicopter whisked him toward L.A., and he knew he had no reason to be surprised. He had done a great deal of business with NASA and other government agencies, and it was accepted wisdom in the space program that nothing was ever done on schedule or within budget. The larger and more cumbersome the operation, the greater the opportunity for something to go wrong. For the same reason, corrective measures were slower and took a more circuitous route. Just as Reed's Space Technologies was closely tied with NASA, so du Mont's European Space Enterprise was tied in with the European Space Agency. Neither government agency had been accused of excess agility in recent years.

Carlson's Lone Star suffered from none of these bureaucratic handicaps. But then, Reed thought, Carlson had enjoyed a phenomenally long string of good luck. Like a gambler sitting down to a high-stakes game with only enough money for a single hand, he had to win immediately and continuously. The big players could afford to lose hand after hand, secure in their larger bankrolls. Now it looked as if Carlson's legendary luck was finally deserting him, leaving the table to the high rollers.

The possibility of a Japanese bailout of Carlson's operation gave him some pause, but he shrugged it off. All it would mean was that Lone Star would be a cumbersome operation like the others, with many hands on the helm instead of one. It might solve Cash's money problems, but at the cost of saddling him with worse ones.

No, Reed thought, right now everything was going his way. He sat back and enjoyed the spectacle of the lights of Los Angeles, spread out below him in unparalleled splendor.

18

CASH CARLSON WAS a man with a lot of worries, but overcomplexity in his organization wasn't one of them. He saw Lone Star as an organism: a living thing, with him as its brain, controlling its intentions and actions. Lately, the organism had been suffering from starvation and oxygen depletion. The Japanese contribution of financial and industrial backing was like an infusion of healthy new blood, carrying nutrients and oxygen to the body. Cash intended to keep the body lean and mean.

It also opened up options and fallback positions Carlson had lacked before. The Japanese were proceeding with the construction of their equatorial launch site in Indonesia as their primary facility for Japan's geosynchronous orbital satellites. That relieved Cash of one worry: The O Navigador launch facility was vulnerable to Brazil's endemic political instability, as well as to devastation by a once-in-a-century hurricane. The option was equally beneficial to Japan. Indonesia was no model of political stability either, and it was subject to typhoons. Each facility could assume the other's launch schedule if necessary.

Just now, his problems lay with his own staff. It looked to him as if during his recent prolonged bout of globe-hopping, it had gotten out of hand. Parker, in particular, had apparently gone clean off the reservation.

"Adam Altieri?" he said. "That's why Alison couldn't look at me this morning and mumbled until she found an excuse to get away?"

"That's it," Parker said. "Not that it's any fault of hers, but she thinks she let you down."

"Of course she didn't," Carlson said. "You did, Jack. I told you I didn't want any mole-hunt in my organization."

"That's not fair, Boss," Pat protested. "That creep almost got you killed or kidnapped, and he's tied in with what's going on in Brazil."

Parker stood up. "You took me on to keep you safe. I can't even keep you half-assed safe if you order me to lay off an enemy agent because you want to keep your employees one big happy family. I had my differences with the Navy just like you did with the Air Force, but we both know they had one thing right: Morale is important, but security is a hell of a lot more important. You want a security chief who'll keep his hands off a rat like Altieri, you can hire one. I'll resign first."

"Oh, sit down, Jack," Carlson said wearily. "Don't try to blackmail me. I know I can't risk my whole organization over someone like Adam Altieri. What I don't like is you doing this behind my back."

"It was your back needed watching," Parker said.

"This is serious trouble, Boss," Pat said. "Altieri is a nobody but he's tied into what's happening in Brazil, and that's deadly. The fire, the attempted bombings, and the attack on Sachi at Iguazu Falls are all connected. The man running the Brazilian operation has to be neutralized."

"I agree," Bob Thibodeaux said. "You have to give Jack free rein in going after this man and his team. It's no time to be delicate. I can work with the Brazilian authorities, see to it that they look the other way if anything rough goes down. Hell, give me a little money to pass around, we'll have their wholehearted cooperation."

Carlson was uncharacteristically grim and quiet. "I don't like it." He waved a hand for silence before anyone could say anything. "I know, I know. It's unrealistic. I got out of the spook business years ago, thought I'd put it behind me. I figured that if there was one place I could escape all that, it'd be in space. I hoped all the competition would be open, free-market scuffling. I guess I was naive."

"Nobody likes it, Boss," Thibodeaux said. "But it's your call."

"Well, I've wasted too much time already," Carlson said, stone-faced. "No sense wasting more of it now. You win, Jack. Go get 'im. You find the bastard behind all this, bring me his scalp."

Without a word or change of expression, Parker got up and left the room.

"Any more good news?" Carlson asked.

"I've traced the raid on our financing back to its source, Mr. Carlson," Auguste Chamoun reported.

"Preston Reed?" Cash asked.

"Yes. Did you suspect him from the beginning?"

"I did, but I didn't want to prejudice your analysis. It just makes sense. He does business with a lot of the same people we do, and I know his style."

"Do you think he could be involved with the sabotage and all the other dirty work?" Pat asked.

"Uh-uh. That's definitely not his style. Preston Reed probably doesn't know which end of a gun the bullet comes out. Money is his weapon, always has been."

"Mr. Carlson," Chamoun said, "Preston Reed approached some of our most prominent investors and pressured them to withdraw their funding. In some cases, he offered them lucrative contracts for future operations. In others, he threatened to withdraw or cancel contracts already agreed upon between them, although our staunchest friends, like the Talbots, ignored his threat. Besides being flagrantly unethical, much of this is in violation of the restraint-of-trade laws. You must take Reed to court, charge him with lawbreaking and recover damages."

"That'll tie us up for years," Cash said. "And I'll bet Reed covered his tracks well enough that we'd have a hard time proving anything against him. He went after our overseas financing, and you know what the international courts are like. Even if we won, it'd be a distraction from important business. And no matter what the provocation, a company that goes after another in court just looks greedy. I don't want Lone Star to have that reputation."

"I think you are wrong," Chamoun maintained. "This is just like leaving the mole alone for too long. Reed will take this as a sign of weakness and continue his blackmailing tactics."

"I don't think so," Carlson said. "He used up a lot of his influence in this little operation. And he must have offended a lot of people while doing it. I guess he thought it was worth it if he could get rid of a rival like Lone Star. Kind of flattering, in a way. Now I've spiked his guns with this Japanese deal. I'd like to hear what he's saying right now."

Thibodeaux smiled his wolverine smile. "He must be gnashing his teeth. I hope he promised those people a lot more than he can afford to deliver. It could ruin him far quicker than some court decision, even with heavy fines."

"I suspect he's done just that," Carlson affirmed. "He must have predicated everything on the prospect of knocking me out of the SolarSat race."

"Why is he so confident?" Pat asked. "Even with Lone Star out of the picture, there're still the Europeans and Japanese as strong contenders, and half a dozen other shoestring operations that might pull off a coup."

"That's a good question," Cash said, leaning back and lacing his fingers above his belt buckle. "And it has a number of possible answers. For one thing, you don't get into positions like Reed and du Mont—and me, for that matter—without having a hell of an ego. He doesn't like my personal style, and he sees me as his main rival. I don't think the Japanese worry him very much. He knows he's been ahead of them in several crucial areas. As for Europe, I can't really say. It could be that their financial backing isn't vulnerable to his sort of blackmail."

"Or maybe he's already come to an agreement with du Mont," Thibodeaux pointed out.

"That would occur to you," Cash said.

"It's what you pay me for, Boss."

"Do you think it's likely?" Pat asked.

"Let's say it's not unthinkable, but I'm reluctant to give it much credit. Du Mont's too vain to think he needs help from Reed. More likely, Reed expects to coexist with the European operation. After all, it's going to be a long, long time before any of us can hope to meet the whole world's energy needs. No, Reed wants to be the first with the biggest chunk of the market, but he can live with competition from Europe, maybe even from a smaller Japanese operation. He just doesn't want any competition from America. Especially not from me."

"I still think," Chamoun grumbled, "that we should take him to court."

Later, when all except Pat were gone, Carlson sat in his private hideaway brooding. His shoeless feet were propped on a hassock and a frosted glass sat forgotten on the lamp table next to him.

"Why so gloomy, Boss?" Pat asked. "The Japanese bailed us out, the mole's been found and neutralized, and Jack's going to destroy the sabotage operation. You should be dancing."

"I know. It's the whole scene that depresses me. Is it always going to be like this? Always watching my back, worrying about some little rodent in the system selling information to rivals, watching out for saboteurs? My God, Pat, space is the deadliest environment humans have ever worked in. Isn't the natural danger enough? Why do we have to play war out there? This isn't what I wanted!"

She shrugged. "You got me, Boss. We're humans. When we go out into space, we take our baggage with us. I may be your secretary, but I'm still a cop inside. When we go out there, I fully expect to run into the same sleazeballs I used to deal with every day. They may be a little smarter, but they'll be just as bad. It's not going to be Tom Corbett, Space Cadet, up there."

Cash mused for a while. "Now I think of it, the old Tom Corbett books had crooks in them, too."

She made herself a drink and sat down in a chair facing him. "Are you missing Sachi?"

"Yes," he admitted. "I know France is relatively safe, but I still worry. If they send another team, it won't be coked-up Colombians."

"She's got Toby and Thad watching her. She's safe. You just miss having her with you."

"I guess that's true." He looked at her steadily. "Does that bother you?"

She looked back as steadily. "It did at first. I didn't trust her when she showed up, and I was prepared to dislike her. But she convinced me she's the real thing. You're a lucky man."

"I'm glad to hear you say that, Pat."

"Are you going to pop the question anytime soon?"

He frowned. "You're getting a little ahead of yourself, girl."

"No I'm not. You'd better not waste much more time. A woman with as much going for her as Sachi has isn't going to wait around for you very long, any more than I did."

"You lost me there. What are you trying to say?"

"I've been your secretary for a while, Boss, and I've liked the job, but this is going nowhere. I like Sachi, but I don't want to be her secretary, too."

Cash and Pat had become lovers shortly after she came to work at Lone Star several years ago, but they had soon realized that their strong personalities did not mesh too well; neither could follow the other's lead gracefully. With mutual consent, their relationship ceased to be an intimate one, but Pat still cared for Cash's well-being deeply. Conversely, if any evil-doer should manage to do Pat harm, Cash would move heaven and earth to get the perpetrator, although he had successfully concealed his private feelings toward her from everybody, including himself.

Cash pondered Pat's last remark for a while. "I can appreciate your position, and I thank you for your candor. Do you want to resign?"

She shook her head. "We just talked about how we're going to be facing a lot of the same problems in space that we have here. Within the next year, we'll have a fully functional solar-power satellite beaming down power. Within five years, we'll have another eight or more. The population of workers and scientists will be in the thousands soon. You're going to need a police force. I want to be your chief of police."

"I see. You've been giving this some thought. How soon would you want to begin setting up an organization?"

"As soon as Lone Star One is fully functional. The earlier I have a handle on things, the better. That way, I can tackle problems as they come up, before they have a chance to get out of hand. It's easier to do it that way than to try to sort out the situation after the problems are entrenched. Look at O Navigador. That place will be a Wild West boomtown for the next ten years. The organized crooks are already firmly in place and there's hardly any law enforcement."

Carlson nodded. "Well, I hired you people to think for yourselves. You've been a damn good secretary, Pat, and I'll hate to lose you, but I don't want anyone in a job where she thinks she can do better in another one. Chief of police sounds sort of prosaic, though. Sheriff's a county office. Let's make you marshall. I'll have a big silver star made up for you to wear on your vest. Littler ones for your deputies, too."

"Marshall Pat Coogan," she said, savoring the sound of it.

"The law above the Pecos," Cash said. "Let's drink to it." They clinked glasses.

19

SACHI WASN'T LOOKING forward to this. Parker's two security men had checked out the restaurant and the street in front, but enemy action was the last thing on her mind. The confrontation was sure to be unpleasant. Du Mont was far too urbane and civilized to indulge in anything so vulgar as a public scene, but he had subtler ways of hurting her. She knew she had wounded him in his vanity, and he would exact retribution.

The restaurant was small, understated but exclusive, located on the Left Bank. Had she not been so nervous, she would have enjoyed the luxury of dining in a first-class French restaurant for the first time in months. Although he was far from uncultivated, Cash Carlson had little appreciation for the subtleties of fine cuisine, and even less patience with the slow service that was the hallmark of most French restaurants.

Du Mont confined himself to small talk for the course of the meal. He would have considered it a serious breach of etiquette to bring up a weighty subject before the cheese arrived. He spoke of the various space programs of Europe, the U.S., and Japan, never mentioning Lone Star. He dismissed the small ventures slightingly, with a Gallic wave of the hand.

Sachi had insisted on coming to Paris to cover the international meeting on solar satellites. Du Mont had "happened" to encounter her there and had invited her to dinner. She was reluctant, but had seen no convenient excuse to beg off. Besides, she had decided that a final dinner might be a convenient opportunity to end their relationship in a civilized fashion.

She forced a smile when the waiter wheeled to their table a cart bearing a multitude of French cheeses, each as distinct and individual as a human face.

"What was it de Gaulle said about the impossibility of governing a nation that had two hundred varieties of cheese?" she said. The waiter left for a moment, returning with a bottle of vintage Courvoisier, which he poured into two cognac glasses.

Du Mont began to say something, then hesitated and raised his glass for a sip to cover his indecision. It was uncharacteristic of the self-assured du Mont to hesitate. Abruptly, he broached the subject that so agitated him.

"Sachi, Brigitte has agreed to a divorce. She is to have our estate in Brittany, along with a substantial financial portfolio, and she is to keep her title as countess. I shall be free to marry you as soon as our divorce is finalized."

Somehow, she had seen this coming. How like du Mont, she thought, to open by enumerating the disposition of property. And the absurd importance put upon an obsolete title, as if it meant anything in the modern French Republic. She realized that for all his aristocratic posturing, Jean-Claude had the soul of a petit bourgeois. It was a saddening revelation, as was the knowledge that she might have been taken in for far longer without her recent months of close contact with the unpretentious men and women of the Lone Star operation.

She wondered whether she might have accepted the proposal had it been made earlier. Maybe a couple of years ago, but then again, maybe not. Not now, anyway. With rising anger, she realized that he had not even phrased it as a proposal. He had simply informed her that she would be allowed to marry him now. She decided that she needn't be so solicitous of his feelings.

"Was that meant to be a proposal?"

He seemed taken aback. "Why, yes. What else could it be?"

"Then I am afraid that I must decline. I am very appreciative of the honor you do me in asking, but I can't marry you, Jean-Claude."

He was thunderstruck. This was a development he had never foreseen. He would not meet her eyes, but toyed with his cognac glass. When he spoke, his voice was thick with repressed emotion.

"Then it's Carlson? Sachi, how could a woman of your refinement consider seriously a cowboy oaf like Cash Carlson? Has he asked you to marry him?"

"That is none of your business, Jean-Claude!" She could feel her face flaming. "This has nothing to do with Mr. Carlson. I am saying that I do not wish to marry you, nothing more."

Du Mont, back in control of himself, raised an eyebrow contemptuously. "Indeed? I cannot accept that, Sachi. You are an opportunist, and Carlson has flattered you by giving you a supposedly important position within his company. A position that keeps you physically near him. Oh, I do not blame you for trying to make the best of your opportunities, but really, you must not deceive yourself. He wants a mistress, not a partner."

"Speak for yourself! Mr. Carlson is a man of vision, and it is a vision I happen to share. He wants to help create a new world, not to resurrect an old one."

Sachi signaled and the maitre d' appeared as by magic. "Please call me a cab." She rose and addressed du Mont for a final time. "Thank you for dinner, Jean-Claude. You need not call me again." She whirled and stalked out, congratulating herself on her composure. Only when she was outside did she remember that her bodyguards were waiting with a limousine and she didn't need a taxi.

Kuprin had a feeling that this meeting with du Mont would be the crucial one. The man's orders had been growing more extreme and, to Kuprin, more deranged. Mere espionage had expanded to sabotage, to attempted kidnapping, and now what? It meant little to Kuprin. He had done far worse for the KGB. What was important was that he be allowed to carry out his instructions with reasonable safety, and that he was adequately paid. He had upped his price with every escalation of the subterranean war, and so far, du Mont had acceded without argument.

Of course, a bigger operation meant more personnel, with consequent increased risk of betrayal. That part Kuprin did not like. A few of his people had disappeared, and he did not know whether they had fled or been apprehended. If the latter, he was not too greatly apprehensive. The underlings did not know enough of what was going on to truly endanger him, and he was certain that Parker lacked the ruthlessness to wring every last bit of information from a prisoner.

Sergei Kuprin was a man who thought ahead, and he had been giving some thought to du Mont's future plans for him. It was obvious that the Frenchman regarded his current eminence as a mere stepping stone to higher office. Undoubtedly he aspired to the presidency of France, possibly even to that of a united Europe, should the disputatious nations of the continent ever achieve that degree of comity.

In a position of such prestige, it would be disastrous for du Mont to be confronted with these events. It would be profoundly embarrassing for him to admit that he had once fostered activities that were criminal and sordid. It would not take him long to perceive Kuprin as a potential blackmailer. Kuprin had already taken measures to forestall any ambition du Mont might have of eliminating him. But there were other possibilities. He could do worse than attaching himself to a rising European politician. Such men always had need of able, unscrupulous helpers, men who would never be questioned by the press or have to answer to meddling parliaments. Perhaps it would soon be time to have a discussion with M. du Mont about these things. Best not to let him get any unrealistic and dangerous ideas.

Du Mont looked up from his desk with the customary expression of distaste, but this time, there was something else in his eyes. There was genuine anger, and it didn't seem to be directed toward Kuprin.

"We have toyed with this man long enough, Kuprin."

The Georgian eased himself into a chair and lit a cigarette. "I take it that there is to be a further escalation of hostilities?"

"It is time to end the game altogether. I want Carlson dead. And I want one of his rockets destroyed, preferably upon launch, with the world's television cameras covering the event."

Kuprin knocked the ash off his cigarette onto the expensive carpet. Du Mont did not even wince.

"I can foresee, Monsieur, that this is going to be a very expensive operation."

20

KUPRIN STUDIED HIS computer screen, abstractedly reading reports and offers of information coming through on the ever-shifting underground message boards. Personal computers were wonderful things, he thought. They had revolutionized the intelligence business in every way imaginable. Of course, they allowed all sorts of amateurs to enter the business, thereby lowering the value of the old pros' carefully cultivated network of informants, but that was more than offset by the ease with which they allowed one to browse through the world's licit and illicit information services. In any case, the important and high-paying assignments would always be left to experts like himself.

Kuprin knew that the personal computer had hastened the fall of the old Soviet Empire. The East could not hope to compete with a West in which everyone—not just the government and major businesses—had access to computers. But to allow Soviet citizens to have personal computers connected by the information net would break the Party's monopoly on means of information dissemination, one of the most jealously guarded of all Party privileges. In an empire where possession of an unlicensed mimeograph machine could mean years in the Gulag, it was unthinkable.

As always, the appearance of pertinent information on the screen jerked him from his reverie. His month's drop from the Carlson Tower mole was ready to come through via his fax drop, which was connected to another computer. He punched in his access code and recorded the information onto a disk before the data disappeared forever. He transferred the disk to another computer that began decoding it. While that machine performed its task, he returned to his scan of the information net.

Suborning moles in large corporations was so easy that he almost resented the lack of challenge. Such organizations were usually sloppy about protecting important data and kept little or no surveillance upon their employees. There were always people who could be reached through money, sex, or fear of exposure. Getting Carlson's traveling schedule had been laughably easy. Kuprin had evaded Parker's periodic bug sweeps by planting his tap in a nearby telephone relay station. It was not necessary to listen to all the thousands of calls made daily from the Tower, because only a few departments would have access to the schedule. He had chosen the public-relations department as the most promising, and within a few days he'd had three excellent prospects.

One was a young woman who was having a torrid lesbian affair with her aerobics instructor and was terrified that her husband would find out. Another was a man with a taste for very young boys. It always amazed Kuprin what Americans would say right out loud over the telephone. The woman seemed likely to get hysterical, and the man showed signs of suicidal depression, but Adam Altieri was perfect: a weak man with no discernible morals and a long-term addiction that cost him great sums of money. If he had been in the accounting department instead of PR, he undoubtedly would be embezzling. Such people were made to be the tools of men like Kuprin. When he had heard the man placing bets with a bookie over three consecutive days, twice on the third day, and always losing, Kuprin had known he had the mole of his dreams.

The decoder began to eject a printout of the month's schedule. Most of the activities listed were of no use to Kuprin, and much of the schedule was subject to change at short notice. But one item caught his attention. There was to be a launch late in the month. Carlson attended as many launches as he could, and he would make this one because the president of the Brazilian Federal Commission on Space Exploration would be there. A Brazilian electronics engineer would be going up on this flight and there was to be much fanfare from the local press and television.

Immediately, Kuprin began to contact his sources in Brazil. He wanted to know everything that could be found out about this launch. Within a few hours, he knew that this was just the sort of event he needed. The official was not important enough to rate heavy security, such as would have accompanied *O Presidente dos Estados Unidos do Brasil*. The engineer-astronaut was a woman, a good-looking blonde from the southern city of Porto Alegre—a *gaucha*, as Brazilians called women from their southernmost state of Rio Grande do Sul.

Among the journalists granted press credentials for the launch was a Russian. The Russians took pride in the fact that their Energia was playing so prominent a part in the project. If a Russian, why not a Ukrainian as well? Ukraine had been a republic of the old Soviet Union, and its citizens had certainly paid their share of the tax money that had developed and built Energia in the 1980s. Kuprin spoke Ukrainian well enough to pass as a native.

This was a task he could entrust to none of his subordinates. He would take along a trustworthy mercenary type as a photographer. There would be no problem getting forged but authentic-looking credentials as a reporter for the *Kiev Bulletin*. Nor should there be any difficulty in getting on the official list of the minister. His contact in Brasilia, capital city of the Federal Republic in the Middle of Nowhere, could take care of the necessities for a small fee. That was the beauty of working in what was commonly called the third, or developing, world: Officials were for sale so cheap! In the U.S. or Western Europe, they were almost as corrupt but greatly overpriced, wanting astronomical sums for minimal services. The third-worlders had a more realistic concept of their own worth. And it was never necessary to justify anything to them. Kuprin would tell them "Fix it!" and it was fixed. The local expression was *"Dá um jeito."* Brazilians used it whenever they needed something arranged, legally if possible, illegally if necessary.

Kuprin swiftly put the plan together in his mind. It would be quite simple as such things went. The inherent fragility of spacecraft and their great visibility made baroque plots unnecessary. The only problem lay in defeating security systems. After that, the task of execution was routine. The required hardware was available to a man with Kuprin's contacts. Using his computer, he made the necessary arrangements in a matter of minutes.

Then he updated his safety file. It was a precaution he always took. Kuprin charged a high price for his services, in return for which, he gave good value. However, there were always unethical clients who might try to get out of paying him by killing him first. He made sure that should any of them succeed, they would be fully exposed. If du Mont should have Kuprin killed, then the full story of their dealings would be all over the world press the next day. That was another advantage of the computer. Of course, it also meant that should Kuprin happen to be killed during an operation, his employer would be exposed. That didn't bother him a bit.

*   *   *

The day was a hot one. They were all hot days at sea level on the equator, regardless of the season. Not that it made much sense to speak of seasons when the sun did no more than swing twenty-three and a half degrees to either side of the celestial equator, which was straight overhead, in the course of a year. Sometimes the sea breeze helped a little, but not much.

Parker detested the muggy climate. He was raised in the arid Southwest, and it seemed that he had spent an inordinate amount of his life in torrid, humid parts of the world: Southeast Asia, Central Africa, Central America. Why, he wondered, did so much of the world's trouble erupt in such disagreeable places? Maybe the heat and bugs drove people to extreme behavior. North Africa and the Middle East were hot, but he found them far more congenial. Or maybe it was just that the developed nations in the temperate zones fought big, conventional wars and didn't have much use for men like Jack Parker, putative great-grandson of Quanah Parker, Comanche chief.

"I think this dude's about ready to talk, Jack." The speaker who shook Parker from his brief reverie was Clyde Garrison, an old member of Parker's team who was assigned to full-time O Navigador security.

"About time," Parker answered. They were at the Estancia, an old ranch house about fifteen miles from the city. Carlson had bought it as a likely Brazilian home but had yet to move in. Parker had commandeered it and altered it to suit his purposes. Built in the early nineteenth century, it boasted a vast wine cellar that Parker had remodeled into a "dungeon." A century of neglect had given it the requisite damp-walled seediness, and Parker had added several cramped cells, complete with rusty bars. Even though the dungeon held only a single prisoner at the moment, it seemed to be crowded. That was because realistic recordings of groans and screams played night and day.

The man in the only occupied cell had been caught in the space center's fuel depot carrying a satchel of explosives and incendiaries. The charges had been quite sufficient to send the whole place up in a single gigantic fireball. Besides the damage to the program, the loss of life would have been in the scores, at the most conservative estimate. Parker felt no real inclination to be easy on him.

From O Navigador, they had taken him, blindfolded much of the time, on a circuitous route by helicopter and Jeep, ending up just a few miles from where they had started. The prisoner believed that he was somewhere deep within the fastnesses of the Amazonian jungle. There was something about isolation in the wilderness that made confinement even more unnerving than usual.

Over the months since commencing operations in Brazil, Parker had been careful to establish a reputation for himself in the local underworld. Carlson's Comanche madman, it was said, killed enemies without compunction. That much was common in the semi-lawless Brazilian frontier communities, but there was much more. He reveled in torture. He scalped his prisoners, and employed a dull knife for the purpose. His secret lair in the Amazonian jungle was full of suffering wretches who had fallen afoul of him, many of them mutilated beyond recognition.

And there could be no escape for them, because Parker was blood brother to all the tribes of wild Indios who infested the jungle, blowguns at the ready to bring down anyone foolish enough to attempt flight.

Parker had constructed this myth with great care. He wasn't above getting rough with a prisoner when he needed information badly and had no time to waste, but he had no use for torture. Above all, his long training in covert military operations had taught him that the most effective torture instrument of all was a man's own mind. Set up the circumstances with enough care, then leave him alone with nothing but his own thoughts and fears. Most would break in time. As a rule, only those with very strong ideological or religious convictions could resist such treatment. Hired thugs generally lacked such advantages, although one who had spent extended stretches in brutal prisons might hold out for a surprisingly long time.

The man in custody, one Martin Parra, was no such hardcase. He was a Mexican national with a history of petty crime dating from his childhood in Juarez. He had been arrested on numerous occasions on both sides of the border, but had done no serious time. He had escaped arrest yet another time by signing up for a crew that was being recruited in Mexico for the construction work at the space facility. Upon arrival in O Navigador, he had disappeared into the shantytown and never reported for a day's work.

The two men clumped down the iron-tread stairs Parker had installed in place of the old stone steps. Their boot heels rang on the metal—an ominous sound to anyone waiting below. At the bottom, they crossed the few steps to the door, and Garrison's big key rattled loudly in the old-fashioned lock. The massive door creaked open on pre-rusted hinges.

Inside, Parra sat disconsolately on an iron-pipe bunk, hands hanging limply between his knees. His sweaty face, numb with apprehension, turned toward them as they entered. Overhead, a single fluorescent tube flickered maddeningly behind a shield of unbreakable Plexiglas.

"Want to talk to us, Martin?" Parker asked in border Spanish, a language he had grown up speaking as fluently as English.

"What you goin' to do to me, man?" Parra hedged.

"Maybe a lot. Maybe nothing. Depends on what you say."

"You can't fool me, man. I know you gonna kill me anyway."

"You don't know that, Martin. See, you know something I need to know, and it's just a matter of how much I have to put you through to get you to tell me."

"I got caught with the explosives. I don't believe you gonna let me live after that."

Parker sat down on the bunk beside him, putting an arm around the man's cringing shoulders. "You got it all wrong, Martin. You know I work for Señor Carlson. He's a great man, does business on five continents, is friends with kings and presidents. You think he cares if a man like you lives or dies? Hell, he don't even know you exist. I told him we caught a guy in the fuel dump with explosives, he says find out who the guy works for. Simple as that. He don't care if you die or I turn you loose afterward. What he wants, and what I want, is whoever's running you. Give me that and you can walk out of here."

"Into that jungle? With all those Indios and jaguars? They're cannibals! They don't even bury you like a Christian."

Parker shrugged. "Some have made it out alive. You don't tell us, you don't go anyplace, except to a little room down the hall where we keep our equipment. I guess you've heard the guys we've taken in there the last couple of days."

Parra turned even paler. "All right! I'll take my chances with the jungle. Now, see, I don't know the boss of this operation, just the people he—"

"Easy, Martin, take it slow." Parker patted him on the shoulder. "There's no rush now. Just tell us everything, starting from the beginning, and you'll walk out of here alive. We'll even throw in a canteen of water and a few days' food to get you back to civilization." He nodded to Garrison, who turned on a recorder. At first shakily, then with growing confidence as he began to hope he might really live through this, Martin Parra began to tell his story.

The plane from Mexico had delivered him to the O Navigador airport, next to the space facility, and a bus had taken him and fifty other contract laborers to a warehouselike barracks near the Mexican barrio. The new workers had been given a meal and an orientation lecture. Most had listened attentively, elated at the prospect of good wages after workless years in depressed Mexico. Martin Parra was already planning his way out. He had never worked except on jailhouse chain gangs and didn't propose to start now. After the talk, he had been assigned a bunk like the others. They were to start work on the new landing strip the next day. Parra slipped out while the others snored.

The sounds of loud, familiar music and Mexican Spanish led him to the neon-lit heart of the barrio, a district that never closed. He had no money, but that was no problem. The boomtown was full of drunks with money in their pockets, and Parra was an old hand at rolling drunks. Within an hour, he had enough to enter the cantinas, drink and participate in card games and pool. He quickly made contact with men of his own temperament and acquired a cot in a shack in the shantytown between the city and the space facility. It held a shifting population of five to ten drifters who did no work but who usually found ways to get money. Except for the shortage of women, it was like heaven to Martin Parra. Lots of money floating around and virtually no law enforcement.

He soon learned that there were drawbacks to his new life. Even a drunk might draw a knife, and many men were packing guns to protect their bankrolls. Within his first two months, Parra saw a dozen fatal shootings and stabbings, and men sometimes returned to the shack groaning, badly cut or shot up. Martin began to look for something safer.

With three other men, he formed an organized gang. Armed with guns, they would go out at night to one of the other parts of town and rob small businesses or break into houses. They were so successful that they rented a three-room apartment above a cantina called *La Cucaracha*. This lasted for a month, then the sort of people they victimized took to pooling their money and hiring security guards, men who believed deeply in drastic measures. In one week, three gangs like Parra's were found in public parks, their hands bound behind them and bullet holes in the back of their skulls.

The little gang began to plot something different and even more remunerative—perhaps a bank or payroll robbery. After all, if you were going to get killed, it might as well be for a big score as for the sort of penny-ante capers they were involved in. At this desperate moment, a man had come to their table in the cantina and said he was looking for men of great courage and few scruples, men who didn't mind a little risk in return for much money. Parra had seen the man around the barrio from time to time. He wore flashy silk suits and much jewelry. His name was Santos, a big shot in the Brazilian underworld. He was rumored to be Colombian, but Parra could not say for sure as he had not yet learned to distinguish among the many Spanish dialects and accents spoken in that part of the world.

This man had told them that he recruited for a very special gang, and to belong to it, a man had to have very big *cojones* indeed. The pay was high and the work involved sabotage against Lone Star. He wanted only the best men because it meant running up against not only the port security, which was tough, but from time to time, the Indio *Norteamericano,* Parker. The name had given him pause, but Parra had imbibed enough tequila to proclaim that he, for one, feared no scruffy Texas Comanche. The Comanches were a contemptible people who had allowed themselves to be beaten by mere gringos. Hesitantly, the others had agreed with him.

They were taken to a house in the shantytown. Outwardly, it was a shack like all the others, a rickety structure of tarpaper and sheet metal made from flattened beer cans. On the inside, it was well-constructed, had five good-sized rooms and was furnished with electricity, running water, and a telephone line. There was even a television set. Parra had realized that what appeared from outside to be five or six shacks built against each other was this one house.

They were shown the room where the weapons were kept—modern arms that looked unused, with plenty of ammunition. There were stacks of explosives and sophisticated timing devices. Parra was very impressed. Back home, he could never hope to join a gang as important as this one. Mr. Santos had told them that having seen all this, there was no backing out. Except when preparing for jobs, they could come and go as they pleased, but there was to be no loose talk in the bars. They assured him that they were firm in their resolution to be faithful members of his gang.

For three days, they lazed about the new house, getting acquainted with the others there. There turned out to be about six regulars, all of them men, all Spanish-speaking. In the mornings, when they were sober, they were given instruction in the planting of explosives and the use of the timers. Parra, who had never used a weapon more sophisticated than a revolver, learned to dismantle and reassemble a fine Austrian submachine gun.

On the fourth day, they were told to be sure to come in early that evening. There was to be a foray against Lone Star that night. Parra was there, but two of the *La Cucaracha* gang who had joined with him did not show up. Mr. Santos told them not to worry, this was a shaking-out mission, to see who had the *cojones*. They were to ambush a truck convoy bringing supplies from the south.

The ambush was exciting and enjoyable. Spraying bullets from the submachine gun gave Parra a great sense of power. It was to look like the work of bandits, so they were allowed to loot the trucks and rifle the bodies for valuables. Back at their safe house, they were highly praised.

The next morning, Parra's erstwhile friends were found on the beach with their throats cut. Mr. Santos was a very, very serious man.

Parra enjoyed the life of the gang. He pulled a number of jobs, one of which was the arson against the silicate plant. The gang's only link with those higher up was Mr. Santos. There was rumored to be a "bad Russian" in charge, but they had never seen him. It was agreed that this Russian must be employed at the space facility, because they always had the schedules and keys they needed to get in and out safely. Sometimes someone would be caught and killed on a job, but that was what they were being paid for. In the meantime, the accommodations were comfortable: The kitchen was always well stocked with food and beer, there was television with a satellite antenna, and the whole town lay open to prowl in when there was no job being planned.

Then had come the assignment to destroy the fuel dump and Parra had been apprehended. Security measures had been stepped up and he had been caught in the convergence of half a dozen searchlights, and everywhere he had dodged, he was bracketed with machine-gun fire. He laid down his gun and satchel of explosives and raised his hands. Minutes later, he was on his way here.

"You're doing fine so far, Martin," Parker said. "How many people did you say you killed?"

Parra shook his head vigorously. "By God, Mr. Parker, I swear I have killed no one! I fired the gun a lot because that was fun, but I did not try to hit anyone. I left that to the others. I am not a vicious man."

"I can see that, Parra. But a lot of people would have died if you'd blown up the fuel dump."

"Oh, no! No!" Parra was sweating heavily. "I was assured that a call would be made, like the *terroristas* do, so that everyone would have plenty of time to get clear. I would never have done it otherwise, I swear!"

"I know, Martin. You're a saint." Parker got up.

"So you will let me go now?" The man was trying to whine and smile at the same time, producing an almost demented expression.

"Not just yet," Parker answered. "First I have to find out if you've told me the truth."

"But, Mr. Parker, suppose in finding out, you get killed? Forgive me, but there is that possibility."

Parker looked around at the cell. "I don't know, Martin. You might get to like it here. They say you can get used to hanging, if you hang long enough." He turned to Garrison. "Let's lock up and go." They ignored Parra's pleading cries as they went back up the stairs.

"That one's a real sweetheart," Garrison said when they were outside. His Spanish was adequate to understand what Parra had said. "What're we gonna do with him? You can't just turn an animal like that loose."

"Can't just shoot him, either. The boss wouldn't like it. If we give him to the local police, he'll probably be working for them inside a week. They'll recognize a kindred spirit." Parker's opinion of the local authorities was even lower than the opinion he held for the Secret Service. "Maybe we ought to just chopper him to the Mato Grosso and set him on foot. That's all he expects anyway."

"Or," Garrison said, grinning, "we could turn him loose right here. First we plaster his picture and history all over O Navigador and the nearby towns. We could take bets on how long he'll last."

Parker smiled. "I like the way your mind works, Clyde. We'll do that. Give him a little money and drop him off in the town square. That's lenient enough to suit the boss. Assuming," he amended, "that he's told the truth and it's of use to us. If he's lied, we'll have to think up something really mean."

The two men piled into a Jeep and headed for the launch facility. Parker sent Garrison to round up a raiding party. "Keep them ready to go at a second's notice. While you're doing that, notify all our contact people in the barrios. I want to know the minute this bastard Santos shows his face. He ought to be easy to spot."

"Check. Where'll you be?"

"Over at Personnel headquarters. I've got a 'bad Russian' to catch." He could raid the hideout immediately, but he was more interested in capturing Santos than in wiping out a single nest of saboteurs. The man he was after probably had several such cells. Maybe Santos would know where all of them were. More important, Santos probably knew who was running the entire operation.

He stopped in front of the office that housed the Personnel section and flashed his ID to a woman who sat behind a big desk. She was a Brazilian beauty he might have taken the time to cultivate, if he had had any time to spare.

"Parker, chief of security. I need to see all your personnel files."

"I have no authorization to release such information—"

"Yes you have." he interrupted. "Check your SOP. I have priority access to whatever is in your files."

She tapped the proper code into her desk set. "It seems that you have. Is there some sort of trouble?"

"You might say that."

She got up. "Then if you will follow me." Despite the urgency of his mission, he found her very easy to follow. A true daughter of Rio, she clicked along on four-inch heels, even on the job. Two computer operators looked up as they entered a tiny, atmosphere-controlled room. The local climate was not kind to computers.

"Send them out," Parker said.

She spoke a few words and the technicians left. "Now what?"

"Find me all the Russians," he said.

The problem was not an easy one. For one thing, there were more than a hundred Russian technicians and scientists at the facility, specialists in handling the Energia. But worse, the "Russian" was little more than a rumor. Parra claimed he had never seen him, and who knew about the others? To uneducated Mexicans, any Eastern European might seem like some sort of Russian. Just selecting Slavic names added another hundred to the list. Parker knew that in time he could narrow the list considerably by finding out who had access to the information necessary to set up the jobs being carried out by Parra's cell. But time was something he had little of.

Where was Max when you needed him? Parker fumed. If only the little nerd wasn't so terrified of traveling. He'd find the bastard in about fifteen seconds. He wondered if Max could tap directly into these computers from his Warren in Houston. His communicator buzzed.

"Parker here."

"We're ready, Chief. And Santos was seen in town this afternoon."

"Damn!" Parker said, uncharacteristically animated. "It's about time we had some luck. I'll be right there." He turned to the woman from Personnel. "Find this guy for me, honey. I'll buy you the biggest lobster dinner in O Navigador."

She looked him up and down, her eyes bright. "Okay. I'll hold you to that."

He dashed out of the building and into his Jeep. Grinding gears, he roared to Security headquarters, leaving a crowd of staring workers behind him. Somehow, he reminded them of old movies of painted warriors on horseback.

Garrison was waiting at headquarters with eight other men. All of them wore the long "raincoats" that had replaced the old, bulky, bulletproof vests. They carried a variety of weaponry: submachine guns, shotguns, and a couple of scoped sniper rifles. They all carried pistols and grenades as well.

"We don't want 'em to know we're coming," Parker said as he dismounted from the Jeep.

"They won't," Garrison said. "Here comes our transportation." As he spoke, a bus bearing the Lone Star logo pulled up beside them. It was one of the regular shuttles used for taking workers back and forth between the town and the space facility.

"Good thinking," Parker said. "You show 'em the map?"

"They know where we're going," Garrison said. They had made a sketch map from Parra's description of the hideout.

"Listen up, everybody. You know what that shantytown's like. Everything's one-story and the windows are just holes in the walls, so you can forget about the sniper rifles. Turn them in for shotguns or SMGs. No grenades, either. We know they have explosives in there, and we don't know how much. There could be enough to blow up the whole neighborhood. It's a rabbit warren with a hundred ways in and out—it'll be no use blocking off any streets."

He looked them over, his eyes invisible behind his wraparound shades. "So it's going to be real simple. We kick the front door in and we go in shooting. Anyone makes a move for a weapon, shoot him. Anyone tries to run, shoot him. Hold your fire only for raised hands and then don't take any chances. We don't owe these people any favors. There's only one I really want to see alive. He'll be wearing a flashy silk suit and a lot of jewelry. If you have to shoot him, make it in someplace that won't prevent him talking for a while."

He broke them down into teams. The two burliest he assigned to the ram; a massive iron bar with handles, capable of smashing through most doors by sheer inertia. Two others he assigned as outside security. They would catch anyone who tried to escape and prevent reinforcements from arriving. The rest would storm inside.

"Ready? Then let's go." They piled into the bus in reverse order, with those to come out first getting in last. Garrison replaced the driver. For the first time, Parker was glad that the shantytown started just outside the facility's gates. It was getting late and he wanted to get this over with before dark.

"We've been pretty damn visible," Garrison fretted. "I hope they don't have any spies here that can tip them off we're coming."

"We didn't have time to be discreet," Parker said, setting his heavy machine pistol for single-shot fire. It was going to be too crowded in there to be spraying lead indiscriminately. Precision was called for in such situations. "We'll just have to be quick."

They attracted little attention in the shantytown. The bus was a familiar sight. A few workmen held out a hand for a ride, and cursed when they were ignored. The men inside were tense, sweating in their heavy protective coats.

"Getting close," Garrison said.

"Maneuver us so our door's right opposite theirs," Parker directed. "I don't want to have to run around the bus."

"I know how this is done, Chief," Garrison said. He made a turn, then two others so that the doors would be properly aligned when they stopped. He put on a final burst of speed, then ground to a halt. Seconds before the bus stopped, he yanked the lever that opened the folding doors.

"Go! Go! Go!" Parker shouted. The two rammers leaped off the bus and took a half-dozen short strides, swinging the massive ram between them. It hit the door and sent it hurtling inward amid a great crash and a cloud of flying splinters. All up and down the street, people yelled delightedly to see this novel spectacle.

Parker was close behind the rammers. The instant the door was down, he leaped between them and over the ram, clearing the splintered wood. Faces turned toward him, blank with utter surprise.

"Everybody down, on your faces!" he yelled in Spanish.

Somebody raised a gun and Parker shot him. Then all hell broke loose. Nobody, it seemed, trusted an order to surrender. Everyone who didn't already have a gun was diving for one. Parker took out two more while the men who crowded in after him shot at others. Some of the gang members were getting off return shots, spraying bullets heedlessly on full automatic.

Fire was coming from a room opening off to the left, and Parker stormed it while Garrison led a team into another room on the right. Two men fired pistols while another raised a heavy assault rifle. Parker shot the rifleman first, then one of the others, while a man behind him took out the third with a shotgun. In the confined space, the noise was deafening.

A flash of yellow caught Parker's eye. He dashed into another room and saw a man in a gaudy yellow suit wrestling with a light machine gun, slamming the cover shut over a belt of shiny brass cartridges, raising it with his finger on the trigger. Parker shot him in both legs and he fell back, dropping the gun. As he slammed into the wall, his right hand flashed beneath his coat and came out with an automatic pistol. Parker shot him in the right shoulder and arm. The pistol dropped to the floor and so did the man.

There was a sudden silence. Parker stepped over to the yellow-suited man, who sprawled amid a disarray of bloodstained yellow silk, gold chains, and diamond rings. He leveled his machine pistol at the man's head.

"Pleased to meet you, Mr. Santos. Now tell me who your boss is."

Santos snarled something and his left hand came up, silver winking from between thumb and forefinger. Without hesitation, Parker shot him through the forehead. Men crowded behind Parker.

"All secure, Chief," Garrison reported. "We didn't have any takers for our amnesty offer. Three of our guys are nicked, not badly." He caught sight of the yellow-suited figure crumpled on the floor. "Aw, hell! This is the one we wanted alive."

"No help for it," Parker said. "I had to waste him myself." With the toe of his boot, he nudged Santos's left hand. It opened, and a tiny chrome-plated, two-shot derringer slipped out.

"Damn!" Parker said, shaking his head in wonder. "Shot to hell, all the firepower in the world staring him in the face, and he tried to take me out with that popgun. This guy definitely knew what *cojones* are all about."

"Okay, guys," Garrison said. "Let's search this place, see if we can learn anything." They began to shuffle slowly among the rooms, lifting some things, opening others, making a thorough job of it. A haze of thin, acrid smoke hung in the air. Blood and expended cartridge cases made the footing treacherous.

"Holy shit," one man said. "Good thing we didn't use any grenades. Look at this." In a corner of the armaments room were stacked several cases of plastic explosive. Parker examined the boxes of timers and other demolitions gear. They were lettered with numerous alphabets.

"All good stuff," Garrison said. "I see at least six countries of origin."

"A pro," Parker grunted. "But we knew that. He's got contacts on the international arms market."

"This must've been their operations table," said one of the team. Parker went over to look. The table was spread with maps of the space facility and the roads used for its supply. There were books containing timetables and other data. On one corner was a large ring of brass keys. Parker picked it up and examined them. There were dozens of them, shiny and new-made from identical blanks.

"Keys!" Parker said, clutching the ring tightly. "These bastards always had keys!"

"What's that, Chief?" Garrison asked.

"You guys gather up all this stuff, bring it to headquarters. I'm going there now myself. I'll send the bus back for you."

"What about all these stiffs?" Garrison asked.

Parker shrugged. "Let the dogs have 'em. I've got a bad Russian to catch."

He climbed into the bus and began to bull his way through the crowd that had gathered at the sound of gunfire. He cursed and slammed his palm against the horn, but the crowd parted only slowly and reluctantly. He knew that every minute counted. In a place like this, news flew around faster than fiber optics could transmit it.

At last he was clear of the crowd and could put on speed. He flashed his ID at the guard on the gate and drove up to the Security building. The bus driver stood in the same spot where he had been left no more than half an hour before. Parker told him where to take the bus and then jumped into his Jeep. With people scattering in front of him like chickens, he tore over to the Personnel center, screeched to a dusty halt, and ran into the building.

To his relief, the woman was still sifting through the files, looking for the Russian.

"Forget all that!" Parker told her. "Pull up the Maintenance personnel."

"You learned something?" she asked, fingers dancing across the keys.

"Our saboteurs had shiny new keys for every lock in the facility," he told her. "Only Security and Maintenance have all those keys, and the kingpin's sure as hell not one of my guys."

"Let me see, there are a lot of names, but your man would probably be in a supervisory position, right?"

"I think so. We're looking for a Russian or anyone from the old Union, maybe from the Balkans or Eastern Europe."

"That is a great deal of geography." She leaned forward as the files flickered past. Probably too vain to wear glasses, Parker thought. "Just a moment. There is a Russian: Ivan Stepanovich Chaliapin, overseer of maintenance, night shift."

Parker's fingertips tingled. "Did he come in with the Russian rocket technicians?"

"No. He was sent here with a recommendation from the Department of Labor of the United States of Brazil. It is part of the agreement between Lone Star and my country that a certain proportion of the personnel must come through our Department of Labor."

"Even if they're not Brazilian nationals?"

"I suspect it was assumed that they would be." She sat back in her swivel chair, hesitating. "I think I must tell you that the Department of Labor is very susceptible to bribery. We have had to fire a number of incompetent or dishonest people who purchased their recommendations from that department."

"Time to pay a call at Maintenance," Parker said, grinning.

"Do I still get the lobster dinner?"

"Soon as I have an evening free!" Parker told her as he ran out the door.

Five minutes later, he pulled up in front of the Maintenance building, a hangarlike structure of corrugated steel. It was fully dark now, the tropical stars bright overhead. Whistling, he slid the depleted magazine from the butt of his machine pistol and inserted a full one. In his urgent rush, he had neglected to reload, for the first time in years. He got out of the Jeep and went into the building.

The main floor was covered with equipment and forklifts for moving it about. On the second-story level, offices opened off a catwalk. Parker beckoned to a workman, who stared wide-eyed at the weapon dangling from his grip.

"Where's the shift overseer's office?" Wordlessly, the man pointed to a doorway on the catwalk through which light streamed. Parker went quietly up the iron steps and along the catwalk, which creaked faintly beneath him. As he neared the door, he heard music coming from the office. He couldn't place the style, but it sounded vaguely Brazilian.

Inside, a man sat with his back to the doorway, a plastic hard hat perched atop his coarse-haired head. He shuffled some papers as the radio blared in his ear. This was so easy it was almost disappointing.

"Turn around!" Parker barked in English. The man whirled in his swivel chair and his eyes widened at the muzzle leveled at his coffee-and-cream-colored face. He was of that Indian African-Portuguese mixture of races so common in Brazil.

"I was looking for the Russian," Parker said, bitterly disappointed.

"Myself, I would like to see him, too!" the man said in heavily accented English. "More than thirty minutes ago, he supposed to relieve me!"

Parker lowered the gun. He could wait here, but he knew it would be futile. The bastard had gotten word of the raid and skinned out. It would be no use to hang around and go through his desk or question the staff. He would send somebody to take care of it for his wrap-up report, but he knew he wouldn't learn anything here. The man was a pro and this job was his cover. He would have done nothing to jeopardize it.

"I guess you're in for a double shift, buddy," Parker said, reholstering the machine pistol beneath his arm. "Don't forget to put in for your overtime." He turned and walked away, dejected. Another damn dead end.

21

YOU LOOK TIRED," Sachi said. Actually, Carlson looked worse than tired. He looked haggard. He had lost weight in recent months, and the lines had deepened in his face. There were dark circles beneath his eyes. The effect was not entirely unbecoming in a man with a cowboy reputation, but she was accustomed to his boyish ebullience, a manner that shaved ten years off his age.

"It's been a bad time," he said. "Too bad it can't always be barbecues and visits to Lone Star." He smiled ruefully into his margarita glass and turned to her. Through the picture window, Manhattan put on its dazzling display below them. "I guess you weren't expecting this when you signed on: corporate intrigue, kidnappers, assassins, sabotage . . ." He paused, unsure of how to go on. "I'm just trying to say I'm sorry. I thought I was letting you in on the big adventure, and I made you a target."

Her eyes went wide. "You mean that has been bothering you?" She tried to say something, but erupted into girlish giggling instead. Carlson's expression was so puzzled that it sent her off into further peals.

"What's so funny? This is a serious situation."

"Of course it's serious! This may be the biggest, most important venture in history. Certainly it is the greatest of my generation. I never expected it to be easy or without danger."

"Yes, but—"

"But nothing." She crossed the room, set her wineglass on a table, took his glass and set it beside hers, then took both of his hands in hers. "Cash, all my life I have searched for something important, and I did nothing to amount to anything."

"The hell you—" She placed her fingertips across his lips, silencing him.

"No, let me finish. Yes, I know I had a lot going for me. I'm not modest about my looks. I have never been some simpering coquette. By the time I was fifteen, I knew what I was going to look like as a grown woman. When I was seventeen, I had every opportunity to become a model. I took part in international aikido events in America and Australia and Europe and I always got swamped by photographers. Pretty soon the offers came in from the modeling agencies, the big ones.

"Well, I gave it a try. I did a bit of modeling to earn extra money while I was in school. But I was repelled by the triviality, the sheer superficiality, of the fashion world. Believe me, I am losing nothing by giving that up. I majored in science with a minor in journalism because I knew what really *is* important. I even specialized in closed-system ecologies because I thought that by the time I had my Ph.D., there would be a demand for that specialty in space settlements or on the moon.

"As you see, I was young and enthusiastic. But the worldwide interest in aerospace was not up to my ambitions. Do you understand what I am saying, Cash? I am a serious person."

She paused momentarily before continuing, as if to collect her thoughts.

"Jean-Claude knew how to flatter me, and I was all too ready to be flattered. I couldn't see then how he was patronizing me, how he played on my weaknesses. That was his real sophistication, the kind I was too young and inexperienced to recognize. He saw to it that I received final polish in continental upper-class manners, that I met the best designers and the right photographers . . . he was molding me into the perfect ornament. He only tolerated my silly enthusiasms. That is all they were to him. To him, the space program was his ladder to power but he saw it as only a hobby to me.

"He seduced me, but I won't be a hypocrite and claim that I put up much of a fight. I was eager to be seduced. But I never saw myself as his mistress. Of course, he always hinted that he was about to divorce his wife—not that I ever asked or expected him to. There was no love between them, but there were children, and at least she was his social equal, as he saw such things. Actually, she was well above him socially—some sort of countess—but he would never admit it, not even to himself." She turned and faced Carlson.

"I was young, I was naive, but I have never been stupid. In time, the dazzle faded. I saw that he was not the man of the future. If anything, Jean-Claude is a man of the past. He wants a resurgent Europe, and he wants it dominated by France. He wants to have the late nineteenth century back, the Belle Epoque. That could be dismissed as a childish fantasy, even tolerated. But the clincher for me was that he had no core belief in anything that really mattered."

"You've proven that," he admitted.

"Then you should understand that I don't expect any of this to be easy, or even safe. And if you think your world of big business is full of politics and intrigue and treachery, you should try the world of haute couture for a while. It doesn't often resort to murder, but it's just as nasty as if it did."

"You have a point."

"Anyway, having determined what the great work of this century was going to be, I made one big mistake. I thought that the man who was going to lead the way would be Jean-Claude du Mont."

"Sachi, I know all about du Mont. You don't need to do this."

"Yes I do. I suppose my history has been a mixture of intellect and hormones. I was always drawn to powerful, ambitious, dynamic men. But I despised the women, and the men too, who spend their lives in the shadow of politicians and the wealthy, the sycophants, the followers, the—what is the word I always hear?—the groupies! I didn't want to be like them. I wanted to be a partner in the work, not a hanger-on.

"When I was twenty-four and recovering from the breakup of my first serious affair, I interviewed Jean-Claude for *Paris Match*. He was a recognized leader in the space program. I thought he was the man of the future. He was brilliant—poised and sophisticated in a way that dazzled me." She released his hands and turned to look out the window. With her forehead against the window glass, her breath lightly fogged the pane.

"And he wasn't about to divorce his countess, was he?" Cash asked gently.

Her laugh was brittle. "Oh, but he finally decided to. He proposed just a short time ago, on my last trip to France. It was a masterpiece of conceit. Apparently it never occurred to him that marriage—to him— would not be all I could ever want from life. I was forced to be blunt. I turned him down, period."

Cash moved to put his arm around her, but she pulled away.

"No, not yet. You must hear all of it. Pat was right, you know. She was right to be suspicious of me when I first showed up here. I hadn't yet made up my mind about Jean-Claude, and I was looking for new opportunities."

"How did you settle on me, then? You had plenty of opportunities. Or have you settled on me?"

"Guess."

"Because I invited you to a barbecue."

At last she smiled. "Exactly. I always wanted to go to a real one."

Carlson picked up his glass and sipped. "Do you think I wasn't evaluating you?"

"Oh, I knew you were. That was part of the game. But then something happened that I didn't anticipate. That first night at *Las Estrellas*, I expected that you would want me to go to bed with you. I might even have acceded, because I was attracted to you and because that is how the game is played. But instead, you did something I did not expect at all—you offered me a job."

He grinned. "I caught hell from my staff for doing it, too. But you won them over. See, Sachi, I'm no spring chicken myself. I used to have a reputation as a ladies' man. I made a fool of myself over more women than I care to remember. But even a fool can wise up if he gets kicked in the teeth enough times. I saw from the start that you were something special, but I had to know more about you. I couldn't move fast when I was in the middle of the most important project of my lifetime."

He put his glass back on the table and took her in his arms. This time, she did not pull back. "Du Mont's the past, Sachi, put him behind you. I think we've learned enough about each other to make a grown-up decision. What do you say?"

She raised her face to his. "Well, as long as you are not too tired." They did not speak again for a long time.

One wall of the bedroom was a huge plate of glass overlooking Manhattan. In the distance winked the lights atop the World Trade Center. Sachi sat up in the bed, contemplating the view. Carlson lay back, contemplating her.

"You know, Cash, just a little while ago, I figured out something important. Once I thought that you accomplished the things you have by your enthusiasm, your cleverness, your skill at bargaining and all those business matters. But that isn't it, is it?"

"Nope," he answered. "Those things will get you where Preston Reed is, maybe where du Mont is, too. It's all right if what you are is a businessman, with a big ego to satisfy. But that's not me. By now, you know I'm really not much of a businessman and that I'm a poor schemer. I'm just a man who wants to build spaceships." He sat up beside her, putting an arm around her shoulders.

"When I got out of the service and began putting together my own outfit, I remembered something my father and grandfather taught me when I was very young: If you want to accomplish something really big and feel good about it when it's done, you have to surround yourself with the best people."

"That is what I finally figured out," she said. "Pat Coogan, Jack Parker, Chamoun, Alison, Thibodeaux—they are the best. None of your rivals has such people. And in the time I have been with you, most of them have defied your orders and acted on their own initiative, always on your behalf. They are fiercely loyal, but not slavishly obedient."

"That's right. The world's full of yes-men and people who're terrified to use their own initiative. I have no use for them. I have my capabilities, but I have my blind spots, too. I get carried away by my enthusiasms, and I know I can make dumb mistakes. I depend on those people to bail me out when I do."

"I think that more than anything else, it gives me pleasure to know that you wanted me to be one of those people." She grinned at him. "Well, maybe not the greatest pleasure." They came together again.

Afterward, she lay with her eyes open, looking at the ceiling but not seeing it. "It is Jean-Claude, isn't it? He is the one behind all the things that have been happening."

Carlson sighed, tired and contented, but not entirely at ease. "That's the only way I can read it. Preston's had his try by raiding my financing. He has no stomach for the rough stuff. The Japanese have come in on my project. Du Mont's the only one with the resources and the motive to pull off something like this."

"It is so hard to believe. I knew he was capable of indirect, subtle cruelty, but not of open violence."

"You never know what a man's capable of until you try to stop him from getting something he really wants. Du Mont may not be quite sane. He wants to be the Napoleon of the twenty-first century, and he knows that Napoleon didn't get his way without killing a few people. I can see him doing it, as long as he can keep his own hands clean."

Abruptly, she sat up. "The falls! I thought that man was trying to kill me. Then it seemed to make more sense that he was going to kidnap me. That was Jean-Claude's doing, too. He was trying to get me back! How could he do something as desperate as that and then calmly propose to me over a dinner table in Paris?" She dropped back to her pillow, staring again at the ceiling. "Oh, Cash, what kind of madman are we dealing with? How far is he willing to go?"

This time, he said nothing.

22

WHAT A BEAUTIFUL day for a launch, my friends!" The voice of the Brazilian commissioner boomed out over the field through the loudspeaker system.

"What a miserable day for anything else," Pat said. She stood near the press stand: a glass-fronted building on stilts, bristling with spiky antennae and satellite dishes. Parker had co-opted her for security duty, wanting to have her cop instincts on tap during what he was sure was going to be the most dangerous period so far in the whole disaster-ridden project.

Despite all the antiperspirant she had applied, sweat trickled down her ribs beneath her light, armored vest. The automatic pistol in its shoulder rig was uncomfortable as well, but she was willing to put up with the discomfort for the extra margin of safety. None of this was especially visible. To the casual viewer, she merely appeared a little over-dressed for the climate.

"Our boy's gonna like it, if he comes here. He's probably here already. Look at this mob," Parker said.

The crowd sprawled for half a kilometer around the press stand. They had been gathering since the day before. The presence of the Brazilian woman on this mission had drawn three or four times the crowd that usually assembled to witness a launch. Vendors from the town had set up stands, taking advantage of the opportunity.

Parker had his men everywhere. Like them, he was in full gear, with his "raincoat" draped over an arsenal of sophisticated weaponry. He wore an extra-large pair of wraparound black glasses, stuffed with instrumentation for communication, detection, and analysis. A constant, almost subliminal, hiss and crackle came from his direction as he monitored everything around them.

"The question is, what's he going to try?" Pat said.

"I just wish I knew what he looks like." They had the description from the people who worked night shift on maintenance, which tallied with Adam Altieri's description of the man who had bribed him, but a pro could alter his appearance easily enough.

"I'm going back to the SCC," Parker said, referring to the Security Control Center. "Keep your eyes open here. Put your woman's intuition to work. We have to stop this guy before he can do anything. We can't wait till after it's done."

"Thanks for pointing out the obvious, Jack. Go ahead." Parker left and she scanned the crowd, trying to think of herself as *Marshal* Coogan. It wasn't easy when irrepressible Brazilian males kept making passes at her. All in a day's work, she decided.

Parker climbed the steps to the SCC and went into the control room. He was too tense to be grateful for the air-conditioning. The room was lined with screens on three walls. The fourth was a window overlooking the new auditorium, which had been built to accommodate press interviews and shows for tourists to the space center. Today it was to be the scene of a speech by the Brazilian commissioner and a brief address by Carlson, followed by a showcasing of the shuttle's crew and their centerpiece, the glamorous young woman from Pôrto Alegre.

"Hell of a time for the boss to be putting on a show like this," one of the screen-watchers groused, "with some sort of crazy killer out there."

"This is just the kind of show to draw him out," Parker said. "If he's gonna come, it might as well be now, when we're ready for him. Now pay attention to your work." He looked over the screens. They scanned the auditorium below, the press area, the gates to the space facility, the preparation hangars, the launchpad, and just about everywhere else a human being could go, hide, or simply hang out. Ordinarily, Parker would have been confident that his surveillance would reveal anyone with foul play on his mind. He knew that it was adequate to catch any ordinary saboteur or would-be assassin.

The trouble was, the man they were looking for was a top pro, one who knew all the tricks. He was as likely to try something obvious as something subtle, and Parker knew how difficult it could be to second-guess the obvious.

"Hey, lookit here, Chief." On a screen, a man was stealthily sliding beneath the hurricane fence that surrounded the facility. He carried something in a long, dark case and looked as if he had been trained in avoiding detection. Parker checked the monitor's number. That area had been a blind spot until just a few days before, when Parker's camera specialist had updated their surveillance system. As the facility expanded, it sometimes outgrew its own security.

"Elmont, Duane," Parker said.

"Check, Chief," said a voice through his communicator.

"Head out to Sector Two, the northeast angle of that new fence. We have a bad guy coming in under it. Probably just more chaff, but he's got what looks like a weapon. Neutralize him and bring him in."

"Check. Out."

"Chaff" was a term borrowed from the Air Force. Originally, it meant scraps of metal foil dumped from aircraft to confuse radar with false readings. In security work, it meant nonfunctional distractions designed to mask the actions of real operators. Lately, the air was full of chaff. The day before, they had picked up a man at the O Navigador airport trying to get through the security check with a firearm that would have been undetectable a year or two before. His ID identified him as part of the Brazilian commissioner's entourage, but the forgery was inept enough to tip off even airport security. Twenty minutes of Parker's interrogation had revealed that the man had been hired to take a shot at Carlson during his speech. He had been approached through a third party, and the whole thing was so inept that Parker knew it was nothing but a distraction.

The fact was, Parker had little fear of assassins. He and his team could cover most eventualities, and Carlson, nobody's patsy, was packing a gun himself. No, what had Jack Parker sweating was the damn rocket. It was sitting out there on the launchpad ready to take its crew aboard, loaded with enough fuel to blow up a good-sized town. Space rockets were so huge that people tended to forget how terribly delicate they were. It didn't take a ground-to-air missile to send one up in a huge fireball. From close range, a single tracer round with a hot charge burning in its base could do the job. And whoever had been running him ragged was sure to have something a hell of a lot more effective than a tracer bullet.

He was all but certain that his team was wasting time watching the gates and fences, but it had to be done. The man had worked inside the facility for months, had access to go almost everywhere. He probably had planted everything he needed long ago. He was unlikely to be smuggling anything in when he came.

Parker went outside and watched the air traffic. Helicopters patrolled constantly, ranging far out to sea, keeping all vessels well away from the launch area. The bastard could have a submarine out there, for all he knew. No, his backing couldn't be that lavish. This was the work of a crazed business rival, not of a rival nation. Where was he?

The jet wasn't one of those bearing the Lone Star logo. That was a precaution Parker had insisted upon, and Carlson didn't like it. But he had given the Comanche complete authority until the matter was resolved, and he had to play along like everybody else. The pilot landed them smoothly at the O Navigador airstrip, just three miles from the launchpad.

The car that met them was made like a tank, its thick windshield slanted like the glacis plate of a Panzer Mark V. Toby was driving, his brother Thad seated next to him. Rog and Charlie stood outside, their faces as blank as robots behind their black shades. They were on top alert. There would be none of their Laurel-and-Hardy banter today.

The pilot kept his engines running, ready for an instant takeoff should he receive the signal. Rog gestured and the engines wound down. The stairway descended and Carlson and Sachi went down quickly, to be hustled into the car by the guards.

"How's it going?" Cash asked as they pulled away from the jet.

"Smooth so far," Charlie said, "but the chief thinks our boy's being clever, throwing out chaff. We've picked up some hired guns that never had a chance."

"This is awful," Sachi said.

"I've got a feeling it'll all be over pretty soon," Cash said, squeezing her hand. Over one way or another, he thought. "Toby, take us out by the launch site first."

"That's not on our route, Boss," Thad objected.

"So, a change of route won't be anticipated. Go on ahead, Toby. Jack won't object."

Ten minutes later, they stopped at one of the remote camera positions five hundred meters from the Energia. The booster waited like a racehorse at the post, fretting to be off. The Lone Star logo blazed along its sides.

"I wish we were going up today," Sachi said. She longed to be in space and away from all this fear.

"God, so do I," Cash said. But his thoughts were darker. So many attempts had been made on his life that he hardly thought about that anymore—but a threat to his ship filled him with rage. To think that someone might try to destroy his beautiful spacecraft! It was intolerable.

"Okay, Toby, take us to the auditorium," he said when he had looked long enough.

The president of the Brazilian Federal Commission on Space Exploration met them at the auditorium. He beamed happily, shaking hands as if he were running for office. He had lobbied hard with Lone Star to get a Brazilian on one of the early launches, and this event secured his career. For this day and for the duration of the mission, his would be one of the most frequently seen faces on Brazilian television. He would be quoted widely, and interviewed by all the major journals. He had every reason to be happy. As long as nothing went wrong. The heavy security outlay had him worried.

"Mr. Carlson," he said quietly, "I hope this does not mean you anticipate trouble today?" He was sweating, but not because of the climate.

"Not at all, Senhor Commissioner," Cash assured him. "But you know that our mutual project has been plagued with petty sabotage. We just don't want anything to go wrong on such an important day."

"Yes, yes, of course. I understand." The minister was trying hard to convince himself.

"Alison's giving you the high sign," Cash told him. "Time to begin your speech."

The minister hurried off, straightening his clothes, smoothing back his hair. From now on, the only emotion he would radiate would be enthusiasm for the forthcoming venture and a modest satisfaction for his own part in it. Alison Baird came rushing over to Cash's side, flushed and agitated but in her element, managing a massive media event. She smiled at Sachi, then turned to Cash.

"Boss, you have to do something about Jack. He's messing up my camera angles with his shield systems, he's shaking down my camera and sound people for weapons, he's—"

"He's just doing his job, Alison," Cash soothed.

"But he's . . . he's acting almost excited!"

"That sounds ominous, all right. Look, you just take it easy. I'll go straighten Jack out." He turned to Sachi. "I'll be back in a minute."

When he was gone, Alison took Sachi's hands. "I'm so happy for you both!"

Sachi was taken aback. "How did you know?"

"Oh heavens, girl, your body language was practically X-rated. I've been trained in spotting all the signs. It makes me so glad to see this. He was linked up with such a string of losers before you came along."

"Ah, well, I'm glad you like me, Alison."

"Dear, I love anyone who photographs the way you do. Now, you and I are going to have to get together to work on your wardrobe. You always wear such fabulous clothes, but sometimes the colors aren't right for the best camera effect, and glittery fabrics can be a real pain in the editing room."

Sachi could tell that she had acquired a new handler.

"What the hell's the problem, Jack?" Cash asked.

"He's close, Boss. I can smell 'im." Parker looked both grim and fidgety. "And you should put your raincoat on."

"I'm damned if I'm going to look like some paranoid Banana Republic dictator just because you're getting antsy. You've been like this since you shot up that place in the shantytown. Don't flip out on me, Jack."

"He's close, and this is the day," Parker insisted. "If he doesn't make his play now, it's all over. It's him and me now."

"Jack," Carlson sighed, "you need a long vacation."

"And I know just where I want to spend it," Parker said, "but right now, you need to make a speech and I have to keep you alive and see that the damned rocket stays in one piece."

Carlson turned and began to descend the steps to the auditorium. He paused and turned. "Jack, I'm glad I have you watching my back, but the ship comes first."

Parker waved him away. "Go make your speech, Boss."

A few minutes later, Carlson emerged on the stage. From the security room, Parker swept the cavernous chamber. His men on the floor watched the seated crowd with cats' eyes. They had all been swept, frisked, and x-rayed for weapons upon entering. He wasn't anticipating trouble from that direction. Above, in the maze of catwalks and support trusses, hung lights and cameras, both television and security. An alarm flashed in Parker's mind as something up there moved suspiciously.

His attention sharpened, centering on a single camera, mounted on a boom with six others. Its movement was slightly out of synch.

"Alison!" he barked. "The camera boom up in the northwest quadrant, just over the old klieg lights. Third camera from the end. Is that one of yours?"

Her voice was thin over his personal comm set. "I can barely see it from down here, against all the glare." She cued one of her assistants, the chief cameraman. "Chet, is that one of ours?"

"I thought it was one of the security cameras," Chet said.

The camera stopped moving. Parker slammed his hand down on a switch. Angled shields slid up in front of the speaker's podium. Tiny sparks flared briefly on them as Parker leaned out of the security room and fired a burst from his sound-suppressed machine pistol. The fake camera erupted in a burst of sparks that showered down on a catwalk below.

The audience began to shout, but Carlson stepped around the shield and quieted it down. He looked up at the security booth and his words rang out loudly over the address system: "Another glitch in the security system, Jack?" He was speaking for the crowd's benefit and Parker took his cue.

"Uh, right, Boss. Some sort of short circuit in the wiring up there. It blew a camera and made the shields come up. Sorry."

Carlson chuckled and shrugged broadly to the crowd. "Third time this week. Well, as I was saying before I was interrupted, this adventure signals a new relationship between the United States of America, Brazil, and Japan. But in a broader sense, the whole world is a part of . . ."

Up in the security booth, men sat back, eyes still on their screens, mopping sweat from their faces. "Jesus, that was close," one said. "It happened so quick."

"That wasn't it," Parker said, fuming.

"Huh?"

"That wasn't the real hit, any more than the guy coming under the fence was. This bastard puts more chaff in the air than a whole wing of B-Fifty-twos." He thought for a moment. "Listen, don't say anything to the boss. As far as he's concerned, this was the real thing and we stopped it. It's all over here. I'm going out to the launch site."

Parker ran down the steps and jumped into his Jeep. What next? An ICBM? But he was sure that the Russian would show himself soon now. This was one job he would tend to personally. The extensive, almost obsessive, use of third parties and throwaway flunkies meant that he considered others useless for anything important. He was a game-player, and such men were always vain. He would want to perform the kill in person and vindicate his sense of superiority.

Kuprin drove up to the gate guard in a battered old Volkswagen. He flashed his press credentials to the Brazilian guard, who studied them closely. "Please get out of the car," the man said. Genially, Kuprin complied. The team that went over the car was local, but they were supervised by a man in a long coat who wore wraparound black glasses—one of Parker's men.

"Is thorough, no?" Kuprin said, laughing jovially. "Reminds me of old days in Ukraine, Brezhnev's time."

"Would you open that, please?" The American security man pointed to the camera case on the passenger's seat. It was the size of a small suitcase.

"You must be very careful," Kuprin said. "Is very delicate. Finest new Japanese technology. Makes television film and still pictures for newspaper and journal." He added, proudly, "Is first ever seen in Ukraine." He lit up a cigarette, not the least nervous.

"I know what it is," the security man said, thoroughly checking both the camera and its case. The Brazilian guards signaled that the car was clean. He handed back the camera. "All right, you're clear to enter. Press parking is in Sector Five, nearest the press stand. I hope you get some good pictures."

"Thank you." Kuprin got back into the Volkswagen. He had known, of course, that the security check would be rigorous. He was not carrying so much as a pocketknife. There was no need, since he had had free run of the space facility for months. He parked the Volkswagen and carried his camera toward the press stand. Most of the audience was already in place, as the scheduled launch was only minutes away.

Unhurriedly, Kuprin made his way to a public toilet that stood near the stand. As he had anticipated, it was empty. All the press people were in the stand, elbowing for a good viewing angle. He went to a paper-towel dispenser, lifted it slightly and pulled outward. It swung away from the wall on hidden hinges. In the space behind the dispenser was a case identical to the one he had carried in. Swiftly, he exchanged cases and closed the secret compartment. He stuck his head out the door and looked both ways. Nobody coming. Opening the case, he drew out an automatic pistol and stuck it under his belt, beneath his multipocketed photographer's vest. The camera inside the case was, to all outward appearances, identical with the one he had hidden. He reclosed the case and carried it outside.

For the benefit of any surveillance cameras, he went through a pantomime of disappointment, as if he had been held up in traffic and now would have to be satisfied with a position outside the press stand, near one of the corners. Actually, this was exactly what he desired. The last thing you wanted when launching a rocket was something solid behind you. The backblast would be as dangerous to the launcher as the missile was to the target.

The dummy camera he took from the case was a launcher for a small but sophisticated rocket. It was not a ground-to-air missile. The range was not great enough to require one, and all such missiles were too large to carry in a shoulder-held camera shell. This one was an anti-tank missile, the latest from France, the world's leader in anti-armor missiles. Instead of an armor-piercing tip, it contained a shaped charge that fired instantly upon impact, blasting a jet of super-heated gas straight into the target. Against a tank, it would vaporize steel armor and turn the interior into an inferno, killing the crew and often exploding stored ammunition.

The paper-thin metal skin of the space rocket would scarcely slow the missile down. It would penetrate into the main fuel tank and ignite all the fuel in the rocket in a fraction of a second. It would make the Challenger catastrophe look like a leisurely process.

His rocket possessed a new venting system that caused far less noise and flash upon launch. It was far from silent, but amid the hellish thunder of a rocket launch, it would go unnoticed. His chances of being detected were minimal. Escape would be easy in the pandemonium that would follow the explosion.

Kuprin wanted this to be a work of art, the epitome of the terrorist's craft. An explosion directly on the launchpad would remind people of the near-comical early V-2 experiments and the earliest American attempts to launch an artificial satellite. The Challenger explosion, on the other hand, had been at an altitude so high that it was not immediately apparent what had happened.

He planned to destroy the rocket just as it cleared the gantry, when the long, sleek shape of the fiery-tailed Energia emerged from the huge ball of flame and smoke that obscured it for the first few seconds. It would be incredibly dramatic, worthy of Eisenstein at his best.

After that, killing Carlson would be easy. Immediately following the blast, there would be utter pandemonium. Tons of fiery debris would be arcing through the air, coming down in all directions. And Carlson would not sit tight in the press box, where Parker would try to keep him. No, the cowboy would come running out, shouting and attempting to take control. He would undoubtedly make a beeline for his car or Jeep or whatever was waiting to take him to his next stop after the launch. Then Kuprin would kill him the old-fashioned way: nothing elaborate, no super-modern weaponry, just a pistol shot to the head.

There was always, of course, the chance that the Texan would be killed by the camouflaged gun on the camera boom, but that he neither expected nor desired. It was a ruse to make Parker think that he had tried to assassinate Carlson and failed. The ensuing relaxation of vigilance would make his work that much easier.

The thought of Parker stirred a vague uneasiness in Kuprin. So far, the man had proven to be far more formidable than he had anticipated. Anticipation—it could be a dangerous thing in Kuprin's business. He had let a generalized contempt for American security procedures and personnel color his evaluation of a deadly opponent. Parker had been taken in by none of the ruses and chaff Kuprin had spread, and the raid in the shantytown had been an exemplary use of force: swift, decisive, and ruthless.

Kuprin now understood that it was Carlson who had been reining Parker in. The Comanche might have cleaned out the Brazilian sabotage operation long since otherwise. Well, Kuprin thought, he would not be the first good man brought to grief by an incompetent employer. But now Carlson had turned his Indian loose. The Cowboy and the Indian— what a strange pairing.

A change in the crowd noise shook him from his musing. A motorcade was approaching from the direction of the main facility. Carlson and the Brazilian dignitary were on their way. Then he saw something that chilled his blood: Parker, dressed in his long black coat, was standing on top of the press stand, surveying the crowd below in long, crescent sweeps, back and forth like a radar dish. He hadn't been taken in by the camera gun and he knew where the real assassination attempt would come from.

Kuprin took a deep breath and forced himself to be calm. *Keep your attention on the rocket, like everyone else. He is looking for someone trying to kill his precious boss, not for someone trying to shoot down that rocket. The Ukrainian journalist is not interested in the Texas tycoon or some Brazilian fool. He just wants pictures of the launch.*

The motorcade pulled up in front of the press stand and the dignitaries got out amid much cheering and the *click-whirr* of still cameras. Kuprin gave them only a glance, intent upon the Energia. He saw the Texan exchanging a few words with a tall, chestnut-haired woman who looked vaguely familiar. The Sasano woman was close beside him. Carlson and the Brazilian went up a flight of stadium-type stairs between a double file of uniformed guards, leaving the tall woman to wander along the front of the stand. He looked away, being a Ukrainian journalist. He fiddled with his dummy controls, as if trying to adjust his picture. The missile's controls were preset. He had only to lock it onto its target and pull the trigger. The rest was automatic.

There was a brief address from the stand, to which Kuprin paid no attention. Then the countdown began, starting at sixty. Even after all his years of experience, his palms began to sweat. This was a far greater feat than any he had ever attempted. Things began to drop loose from the rocket and something like a crane swung away from it. A cloud of steam rose from below it as tons of water sprayed into the pit to cool it and damp the sound.

Main ignition began.

An instant after the first flame and smoke shot from the base of the Energia, the ground began to shake, and the sound, low at first, swiftly ascended to a deafening thunder. The crowd was cheering wildly but Kuprin could not hear a thing. *All to the good.* He began the targeting sequence, and the illuminated square in the middle of his range finder began to blink, framing the center of the rocket, which was instantly obscured by a billowing cloud of smoke. His finger tightened on the trigger.

Then something loomed in front of his range finder.

Kuprin jerked his eye away from the eyepiece to see Parker standing before him, waving and shouting something. *Where did he come from?* Kuprin knew he had been distracted by the chestnut-haired woman. He had been trying too hard not to look suspicious to her. He had neglected to keep his surroundings covered. Parker had come in from a blind angle. Pure chance, or his own neglect? It didn't matter. Without hesitation, even as the thoughts sped through his mind, he drew his automatic and fired, landing three solid hits on the Comanche's chest. Parker went over on his back, either dead or knocked unconscious—it all depended on the quality of his armor and whether Kuprin's high-velocity ammunition was as effective as advertised. The immediate threat disposed of, Kuprin tried to realign the launcher. There was still time.

Parker dragged a deep breath into lungs that felt punctured, forcing his diaphragm to work despite the agony of what had to be shattered ribs, maybe the sternum as well. No matter. *A man can't fight if he can't breathe*, he thought, his hand already dragging the coat aside, reaching for his machine pistol. He couldn't sit up but he rolled onto his left side and lined up on the launcher, the calculations flying through the part of his brain that wasn't half stunned: "Protect my rocket first," the boss had said. *Shoot the bastard, his finger might tighten on the trigger! Shoot the launcher itself, the rocket might launch, might even go off, taking out half the stands!* The fake camera was mounted on a padded shoulder rest. What was it General Crook had said? *If the Indians had ever figured out what the back sight on a rifle is for, we never would have beaten them.*

Parker triggered a precise, three-round burst and saw the launcher separate cleanly from its mount, saw it fly away as the shooter, a real pro, drew his gun again, instantly. Parker's shooting hand was already going numb. *Well, General Crook, we figured out that business about the sights.* He felt a double impact and he knew the armor hadn't stopped the bullets this time. Then he was looking up at the clear blue sky.

Kuprin saw the Indian fall back, surely dead now. The side of his face stung, peppered with fragments of metal and plastic.

A glance told him it was too late to try launching the missile. Even if it hadn't been damaged, the Energia was already climbing out of range. He wasted no time wondering what had happened. The woman was running toward him, her shouts unheard in the all-encompassing roar of the launch. He jumped into the Volkswagen and gunned it.

At the gate, Parker's man was no longer there, for which he was grateful. The two guards on duty had their heads craned back, watching the ascending rocket. If they were getting any emergency transmissions, they could hear nothing. They noticed Kuprin only as he passed them. He shot them anyway. No sense in taking any more chances.

*   *   *

Pat knelt by Parker, jammed her fingers into the holes in his long coat. No blood, but she felt still-hot lead in all five places. Then she jerked his coat open and gasped through clenched teeth. Two holes, not bleeding much but that didn't mean anything. The bleeding would be internal. They had hit right where Parker had pulled the coat open to get at his pistol. Either the bastard was a great shot under stress or he was just lucky. Even as she called for an ambulance, pink froth began to bubble through one of the holes in time with his labored breathing. He tried to sit up but she pushed him back down gently. Blood began to leak from the corners of his mouth.

"Ran up to this jerk," he muttered. "Tried to tell him his lens cap was on. Catch me doing another good deed. He shot me off my feet. It was some kind of launcher. The camera, I mean. I shot the launcher, but he nailed me. Caught me like a damn amateur. How bad is it?"

"Missed the pump or you'd be dead, but you're lung-shot. Can you move your feet?" She watched them as they spread apart and back together. "Probably no spinal damage. We get you to a hospital, you'll be okay."

"No big deal, then. Go get him, Pat. Bring me his scalp."

"It's yours. Good work, Jack. I'll recommend you for a raise."

Pat grabbed the launcher on the ground and sprinted for the back of the press stand. It was all like something in a dream, because nobody had noticed anything. Everyone was craning upward, watching the rocket diminish to a bright dot on a long tail of smoke amid fading thunder. The radio traffic over her headset was frantic: ambulance heading for Parker, someone yammering that two guards had been shot at the press gate.

She came up to the gate, saw the two men down, the others yelling and pointing to where the getaway car had disappeared into the shantytown. Pat made a mental note: Bulldoze or burn the place down. It would make Parker's job a lot easier.

Kuprin ripped through the shantytown, scattering pedestrians and livestock before him. Mothers snatched toddlers from his path, chickens took to the air squawking, flapping, feathers flying. He gunned the engine, taking random turns, always trending toward the small-craft area of the beach, next to the little fishing cove. Anxiously, he checked his rearview mirror. Nothing so far. Several helicopters were visible in the distance, but none of them were heading toward him. Probably camera aircraft for tracking the launch, he thought.

Then he broke free of the slum and was on the short dirt road to the small-craft port. The shed loomed ahead, a corrugated-iron hut extending onto a small jetty over the water. Its double garage-style door was padlocked. Kuprin smashed through the door without slowing, jamming on the brake as he drew up next to a sleek speedboat. He jumped out of the Volkswagen and scrambled into the cockpit of the craft.

This was a part of his arrangement with Santos—a smuggler's boat with two enormously powerful engines. It would effortlessly outdistance anything the Brazilian Navy or Coast Guard could muster, and even the helicopters would not catch him unless they were alerted long enough in advance to get ahead of him and carried heavy armament to boot. He knew that he had a ninety-percent chance to get away clean, and that was fine odds for a man in his business.

As promised, the tanks were full and the motors rumbled in perfect synch. The boat was beautifully cared for. The little heat-seeking missiles in the cockpit would take care of any boats or helicopters that strayed too close. With a grin, Kuprin revved the engine, engaged the prop and smashed out through the flimsy boathouse doors. Then he was on the waters of the cove and headed for the open sea.

Pat Coogan hadn't caught sight of the VW yet, but she had no trouble following the direction of the staring, indignant Shantytown inhabitants. She looked in her rearview mirror and saw that she was not alone. Thad and Toby were behind her in a car, and Rog was behind them on a motorcycle. Rog had a heavy assault rifle across his back.

She could tell that the Russian was heading for the beach, probably the small-craft cove. She tried to think of whether there might be a shortcut she could use to get there ahead of him. She decided to keep on following. This bastard was so tricky that he might be intending to head for the airport.

Minutes later, she was on the road toward the beach. Even over the roar of her own engine, she could hear the sound of a speedboat pulling away. She brought the Jeep to a sand-spraying stop next to a shiny iron boathouse. The smashed-in doors told her where the Russian had gotten his boat. Out in the cove, a spume of water showed her the boat, heading for the open water.

The car and motorcycle pulled up beside her as she got out of the Jeep. Rog unlimbered the assault rifle and started shooting, but the boat was already out of range.

"Crap!" Toby yelled. "Maybe the choppers'll get him."

Pat reached back into the Jeep and lifted out the phony camera.

"You gonna take pictures of him?" Rog asked. Then he saw the tip of the missile protruding through an aperture below the dummy lens. "Well, ain't that cute. Was he gonna get the boss with that?"

"Nope," Pat said. "The rocket." She fiddled with the controls and lifted the thing to her shoulder, taking a sight through the range finder. "Let's see if this thing works."

She caught the boat in the sight, almost between the artificial breakwater and the rocky headland that formed the entrance to the cove. She tightened her finger on the trigger, and the white square flashed, framing the boat. She tightened some more and there was a loud *whoosh!* as the missile surged from the launcher and the backblast vented from the rear, raising a cloud of sand for thirty feet behind where she stood beside the Jeep.

They watched with interest as the barely visible missile sped across the water, zigging and zagging as the boat maneuvered. It dipped and its last hundred yards were marked by a line of spray as the shock wave following it churned the water below to vapor. Abruptly there was an expanding, whitish ball where the boat had been. The ball turned fiery orange and broke up into long streamers as the debris that had been the speedboat continued to travel in the direction the craft had been headed, then splashed into the water. A few seconds later there came a flat, multiple bang, accompanied by a wave of concussion as missile, fuel, and explosives detonated in succession. Within a few more seconds, the only sign of the boat was a few fragments smoking in the water.

Pat tossed the empty launcher back into the Jeep.

"Yep," she said. "Works fine."

YOU WANT TO go where?" Carlson demanded.

"I need a vacation," Pat Coogan answered, grinning. "And I want to spend it in Paris."

Jean-Claude du Mont stared down the long table and a double row of faces stared back at him, their expressions funereal. The loudest sound in the room was the clock ticking on the wall. The Dutchman pushed a paper toward him as if it might contaminate his fingers.

"We have already prepared your letter of resignation, Monsieur du Mont. You will of course wish to spare the agency and your government as much embarrassment as possible."

"Do you think I need to be reminded of this?" His hauteur was showing signs of cracking, but he was holding up well. The papers before him on the table read like something from the most sordid pages of the popular press: names, dates, transcripts of recorded meetings, the recordings themselves sent in multiple copies to prosecutors and news agencies worldwide. It was all quite sufficient. More than sufficient. The others stood.

"I do hope, Monsieur du Mont," said Lady Elspeth, "that you will not tarry long. Our solar-satellite project is at a most delicate stage and your successor will need to take over operations as quickly as possible."

"I assure you, Lady Elspeth, that I shall not be here much longer. Now, if you will all give me leave." They filed out. He could hear the crowd of reporters beyond the door. The police would not be far behind. It gave him some satisfaction to know that they would all be disappointed. He picked up his interoffice telephone.

"Clear that rabble out of the building."

"Oui, Monsieur." At least someone was still obeying his orders. He sat back and wondered how this had all come about. It seemed so unreasonable. The door began to open.

"I said . . ." But this was not a reporter. It was a tall, chestnut-haired woman—obviously an American, judging by the way she looked at him. She peeled off a pair of dark glasses and regarded du Mont with steady brown eyes. "Who the devil are you?" Strangely, her body language reminded him of Sachi Sasano.

"Pat Coogan. Temporary security chief of Lone Star."

"I see. I might have known that Carlson would not come himself, for all his cowboy posturing. He sent his errand girl instead." Even in the midst of his troubles, he could still manage a sneer.

"He didn't send me. I just like to tie up loose ends myself. And you're the one who's been sending out hired help to kill people."

Du Mont sighed. "I suppose this is what comes of employing a subhuman Slav. Treacherous swine."

Pat pulled out a chair and sat down. "He gave you good service, had us running around in circles for months. The records he left behind were just his insurance policy, in case you tried to get out of paying him by killing him instead. A lot of the pros keep records."

"But I had nothing to do with his death!" The unfairness of it galled him.

"That's right, I killed him. But he had no way of knowing in advance, and he knew he wouldn't be around to sort out the facts afterward, so his last employer would just have to stand the embarrassment."

"Why are you here?"

"I know your board of directors has demanded your resignation. That's not enough for me. You're about to be arrested and probably tried on a number of counts. That's not enough for me either."

"Did you really think," du Mont said icily, "that I would tolerate such public humiliation?"

"You never can tell. Lots of men like you have money salted away somewhere, ready for a quick getaway and change of identity. It's been known to happen. Don't bother to try."

"Must I endure your insolence on top of everything else?" Du Mont shook with fury.

"Take it easy, Jean-Claude. Oh, by the way, it looks like Miss Sasano is about to become Mrs. Carlson. I guess you're just always a little bit late and a little bit stupid."

Du Mont said nothing, but he seemed to sag. Pat leaned forward. "Now, listen to me. I know you know what the right thing is for you to do, what with all that breeding you like to talk about all the time. I'm just telling you not to dawdle too long to do it. I'm going to go out and wait one hour. Then I'm going to come back up here and kill you."

Fierceness emanated from her athletic physique, and du Mont understood she meant every word she spoke. What's more, he instinctively knew she was quite capable of carrying out the threat. Seeing his resigned reaction, she stood, replaced the dark glasses, turned and walked out, closing the door behind her.

Du Mont got up, breathing hard, his hands shaking. He went into his private office and shut the door. The room was full of mementos of his family history, including the revolver his grandfather had carried in the Great War. It had been returned to his widow just as it had been when it was taken from his body at Sedan, holstered with a full cylinder of ammunition. It had not been handled again until Jean-Claude had unholstered it to mount it for his office wall.

He took the gun down and broke it open, his hands once again steady. Good, the cartridges were still there, their brass bases dull and greenish with age. He sat behind his desk and thought about writing out a note. No, let my work be my monument, he thought. It will speak to future generations more clearly than the malicious babblings of my enemies. He raised the pistol, pressed the muzzle against his right temple.

The ammunition was very old and he had to pull the trigger three times before the hammer fell on a live round.

24

THIS IS *DEA Tag*," Quentin Mallory muttered to himself.

"Excuse me?" Violet queried. His student once, she had been his personal assistant for the last ten years and knew him better than most people did.

"This is the big day," he said, for once sounding nervous. "This is when I find out if I'm really as good as I think I am."

"Huh? All those books, the TV show, international celebrity, that isn't enough?" He could still amaze her. Mallory had his failings, she knew that, but weakness of ego wasn't one of them.

"Doesn't mean a thing if I blow it here today. Whether I succeed or fail could determine the future of humanity."

"Oh." That was more like it. If he was worried, it wasn't because the consequences of his work lacked grandeur. "Don't worry. When did it ever take more than five minutes to get any audience in the palm of your hand? Have you ever failed?"

He turned and gave her that famous smile. "Keep talking like that. I need it. I'm serious, Violet—this isn't just about selling a book or exciting kids about science. This is about world policy concerning space, and it's all on me."

"Because you're the best for the job. Most scientists can't convince bureaucrats and laymen—they don't speak the same language. You're the one everyone can understand." It wasn't flattery or idle egostroking. It was true.

"You're right. But I've got to give the best performance of my life."

They were sitting in a basement conference room of the White House—the real White House, not one of the executive mansions called the White House on news broadcasts for the sake of prestige. The event was an emergency session of the National Security Council, and the choice of site emphasized the importance of the meeting.

Presiding over the gathering was the Vice President, ex-officio chairman of the National Space Council. With him sat the chairman of the National Security Council, The science advisor to the President, the secretaries of State and Defense, the NASA administrator, the Joint Chiefs of Staff, and the directors of the CIA, the Defense Intelligence Agency, and the National Security Agency.

Quentin Mallory was the only scientific expert in attendance. This had been at the instigation of Gertrude Talbot, a multibillionaire and a generous contributor to the President's campaign. When she talked, the President listened, and what she had said was that Quentin Mallory was the man to deliver this briefing. Every bureaucrat, politician, and soldier in the room would know his face and name, and everyone in the country considered his the most trustworthy voice since Walter Cronkite's. The President himself planned to attend later in the day.

The Vice President called the meeting to order. "Gentlemen, ladies, in recent days, a great many rumors have been flying around concerning alleged signals—possibly of intelligent, extraterrestrial origin—received here on Earth. I ask you to forget for the moment any unfounded speculations you may have heard and give your closest attention to the following address by the distinguished astronomer and author, Professor Quentin Mallory. He will inform us of exactly what is known about this matter, and he promises that any speculations he voices are of the most conservative nature, adhering strictly to the known facts."

"Admirably succinct," Mallory muttered.

"He's got my vote if he wants to run for president," Violet whispered.

Then Mallory was standing, walking toward the raised lectern at one end of the room. He took the lectern and scanned the figures seated at three sides of the long table, each with a pad, pens, and a cup of something steaming before him. They were unsmiling, serious people. For the first time since childhood, he felt stage fright. None of this was apparent in his famously smooth, almost hypnotic voice.

"There is a great deal of valuable time being spent in this room," he began, "and I propose to waste none of it. To begin: The orbiting observatory *Heisenberg* has detected X-ray emissions emanating from the star *eta Cassiopeiae A* that cannot be explained as the natural X-ray phenomena to be expected from such a star. Instead, these have every appearance of modulated signals, intelligent in origin and directed toward Earth. Note that I say 'toward,' not 'at,' Earth. I will clarify this distinction soon. Please bear with me while I get technical.

"First, some well-established astronomical data on this star system. *Eta Cassiopeiae* is a binary system. Stars A and B orbit a common center of mass with a period of some hundred and eighty years. They are a widely separated pair, so each could have fairly stable planetary orbits around it. Star A is a spectral type G-zero, luminosity Class Five star, quite similar to our sun, which is a spectral type G-two, luminosity Class Five object. The spectral type tells us that its surface temperature is around six thousand degrees absolute, and its luminosity class says that it is an unevolved dwarf star, suitable for supporting life as we know it. There is no reason why it cannot harbor a planetary system similar to our own.

"Star B, in sharp contrast, is a spectral type M-zero, luminosity Class-Five star. It is much cooler and smaller than the sun, and its planetary system, if it has one, would be far different from ours. The binary stars are only about twenty light years from us, a trifling distance in the cosmic scheme of things. Our Milky Way galaxy is one hundred thousand light years across."

He paused and took a sip of water. He had their attention. *So far, so good.* Nobody was asking questions yet. They would hear him out first.

"The modulated signals come from the direction of Star A, the sunlike object. One plausible explanation—and I stress that this is the *most* probable explanation—for these signals is that they are being transmitted by a technologically advanced alien civilization. If the broadcast is being made omnidirectionally, like an ordinary radio broadcast, it implies an immense amount of energy expenditure—in fact, it would vastly exceed the entire daily energy consumption of the human species. Perhaps, with their advanced technology, they can afford to throw away so much energy. After all, our own use of energy is unthinkably greater than that of our ancestors of a mere two hundred years ago, whose energy sources were the same as those of the Roman Empire.

"But the energy requirement becomes far more reasonable, not to say credible, if the X-ray signals are tightly beamed in the direction of our solar system. And if that is indeed the case, the fact that our solar system is in their path can hardly be a coincidence."

He paused to let that sink in and saw a pencil slightly raised. It was the President's science advisor. At Mallory's nod, he asked, "Have you been able to decode the modulated signals?"

"No, we have yet to decipher them. In fact, we haven't a clue even though hundreds—in fact, thousands—of people all over the world have been trying very hard to do so."

"But you and your colleagues are positive that the signals are artificial?"

"Oh, yes indeed. On that one point, we all agree. No natural X-ray source would emit such highly modulated signals."

The Veep spoke next. "Do you suppose the signals are intended for us?"

"That's possible. I've already mentioned the unlikelihood that a tight-beam transmission would fall upon a planet like ours, where it was likely to be received, by pure chance. The odds are quite literally astronomical. But . . . intended for us? If so, why are they sending their signal in X-ray frequency? For one thing, modulating X-ray transmission is not technologically easy. Also, it may be speculated that an advanced civilization like theirs would be capable of intercepting our past radio signals—after all, the distance is only twenty light years. Our earliest, admittedly very crude and weak, radio signals could have reached *eta Cassiopeiae* around the year nineteen-twenty. By now, they must know that we use radio frequency for communication. If they want to communicate with *us*, then why not send their messages in radio? And why not precede them with a key for their decipherment? It would be a simple task for a species with the most rudimentary grasp of mathematics, and their command of math has to be far more than rudimentary."

"If not us," said the Veep in his faint Southern twang, "then who?"

"You will recall that earlier in this address, I mentioned a distinction between a signal directed 'toward' Earth and one directed 'at' Earth. Here is where I clarify that distinction. One directed *at* Earth must be intended to be received by Earth. But one directed *toward* Earth may well be intended to be received by someone or something that is between that star and us."

He paused again. One segment of his audience had grasped his implications instantly. He had the fullest attention of the Joint Chiefs. *They may be military bureaucrats*, he thought, *but those are people who know how signals work.* A hand went up from the group. It was the Air Force general. "You're talking about a ship headed this way?"

Mallory nodded. "Yes, a ship. A starship. Perhaps a fleet of them."

There was a shuffling of papers, feet, and chairs. This time, the Army general spoke. "How close?"

"Here we can only speculate, but we have reasonable data upon which to found our speculations. They may well be traveling at close to the speed of light. In that case, the X-ray signals will be Doppler-shifted to radio frequency when received by the starships. That would explain why they use such a high frequency to communicate. We have no idea of how fast their ships may be traveling. What we do know is that if they are traveling near the speed of light, they can get from their system to ours in a little over twenty years, by our clock. Thanks to the relativistic time-dilation effect, it would be only a few years by the ships' own timing. At any rate, since the detection occurred only about a year ago, and even if traveling at near the speed of light, it would likely be a couple of decades or more before the putative alien fleet's arrival in our solar system.

"Of course there are other variables involved. The ship, or fleet, might have been launched long before the signals began. Or it might have begun its voyage from someplace other than *eta Cassiopeiae*. After all, if you order a ship to sail from Norfolk to Japan, it will take a while to reach its destination. If you order a ship that is already docked on Guam to sail to Japan, it will be a far shorter voyage. We might not have all that much time."

"Have you considered any other explanations for the signals?" the CIA director asked.

"Naturally, we have. These signals may have nothing to do with what we are speculating about here. They could be the interstellar equivalent of 'Hi! How are you doing?' There is even the possibility—which I and most other astronomers consider vanishingly small—that it is some sort of natural phenomenon. But what I came here today to say to you, what I beg you to give your deepest consideration to, is this." Here he swept the audience with his intense, burning gaze. "Can we afford to ignore the possibility that we are soon to encounter an alien star fleet headed this way? Can we afford to assume that such a fleet's intentions will not be hostile? I hope that will be the case and that they will be peaceful, but such hope must not be founded on wishful thinking. If we assume they are not coming, or if we assume they are coming and their intentions will be friendly but it should prove otherwise, then we may have, here today, made mankind's last mistake."

The Veep called a half-hour break and Mallory went out into the hallway. He was astonished to note that his hands were shaking. For the first time in fifteen years, he regretted having given up smoking. Violet was patting his shoulder, assuring him he had delivered the performance of his career. A man wearing a blue uniform approached them. It was one of the Joint Chiefs, the Navy admiral. He was slightly built but as erect as an antenna, with a horseshoe of white hair surrounding a shiny dome, and a narrow white mustache that looked as though it had been trimmed by computer. He held out a hand.

"Professor Mallory, I'm Bob Anson. That was a hell of a show you just gave us, but I'd like a bit more clarification, if you don't mind."

"That's why I'm here, Admiral." He sensed no hostility.

"I hope you won't take offense if I note that some of your colleagues of the scientific community, naming no names of course, are not averse to hyping their discoveries far out of proportion to their actual merits."

"True," Mallory said ruefully. "All too true. I say this most sincerely, Admiral: There is nothing I detest more than professional dishonesty among scientists. It's led to a great distrust of scientists by the public, and it's justified. From being the most trusted voices of the world community, scientists have come to be lumped together with showmen and charlatans."

The admiral nodded. "I recall the cold-fusion enthusiasm of some years ago. For about five days, it looked like the answer to a lot of military prayers, before it dissolved into hokum and snake oil."

"That's become a common disease. I call it 'Nobelitis.' "

Anson grinned briefly. "The first one into print with a new discovery gets the prize, eh?"

"Exactly. And media hype can do a lot to advance one's scientific career, too. Once, scientists devoted years to their work, then published their findings in the professional journals and waited for the critical reviews of their peers. Publicity was not a routine part of the professional life; it was a matter left entirely to the news media. A lot of my colleagues still do abide by the traditional principle, but there are far too many who rush straight to the reporters as soon as they think they have something—often exaggerating their results beyond reason. They're terrified that somebody else will get on TV first and garner the fame."

"Of course," Violet put in, "it works the other way, too. The media love sensationalism, even when they're reporting science. Some astronomer makes a cautious, conservative statement that he's found intriguing evidence of a planetary system surrounding a distant star and the next day he's quoted as having found *proof.* Or a medical researcher says he's had promising results from lab-rat experiments and he's reported as having discovered a cure for cancer."

"So what is it, Professor?" The admiral waited expectantly.

"Admiral, what I've said here today is absolutely without hype or any trace of political bias. I, and a great many good scientists, believe that the best explanation for what has been discovered is that these signals are intended for an alien vessel headed our way."

Anson nodded. "Then I can promise you my support." He paused for a moment. "You realize that your connection to Cash Carlson will come up."

"Can't be helped, but I can answer any charges of conflict of interest. I have nothing to hide."

Anson nodded. "I knew Carlson slightly when he was in the service. He's a good man. He wasn't treated right." He nodded a brief good-bye and turned away.

"I hope the admiral swings a lot of clout," Violet said.

"So do I. The next part may be an even harder sell."

The Veep reconvened the meeting, and now the President sat at the long table. For another half-hour, Mallory fielded questions, most of them pertinent. He was in his element and he didn't mind that some of the questions were repetitious; these people wanted to make sure they had their facts straight. Then he went into the second phase of his address.

"We now come to a momentous question: What are we to do in order to protect our planet? What must be our posture when these putative aliens arrive, whether their intentions prove to be benevolent or otherwise?

"The strategy I now present to you is the synopsis of work done by an untold number of dedicated scientists and engineers who have been involved in these issues over the past few decades. Their conclusions are outlined in the handout before you. Before discussing each of these items in detail, let me address a concern that might color your reception of these proposals: their cost. We are accustomed to thinking of space projects in terms of a tremendous initial expenditure of taxpayer funds, with payback always in doubt.

"If we do this right—if we take the proper, logical steps now—this program should pay its own way, and with fat dividends to boot. This is not just an academic speculating theoretically. We will soon have abundant proof that it can be done. The soon-to-become-operational solar-power satellites are an excellent case in point. The development of highly economical, reusable launch vehicles is another.

"I suppose you recall that not so very long ago, pundits said that there was really little worth sending into space, even if RLVs could be operated dirt-cheap. Well, solar-power satellites can use those RLVs as soon as they are put up in service, and the demand for them will continue to increase. And then there is the budding but highly profitable field of space tourism. These enterprises have all been accomplished without a penny of government money. In fact, the space entrepreneurs have preferred that the government neither help nor interfere in their work. There is no need for a government bureaucracy to oversee this area of endeavor. In fact, by following this course, the recent space projects have created large numbers of jobs and stimulated the economy. A byproduct that is of national interest, although hardly necessary as planetary concern, is that the United States has remained at the forefront of the space sciences and technology.

"The program before you is still incomplete. But it represents a first step in making our species a truly spacefaring one, so that in a few decades, we will at least have a chance to greet our potential visitors from *eta Cassiopeia A* as their equals, not as primitive tribes they can exploit, conquer, or annihilate at will. There will, of course, be collateral benefits from the program. Among these will be a system for protecting our planet from collision with asteroids or comets, and another for the exploitation of mineral resources in space. There will, naturally, be many more spin-offs from the program that we cannot even anticipate today. Remember that the rather simpleminded race between the United States and the USSR to be the first to land a man on the moon produced technological developments that changed the world in profound ways unforeseeable to those statesmen of nineteen-sixty. Expect the unforeseen benefits from this program to be as great. In fact, they will probably be far greater.

"All the government is being asked to do is to not interfere with the entrepreneurs in their exploration and exploitation of space for the common benefit. The government can help this process along by investing in high-risk technological ventures that may still be beyond the reach of the private sector today—there actually aren't very many in this category anymore. Developing an interstellar spaceship might be one of them. And, of course, there is the building of our space defense forces; this is definitely a proper course for our government to pursue."

He leaned back a bit from the podium. "And there, briefly and baldly, you have it. The boons certain to accrue from these proposed activities in space are tremendous. The consequences of *not* taking action now will likewise be tremendous, quite possibly fatal and final. Can we afford, as a responsible nation, not to embark upon this path? My distinguished audience, the future of our planet, of our very species, is in your hands."

25

L ET'S MOUNT UP. "Carlson maneuvered himself onto the space scooter with practiced ease. Sachi got on behind him somewhat more awkwardly. She had only recently been allowed to take part in EVA and she was still unused to the necessary gymnastics. She never missed an opportunity to get out of Lone Star and into open space. Being in the space station was a bit like being in a submarine, but without gravity. EVA was what being in space was all about. She loved the scooter as much as Cash did.

Near them, other crews—workers and camera operators—were readying their scooters. The final preparatory stages were to be recorded for posterity. All around them bulked the greatly expanded Lone Star Space Station, which now included six external fuel tanks linked in a hexagon. Spiderweb struts were laced between the long cylinders. At "night," when Earth blocked the sunlight, the tanks and their supporting struts twinkled with multicolored lights, a sight of literally unearthly beauty.

"Let's go." With Cash in the lead, the little flotilla sped silently toward the SolarSat, which now neared completion.

As they left Lone Star, Prometheus 1 was nothing but a glitter in the distance. With the cameras recording their approach, it grew to a complicated structure of triangular aluminum struts supporting broad, black solar cells. During the last two kilometers of their approach, Cash began his narration.

"What you see is the future of man in space, and possibly the salvation of human life on Earth. The immediate future, that is. Our descendants will find it laughably crude. The functional beauty of Prometheus One is clear from the picture you see before you. What is not clear is the sheer scale of it. Prometheus One is three kilometers by four kilometers, and most of it is a framework supporting solar-power cells with a total surface area of twelve square kilometers. To help you visualize this, that's larger than most small towns. As we get closer, you'll be able to see the people working on it, and then you'll have a faint idea of how huge it is."

This was being recorded live for the sake of immediacy. The inevitable hiss, crackle, and pop lent authenticity to the narration, as did the mysterious pings and beeps and the voice distortion that always occurred when speaking from within a space helmet.

"Cue remote," said a technician's voice; then, "Cue Quentin Mallory." Mallory was in the Houston facility, sitting before a gigantic television screen recording the rough version of his voice-over narration. It could be done in its entirety later, in the editing room, but Mallory, too, liked the excitement of immediacy. He did not like it enough to go into space himself, however, and was quite satisfied to leave that end of it to the adventurers.

"From the burly, workmanlike simplicity of Lone Star," crooned Mallory's mellifluous, hypnotic voice, "we now go to a far different island in space: the delicate, ethereal beauty of a solar-power satellite."

They drew closer, and now the workers were visible, some pulling themselves along the connecting struts, others crossing greater distances on space scooters. Mallory's voice continued.

"Among the solar cells, the astronauts swarm like bees in a vast field of black flowers. All that is missing is the buzz, but that is only from our point of vantage. Space itself is silent as far as human ears are concerned, but this task is anything but silent for the men and women working on it."

"Cue radio traffic," said the technician. Immediately, their speakers erupted into a babel of voices as foremen issued instructions, workers reported, orders were sent from Lone Star and from Houston, all overlaid with the pings, beeps, warbles, bongs, and other electronic sounds that had meaning for astronauts and were incomprehensible to the Earthbound, save that they carried the unmistakable feel of man in space.

"Squelch radio traffic," said the technician.

"Yes," Mallory said, "this is a noisy, busy place. The swarms of workers who built the pyramids, the Great Wall of China, and the cathedrals of Europe, the high-steel workers and roughnecks who built the Empire State Building and the Hoover Dam in the nineteen twenties and thirties, all would have felt at home here, after a certain inevitable period of adjustment and orientation. For make no mistake about it: All of these vast projects were masterminded by the scientists and technicians of their times, and brought into being by the wealthy and powerful, but they were actually made real by the workers and foremen, whether wearing the linen kilt of the ancient Egyptian or the high-tech space suit of the astronaut.

"Now let's go closer and see who these people are, what they are doing, and how they feel about their work. Soon this will be commonplace, but like all historical events, it happens for the first time only once."

"Cut introductory sequence," said the technician. "Ready sequence two, cue time in forty-five minutes."

"Great pitch, Quentin," Carlson said. "You sure do talk pretty."

Mallory laughed. "It's a once-in-a-lifetime chance, Cash. I want to get it right. I just wish I had the nerve to ride up in one of your sky rockets. As it is, just sitting here in front of this screen is enough to get me a little queasy. This new high-resolution TV process is phenomenal. It's like looking out a window on a spaceship."

"Believe me, Quentin, it's not a patch on the real thing. You miss the whole ambience down there."

"I can live without that. Just seeing it clearly and from a distance is good enough for me."

Minutes later, Cash's scooter was tethered to the largest structure on the immense satellite. The program would be broadcast worldwide in several versions. Sachi would do the principal narration for the Japanese presentation. As the film and video teams fanned out to shoot their footage, she recorded the program in her most elegant Japanese. Tiny monitor screens on a panel mounted to the scooter showed her the view from each camera team and let her key her narration accordingly.

"We are now atop the power generating structure, although 'atop' is merely a relative term in space, where there is no up or down. However, people who work in space use those terms all the time, just to keep themselves oriented. These extremely long, thin, spokelike objects you see extending from the power-generating structure are antennae. When the satellite is operational, they will beam energy to the receiving antenna in the Mojave Desert. Actually, the proper term for a receiving antenna is "rectenna." The power-sending antennae are several kilometers in length. The Mojave rectenna is about ten kilometers by fifteen kilometers in extent. It will convert the energy, transmitted from the power satellite in retrodirected microwave at 2,450 megahertz, into electricity." She shut off her recording mike and spoke privately to Cash.

"I wish Quentin Mallory could speak Japanese. These sentences sound just as awkward in Japanese as they do in English. I'm a writer, not a public speaker!"

"You're doing just fine, Sachi," he assured her. "And you're here, which he isn't." He put an arm around her waist. Wearing bulky space suits in zero-gee, it was an almost ludicrous gesture, but the sentiment was appreciated.

Surveying the technological marvel he had brought into being, Cash felt as if he glowed out to his fingertips. It wasn't finished yet, but he had accomplished something one expert after another had said was impossible. With a one-man business operating on a shoestring, he had raced national space agencies and big corporations right down to the wire in developing a space project of unprecedented magnitude. And he intended to beat them all to the finish, too.

In just four more months, this whole, unthinkably vast machine would lift from LEO and be on its way to its designated geostationary orbit some thirty-six thousand kilometers from the ground.

Pat Coogan knocked at the entrance to Carlson's private compartment. The greatly expanded Lone Star was still under construction, but the living quarters were almost finished and were far roomier and more comfortable than they had been. The original tank was still called the Igloo. The section where Cash and his close associates had set up had been dubbed "the Ranch."

"Come on in. The door's open."

As she floated in, Carlson was checking a three-dimensional holo projection of Prometheus 1 against an engineering report. Near him, Sachi worked at her computer terminal. Her task was to figure out the most economical way to maintain the living quarters for the crew in orbit: a never-ending job in the ever-expanding and mutating Lone Star.

"Message from Max," Pat reported. "Eyes only, via scrambler." She added, "Not that he ever sends messages any other way."

"Let's hear it," Cash said, not taking his eyes from the projection. "We're all friends here."

"He says that Reed's Space Technologies will be completing construction of its SolarSat in three months. They'll start installing their boosters even before that. Their expected LEO-to-GEO insertion date is three months from now. Thibodeaux's agents also confirm Max's predictions." She looked and sounded gloomy. They all knew that Prometheus had four months to go.

Carlson was poker-faced. "I take it that's the good news. What else has Max got to say?"

"I quote: 'Despite Jean-Claude du Mont's unorthodox and melodramatic departure from the scene, the European Space Enterprise hasn't even added a week to its SolarSat schedule."

"No surprise there," Carlson said. "The business end of the ESE is run by plutocrats. The technical end is handled by a bunch of Eurotechnocrats. They don't need a megalomaniac like du Mont in order to keep operating. If anything, he slowed them down with his unending ceremonies and tours with foreign dignitaries. The man was Charles de Gaulle reincarnated."

"Louis the Fourteenth," Sachi said. "De Gaulle was self-effacing by comparison."

"Better than Napoleon, I guess," Carlson said. "At least du Mont didn't have any military ambitions. Oh well, the man's dead, I guess we shouldn't speak ill of him. Anyway, it comes as no surprise that his passing hasn't disrupted their schedule any. What else?"

"Max says the ESE will be ready to lift its SolarSat into geostationary orbit within a fortnight of the Space Technologies team."

Finally, Carlson looked up at her, frowning slightly. "Max didn't say fortnight."

"Well, actually he said a couple of weeks. I thought it might lighten up the bad news to dress up his language a little."

"That sounds more like Max. Anything else?"

"Well, he adds a little addendum. It sounds kind of strange after all the rest: 'Boss, we're going to win this one.' "

Carlson nodded. "That's right, we are. Max is almost always right."

"If you say so, Boss," Pat said, smiling. She knew that if there was a way to salvage this situation, Max and the boss would do it. Confidence is as infectious as defeatism, and Carlson exuded confidence the way a lamp gave off light. She left the compartment. Outside, she surreptitiously stroked the hard, metallic bump beneath her coverall just above her left breast. When she had come up to Lone Star, Carlson had ceremoniously presented her with a five-pointed silver star engraved with her name and the title, "Space Marshal." The position didn't officially exist yet, and she wouldn't wear the star publicly. But she wore it pinned to her undershirt beneath her coverall. Humming, she floated back to her temporary post at the command station.

"Are you as sure of this as you told her?" Sachi asked. She could ask Carlson questions that might be impertinent coming from any of the others.

"Absolutely, and that's not just dumb optimism. It's not that my technology is better than theirs; in some ways, they're more advanced. I'm counting on the built-in inefficiencies of their organizations, and so is Max. The only thing that's ever gone wrong with this project was sabotage, and we took care of that. The others have had far more foulups than we have, and they'll have more in the next three months. They've been able to keep close to schedule only through sheer size and resources. As we get down to the finish line, their backup systems won't be able to take up the slack quickly enough. They'll have delays and setbacks. It's inevitable. It's a matter of mentality."

"Mentality?" she echoed.

"Yep. You see, they make their plans anticipating, actually counting on, a thousand things going wrong. When you plan that assiduously for foul-ups, you get them."

Dalton Cooper was chief engineer in orbit for Space Technologies. He stared at the figures on his screen grimly, his expression noncommittal. But beads of cool sweat formed on his forehead when he thought of what might have happened if he hadn't caught this.

"Perez," he said.

"What?" his deputy responded.

"The attitude-control system of the second booster we tested malfunctioned in exactly the same way the first one did. You know what would have happened if I hadn't checked them out first? Three months from now, we'd probably end up boosting our power station into a lunar orbit. What do you want to bet the third one's going to misbehave just like the other two?" He glared at Perez as if his deputy were personally responsible for the fiasco.

Perez turned away from the accusing gaze. "I won't put any money on it. Let me query L.A." He tapped the keys on his console and waited while his boss stared glumly at the figures on his own screen. A few minutes later, the answer from headquarters came up.

"They went through their quality-assurance files and reported that everything checked out perfectly before their shipment to the orbital assembly plant. They think we must have done something wrong in the testing up here."

"I don't give a good goddamn about their QA files! All that means is that their asinine procedures were followed to the letter. At every stage, some idiot solemnly signed them off, just like the regs say. Don't those desk people in business suits know what we're doing up here?" For the usually phlegmatic engineer, it was an unusual display of temper. "What I want to know is how the lab tests went on the ground! Tell them to check. There must have been some indication of trouble in the post-integration lab data if they look closely enough."

Glumly, Perez did as he was told. Once again he waited for a response from L.A. When it came up, he wiped a hand across his face. Cooper didn't miss the gesture.

"What is it, Perez?" he said quietly.

Perez tried to show professional calm and detachment. "Uh, apparently, since all the QA reports looked okay, they figured no problem would be encountered after integration with the booster."

Cooper turned very pale, then red. "What? Do you mean to tell me those idiots didn't test the attitude-control system at the integration?" All through the space station, heads turned.

"No, the idiots themselves are telling you that."

Cooper drifted quietly for a while, thinking. Perez didn't dare say anything. "I wonder," the chief engineer said finally, "if we fired up those low-yield boosters and reprogrammed them for L.A.—you think we could hit the headquarters building?" The low-yield rockets were intended for boosting the solar-power satellite from low Earth orbit and were now useless for the purpose. "We could call it a misfiring."

"Probably miss the eighth floor," Perez commented. The Eighth floor held the management offices. "Maybe miss the headquarters building entirely, just kill a lot of worker bees in the plant."

"Probably right," Cooper said, calming down. "Well, this is going to hurt them about as bad. Tell them we are immediately sending back for repair all the boosters with attitude-control systems. Tell them to do fix-up as a crash program." He smiled humorlessly, remembering von Braun's definition of a crash program: "Get nine women pregnant in hopes of producing a baby in one month."

"But we're within three months of GSO insertion," Perez protested. "This'll set us back another three, at least!"

"That's what's going to hurt. And it wouldn't have happened if those bozos hadn't confused signing papers with carrying out tests. Tell them. If they ask you why it happened, refer them to me. I'll be happy to tell them. More than happy."

While Perez sent the message down, Cooper wished for the hundredth time that he had the facilities and trained manpower to carry out the necessary repairs in orbit. He detested being dependent on the paper-pushers on the ground.

"Now aren't you sorry you turned down that job offer from Lone Star?" he said to Perez.

Roel van der Boss knew what the chief engineer for the Tower of Babel must have felt like. He too was running a multilingual project. Such a project had unique problems. It was bad enough to be saddled with the centralized but unfocused Washington-style bureaucracy that Space Technologies had to live with. In addition, van der Boss had to contend with the top-heavy bureaucratic cultures of a dozen European states that often did not mesh well with each other.

Van der Boss had lived for a few years in America and France. He had no trouble communicating in both English and French. Most of his Dutch and Scandinavian coworkers were fluent in English and managed passably in French and German. Many of the English, on the other hand, thought that everyone else should learn their language if they wanted to work in space. The French were not far behind the English—or the Americans, for that matter—in linguistic parochialism, but at least they made the effort to speak English while working in the space program.

The European Space Enterprise was officially a private enterprise, as the name suggested. Most European governments, however, had a substantial investment in it. This was in part to make sure that their countries got their share of contracts in the space program. Unfortunately, as van der Boss had found so often since assuming his post of chief engineer, all European countries were not equal when it came to space technology. There was a great deal of gerrymandering to assure each country an equal share, and the results were not always in agreement with the technical expertise of a participating nation.

The net result was that some hardware—or software—worked better than others.

Just now, his problem was the microwave transmitter that was to beam power to the rectenna on the ground, which was located in the Spanish plateau a hundred kilometers from Madrid. It seemed that the components produced in England and those manufactured in Italy refused to work together, although each had worked perfectly when tested on the ground.

He first had to determine whether the failure was in the hardware or was caused by workers who were unable to understand one another with perfect clarity. Communication upon such highly technical matters was difficult enough even among people who spoke English—the official language in space—as their native tongue. When working with a mixed crew of a dozen nationalities, the result was a recipe for disaster.

He looked out the window of his stateroom in Yggdrasil. ESE's permanent orbiting space station was a palace compared to Carlson's jerry-rigged Lone Star, but at that moment, van der Boss would gladly have traded his comfortable accommodations for the Texan's spartan Igloo, if only he could have a similarly lean, purposeful organization to work with. Floating ten kilometers away was the pride and joy of the European Space Enterprise. The first European solar-power satellite was a picture of majesty and serenity, waiting only to be lifted into its working orbit to begin snatching power from the sun and sending it down to Earth, there to drive the engines of civilization.

Van der Boss had more personal reasons to want to keep the project on schedule. First, there was professional pride. Like most top professionals in any field, he liked to think he was the best in his line of work. More practically, there was a special clause in his contract with ESE that promised him a bonus of two million Euro—the European currency unit—if his team succeeded in beating its competitors to the prize.

If this new problem proved not to be easily solvable in orbit, it would set back his schedule by several weeks at the very least, weeks he could not afford.

The control room of Lone Star was not exactly spacious, but it was no longer as claustrophobic as it had been. Astronauts nostalgic for the science-fiction entertainments of their youth had dubbed it "the bridge," in honor of the legendary command post of Captain Kirk. It looked nothing at all like the famous command center of the *Enterprise*. Instruments protruded from the walls at every possible angle, seemingly planless but actually carefully worked out for the utmost efficiency and easiest use by people working in free fall.

Cash Carlson hovered before his command console, anchored to it by Velcro pads sewn to the knees of his coverall. The console was roughly U-shaped and consisted mainly of screens giving him a nearly complete overview of everything going on in Lone Star and out at the site where Prometheus 1 was being readied for launch to GSO.

For several hours, the precountdown checkout had been going on. On a launch of this sort, the procedure was not the same as for a launch from the ground. On the ground, when a countdown was stopped at, for instance, T minus four minutes, it usually could be resumed at will and at the point of interruption. But Prometheus 1 was not sitting still. It was orbiting Earth, and if the countdown were to be interrupted, it could not be resumed until Prometheus again reached a point in the orbit where the injection into a preplanned geostationary orbit could be accomplished within the fuel budget of the kick-stage rocket.

In consequence, a careful checkout before the countdown was essential. If the satellite ended up in a geostationary orbit above the Indian Ocean when the rectenna was located in the Nevada desert, the results could be more than embarrassing.

"Boss, don't you think we ought to start the countdown as soon as possible?" The speaker was Robert Arnold, Cash's operations engineer. He was sweating the launch because the latest intelligence from the ground said that the Space Technologies team was ready to boost its own SolarSat, Helios 1. Since S-T would be using chemically powered kick-stage rockets, their acceleration would be much faster than that of the electric-impulse engines Prometheus 1 would be using.

"Chemical boosters are fast, Bob," Carlson said, "but they don't leave much margin for error. If S-T gets in a hurry and launches now, it runs a high risk of blowing its whole operation. And it's not the only one out there. The Europeans are pretty close to launch date."

"If we're to believe the latest intelligence from the ground, ESE's being held up, waiting on delivery of a memory board or something."

"Don't count the Europeans out just yet. Their chief engineer's a man who knows how to get things done. I know. I tried to hire him myself. And he's got good backup on the ground, now du Mont's out of the picture. This one's going to be right down to the wire no matter what, so we do ourselves no favor by acting too fast. We opted for the slower drive long ago. We counted on running a more efficient organization to make up for any disadvantage in launch-to-insertion time. We're still going to make it."

"If you say so, Boss," Arnold said doubtfully.

Carlson didn't mind his subordinate's anxiety. It was an operations engineer's job to worry. Blind faith was too much to expect. But Carlson had been planning this operation for a long time; he knew how it should proceed, and he saw nothing at this point to make him change his plans. Flexibility was one thing. Panicky response to a fluidly changing situation was quite another.

Dalton Cooper felt a flush of satisfaction and it was better than a double shot of whiskey to a thirsty man. He couldn't have been more pleased with himself as he pulled his way out of his stateroom, using the fabric loops favored aboard Space Base 1.

Those people on the ground had really come through for him, for a change. When he had told them that he was sending back the malfunctioning attitude-control system, James Willcox Chalmers himself had stepped in. Chalmers was the executive vice president of Space Technologies. First off, he told Cooper to keep the defective kick stage at Space Base 1. He then ordered the backup boosters and attitude-control systems brought up from the storage area and instructed that an integration-and-testing program be commenced immediately in the vacuum chamber. By working his crew twenty-four hours a day, seven days a week, he had the new boosters and attitude control systems integrated, tested, and ready to be shipped to Space Base 1 within a record-breaking four weeks.

"You look happy," said Jimmy Huang as Cooper pulled himself into the control station. Huang was duty engineer for this shift.

"We're going to win this one, Jimmy. It's all done and we're ready to go!"

"Yeah, they Lone-Starred it this time," Huang acknowledged.

"Hell, we can't even win without Carlson getting half the credit," Cooper said, scowling.

"Face it, Coop. If Carlson wasn't in the race, none of us would be doing half as well. It'd still be executive board meetings and projections and analyses, and everybody would be afraid to do anything for fear of being the first to screw up. That crazy cowboy got people off their butts and working. Without him, Reed would never have given Chalmers a carte blanche to fix our attitude-control problem without interference and with the resources of the whole company."

"Yeah, I guess you're right," Cooper acknowledged. "Sort of makes you wonder what an outfit this size could accomplish with Carlson in charge, doesn't it?"

"I didn't hear that," Huang said, looking all around as if trying to spot bugs.

"Okay, enough chatter," Cooper said. "Let's get this baby on its way. The Mojave rectennae is now operational and ready to receive microwaves. Let's give it some." His fingers danced across his control board, and figures and diagrams flashed over his screens. He punched into the space-station intercom system. "PowerSat One launches in six hours." Cheering erupted all through the station. He could taste victory already.

Roel van der Boss forced himself to relax for the first time in twenty-four hours. The decision to launch Helios 1 had been made, despite a malfunctioning memory board. It had been spotted during a precountdown test run the day before. Delivery of a new board from the ground would take at least another week. By that time, Prometheus and PowerSat would both have been launched. Since Helios would also employ electric-impulse kick-stage rockets for GSO insertion, there was no way he could beat the other two competitors under such circumstances.

Of course he could not be absolutely sure of precisely when his competitors would be launching their SolarSats, but according to the latest reports from reliable sources, Lone Star would be ready within a few days. Space Technologies would be ready within a week or so, and with faster, chemically powered boosters. Barring accident to the others, waiting on the memory board would cost ESE the race.

So van der Boss had contacted Jean-Claude du Mont's successor, Paul Dirksen, with a heroic proposal: Launch immediately, without the computer memory board. Since it would be several weeks before the satellite could reach its designated orbit, he would have ample time to dispatch a Hermes shuttle from his space station. Hermes could reach the geostationary orbit within hours and match it with Helios 1 just as the SolarSat attained its own orbit. The engineers on Hermes could then install the memory board while in geostationary orbit.

The whole procedure should not take more than a couple of hours. It was a little risky, he thought, but it was his only chance to beat the competition. He had to win. The European Space Enterprise had gone to great lengths, even without du Mont's extralegal efforts, to have a shot at the huge U.S. market.

The Europeans, with good reason, did not trust the U.S. Congress. Even if ESE won the race, a new U.S. administration or a shift in popular feelings could result in protectionist legislation, barring Europe from their energy market. To forestall such action, the Europeans had established an American corporation called Atlantic Space Enterprise, with a charter to build and operate a series of U.S.-based rectennae for the American market. A rectenna had already been built in Georgia, and it was toward this receiving station that they planned to beam the energy in microwave even before sending it to their Spanish rectenna. Its strategically chosen orbit would enable Helios 1 to use either rectenna for beaming down solar energy. There were plans for building other power satellites specifically dedicated to either the American or European market.

This represented capital outlay on an epic scale, something unheard of in European history save during major wars. And responsibility for all of it was squarely on the shoulders of Roel van der Boss.

"Good evening, America and the world." The woman's flawless, classic face carried that combination of cheerfulness and seriousness that viewers had come to expect from anchorpeople. "As we approach the finish line of the unprecedented and often controversial race to put the first working solar-power satellite in orbit, it may be that some of us, numbed by the flood of spectacular images and their attendant rhetoric, may be missing the historic significance of these events. With us this evening to help put these matters into perspective, we have been joined by Professor Quentin Mallory, world-famed expert on matters pertaining to space exploration and best-selling author. Professor Mallory, thank you for joining us tonight."

The handsome features of Quentin Mallory beamed from screens all over America and much of the rest of the world. "Thank you, Amelia, for having me and giving me this opportunity to communicate just a little of my enthusiasm for this marvelous project."

"Professor Mallory, very soon we will know who is to be the winner of this race, if indeed there is a winner since it's possible that all three major contenders could fail. How do you interpret this endgame phase? All three seem to have accomplished miracles, far surpassing the predictions of everyone but the most optimistic of experts."

In his element, Mallory spoke as much with his eloquent body language as with his voice. "Amelia, this race to tap the energy of the sun is not unlike other races of the past, when competitors suddenly found it possible to surpass the human limitations set by the conventional wisdom. Once it was thought impossible for a human runner to run a mile in under four minutes. When that mythical barrier was broken by an outstanding athlete, others found no difficulty in surmounting it.

"Time after time, Amelia, we encounter difficulties and exalt them to the status of immutable laws. Once it was thought that aircraft could not exceed the speed of sound. Then Chuck Yeager broke the barrier in the Bell X-One and now aircraft routinely go many times the speed of sound. The so-called sound barrier was merely a problem of aerodynamics, not a law of nature.

"What is happening now, in orbit, is the equivalent of the final seconds of a long, grueling marathon. Three competitors remain after all the others have fallen out. Egged on by the competition and by the urging and cheering of the crowd, all three strive with inhuman fervor.

"The fact that those three are so close to launch date at the same time is miraculous when you consider the unbelievable complexity of the project. The sheer audacity of it staggers the imagination, and it tells us something about what the human species is capable of."

"I take it, Professor Mallory, that you are not entirely unbiased as to the outcome of the race? There are those who say that your attachment to Cash Carlson makes your assessments somewhat less than detached."

He gave her his famous boyish smile. "My association with Mr. Carlson is well known, and for purely selfish reasons, I'd like to see Lone Star win. But believe me, Amelia, whoever is first to beam down the kilowatts, all of us, the whole of humanity, will be the real winners. Besides guiding us into the next phase of our epochal leap from this planet to the stars, these brave, visionary adventurers will have taken a giant step toward freeing us on this planet from dependency upon the ancient, inefficient, and dangerous sources of energy that for so long we have had no recourse but to employ."

He leaned forward, supposedly toward her but actually toward the millions of viewers worldwide. "Amelia, the end of this race is the beginning of a new era. None of our lives will ever be the same again. This planet is about to change irrevocably, and the consequences will be beyond our imagination. There will be no limits to what humanity can accomplish."

"Helios One ready for launch."

"Begin countdown at T minus four minutes," van der Boss instructed. He was eminently calm and confident. Everything had checked out perfectly except for the malfunctioning memory board, and that problem had been taken care of. He was getting Helios 1 launched ahead of Prometheus, and by the inexorable logic of physics, he would beat Lone Star. Only Space Technologies remained as a competitor. PowerSat was as yet unlaunched, but it was much faster with its chemical-powered engines than was Helios.

Van der Boss had little faith in chemical rockets. They were fractious enough when launching from the ground. He wouldn't want to be the engineer who had to depend on the temperamental things for a task as delicate as pushing a huge solar-power satellite into geosynchronous orbit. Surely, he thought, PowerSat must come to grief during its launch-to-insertion phase.

"Helios One just launched." The voice over the intercom sounded resigned.

"Right on time," Cash said.

"And we're right on time, too," Pat said. "Behind them."

"Only by twelve hours," Cash said, not at all perturbed.

"A twelve-hour lead . . ." Sachi mused. "That gives them a lot of leisure to get their power-generating station on line."

"If everything works out the way they want it to," Cash said. "But it looks like they've launched without the memory board. So they're going to send up a shuttle to wait for Helios in GSO and install it there.

It's a splendid effort and as ballsy as you could ask for, but it'll be a delicate operation getting it installed, one they didn't expect to have to do and, more important, one nobody's trained for. If they can get it done within their launch-time advantage, I'll be surprised. It'll be close at best."

"You're taking this pretty calmly," Pat said.

"Why not? At this point, there's absolutely nothing I can do to affect the outcome. That's a pretty good feeling, after all we've been through. And one more thing: Before much longer, somebody's going to have a working solar-power satellite in orbit. That's a pretty good feeling, too."

"Professor Mallory," Amelia said, "isn't this about like watching a yacht race?" The images of the anchorwoman and the scientist were super-imposed upon the huge solar-power satellite, Prometheus 1. After a dramatic countdown, nothing seemed to be happening.

"It is something like that, Amelia. As we saw yesterday at the launch of the European Space Enterprise's Helios One, there is no visual display when these ion-drive engines are activated. There is no true ignition as such. I know it seems disappointing to a public weaned on the spectacular fireworks of the great Earth-to-space launches, and the unrealistic but picturesque special effects of popular science-fiction films, but these spacecraft use a power source as invisible as the wind that powers the racing yachts you mentioned."

"Is it moving at all?"

"It is, but the movement is nearly imperceptible to a remote viewer. These vast structures are extremely delicate and they have to be accelerated very slowly, their engines kept in perfect balance and synch."

"You say they're delicate, yet they seem so massive. It's hard to imagine." Of course she knew the answer, but Mallory had listed the questions she should ask and the sequence in which she should ask them, to give the viewers an accurate, or at least an understandable, idea of what was happening. Quentin Mallory, she thought, was such a dream to work with.

"It's because of the extreme attenuation of the structure. The members of which it is built are very strong, but they are so stretched out that they become flexible and the slightest imbalance of thrust can twist the whole fabric."

He looked straight into the camera, at the audience of millions. "Try this simple experiment, if you have the time, the resources, and the inclination. First, go to a closet and take out a coat hanger or two. A steel one, plastic won't work. Coat hangers are made of stout wire formed from high-quality steel of hard temper. With a pair of wire cutters, cut off a half-inch piece. Carefully, being sure not to hurt your fingers, try to bend that piece of wire. You can't do it. All the strength of a strong man's hands won't bend it. Now cut off a piece six inches long. You can bend it easily. Take another coat hanger and open it out to its full length. A child can tie it in knots."

He turned back to Amelia. "What we are seeing is the equivalent of a structure made of coat hangers that is miles in extent. That is why they must accelerate very slowly. In the absence of gravity, a structure like this is perfectly strong in a stable orbit, but it has to be handled with care when moving from one orbit to another."

"But the Space Technologies satellite, PowerSat One, will be using chemical rockets."

"Yes, and at a considerable risk. They will move faster, but still with far less acceleration than most rockets provide. In this tortoise-and-hare race, Space Technologies has chosen the role of the hare, with a faster transit making up for a later start. If all goes well, they will win the race. But if anything goes wrong with one or more of their kick-stage rockets, they will have far less chance than the others to make corrections before tumbling becomes irreversible."

"Will the Space Technologies launch be more visually impressive than this?" she asked wistfully, gazing at Prometheus 1, which still showed all the dynamism of a rock.

Mallory laughed. "I'm afraid the most we can hope for is a little glow in close-up pictures of the nozzles at launch. Unlike the ion-drive engines, these rockets will have true ignition, but we won't have the flame and smoke we all associate with the Earth-based launches, which consist mainly of a huge amount of fuel expended before the craft even begins to lift. What we see in those instances is mainly fuel lifting more fuel. This will be a process not of a single boost, not even of a single, continuously accelerating boost phase, as some of the popular magazines have reported. Rather, it will be a series of short, gentle boosts, with corrections made whenever needed."

"And if something goes wrong, and corrections can't be made?"

"Then, Amelia, you have a very expensive piece of hardware up there doing nothing. It will be a disaster."

"Everything copacetic, Mr. Reed." The engineer's voice echoed through the huge boardroom of Space Technologies, improving the already complacent mood. Reed beamed at his subordinates, mentally seeing himself on the cover of *Time Magazine*: "Preston Reed, Man of the Year." Or did they say "Person of the Year" these days? No matter.

"Ten days into kick phase and it couldn't be better," said Reed's personal secretary. "No doubt now that PowerSat One will be in GSO and beaming down the gigawatts well ahead of Lone Star and ESE."

"S-T shares are still climbing," reported the chief stock manager. "Investors in markets all over the world are scrambling to buy before they go through the roof."

"I never had any doubt," Reed said, savoring the moment. "Never once."

The following day, however, the mood was not quite so upbeat. In fact, it was somber. It could even be described as gloomy.

"Can the tumbling be brought under control?" Reed demanded, his face a rigid mask.

"Yes, certainly," Owen said. He was chief engineer of the project, and to him, an engineering problem was just that. He left the historical and business implications to others. He was the only man in the room not frowning or sweating.

"How long?"

"It will take at least two days to bring the tumbling under control, and probably another five days to orient the satellite properly for reboosting to its geostationary orbit."

"Damn! Couldn't you continue the boosting while you . . . you detumble the satellite?"

Owen remained bland and patient. It was always difficult explaining orbital mechanics to someone whose background was mostly in law and business management and who possessed neither the basic scientific training nor the temperament for it. On the other hand, he had not achieved his current position without doing plenty of exactly such explaining, usually with a high degree of futility.

"PowerSat is in an outbound orbit now, although it will require several more mid-course corrections, especially because of that misfiring at the last mid-course correction. Actually, it was the boosting that started the tumbling. The chemically powered rockets are powerful, but fine-controlling their boosting power is more difficult than with the ion drive. It was when we did the third mid-course correction that one of the rockets overcompensated."

"Any idea why that happened?" asked J. W. Chalmers.

"It was a computer failure. We can't discern the cause just yet, but my guess is that it was a cosmic ray hitting an onboard computer. OBCs run risks that ground-based computers don't need to contend with. We stopped all rockets as soon as the attitude-control system told us that the satellite had started tumbling."

"And stopping the rockets didn't stop the tumbling?" Reed persisted.

"Not in space, not in free fall. Unless a force is applied in the opposite direction, the tumbling will continue in free fall. And that force must be precisely calculated and applied with utmost precision. Otherwise, the satellite can start tumbling in the opposite direction."

"If the damned things are so difficult to control in delicate mancuvers, why are we using them?" Reed asked.

Seemingly oblivious to his boss's growing anger, Owen went blandly on. "Well, if you'll recall, when we were selecting the kick-stage rockets, the electric-impulse engines were still in developmental stage. It wasn't clear if they would be available for practical use in a decade, or even two."

"As I recall, that was your decision, Preston," said Chalmers. "You said that Lone Star and the Europeans and Japanese were being foolish in going for an untried technology like the ion drive instead of sticking with reliable rocketry."

"Thank you for that hindsight, James," Reed said through clenched teeth.

"The difficulties we're experiencing now," Owen calmly continued, "stem from the fact that we are lifting an immense object with a large moment of inertia."

"Moment of inertia?" Reed asked, as if immersing himself in the minutiae of physics would bring his blood pressure down.

"You might say it's an object's capacity to tumble in space. The greater the length over which its mass is distributed, the greater is its moment of inertia. When an object with a large moment of inertia starts tumbling, it's not easy to correct it."

Reed let out a long-held sigh. "Fix it, Owen. Do whatever you have to do to save our satellite."

"We've lost," Chalmers said when the engineer was gone.

"Not necessarily," Reed said when he had regained his equanimity. "The others haven't reached GSO yet, nor have they brought their power stations on-line. A great deal can happen between now and then."

It was quite true, but with the prospect of certain victory gone, the air of invincibility was irretrievable. As the bickering and recrimination went on, the silvery, six-kilometer-long PowerSat 1—at a geocentric distance of some thirty thousand kilometers—continued to tumble over and over in space, slowly and gracefully.

26

AT LONE STAR headquarters in Houston, Cash Carlson, Sachi Sasano Carlson, and the whole Lone Star staff, plus as many employees as could crowd into the facility's largest assembly room, sat or stood around in the dark. Standing near Cash and Sachi were his special guests for the occasion—Quentin Mallory, Gertrude Talbot, Dieter Moyer, Yoshino, and the Japanese contingent among them. A few minutes earlier, the whole building had been disconnected from the regular Houston power net and readied to receive power from the Mojave rectenna station. There was a low murmur and a clinking of glass as the squad of bartenders readied for the celebration.

"How's PowerSat?" Carlson whispered into his lapel mike.

"Stabilized and limping toward GSO," Max said through Cash's earplug. "Be there in about two weeks."

"And Helios?"

"They're onboard and installing the memory board now. I figure installation and testing will take another day."

Sachi was listening on her own earset. "We've won!"

Cash grabbed her in a fierce hug. "Everybody won! Hell, they'll both end up with a bigger piece of the market than we will, but we're still in the game. That's what's important! And there's lots more competition to come. That's what I get for showing that you don't have to be a big player to win in this game."

Abruptly, the chandelier overhead flashed into brilliant light. The room erupted into cheers as Cash made his way to the podium amid popping champagne corks, Texas football chants, and index fingers thrust overhead, signifying Number One. People grabbed him, shook his hand, and hugged him.

"Boss!" Chamoun said, uncharacteristically jubilant, "you have to buy a bank now! We'll need one to store all the money people will be throwing at us!"

People grabbed and kissed Sachi, just on general principles. Jack Parker swaggered around, looking as if he wore a beltful of invisible scalps. Pat Coogan openly sported her Space Marshal's star, and even Bob Thibodeaux looked like a wolverine who had eaten enough raw meat at last. Alison Baird got it all on camera. Far below, even Max poured himself a glass of champagne. Louis Pasteur himself had ensured that the stuff was germ-free.

Cash fought his way up to the podium amid balloons and clouds of confetti. Several minutes of cheers greeted him, and Sachi climbed up beside him, handing him a full glass. Slowly, the noise quieted.

"By God!" Cash shouted. "Hasn't this been fun?" The cheering started up again and required several more minutes to settle down. When he had silence once more, Cash raised his glass high.

"Friends," he cried to the worldwide audience, "Lone Star brings you the fire from the sky!"